THE ROPE CATCHER

Also by Larry Stillman:

A Match Made in Hell:
The Jewish Boy and the Polish Outlaw
Who Defied the Nazis
(nonfiction)

11/22/13

For Keith Kinney —

THE
ROPE CATCHER
A Novel

Proof that there is life after advertising! Best wishes on your up coming surgery —

LARRY STILLMAN

Larry

iUniverse, Inc.
Bloomington

The Rope Catcher
A Novel

iUniverse books may be ordered through booksellers or by contacting:

iUniverse
1663 Liberty Drive
Bloomington, IN 47403
www.iuniverse.com
1-800-Authors (1-800-288-4677)

ISBN: 978-1-4759-5552-1 (sc)
ISBN: 978-1-4759-5554-5 (hc)
ISBN: 978-1-4759-5553-8 (e)

Library of Congress Control Number: 2012919102

Printed in the United States of America

iUniverse rev. date: 11/05/2012

For Loraine, who always believed

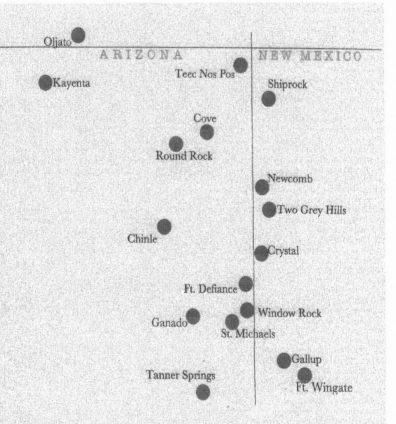

Oljato

ARIZONA   NEW MEXICO

Teec Nos Pos

Shiprock

Kayenta

Cove

Round Rock

Newcomb

Two Grey Hills

Chinle

Crystal

Ft. Defiance

Window Rock

Ganado

St. Michaels

Gallup

Tanner Springs

Ft. Wingate

Eastern portion of Navajo reservation and adjacent area
(not to scale)

Prologue

His dreams always ended with a question.

But only after they spooled across his psyche with imagery beyond the young man's understanding: chimeras that materialized with changing shapes and settings yet seemed to follow archetypal patterns that, he sensed, were somehow interlinked.

Ships at open sea, the ocean he had heard about but never seen, waves roiling like a dire warning against the massive hulls.

Strange phrases uttered in Navajo, his birth language, peculiar because the words made little sense in the context in which he spoke them.

Young men, dying, far from home, flesh turned to ash, the smell of sulfur and cordite fouling the unfamiliar tropical air.

Perplexing impressions; disturbing, certainly. Yet as they wound to their inevitable conclusion, they left the young man feeling vaguely content, rewarded. As if the images were an inescapable part of something significant, something tangible, that had been missing in his life, the fulfillment of long-held desires.

But always, in the murky business of awakening, before the hopeless reality of another listless day consumed him, came the question, hard and insistent.

It asked, "Suppose one day you actually get what you've wished for? Suppose your dreams of acceptance and purpose in life really do come true?

"What then, do you presume? What happens after that?"

In the marines, the guys were really nice to me. Called me Chief. "Chief, how's things going?" they'd say to me. I said, "Why do you call me Chief? If I was your chief, we wouldn't be in this mess."

*—Interview with Wilfred Billey,
code talker, USMC*

PART I:

THE CALL

CHAPTER 1

APRIL 1942

I t is the wind that sets him on the path to war. The wind, given voice by a scruffy Hallicrafters shortwave radio that, almost magically, plucks the words from the air and spills them out like cottonwood seeds bursting from their pods.

Although twenty-eight years have passed since he became a human being, Jimmie Goodluck has little to show for his time in the world. Finding himself out of work again, he idles away the hours by shooting craps with his buddies, paying scant attention to the radio perched on a nearby windowsill. But when a Glenn Miller number is interrupted by a dulcet-voiced announcer, Jimmie holds up on his roll to listen. The broadcaster, speaking on behalf of the Bureau of Indian Affairs, delivers a startling message that only Jimmie seems to hear.

Impulsively, he drops the pair of dice, scoops up his twelve dollars in winnings, and mumbles a hurried good-bye to his puzzled friends.

"Where are you going?" they call as he sprints away. "Give us a chance to win our money back."

3

Without breaking stride, Jimmie responds with a dismissive wave of his arm. He is determined to gather up a few things at home. When his father is out of earshot, he will confide in his mother, explain his sudden plans. She, at least, should understand.

Then, come the first light of morning, he will tuck all of his possessions into his jacket pocket and set out on foot toward the rising sun.

IT TAKES HIM TWO DAYS to reach Ft. Wingate, where Jimmie's forebears forcibly began their exile known as the Long Walk. These days, of course, the fort is long gone. Now the little community is simply a sparse collection of low-slung buildings and log construction dwellings that stand a few miles east of Gallup along the reservation border.

He walks past a little store emblazoned with Coca-Cola, Chesterfield, and Indian pawn signage, seeing no evidence of the place he needs to be. In front of the store, squatting in the dirt, three boys are playing a traditional Navajo gambling game called Seven Cards.

Jimmie approaches them and asks, "You know where the recruiting office is?" It is in this town that US Marine Corps recruiters have set up temporary quarters.

Two of the boys act as if they do not hear him, but the third young man scoops up the game's seven cottonwood dice and nods. He gestures with pursed lips—the Navajo equivalent of pointing—to an old building about a block farther up. It appears to be the remains of a boarding school built here fifty years ago.

"You signing up?" the boy asks, almost as an afterthought.

"Guess so," Jimmie replies.

"Wish I was old enough." The teenager's mouth puckers as if he has just tasted sour fruit. "Anything to get away from here."

Jimmie smiles, understanding the sentiment only too well. "You'll get your chance soon enough."

The boy shrugs, wipes his nose with the back of his hand, and then turns his attention back to the game.

Jimmie hurries on.

The two-story building is long and narrow, constructed of heavy sandstone, with a white portico that extends out from each story. Vertical wooden beams, also painted white, support the porticos, which run in parallel from one end of the building to the other. A sign over the main entrance reads "Post Office." Directly in front of the sign stands a long table, sheltered in the shade of the covered portal. There sit two young, unruffled marines, looking as out of place as fresh tuna in this desolate land adjoining the reservation.

Lined up before the officers, patiently waiting their turns in the warm breath of late afternoon, stand more than a dozen Navajo boys. None look more than eighteen or nineteen. Several seem barely older than the boys who directed Jimmie here. Two of the young men in line are wearing moccasins. Four of them have headbands and long black hair tied behind their heads in traditional hair bundles. One young man is actually sporting an old rifle as if the recruitment posters had read, *Come fight the Japs. Bring your own weapons!*

Jimmie takes his place at the end of the line. He slings his bedroll over his shoulder, along with a leather jacket, worn and faded as an old saddle. Inside a zippered compartment is a pocketknife and a thin wallet into which he has tucked a few dollars, along with a black-and-white snapshot, yellowing with age. A small buckskin pouch, bulging with sacred corn pollen, hangs on a strap around his neck. He carries it so he will always remember where he comes from. He carries it to help him try to understand who he is.

Directly in front of Jimmie stands a kid who looks like he could use a good meal, a long bath, and a few more birthdays before enlisting. "This moving at all?" Jimmie asks him in English.

Nothing more boring than standing in line, after all. Like boarding school all over again.

The kid turns, gives Jimmie a quick glance, then looks down, avoiding direct eye contact. "Uh, I been here twenty minutes, moved up maybe one or two. You here to enlist too?"

"You mean an old guy like me?" Jimmie breaks into a grin.

The boy's face reddens. He kicks at the dirt with the toe of his ankle-length boot, a conventional style. The buckskin looks practically new. Same for the shiny, silver button that holds it closed.

"That's okay, I can still *fight* like a twenty-year-old," Jimmie says, sorry that he embarrassed the kid. "Did some boxing in my younger days. You don't forget stuff like that."

The boy nods, still looking down. His mane of coal-black hair, in need of a good brushing, hangs limply at his shoulders.

"Guess I decided to enlist soon as I heard the announcement over the shortwave," Jimmie explains. "I figured, why not? The country says we can help and I got nothing keeping me here." Pure understatement, the last four words, but he is of no mind to elaborate. "How 'bout you?"

"I ... I dunno. Like you, I guess. Even with my years at Indian schools, there's still no jobs or nothin'. What else can I do, raise sheep? Anyway, can't get no grazing permit. Government seen to that. It's best for everyone that I sign up, go to war. There's hardly food enough to go 'round as is, what with my older sister still at home. Things was even harder when my other two sisters lived there."

"Still, you're lucky," Jimmie remarks. "Me, I got no brothers or sisters. None that lived, anyways."

The boy shuffles his boots in the dirt. "Wouldn't've minded if one of my sisters was a boy. They treat me like I'm their pet lamb or somethin'. Now's I think about it, that's the real reason I'm joining up, if the marines'll have me. I'm not some little kid anymore. I'm seventeen. Practically a man, y'know? And I don't want to become a man for nothin'."

I don't want to become a man for nothin'. Unexpected words, ripe with inference. Jimmie chews on them, like jerky.

The boy-who's-practically-a-man looks down the line toward the recruiting officers who are stamping reams of paperwork. "Naw, I'll tell you what the real reason is," he says abruptly. "It's the uniform. I want everyone to see how good-lookin' I can be in it."

Jimmie, captivated by the kid's good-natured response, holds out his hand—wrist bent, fingers extended upward—in the traditional greeting. "Name's Jimmie Goodluck. *Kinlichii'nii,"* he says, identifying the clan of his mother, the Red House people. Clan association is sacred, after all.

"Ray Begay," responds the young man, brushing his upright palm against Jimmie's. *"Tachii'nii."* This is the Red-Running-into-the-Water Clan. "Born for *Ashiihi,"* he adds for further identification, to indicate that his father comes from the Salt Clan. "I'm from Kayenta. A little north of there, actually."

"Monument Valley, huh?"

"Yeah."

"You're a long way from home." Must have taken him many days to get here.

"Ain't everybody? Long ways from home, I mean?"

"Me, not so far. Area called Two Grey Hills. Two days walk from here, north. Toward Shiprock."

The journey is still fresh in Jimmie's mind: red rock country as far as the eye can see. Defiant sandstone buttes rising, one after another, their eastern planes shimmering in the angular early morning light, a prophecy of fire and blood. His only company was skittering lizards and a few passing motorcars, mostly driven by whites on their way to, through, or from Gallup and places beyond. Jimmie did not bother to hold out his thumb in the hope of hitching a ride. No one would stop for an Indian, any more than they would leave the newly paved roadway to venture forth onto the few dirt roads that crisscrossed portions of the expansive Navajo lands. In any event, there is little reason for outsiders to be on the reservation, where morale weighs heavy as cement and aspiration seems pointless in the face of reality.

During his walk, the only sound Jimmie heard was the steady crunch of his boots on the desert carpet beside the road. Carried on the breezes were the comforting scents of sage and pinón pines and, from time to time, the pungent odor of livestock droppings, all welcome, all familiar.

This land. The only place he has ever known. With any luck, behind him, soon.

"Anyways," Jimmie goes on, "who knows how much farther away we'll get before we come back." Then he adds—callously, as he thinks about it later—"Or if we'll even *come* back."

"Don't know where else I'd go after the war."

"Think you're missing the point."

Ray flushes for a second time. Like many people from the reservation, he is clearly not used to hearing references to death, let alone discussing the subject.

"Oh. Well, I ain't plannin' on dyin', if that's your meaning," Ray says. "Besides, I might not even make it in. Don't know how I'll face my father if they don't take me."

"Don't know how I'll face my father if they do."

Ray looks at Jimmie with a puzzled expression, but Jimmie is of no mind to explain.

"I mean, I'm not sure I meet all the rules," Ray goes on. "You got to weigh in at a 120 pounds, I heard. Maybe even 122. Far as I know, I'm just under that."

Jimmie swipes at a bead of sweat as it works its way down his forehead. "Me, I'm going to take a few years off my age. We got no birth records, so who's to know? And you, you better do the same thing with your weight, only in the other direction."

"Huh?"

"What I'm saying is, give yourself every advantage, kid. Go drink some water. Drink all the water you think you can hold, then drink some more. And don't piss till after they weigh you."

Ray considers the advice. His face, slightly darker and less angular than Jimmie's, hangs motionless, like a half moon thinly veiled by a passing cloud.

"Go on," Jimmie urges. "Do it now. I'll hold your place in line."

Without further prodding, Ray lopes off like an errant puppy while Jimmie stands, parched and restless, under the unsympathetic sun. Far ahead of him in line, a young man steps up to the recruiting table and, in a shaky voice, states his name. It prompts Jimmie to think about how he came by his own name.

His father, Wilson Goodluck, had always bristled at Anglo names, his own in particular. It was given to him by white men who were oblivious to the fact that people of Wilson's generation had little use for proper or family names, preferring descriptive nicknames for reference. Wilson's was "Walks Alone" in the Navajo language, reflecting his appearance as a moody, solitary child.

Wilson got his Anglo surname years later when he was sent down to Ft. Defiance—kidnapped, is how he talks about it—and placed in one of the early government boarding schools. "Good luck with this one," said one school official to another as the feisty boy stood before them. The name stuck. "Wilson" was added from an old army roster, and that was that. Other children were assigned names in similar fashion: white men's names like "McCabe" and "Brown" and "Thompson" and "MacDonald."

As for Jimmie, his first name suits him fine. It was offered up by his mother when he was very young. Said she simply liked the sound of "Jimmie." He cannot recall his father ever uttering it.

"Uh, Jimmie, I done what you suggested."

Ray has come back to the line, shifting his newly enhanced weight from foot to foot. Jimmie can almost hear the *swoosh-swoosh* of the liquid as if it is filling first one hollow leg, then the other. He hopes they weigh the poor boy before he starts leaking like a loosely woven reed basket.

Before long it is Ray's turn at the table, after which he waddles off for his preliminary physical. Jimmie fingers the pouch around his neck—a nervous gesture?—as directly in front of him, a weary-looking marine asks *his* name. And the answer that forms immediately in his mind—though certainly prematurely—is *Private Jimmie Goodluck, USMC.*

He is abruptly aware of a change in perception. Curiously, Ft. Wingate has shaken off its violent history. Its aura of witchery and malevolence has evaporated, somehow, seeping away like surface water after a summer cloudburst. And the notion pours over him, reassures him, saturates his thoughts with a sense of both revelation and calm acceptance:

This is as good a place as any to be reborn.

Chapter 2

April 1942

After undergoing a cursory physical, Jimmie flies through a few simple tests designed to measure his English proficiency. Moments later, an NCO summons him for a lengthy interview in a shabby space that might have once been a boarding school classroom. The room, like the dormitory that houses the would-be recruits, reeks of mold and years of disuse. To Jimmie, it smells of promise and opportunity.

Early the next morning, Jimmie gets the news he has been hoping for. He is welcomed as a candidate for basic training.

Jimmie embraces the new direction his life seems to be taking. He marvels at his good fortune to have been near a shortwave radio when the call for "a few good men" went out. *Navajo* men, in this instance.

Since the attack on Pearl Harbor four months earlier, many young Navajo males— along with a few females—rushed to enlist in the army and navy. Jimmie had entertained fleeting notions about joining up himself, much to his father's chagrin. But this was different. This message made him want to take action. Not only because, for the first time, it was the *marines* who were recruiting on the reservation, but because according to the announcer—and this struck Jimmie as rather odd—they were specifically looking for men with exceptional fluency in both English and Navajo. It was a requirement never mentioned by other branches of the armed forces, and it narrowed down the field of candidates substantially.

Jimmie qualifies as well as anyone.

Still, his spontaneous decision to sign up belies how deeply he is bound by loyalty and by history to his ancestral lands. The impoverished majesty of his Navajo birthplace is etched upon him. Its legends and traditions. Its warm people, largely secluded from the outside world. Its vast acreage, punctuated by deep canyons and high mesas and the sheltering sacred mountains that mark its boundaries in four directions.

But circumstances being what they are, he is compelled to escape the gravitational pull of the reservation. For as much as he loves the desert and respects its sacred ties to his ancestors, he yearns for adventure, needs to prove himself as a fighter, aches to be a part of something important for once, something undoubtedly alien and terrifying and yet, as he envisions it, somehow liberating. This opportunity is what he has been dreaming about all along: acceptance in the world at large. A change in the downward spiral of his life. Release from the despondency that is as commonplace on the reservation as dust in the air.

Becoming a marine, he knows now, is not just a whim. Far from it.

It is a burning need.

EAGER TO SHARE HIS GOOD fortune, Jimmie looks for his new friend, hoping he, too, is one of the chosen.

"Jimmie! Over here!" Ray calls from the former parade ground, where he is writing a letter beside a sumac bush, seemingly oblivious to its malodorous scent.

"I made it!" Ray squeals, pen flying as he jumps up to greet Jimmie. "But lemme tell you, I ain't stopped pissin' yet!"

"Good for you, Ray. I'm in too."

Still, word is getting around that many candidates were turned away for not proving facile enough when switching between English and Navajo.

"Why d'you think talking Navajo is so important?" Jimmie wonders aloud. "In my first missionary school, they tried to force everything Navajo out of me."

Ray shrugs and then stoops to pick up his pen along with the unfinished note that lies on the ground. "I was just writin' to my family. My oldest sister, Katherine, she's real good at readin' and talkin' English. Better 'n me, even. She can translate for my parents. If I know my father, he'll be at our trading post twice a week or more, lookin' for my letters."

If I know my father, Jimmie thinks, *he won't read my letters at all. Not while I fight side by side with white men.*

"San Diego. You know where it is?" Ray asks. "I don't want my family to worry none about me, there bein' no time right now to get home and back. I was writin' 'em 'bout where we're goin'."

"Oh. San Diego's in California. Below Los Angeles, I think."

"Never been to California. Never been nowhere, really, till now."

Jimmie puts his hand on Ray's shoulder and then pulls it away, feeling self-conscious. "I've never seen California myself. So we'll stick together, how's that?"

Ray exhales a great volume of breath, like the release of a pressure valve. The boy, for all his earlier bravado, seems anxious at the prospect of what lies ahead.

"Don't you worry none," Jimmie reassures him. "Just think of me as your big brother. Never had me a brother or sister. Got some catching up to do."

Ray beams like the cat in that *Alice* storybook. The boy's youthful face radiates a joyful glow that comes not just from his gentle features, but from somewhere deeper. Perhaps he simply reflects the pure and simple delight that comes from life's little events and surprises, like this budding friendship.

That feeling is mutual, and it intensifies three days later when the pair is inducted into the Marine Corps along with twenty-seven other young Navajo men. Jimmie and Ray stand together in front of the recruitment office as a sleek Greyhound bus pulls up, the words *City of Redondo Beach* stenciled alongside the Marine Corps insignia on its door. Everyone poses, chests puffed out, as a Corps photographer snaps a group picture. Then they all shuffle onto the bus and take their seats.

There is little conversation at first. With eyebrows furrowed and lips pressed tightly together, most of the young men are lost in their own private reveries. Jimmie may be the only one who feels little anxiety over what is to come. In fact, his thoughts have wandered *back* in time, not ahead. Back to the isolated *hogan*—the traditional six- or eight-sided Navajo dwelling—he passed days earlier on his trek to the recruiting office. It was of recent log construction, that place, positioned a short distance back from the road. Nearby, a small corral of brush and fencing wire held a few calves and about a dozen sheep. Jimmie gave it little notice at first, until he heard voices in familiar Navajo cadence. A father and son had emerged from the *hogan*, each carrying a coil of rope.

"When can I try calf roping?" the boy asked as he walked with his father past the corral. He could not have been more than seven or eight years old.

"First you must learn to handle the rope correctly," his father answered. Their words carried easily on currents of air.

Jimmie slowed his pace and watched with keen interest as the father pushed a wooden stake into the ground. Taking a position some distance away from the stake, the man held the coil of rope in his left hand. The loop was a large one, easily six or seven feet in diameter.

"Now watch carefully," he said to his son, taking the loop in his right hand about a foot below the ring. "Remember to leave enough loose rope between the coil and the loop. And make sure there are no twists in the line or the coils won't slip off easily when you throw."

The boy looked closely at his father's hands and then stepped back. His father raised his right hand and began to expertly swing the rope over his head from right to left.

"See how smoothly my wrist moves? Remember what I told you: pretend the loop is a wheel."

Then the man took a quick step forward, extended his swinging hand to arm's length, and—without interrupting the motion of the loop—let it fly in a steady arc toward the stake. The boy squealed with delight as the loop precisely ensnared the target.

"Did you see how the right side of the loop was lower than the other side?" his father pointed out. "The right side hits first, then the other side falls over the animal's head. We need to work on your spinning and throwing, on keeping your rope level. Then, when you've mastered that, we'll try it with a calf."

The boy nodded. He held his rope well, and while his first attempt at swinging the loop was awkward, he got a little better with each successive try.

"Keep it circling over your head, that's the way," the boy's father encouraged. "Don't let it touch the ground, keep it aloft. Keep it aloft, that's the idea."

Jimmie had smiled then as he does again now. *Someday,* he thinks, settling in for the long bus ride. *Someday, perhaps, that father could be me.*

It is a new feeling for him, as unfamiliar as an ocean voyage. He searches for the precise English word to attach to it. Then it comes to him:

Hope.

SOMEWHERE NEAR FLAGSTAFF, THE MOOD on the bus elevates along with the altitude. Poker games spring up. The jangle of coins accompanies pockets of laughter, harmonizing with the steady drone of tires on asphalt—an unfamiliar sound to most of the young men who have seldom, if ever, ridden on a paved highway, let alone on a Greyhound bus.

In the seats behind Jimmie and Ray, two boys argue over which tribal leader had the most impact on the Navajo people in the late eighteenth century, the turbulent period culminated by the Long Walk. History always has a way of creeping into Navajo conversations.

"Barboncito was our greatest warrior," insists Charlie Yazzie, a lanky boy of eighteen, with prominent ears and a look of mischief about him. He refers to the medicine man from Canyon de Chelly who struck out against Indian-fighter Kit Carson in the 1860s. "A great peace leader, too."

"Yeah, but Barboncito was finally captured like everybody else," argues Carl Slowtalker, who claims to have turned twenty but looks no older than Ray or Charlie. "It's Manuelito who was the best war leader *and* peace leader. His attacks on Ft. Defiance hurt the American soldiers the most."

Before emotions get out of hand, Jimmie turns around in his seat. "Guys, listen to yourselves! You're arguing about who fought better against US soldiers. Yet here you are, heading to join up with those soldiers!"

"Yeah, you got a point," Charlie admits. "We was fightin' for our land back then, and now I guess we're fixin' to do it all over again. Only this time, like you say, the Indians and the cowboys are in it together, all fightin' for the same thing."

Ray turns sideways to better address the boys behind him. "Now's you mention it, I feel pretty much that way myself. Can you think of a better reason to go to war than to help fight for our land?"

Under different circumstances, Jimmie might share that point of view, but he signed up for far less noble reasons. So he turns back to the window, though his eyes barely register the dramatic landscape of northern Arizona that streaks past the dirt-smudged glass in a hypnotic blur. He withdraws into his own world.

Almost mechanically, he pulls out his tattered wallet and stares at the creased photo tucked inside. Looking back at him is a much younger Jimmie: thick black hair, high cheekbones, determined chin that looks to be chiseled not out of flesh and bone, but of sterner stuff—that reddish-hued Colorado alabaster, perhaps, quarried and rough hewn, awaiting the smoothing and polishing that might eventually bring out its individuality. In the photo he is positively beaming, for standing next to him is Chee Dodge, the one Navajo of this era who has reached celebrity status owing to both his immense wealth and his visionary leadership. To Jimmie's left stands Chee's daughter, Annie. She is a big girl for her age and not an outward beauty, but her radiant smile hints at the beautiful person beneath.

Jimmie recalls the day they posed for that photo, and it occurs to him: Funny thing about memories. They have a way of intruding, like a scorpion in empty boots, when you are least prepared to deal with them.

"Can I see?" Ray asks.

Jimmie shrugs and hands over the picture.

"I think I seen that man before. Your father?"

A sound escapes from Jimmie's mouth: a laugh held hostage by a snort. "Not hardly. He's Henry Chee Dodge."

"Chee Dodge, leader of the tribal council? You *know* him?"

When Jimmie nods, Ray's jaw looks as if it might drop to the floor of the bus. "Me, I never met nobody important like Chee Dodge. And, uh, that girl—who's she?"

"Chee's daughter, Annie. Annie Wauneka, her married name. We been friends, her and me, a long time."

Ray is clearly in awe of his new buddy.

"I met her about fifteen years ago on a train taking kids to Indian school in Albuquerque," Jimmie explains, relating how children of all ages, and from different tribes, were shuffled into a coach of the long Santa Fe Railroad train. Indian children were not allowed to mix with white people, of course, and luckily, they were packed into a forward car. The train had stopped to pick up more children at the Laguna Pueblo when suddenly came a jolt, along with the explosive sound of wood splintering. The children were thrown from their seats. Jimmie landed on the floor next to Annie, a raven-haired girl a couple of years his junior. All around, children screamed and cried. Annie was the first to call out, "Is anyone hurt?" She quickly surveyed the shaken youngsters, none of whom were seriously injured.

What had happened was, a late-running freight had rammed into the back of the train. The rear cars lay scattered off-rail like discarded dominoes. The children had to wait through the night to catch another Albuquerque-bound train the next morning. During those trying hours, Jimmie learned a lot about Annie Dodge, about her passion, even back then, to help her fellow human beings.

"An' you got to know her father through her?" Ray bubbles, measuring Jimmie's words as if each one is worth its weight in turquoise.

"Well, eventually. Look, it's a long story."

"An' it's a long bus ride." Ray looks expectantly at his seatmate as the bus hurtles toward the California border. The setting sun casts deep shadows on the fading landscape outside the windows. The snow atop the distant San Francisco peaks glows an otherworldly purple in the dimming light. Inside the bus, few of the boys look out at the scenery. Having talked themselves out, many are slouched down in their seats, although most are too keyed up to sleep.

Jimmie takes a deep breath and explains that he graduated from Indian school in 1930. That unlike his earlier experiences at a misguided boarding school in Toadlena, he has only positive memories of the progressive Albuquerque school. Then, a year or two after he returned to Two Grey Hills and struggled to find work, Annie announced her plans to marry George Wauneka, a boy Jimmie knew from school. She invited Jimmie to the wedding ceremony at her father's winter ranch at Tanner Springs, where she and her husband-to-be planned to stay on as managers.

The ranch sat on acres of lush grazing land dotted with sage, thistle, and sunflower, all framed against the backdrop of LaPinta Mesa. Annie invited Jimmie to stay on a while after the ceremony, but he mumbled vague excuses about needing to be somewhere else.

Three difficult years went by before he saw her again.

"Understand, Ray, there wasn't much work then any more than there is now. I jumped at the chance to dig ditches and wells in the hot sun. For a while I signed on as a fry cook at Sage Memorial Hospital in Ganado, but it was monotonous and lemme tell you, the smell of grease stayed with me long after I left the stove. I remember one winter, I hauled coal to a few government schools. And toward the end of Prohibition—believe me, I'm not proud of this—I got involved distributing corn whiskey. White Mule, they called it. I bought it by the gallon and sold the stuff in Coca-Cola bottles."

As Jimmie talks about his unsettled past, it dawns on him

that it was shortly after his friendship began with Annie that his relationship with his father began to deteriorate. Wilson nurtured a longstanding resentment toward Chee Dodge stemming back to an incident in his youth involving Black Horse, a renegade tribal leader and outlaw who had young Wilson under his spell. Jimmie has often seen his father's anger ignite like dry timber every time news came of Chee serving as liaison to the white man or leasing reservation land to big oil companies. But Jimmie had underestimated, back then, just how deep his rift with his father would become.

Jimmie is about to suggest saving his little melodrama of a life for another time when from the back of the bus, a loud whoop rings out. Apparently, Carl Slowtalker has been caught dealing from the bottom of the deck. Common enough among Navajo card players, long as the dealer can get away with it.

"Look, there's more to the story, but tell me about yourself," Jimmie suggests. He takes back the photo from Ray and stores it, along with his memories, out of the way.

"Actually, ain't much to tell. Dirt floor *hogan,* around a hundred sheep, six horses, three sisters. The younger two got married—sisters, not horses—but Katherine's in no hurry, I guess. My parents been tryin' to marry her up since she was fifteen, but she won't hear of it. She's real close to the family but just ain't interested in startin' one of her own. Not that guys haven't come around, lemme tell you." Ray raises his eyebrows as he adds, "She's real pretty, I got to say. You'd say so too, if you ever seen her."

"Who's to say? Maybe someday I will."

There is a distant look in Ray's eyes as he goes on, "It's tough on my folks, barely gettin' by, tryin' to keep the livestock healthy. I know nobody's got it much better. Some years, though, it seems like the sheep had more to eat than us."

"I hear you. My parents have been scraping by too. My father blames the white leaders—actually, he blames just about everyone—

but y'know, it's lots of things. Mother Earth throws a blizzard at us, our livestock dies, you can't blame a government for that. When a few dozen head of sheep is all you got, times are always tough. Weaving is what keeps my mother going, but of course, that's not possible without healthy sheep."

Ray brightens. "Last couple years, my sisters and mother started makin' baskets an' sold a few. And my father, he learned me how to work leather like him."

"I noticed your boots the other day. You made 'em?"

"My father did. A goin'-to-war present. But I made the silver button. I like workin' silver even more than leather."

"Good for you! Could be your future you're walking on."

"Think so? Guess we better hurry and win the war, then."

"Oh, we'll win the war," Jimmie says, trying to sound confident for once in his life. "How can we lose? The cavalry finally has sense enough to bring in the Indians!"

CHAPTER 3

MAY 1942

The San Diego Marine Recruit Depot is home to the twenty-nine Navajo boys who scarcely have time to absorb their first sight of palm trees, or register the harsh and unfamiliar sounds of the big city, or marvel at the playful breezes, swollen with the damp breadth of ocean, which course against their desert-tempered skin. All these experiences are foreign to them. It is as if they have been transported to one of the strange and exotic countries they learned something about in school. Even Jimmie, who has been short distances off the reservation before, experiences a sense of wonder at something so simple as sweat, which blossoms in the warm, humid air and glistens like starlight on his skin.

The Navajo boys are assigned to a tent because the more standard barracks are already filled due to the surge of new recruits. They have just begun to settle in for an afternoon of unpacking and a couple of hours of free time when George Benally, a stocky, twenty-six-year-old miner from Cove, Arizona, announces, "I can tell already. This place is a fucking prison." Many of the Navajo recruits are amused by George's vulgarity, for that sort of language is seldom heard back home.

One of the boys, Wilfred Smith, had attended the Navajo Methodist Mission School in Farmington. There he heard a young navy man, in town on home leave, talk about his recent boot camp experiences. Wilfred, therefore, has a pretty good idea of what is ahead of them.

"If you think it's a prison today," he tells Benally, "I can hardly imagine what you'll call this place by the end of the week." Then Smith gets a puzzled look in his eyes and says to everyone, "One thing's curious, though. A boot platoon's usually around sixty guys. There's just twenty-nine of us here. And I don't see any white faces bunking with us."

Jimmie notices it too. From all appearances, they are being kept together in one small platoon. He wonders whether he might have been wrong about enlisting. If the Indian boys here are kept separate and unequal, he might as well have stayed on the reservation. Separate and unequal works perfectly well back there.

His concerns ease a bit after his platoon scrambles over to the mess hall. They wait in a line with all the other boot recruits to get their food. The Navajo boys are a bit self-conscious, for they are the only recruits not sporting a short haircut or a uniform. This elicits stares from the others in line, accompanied by a few snickers that might mean, *You just wait, young boot virgins, wait till you see what's in store for you.* Jimmie does not allow his paranoia to define the snickers with a more sinister implication.

Eventually the platoon moves their way up to the long counter where expressionless young women dole out the meal. They wield their oversized spoons like war clubs. Ray says he finds it reminiscent of feeding and watering livestock: the sheep all gathering 'round and jockeying for position so as not to miss out.

Following the lead of the uniformed recruits, Jimmie takes a

metal tray, still warm from its hot water rinsing, as choices unfold
before him, one after another, like the pleats in an accordion he
once saw in Gallup. Here it seems as if there are no shortages, no
rationing, no wartime limitations. Greedily, he selects a salad, a
hot dish, a side dish, fruit, dessert, a slice of bread with a smear of
something yellow, and a cup of black coffee that he dilutes with hot
water. With his plunder in hand, he heads for one of the long tables
feeling as if he were the most privileged man on the planet.

It is a sentiment shared by the other Navajo recruits who sit
down beside him in the noisy hall as they laugh and marvel over the
cornucopia of fare, much of which they cannot remotely identify.
The only foods familiar to most of them are the fruit and the
vegetable—peaches in syrup and kernels of corn, both of which
must have come from a can—and the coffee. They puzzle over the
meatloaf of unidentifiable composition, along with the brown pasty
substance, viscous as motor oil, that gushes over an accompanying
mesa of mashed potatoes like an overflowing wash. Charlie Yazzie
nearly gags when he bites into the butter, apparently thinking it is
a piece of candy. This elicits a huge guffaw from George Benally,
who himself has never seen the greasy substance before, but has
enough sense not to pop it in his mouth as if it were a lemon drop.
Wilfred Smith, meanwhile, examines his slice of bread, holding it
up to the light and turning it over in his hands as if it is some sort
of laboratory specimen. Quiet Stanley Tso takes timid little bites
of his dessert, a gelatinous mound of fruit-flavored something or
other, but every time he approaches it with his spoon it jiggles back
and forth like a living entity. He not sure what to make of it, but
his smile suggests he finds it both tasty and entertaining. Directly
across the table, Ray is busily picking the croutons out of his salad
before they get soggy from the dressing, because as he tells his
buddies, "These little bread thingies are the closest we're likely to
get to fry bread around here, so you need to savor them on their

own." Jimmie eats and enjoys everything on his plate, regardless of shape, texture, or aroma, delighting in the bracing, non-Indianness of it all.

The clamor in the room reaches a crescendo as the hungry boot recruits finish their meals. The clatter of spoons and cups and dishes and trays heading back to the kitchen adds to the din. Jimmie has been at the training depot for only a few hours, and the rigorous schedule has yet to begin. But here—surrounded by hundreds of other recruits who, except for the whiteness of their skin, do not appear so dissimilar—he begins to feel a part of something he has been waiting for all along. Who knows, perhaps keeping the twenty-nine Navajo enlistees as a small and separate platoon is temporary, until they become more adjusted. Anything is possible.

He slaps his buddy Ray on the back and says, "Looks like from now on you'll finally get more to eat than your sheep back home, little brother."

Ray laughs and together they shuffle back to their tent, full and content, looking forward to a peaceful evening followed by a good night's sleep.

ON THE FOLLOWING MORNING, A Monday, everyone in the Navajo boot platoon undergoes a thorough physical. Jimmie smiles, imagining what his narrow-minded father might say if he were present to witness a white doctor's gloved finger worming its way up twenty-nine Navajo asses.

From here they line up to receive shots for diseases they never knew existed. All this takes up most of the morning.

After midday mess, everyone marches off to get haircuts. Most of the Navajo recruits have never seen a barber's chair, let alone a whole line of them. For several of the young men, this stirs up no less anxiety than, say, an impending amputation. Long hair is commonplace among Navajo males, and the marine-issue buzz cut seems nearly akin to cutting off their manhood.

Carl Slowtalker, for one, pledges to circumvent mirrors for days as if they are instruments of witchcraft. "I look like a baby chicken!" he cries.

"Nah," cracks George Benally. "Chicken's got a neck."

Jimmie and Ray, however, are intrigued by their new looks. Ray constantly runs his hands over the alien surface of his scalp.

After getting their hair cut, the young men next head to the supply depot for uniforms and standard-issue equipment, which includes the reliable—but unquestionably obsolete—1903 bolt-action Springfield rifle. Jimmie is not the only recruit who stands open-mouthed as an NCO unpacks the crates in front of him and removes the rifles, one after another, each covered with a greasy coating of Cosmoline. The platoon proceeds to a nearby area where another NCO orders them to clean their rifles in troughs filled with gasoline and then instructs them in how to properly field-strip their weapons.

Finally, they are given a list of required items, such as a bucket and some basic toiletries, which they must buy at the MCX, the base exchange. They enter the place with wide-eyed wonder, gawking like blind men who have gained sight for the first time. Jimmie experiences a sense of incredulity at the enormous variety of scarce wartime items offered for sale. There are bins of chewing gum and candy—everything from Wrigley's to Lifesavers, from Hershey's to Whitman's Chocolates, from revolutionary new M&M's to hard little turds (George's description) called Tootsie Rolls. All together, there must be enough sugar and chocolate to send the entire base into a glycemic frenzy. And that's only the beginning. Cartons of cigarettes are stacked like firewood. Nylons and perfume are piled high for wives or girlfriends or the insurance of a one-night stand. Everywhere Jimmie looks, cases of food items are adorned with the smiling faces of Betty Crocker and Aunt Jemima and Uncle Rastus and Mr. Peanut and Cracker Jack. And what is perhaps the most thrilling sight of all to many of the boys, an immense cooler is filled with bottles of beer, glorious beer, lined up like so many bowling pins. All this and much, much more greet the green recruits, some of whom later admit they have not so much as set foot in a store—*any* store—until now.

Trouble is, every item in the MCX—except the basics on the list, like soap and razor blades—is off limits to them. What is more, they cannot return until they graduate from boot camp.

"Shit on a stick!" George mutters under his breath. "It's like we get the keys to the cathouse but can't touch the whores."

Carl Slowtalker has a more cogent observation. "Reminds me a little of our trading posts back home."

"More than a little," Jimmie reflects, thinking back to his childhood visits to the Two Grey Hills Trading Post. He spent a great deal of time there because his father, unlike most husbands, refused to accompany his mother on her necessary trips to get supplies. True to his xenophobic nature, Wilson nurtured a distrust of all white traders, even though most everyone agreed they were generally fair and were, in fact, essential to the reservation economy and way of life early in the twentieth century. Jimmie was happy that it fell on him to go with his mother.

Over the years he spent countless hours gazing out from the trading post porch, immersing himself in the parched splendor of the nearly barren landscape while Leila traded for food and other necessities. The trading post was more than a supply store and a local outlet for selling, trading, and pawning. It was a social institution, a gathering place for the men and women widely scattered throughout that area of the reservation, a center for news and gossip and entertainment and even medical help.

Then there was the free coffee. Weak and plentiful, the way most Navajos like it.

The trader, Ed Davies, was well over six feet tall. Everyone called him Shorty in the Navajo language, a name they all thought was very funny. Each spring, Leila brought in bags of raw fleece, and every autumn she contributed a portion of her flock to be sold and butchered. In between, she wove blankets for trade. That is how she paid off the debt she had run up buying supplies throughout the year.

Jimmie always had fun rooting about the store, looking for new items among the farm supplies, groceries, Bull Durham tobacco, medicines, and what-have-you. Often he sipped on a nickel bottle of Coca-Cola that came out cool as you please from an outside well. Mostly, he liked the ebb and flow of the place: the comings and goings of the local characters; the snippets of social conversation; the little jokes that were often played, like the time someone put a pawn ticket on Lorraine Tso's crying infant; the notices that were posted by government officials announcing upcoming farm demonstrations or designating days for sheep dips to ward off ticks and disease. He was also fascinated by the steady parade of neighbors who asked Shorty and his wife for advice or on-premise medical help or, on occasion, an emergency ride in their wagon to the nearest hospital down in Ft. Defiance.

Each time Jimmie came in with his mother, Shorty always asked politely about Wilson, and Leila replied, "He is well." She offered no excuses for his constant refusal to accompany her, but Jimmie suspected Shorty knew him well by reputation. Wilson begrudgingly acknowledged that the family's modest livelihood depended on commerce with the white trader, but he insisted on letting his wife be the go-between. It is a matriarchal society, after all. The sheep, just like the weavings, are hers.

"You help your mother, but don't go near the trader," Wilson warned his son time and again, as if the giant man might eat the boy alive if given half a chance.

To Wilson's displeasure, Leila taught Jimmie that there are more good and honest people in the world than bad, even among whites, and that Shorty, in particular, treated everyone with fairness and respect. Jimmie realized early on that his own openness to others had been influenced in good measure by his mother, for Leila is as generous and trusting as Wilson is intolerant and cynical, their personalities as different as a lamb from a coyote. It was an arranged marriage, of course, that put these two disparate personalities together. Darkness and light is how Jimmie thinks of them, not only in their outlook but also in their regard for the outside world that presses closer with each passing year.

Jimmie is startled out of his reverie when he hears Ray exclaim, "What do I need this for?" Ray holds up a razor, one of the items on the supply list.

George sneers, "You don't. It's for men, not kiddies."

In truth, many of the new Navajo recruits can boast scarcely a whisker. Still, Jimmie rises to Ray's defense. "It's on the list, you buy it, Ray. You'll need it soon enough."

His words prove prophetic when, late that afternoon, the platoon stands at attention for their first inspection. The DI zeroes in on poor Ray as his opening target. He studies Ray's face, smooth and unblemished, almost delicate in its features. Ray stands stiff and uneasy, staring directly ahead without hardly blinking, a jackrabbit caught in the glare of a headlight. The DI leans forward until his bulbous nose almost touches Ray's, then he tugs at the one pale straw that stands out half an inch from the boy's chin. Still rigid as a two-by-four, Ray averts his eyes.

"You look at me, shithead," shouts the gunnery sergeant, a solid tank of a man named Shaw who towers over the five-feet-seven Ray Begay. It must take everything in the young man's power to comply, for he was raised, like all the boys, with the admonition that direct eye contact is rude.

"Were you issued a razor, shithead?" Shaw screams.

"Yes, uh, sir," Ray answers in a wavering voice.

"You will start every sentence with 'sir,' and you will *end* every sentence with 'sir,' you understand me, shithead?"

"Sir, yes … sir."

"I don't know what 'yes' means, shit-for-brains. The doggies in the army are all 'yes' men, but here we say 'aye-aye.' You got that?"

"Sir, aye-aye, sir."

"Now then. Did you use that marine-issue razor this morning?"

"Sir, no, sir." A momentary pause. "We still say 'no,' right?"

From the other men, stifled chuckles. Only Jimmie does not find it amusing. He is concerned for his friend Ray.

"So you're a smart-ass, are you?" By now Shaw is so red in the face he could pass for Navajo himself. "When's the last time you shaved, shithead?"

"Sir, uh, never, sir."

"Never? *Never?* Are you a little girl?"

"Sir, no, sir."

"You have a pussy down there?" The sergeant points toward Ray's crotch, pointing being another cultural taboo everyone will have to get used to. Ray's puzzled expression suggests that the crude term is unfamiliar to him.

"Sir, I don't think so, sir."

More snickers emanate from those who understand the word. George Benally can barely stay at attention as he tries to hold in his laughter. Jimmie, to keep from giggling himself, shoots George a stern glance.

"You listen up, shithead," Shaw demands, this time lowering his voice for emphasis. "We don't take no little girls in the Marine Corps. So you go find your razor and shave that face of yours till it's smooth as your mama's ass. Your mama don't have no hair on her ass, does she?"

Ray, unsure how to respond, stammers, "Sir, I ... I never looked, sir."

Most of the platoon is nearly doubled over. Even Jimmie now, in spite of himself.

"Shithead!" Shaw screams. "Follow orders and report back here in five minutes."

"Sir, aye-aye, sir!" Ray practically trips over the words. Then, with an immense look of relief, he runs off to search and destroy his errant whisker.

Day one at boot camp has been eye-opening, to say the least.

CHAPTER 4

JUNE–JULY 1942

"Can't tell if they're assholes because they're white, or because they're drill instructors," George muses back in the tent a few evenings later.

The first ever all-Navajo boot platoon of twenty-nine specially selected young men is primarily overseen by Gunnery Sergeant Arthur Shaw and Corporal Stuart Passon in their roles as drill instructors and arch-nemeses of the raw recruits.

"They're not so bad," Jimmie insists. "We're training to be marines, not sheepherders. Or did you forget?"

Truth be told, Jimmie actually *likes* the sergeant and especially the colonel. The rigid discipline and angry harangue does not bother him as it does George and some of the others. For him, the new experience is generally agreeable even with the verbal abuse and random bullshit that is ladled out daily much like the unrecognizable tastes and textures in the mess hall. Basic training is a ceremony unto itself, and the Marineway, as he dubs it, is far removed from anything he has ever encountered.

"Don't know 'bout you," Jimmie goes on, "but I got treated a whole lot worse at my first boarding school."

He remembers being a frightened youth back then, with the school's flimsy cots packed together wall to wall, with little air, ineffective light, and often no heat during the harsh winters. He remembers the sparse meals, which more often than not consisted of little more than bread and water; on some days, the pigs kept in a sty behind the kitchen ate better than the boys, and on several occasions, Jimmie actually stole scraps from the pigs. He remembers the hard menial labor required of the children, with far more hours allocated to the demanding chores than to the so-called education they were supposed to get. He remembers the bad-tempered teachers and their unyielding rules, which required their charges to act and dress and speak and pray like white people, not "wild little Indians." And he remembers the severe, often brutal punishments that were meted out for disobeying these and other dictums: the acrid taste of the soap used to wash the Navajo language out of his mouth, the feel of chains cinched tightly against his arms and legs for days on end, the sting of the strap against his backside, the enveloping darkness and the smell of earth and decay in his nostrils when he found himself locked in a dank basement storage room.

All this he remembers. All this, and more.

"Look at it this way, George," Jimmie points out. "At least here there's a good *reason* for the discipline and obedience. Who knows, might save our lives some day."

Carl and Charlie nod in agreement. Even Ray admits their DIs have more bark than bite.

This eventually becomes evident to George as well, when Shaw and Passon lighten up a little on the bluster and bravado once "their Indians" easily prove themselves with discipline and the physical demands of basic training. They would have no reason to know that standing at attention under the hot sun and then marching relentlessly is no big deal for most of the Navajo boys, who all grew up in an ascetic and unpampered environment and often talk about it among themselves.

"I ran barefoot at sunup on more winter mornings than I can remember," Ray relates one evening. "Gets cold sometimes up around Monument Valley, but my father, he wanted me to be one with the earth. Besides, the faster you run, the less you feel the cold."

Charlie Yazzie, from Chinle, talks about how he wandered the bends and forks of Canyon de Chelly with his family's flock. "Been doing it practically from the time I was old enough to walk. Lot of those Anglo recruits, they come here soft, I bet. Boot camp's no rodeo for them."

Carl Slowtalker, who grew up in a primitive, dirt floor *hogan* in Ft. Defiance, has his own anecdote. "Hey, I chased jackrabbits nearly every day under the blazing sun. Did it for fun, y'know? So now, a march of twenty miles or more? That's nothing. For me, anyway, it's just like being back home."

Wilfred Smith laughs—guffaws, more accurately—and remarks, "I find boot camp to be hilarious, so far. Hilarious! Love every minute."

Strange as it must sound, Jimmie feels the same way.

AS READILY AS THEY MEET the stringent physical demands of boot camp, the boys' accomplishments really shine once they are transported up to the pistol and rifle range in San Luis Obispo. Jimmie always believed he was a pretty good marksman; Ray and several others are better. The platoon's above-average qualification numbers, in fact, have impressed everyone up through George Hall, commanding officer of the Recruit Depot. Ray overhears the corporal telling "Gunny" Shaw that the CO has taken a special interest in "our Indian platoon" and is "sayin' good shit" about them in written reports.

Naturally, Jimmie and the others take great pride in that news. Early on, they established a stunning esprit de corps built on a foundation of confidence and determination to be the best platoon ever to graduate from boot camp. With just two weeks to go, it appears they might not be far off the mark.

So when they learn the DIs are going to add boxing to their physical routine, they approach the news by trying to muster the same enthusiasm they have given to everything else. But aggressive behavior is not typically part of the Navajo character. In this platoon, only Jimmie has ever boxed for sport. To make matters worse, the boxing regimen has apparently been prompted by a sergeant who makes it clear he harbors no liking for "cigar-store Indians" in his beloved Corps. His name is Carston, but the Navajo recruits secretly call him Carson, as in Indian-killer Kit Carson.

It is after the platoon drills for two hours in full sun that Sergeant Carston saunters over and orders the boots to form a line. Carston is tall, stringy as wild buckwheat, with pale skin and an Adam's apple that thrusts forward, demanding to be noticed. His close-cropped hair is sandy blond, the color of hay. When the sergeant speaks—hollers, more accurately—his drawl sounds as foreign to Jimmie as a European accent might.

"You Injuns think your shit don't stink," the Sergeant snarls. "Let's see how good y'are without the war paint and tomahawks," he says, pronouncing it "tommyhawks." "Who'll be my first volunteers?"

Carston walks along the line of recruits and then turns on his heels and points to Ray Begay and Charlie Yazzie, who both look as if they are willing themselves to be invisible.

"You, Tonto ... and your *kimosabe* here. Jes' like on the radio, you two."

He tosses two pairs of boxing gloves at the invisible men and shouts for them to get into the ring.

"Sir, what ring, sir?" Ray asks. All anyone can see is the dusty parade ground, flat and open as Navajo paper bread.

"I'll show you what ring." He swings his head and glares at the hesitant recruits. "Boot turds! Form a circle here around Tonto and *Kimosabe*. Now!"

Reluctantly, the boys follow the order. Twenty-seven pairs of marine-issue boots kick up the dust as they form a wide ring around the two men in the middle.

"Let's see what you Injuns got," Carston snarls.

Within the circle, Ray and Charlie begin sparring, if anyone would call it that. They bob and weave and throw light, timid punches, neither quite sure of what to do.

"You call that boxing?" screams the Sergeant. "You fight like squaws, like little pansies. Everyone, get back in line, stand at attention while I show you how it's done."

The hesitant recruits quickly break their circle and line up side by side.

Carston puts on a pair of gloves and walks up to Ray, the first man. The sergeant draws back his right arm and lands a punch squarely on Ray's jaw. The surprised recruit cries out and staggers backward from the blow.

Jimmie is sixth in line. He curses the sergeant under his breath, using all of his self-control to keep from breaking formation and running to Ray's aid. But Ray is already resuming his place at the head of the line and rubbing his jaw as the sergeant announces smugly, "*That's* how to throw a punch."

The demonstration is far from over. Carston moves to the number-two man, the quiet boy named Stanley Tso, and sends him reeling with another strong right. In similar fashion, the sergeant moves down the line and delivers a blow to Charlie Yazzie, George

Benally, and Wilfred Smith as they stand, under orders, eyes forward and at full attention, like ducks in a carnival shooting gallery.

Jimmie is next. Although he looks straight ahead as ordered, anger rises in him like stomach acid. And now he stares defiantly into the resolute face of Sergeant Carston, who has positioned himself directly in front, his right arm coiled back.

Jimmie acts instinctively, confidently, deflecting the sergeant's swinging glove and countering with a bare-fisted punch of his own. He catches Carston under the chin with a powerful left hook, followed by a clear blow to the sergeant's jaw with his right.

Carston sprawls backward and hits the ground ass first. Dirt and dust flies in all directions. The sergeant slides on his back, an upside-down turtle, arms and legs flailing.

As the recruits watch with their mouths agape, Jimmie breaks the stunned silence by calling out to the fallen sergeant, "Sir, see what a good instructor you are, sir. I'm getting the hang of this boxing thing already."

The platoon stands in stunned silence. Jimmie can see it in their eyes: concern for him, fear that his actions will get him thrown out of boot camp. Or worse.

Carston brushes himself off and, like an angry bull, glares at his nemesis. "When my report gets to Captain McLeod," he fumes, "y'all will be back on the reservation fuckin' your sheep to make more Injuns." Then he turns and, with a dismissive gesture, mutters to Shaw and Passon who are running over to investigate, "Y'all can deal with these misfits from now on."

Expecting no sympathy and caring little for the consequences, Jimmie tells the DIs what happened. To his surprise, Shaw and Passon simply shake their heads and promise they will put in a word themselves with Captain McLeod, the senior officer in charge of drills and inspections.

Hours later, Jimmie and his buddies learn that Sergeant Carston has been given a verbal reprimand and told to keep his distance from the "important" Navajo platoon. Jimmie receives no dressing down for his actions. To the contrary, he senses that Shaw and Passon regard him with renewed respect.

As for the boxing, it is discontinued as quickly as it had begun.

Up until the Carston incident, the Navajo platoon had not been aware of any ill feelings directed toward them. But Jimmie, for one, is not entirely convinced that this will prove to be an isolated incident. He is well aware that, like the delicate cactus flower that adorns a prickly skin beneath, not everything that seems beguiling, at first, can necessarily last forever. Often the beauty fades and only the thorns remain.

IN SIX SHORT WEEKS, THE twenty-nine boys have become men and now march proudly to the parade ground. They stand in formation, straight as steel rods, for the last time as boots.

Ray playfully punches Jimmie in the arm. "Every one of us made it. Even you, *Cheii*." As a joke, they've taken to calling Jimmie *Cheii*: grandfather.

"And you," Jimmie says, grinning, "made it through basic without having to cheat on your weight. Matter of fact"—he taps Ray's stomach—"it looks like Marine Corps food agrees with you. Or is that mostly beer?"

The previous evening, Shaw and Passon had taken the boot platoon to the canteen and bought them a couple of rounds. A victory celebration. Most of the boys discovered what Jimmie had suspected all along: that their DIs, underneath all the bullshit, are happy to welcome them into their special brotherhood.

The graduation festivities on this twenty-seventh day of June are marked by a company parade and a final formation before the boot platoons are disbanded, scattered, and reassigned. But for some inexplicable reason, the all-Navajo platoon is to be an exception. The men whoop and holler to find out they will be moving on together for special training as the 382nd Platoon.

Capping off the ceremonies is a special address by Commanding Officer Hall, who directs some of his words specifically to the Navajo platoon.

"Over here is one of the most outstanding platoons ever to come through the recruit depot." He looks directly at the twenty-nine young men. "Your physical endurance is exemplary, and I understand you achieved among the all-time highest aggregate scores on the rifle range. I cannot express the pride and privilege I feel in having you outstanding young men join our ranks. Well done, lads."

For Jimmie, it marks a proud moment in what has been an aimless life. He wishes that, during the anticipated ten-day liberty that traditionally follows boot camp, he could express to his father how it feels to be a part of something not just Navajo, but American—American, in the sweeping, multicultural sense of the word; how their platoon is bringing honor to the Navajo people through their accomplishments, singled out in the CO's graduation speech. But Jimmie knows better. Wilson would simply label his son as delusional. The CO's words? More lies and doubletalk from the white man. Nothing could pierce Wilson's armor of contempt and resentment toward the Anglo world and toward all individuals who are either a part of it or, among the Navajos themselves, those who, like Chee Dodge, reach out to it.

No matter. For after the glowing words from the CO, after the snappy salutes and warm gestures of acceptance from the drill instructors, and after receiving numerous welcomes into the brotherhood of the Corps, the platoon learns that their liberty has been abruptly cancelled.

Instead of going home, they are ordered to immediately board buses for the twelve-mile drive up to Camp Elliott. Communications training is scheduled to begin first thing Monday, less than forty-eight hours away. "Special circumstances" is all they are told.

Most of the boys express disappointment and anger. For Jimmie, though, the news comes almost as a relief. He is not eager to face the wrath of Wilson Goodluck anytime soon.

"Looks like we're the only boot graduates not gettin' home leave," Ray grumbles as they climb aboard the bus. "Here I am, lookin' real nice in marine dress blues, and nobody back home's gonna see me."

"I'm sure we'll get our liberty soon. Probably after the next phase of training." Jimmie's voice, however, is flat and unconvincing.

Ray drops into the empty seat beside his buddy. The young man is clearly on the verge of tears. Jimmie pats him on the shoulder but can think of nothing more to say.

"What could be so darned important it can't wait ten more lousy days?" Ray wonders aloud, his trembling voice barely audible over the strident complaint of the bus doors as they close on their indispensable cargo.

CHAPTER 5

JULY 1942

C amp Elliott, host to thousands of marines on their way to combat in the Pacific, is a seemingly random sprawl of buildings and Quonset huts hunkered down in the Kearny Mesa district north of San Diego. The new 382nd Platoon spends part of their Sunday arrival day getting acclimated to their barracks, a long wooden structure painted the color of dried mustard. At first blush their new home appears to be a step up from their drafty tents at the training depot.

Throughout the unremitting challenges of boot camp, the young men have formed a bond, and now they take advantage of their free time to socialize, laugh, bullshit, and become even closer. They have been ordered not to leave the compound, so they sit on their bunks and swap stories about their lives back home.

Jimmie has no interest in contributing anything about his own background. The personal insights he might be willing to share privately with Ray are not for widespread consumption. He guards them fiercely, like a military secret. Instead he listens to the others, enthralled by their anecdotes and yarns.

George Benally, for all his rough-edged wit and sarcasm, starts things off with a story about the time he ran away as a lonely, frightened child from his strict boarding school.

"I walked all the way home to the Red Valley—took me a good couple of days—and my grandfather, he was not happy with me. 'Like it or not, times have changed,' he said to me. 'Without the white man's education, you will end up hungrier than you are already.' Hate to say he was right, but I didn't think so at the time. He sent me right back to school, I can tell you that. Not long after, I wanted to run away again, but out of respect for my grandfather, I didn't. I stuck it out."

George seems to be finished, but then he adds with a smirk, "Besides, by then I was starting to learn all the good white man's words, like *fuck* and *shit* and *cocksucker* and *asshole*."

Next, Carl Slowtalker, already homesick for his mother's paper bread, makes everyone's mouth water as he reminisces how he squatted by her side while she pounded corn into flour.

"After she mixed the flour and water together, she poured blobs of the batter onto a hot stone slab. I loved to watch as she pressed them down and smoothed each one with her bare hand until they got paper thin. When the bread started to brown and crisp along the edges, she folded them just so"—he makes motions with his hands as if none of his platoon buddies have ever seen or tasted the staple before—"and she always handed me the first warm bread to come off the stone."

Jimmie can almost see it frying, can inhale the steam and smell its heady aroma. His eyes grow moist as he pictures his own mother in much the same way.

For Charlie Yazzie, life alongside the Chinle Wash was more idyllic in retrospect than it probably was in reality, the boy admits.

But Carl's mention of paper bread reminds Charlie of his own personal favorite.

"During the rainy season, my friends and I went out with long wooden clubs and pails of water. We poured the water into prairie dog holes—they were already soggy from the rain—and when the little rascals scrambled out to keep from drowning, we took turns clubbing 'em. Sometimes we returned home with a dozen or more. Man, we ate pretty good when that happened."

Ray is quiet as the boys swap stories. So Jimmie asks his new best friend how he got interested in becoming a silversmith.

"Well, I ain't no smith yet, just done a few buttons, really, seeing as I'm still learnin'," Ray admits. He explains how his father works leather and needs buttons for some of his boots, so Ray thought it might be a good thing to try.

"I started by building a forge in our outhouse using wood sticks and mud and a big, flat rock. Then my father built a goatskin bellows. He even found a chunk of iron someone threw away. Used that for an anvil."

One thing led to another, Ray goes on, and before long he was polishing his first button. "'Course, silver takes money, so my buttons have been mostly copper and nickel mixed together. Someday, though, I'm going to make bracelets and necklaces and conchos out of real silver, you wait and see. To go with the leatherwork my father does."

Jimmie tries not to think about his own father, although there was a time, long passed, when they were close. Wilson used to patiently explain the *Dineh* traditions to his young son—*Dineh*, or the People, as the Navajo refer to themselves. Wilson instilled within Jimmie a deep love of nature, of the tribal legends, of *Dinetah*— sacred land of the People. He showed his son how to build and repair brush corrals for their livestock. He worked with him on the Navajo songs that were part of their everyday lives. He taught him how to spin a rope, much like the father and son Jimmie passed on his way to Ft. Wingate. But those times did not last, for Jimmie eventually became aware that in spite of all his father cherished, the man was consumed by the intolerance spewed by the likes of Black Horse and his followers.

Eventually the stories stop, so Jimmie heads outside for some fresh air. He is followed by Charlie and Carl, who amuse themselves playing horseshoes. George, Wilfred, and two others begin a marathon poker game at one end of the barracks. Ray begins a long letter to his family, promising them a picture of himself in uniform. That is, he writes, if he ever gets time off to go into town, where there is rumored to be a box you can go into and, for a quarter, get your picture taken. Then Ray spends the next hour with some illustrated magazines called comic books that someone discovered among the treasures in the now-accessible MCX.

Ray shows his remarkable find to Jimmy, who has returned to the barracks fifty dollars richer after stumbling onto a craps game behind the mess hall. From the back of the barracks there rises a distinctive whoop, conjoined by several disgusted moans. Carl Slowtalker has won another big pot.

Jimmie says, "Hey, little brother. How's about I teach you how to shoot craps? Not for money, though. If you're as lucky as you are on the rifle range, you'll clean me out."

"Naw, I don't want none o' your bad habits," Ray chides. "B'sides, you didn't talk up earlier, an' you owe me the rest of your story. Y'know, the one you started on the bus ride from Ft. Wingate."

"My story's not like your ... picture books? What do you call them?"

"Comics."

"Yeah, nothing comical about my life."

"You said you knew Chee Dodge. Sounds pretty good to me."

"I worked with him. Back in the thirties, when the government stirred things up by ordering Navajos to cull down our livestock."

"My dad talks about those days a lot," Ray sighs. "Those orders hit our family pretty hard."

"Hit everybody hard. I got involved with Chee around the time I quit my bootleg whiskey business. Had nothing lined up for the future, and I wasn't getting on with my father anymore, so I rode to Chee's summer ranch to see how Annie was doing. It'd been three years since I saw her at her wedding."

Jimmie talks about how Annie did not have an easy life, in spite of her father's wealth and position. Chee expected a lot from her and her husband. She told Jimmie she did not mind the hard work, but she wanted to do more, perhaps get involved with her local chapter, whose elected officials and delegates represented the area's interests in the tribal council. When Annie's father was at the ranch, he often took her to chapter meetings at nearby Wide Ruins and Klagetoh. After a time she started going to meetings even when he was away.

"As you know," she told Jimmie, "the Indian Service isn't very popular around here, with the livestock issue and all. My father believes Washington isn't entirely wrong, so you can imagine, he carries a heavy saddle at those meetings."

As Annie got dinner going, cleaning four prairie dogs and singing off their hair over an open fire in a pit behind the house, she listened as Jimmie spoke of his relationship with his father, sour as last week's milk, and of his despondence over being unable to find steady work.

"I have the answer for you!" Annie said abruptly. "You know what my father's going through, trying to get people to understand the government's position on livestock and grazing. Take the chapter meeting I went to last week—the government agent's translator didn't put the English words into Navajo very clearly. But Jimmie, *you* could. You'd be perfect!" She insisted her father could get him a position with the Indian Service. One word from Chee is all it would take.

"It's settled then," Annie declared, without waiting for his answer. "Father will be visiting next week. You'll stay here and meet with him, of course."

And of course, he did.

Jimmie and Chee sat together on the veranda of the Anglo-style ranch house. The porch itself was unusual on the reservation, let alone the two cushioned chairs and the swing wide enough to seat three people. Chee was nearing eighty, although his energy suggested a younger man. He fanned himself with his wide-brimmed hat and then took a hearty swallow of scotch and explained, "It's not easy, trying to ride two wild ponies at once. I speak for the government when I'm with my people. I speak for my people when I'm with the government."

Chee explained that the people would not admit there might be some truth in the agents' words, while at the same time, the government agents were not sensitive to the needs and emotions of the people. "The agents do not understand that sheep and horses are to the Navajo what money and social standing are to the agents. Expecting a Navajo to destroy some of his livestock is like asking the agent to burn some of his money."

Jimmie was confused. "So you don't think the government is right, then?"

"That's not what I said. Fact is, the white man is usually right."

Jimmie struggled to keep Chee's rambling discourse straight in his mind. "Let's see if I understand you correctly. The government is telling us that we Navajos have too many sheep, too many horses. That our grazing land can't support our increasing livestock. And so this John Collier, as commissioner, is calling for a straight 10 percent reduction of everyone's flock?"

Chee nodded. He removed his spectacles and rubbed his eyes, as if he did not care for the vision lodged there.

Collier's demand hardly seemed fair to Jimmie. Many families, his included, had only small flocks. Asking them to cut back 10 percent would be a tremendous sacrifice.

In the brief silence that followed, Chee looked into his scotch, transfixed, as if the glass spoke to him in a peaty voice only he could hear. Of course, alcohol was illegal on the reservation, but Chee Dodge was not one to bother with trivialities.

"Look," Chee said, replacing his glasses on his face, "overgrazing is a fact. *Something* has to be done. So it falls on me to make the people understand."

Maybe Washington's intent was right, but it would be bitter medicine for most Navajos to swallow. The old ways were not easily changed.

Chee looked at Jimmie and confirmed that he was looking for a good translator. He intended to tell Collier to put Jimmie on the government payroll.

"It was like this," Jimmie says to Ray, summing up his recollections of those turbulent times. "I realized Chee was used to getting what he wanted. And only a fool would turn down the opportunity. So I told him I'd do my best."

"I bet you were great at it," Ray gushes. "Bet they loved you at the chapter meetings."

Jimmie is about to explain how wrong Ray is but then thinks better of it. He flops down onto his bunk, exhausted.

"If that's your idea of a good bet, my friend, maybe you better stay away from craps after all," he says.

CHAPTER 6

JULY 1942

The windows are covered with heavy iron bars like those found in a prison. That is the first thing Jimmie notices as the platoon walks from the mess hall to the low-slung building that will house their classroom over the coming weeks. There are no bars on the windows of other structures at Camp Elliott, and Jimmie wonders if anyone else in his platoon finds this as unsettling as he does.

Escorting the platoon is a sandy-haired and expressionless young staff sergeant whose tag identifies him as Sgt. Rick Anderson. He appears to be in his early twenties. He stands by the door, which is also protected with iron bars, as the men file inside. When they all pass through, he locks the door behind them. Then he leads the way down a long, dimly lit corridor, past closed-door offices identified only by small, numbered plaques beside each doorway. The transom above one of the doors is open a few inches. From the other side Jimmie hears the faint sounds of a typewriter, the only audible evidence of human occupancy within the building.

Moments later, Sergeant Anderson ushers the men into a room at the end of the hall.

"This is where I leave you," the sergeant tells them. "Make yourselves comfortable, 'cause you'll be spending a lot of time here. The colonel will be along in a few minutes to brief you and get you started." With no further explanation their escort walks out, closing the door on twenty-nine puzzled and anxious men milling about inside.

The room is rather plain. In the center, a large folding table looks like it came right out of a Sears catalog. Thirty or so metal folding chairs lay scattered haphazardly around the otherwise empty space. The walls are unadorned, painted off-white, and dappled with numerous marks where items have apparently been tacked on and then removed. At one end there is a freestanding chalkboard and chalk. From the ceiling dangles a poster depicting a US Marine with full pack, his posture in forward movement, his face determined. He is positioned against a red background with the words "Let's go!" boldly printed in black capital letters.

"This looks a lot like my classroom in boarding school," Carl Slowtalker says, casting a suspicious eye on the clean chalkboard. The reservation schools attended by Carl and others of his age have reportedly improved since Jimmie's time at Toadlena. Maltreatment is largely in the past. But now, from all appearances, the young men are back in school again, although as Jimmie looks around he realizes that something is missing.

George Benally is the first to put it into words. "Shit sakes, there's no windows in here! Even a fucking prison cell's got a window."

"Yeah, and you would know," chimes a voice from somewhere in the room. George feigns anger at the remark and the men break into laughter, a culmination of nervous energy that has been building like atmospheric pressure since morning roll call.

Suddenly the door swings open and a lieutenant colonel enters.

He carries a rectangular case and a stack of printed material. The laughter in the room stops abruptly as the men snap to attention. When Carl leaps to his feet, his chair overturns and collapses with a loud metallic clatter on the hard floor.

"At ease, lads," says the officer. "Please find a seat."

He sets down the items in his hands and waits patiently as the men scramble for chairs. Then he introduces himself as Lt. Colonel James Jones, Area Signal Officer. He commends the platoon on their exemplary record at the training depot and welcomes them to Camp Elliott. As he speaks, twenty-nine anxious Navajo faces look up at him.

The officer is tall and trim, his hair clearly graying at the temples. His uniform is so neatly creased, Jimmie wonders if he ever sits down. His voice is deep and resonant, like a radio announcer. Not Edward R. Murrow, exactly, but Jimmie can almost picture the colonel in a studio somewhere reading the latest news or selling war bonds or something.

"First, let me go over some rules about how we're going to proceed here," the colonel says, making eye contact with the young men. "Any time you need to leave this room—to use the bathroom, or take a break, or simply get some air—you'll go with a buddy. You'll exit this classroom in pairs only, never alone. And you will not leave this building for any reason without prior permission from an officer, is that clear?"

Heads nod slowly. Some of the men glance warily at one another.

"You may wonder if this heavy security is standard operating procedure here in Communications School, and I will tell you now, it is not. Your platoon will receive all the standard training required to become Marine Corps radiomen, which will be your designation when you leave this camp and go into areas of enemy contact. But you weren't recruited to be exactly like all the other radiomen. The

Corps has a particular mission for this platoon, one that requires specialized training. It will begin at once and must proceed quickly, under tight security and the strictest secrecy.

"What happens in this room is strictly classified, gentlemen. That means you won't breathe a word of what you'll be doing here to anyone—including your mothers or wives or sweethearts. While you're here, you won't even discuss it with your fellow marines or with *any* serviceman, for that matter, under the rank of lieutenant colonel, unless they're designated by me to enter the room. Any questions so far?"

Jimmie raises his hand. Tentatively, halfway up. The officer acknowledges him with a nod. "Sir, just what is it we're supposed to be doing?"

For the first time, the colonel forces a weak smile. "All right, let's get into that." He clears his throat and pauses to choose his words. The smile vanishes.

"Gentlemen, you have been handpicked to create and implement what a few of my superiors think could be the most powerful weapon ever used in US military counterintelligence." The colonel coughs—nervously, it seems to Jimmie—and then he continues. "Me, I'm not so sure about that. But I do know this: the success or failure of this program rests entirely in your hands."

WALKING OVER TO THE CHALKBOARD, Lieutenant Colonel Jones writes out two words: *code* and *cipher*.

He begins. "Let's start with the basics. In any war, it is imperative to send messages that the enemy—if he intercepts the communication—can't understand. Conversely, intercepting and understanding the enemy's transmissions is essential to any victorious military force. That's why codes and ciphers are used. We try to break theirs, they try to break ours."

He walks slowly back and forth in front of the room as he talks, pacing between a Marine Corps flag on the right, the Stars and Stripes on the left.

"When words or phrases in a message are simply replaced with other words or phrases, that's a code. But when you mask a coded message by varying the ways in which it can be understood—multiple keys, in other words—that's a cipher."

The colonel stops pacing. He must see some confusion in the eyes of the men, because he says, "Let me try to explain with an example. In the days of the Romans, Julius Caesar created a simple code for his armies by substituting a letter three higher in the alphabet than each letter in the original. He used a *D* for an *A*, an *E* for a *B*, and so on. But suppose Caesar constantly *varied* the way to *understand* his messages? Suppose one day it was necessary to note every *other* decoded letter; another day, every *fourth* letter, let's say. You see? Those are examples of the multiple keys I was talking about. With this variable, Caesar's code becomes a cipher, and then it doesn't matter so much if his enemies figure out the basic word substitutions, as long as they don't discover the keys needed to decipher it."

He barely pauses to catch his breath as he continues, "Thing is, a code—and from now on, I'll just stay with that word to make this simpler—a code is either rendered useless when it's broken by the enemy, or else it evolves into something newer, stronger, better. Let me tell you something, men: in this war, the codes being used on all sides have never been more complex or more difficult to break. Today many of these codes are encrypted by machines and can only be broken by machines.

"The Germans are using a machine called Enigma. We haven't cracked it yet, but we will. The Japs have something we call Purple, a variation of Enigma. Just last month, we made a breakthrough in starting to crack that one, and you know why? Because we discovered their diplomatic messages all began with 'I have the honor to inform your Excellency …' See, it's *repetition* that gives us a peek under the tent, so to speak, that helps us not only to understand their code but, ultimately, to find the keys they're using."

Instead of waiting to see if the men have any questions, Lieutenant Colonel Jones pushes on. "Now, I've talked a little about the codes of our enemies. What about ours?"

He walks back to the chalkboard and writes out the letters SIGABA. Then he goes over to the carrying case he had set down on the table when he came into the room. He unlatches the cover and pulls out a strange-looking machine, a large box-like object with typewriter keys in the front.

It is like no typewriter any private in the room has ever seen.

Within the box, behind the keys, is a large cylinder of some sort. A dial sits on top of the box, and in the front, just above the typewriter keys, four rollers feed tape or ribbon across the front and into the mysterious workings inside.

"Meet SIGABA." The colonel looks down at the machine like a proud papa. "This is the primary cipher machine used by our armed forces. With it, we can send a message and decipher it at the other end in a matter of hours. But that's agonizingly slow during the heat of jungle warfare. Messages have to be typed into this machine letter by letter and then typed out letter by letter. After that, the completed cipher text has to be transmitted by a radio operator. The radioman on the other end then has to pass it on to a cipher expert, who selects the correct key based on that day's key list and then types the cipher text into his machine, which deciphers the message letter by letter.

"Time isn't the only drawback, though it's a big one. You see, amazing as these code machines are, there are too many chances for human error. Still, it's all we've got. Right now, on Guadalcanal, the Japs are breaking every other code we throw at 'em. Who knows how long SIGABA will be safe?"

Once again, the colonel abruptly stops his pacing and stands at direct center in front of the men. This time he takes a deep breath and speaks in a voice slightly softer than the didactic tone he has been using. "Our search for a whole new kind of code, one that can be fast and effective under battle conditions, one the enemy can never break, is what has brought you twenty-nine men here today."

Within the room there is silence, punctuated by a collective intake of breath. Jimmie sits up straight, listening intently. Faintly, from outside the walls of the room, comes the muffled sound of marching boots.

"It will be up to this platoon to come up with that combat code, and to memorize it. There will be no code book outside of here. When you put messages into your code, no one but you will understand it. Not the enemy. Not your fellow marines. Not me. Not even the commandant himself." Jones takes a deep breath, exhales. "You see, lads, your code will be in a language the rest of the world has never heard. It will be in Navajo."

The officer turns to the chalkboard. Only the squeaking of the chalk shatters the stunned silence. Everyone's eyes are riveted to the board as Lieutenant Colonel Jones scribbles four rules for the privates to follow in the days ahead.

The colonel points to them one at a time. "First, you'll need to construct an alphabet. You'll choose a code word—one that has a comparative word in your own language—to represent each letter of the alphabet. Second, you'll take the frequently used military terms on the hand-out I'll leave with you, and you'll choose common words to serve as accurate equivalents for those terms. Third, you'll make sure to think up short terms only, to ensure speed of transmission. And finally, you'll memorize each and every code word you create. There will be hundreds before you're through." He turns away from the board and faces the platoon. "That, my fellow marines, is your assignment."

The privates look at one another with wide-eyed wonder as the officer distributes a leaflet listing military terms and equipment. He follows with a second sheet that depicts picture charts of planes, ships, and weapons.

"Every scrap of paper in this room will be locked up at the end of each day. And remember what I said about leaving the room only with a buddy, or about leaving the building only with an officer's permission. If there's any additional material you need, just ask and we'll get it for you.

"Privates, you've distinguished yourselves in boot camp. But what you did there was nothing compared to what we expect of you now. I know you won't let down the Corps."

Lieutenant Colonel Jones pauses a moment to let his words sink in. Then he adds, "Lunch will be brought in at 1200 hours. Either I or one of my men will be back at the end of the day to see how you're coming along. Thanks for your attention this morning. I, along with your Corps and your country, wish you the best of luck."

He does not smile as he says these words. He does not ask if there are any questions, or if the assignment is in any way unclear. He simply scoops up the SIGABA machine, turns, and leaves the room, closing the door tightly behind him.

CHAPTER 7

JULY 1942

"What the fuck was *that* all about?"

The question is put forward by George Benally, who surges from his seat as if he has just backed into a cluster of thorny blackbrush back home. He looks around at the other twenty-eight faces. "Best of luck?" he exclaims. *"Best of luck?* If I could go back to the spot where I was born, roll around there a little, *that* would bring me luck. My grandfather told me that. Hard to find luck in this fucking prison, though."

For several moments, no one can think of anything to say. It is Carl Slowtalker who finally speaks up. "I don't get it. We're supposed to come up with some kind of code in Navajo? Didn't the boarding schools once *punish* our young people for speaking Navajo?"

And then everyone talks at once, some complaining, others marveling at the irony of it all, until Jimmie stands up and, putting two fingers against his lips, whistles loudly. Immediately the noise level drops. As the oldest member of the training platoon, the mantle of leadership has fallen on him. The men clearly look up to Jimmie, like Ray does. It makes him uncomfortable until he realizes his friend Annie would have taken charge in this situation without a moment's hesitation, and with this comprehension he knows what he must do.

"They want us to create a combat code," he says in an even tone. "In Navajo. Sounds fairly clear to me."

"Can we *do* that?" Ray asks. "Is it even possible?"

Jimmie shrugs. "We'll know soon enough. We have to try and work it out together. The colonel said to begin by putting the alphabet into code, and that makes sense to me. Let's start there and see how it goes."

Charlie Yazzie raises his hand as if he is back in school and Jimmie is the teacher. "I think we should agree on words and terms that are familiar to us," he says, "things we know from home."

"Good idea," Jimmie agrees. "So let's start with *A*. We'll pick a familiar English word starting with *A* that would have a Navajo equivalent."

"Navajo equivalent? That would leave out 'asshole,' I guess." That from George, naturally. They all chortle, Jimmie too, though he quickly regains a straight face.

"Seriously."

"How 'bout 'ant'?" suggests Ray.

"Ant," Jimmie repeats. *"Wol'la'chee.* That's great, Ray. See? This isn't so hard."

Charlie offers to write down the words they come up with. He will have to do it phonetically, as Navajo has traditionally been a spoken language, not a written one.

"Hey, I got a *B*," Ray says with all the excitement of a boy who has just ridden his first pony. "How 'bout 'bear'? We'd say *shush*."

Charlie writes down *s-h-u-s-h,* although he undoubtedly knows that an outsider would pronounce it quite incorrectly, as if they are telling someone to quiet down.

Jimmie is encouraged. "Okay, this is really good. Let's move on to *C*. We need a word starting with *C*."

George begins to snicker, so Jimmie quickly jumps in with "cat." In Navajo, *moasi*.

And so it goes. By the time lunch arrives, they have continued on to deer, elk, fox, goat, horse, ice, jackass, kid, lamb, mouse, nut, and owl. By midafternoon, they have added pig, quiver, rabbit, sheep, turkey, Ute, victor, weasel, yucca, and zinc. The platoon has their coded alphabet, and it is only 3:00 p.m.

For the rest of the afternoon they practice and memorize the twenty-six code words. It is important that everyone's Navajo pronunciations are identical, for many words change in meaning with even the slightest variation in pitch or lilt of the voice.

Shortly after five, an NCO reporting to Lieutenant Colonel Jones comes into the room to gather up all papers the men want to save. The rest, he says, will be destroyed. Moments later, after the room has been checked and double-checked, the platoon pours into the mess hall, exhausted and exhilarated in equal measure.

After dinner, the men head straight to barracks and relax until lights-out. One of the group, Samuel Nez, takes out a beautifully crafted wooden flute and plays a soulful tune of his own composition. Charlie Yazzie finds no takers for a card game, so he amuses himself by looking at George Benally's growing collection of pin-up photos. Ray, meanwhile, writes another letter home. As Ray seals the envelope, Jimmie asks what he finds to talk about in his letters, since there is not much they are allowed to tell their families.

"Just that I'm well, stuff like that. An' about my buddies. Even you, big brother." Ray beams and then becomes more somber. "I can't stop thinkin' about how my mother cried when I told her I was goin' to enlist. As for my father, well, he knows why I did this. He worries about me, but he supports me."

"You're lucky there."

Ray's face melts into a look of dismay. "Oh, jeez, I'm sorry, I wasn't tryin' to—"

"It's all right, Ray. Really. My mother cried, too. And like your father, she understood that I *had* to enlist. That I needed something more than—let's face it—the stagnant future I faced at home. See, by sending me to school when I was younger, she'd opened my eyes to how much in this country is always out of reach to people like us. But my father, well, he was madder 'n a tick at a sheep dip when I told him I was thinking 'bout joining up. How could I fight for the white man's government? Only he used the pejorative word, *bilaga'ana*. 'It's not our problem,' he says to me. 'Not our enemy. Not our war.' I tried to explain it *is* our enemy, our war. That if America was defeated, it would be the end of Navajo life, too. But you can't reason with a man like my father. To him, our enemy is the *bilaga'ana* government. Period."

Jimmie pauses to rein in his emotions as Ray sits on his bunk and waits for his buddy to continue. The sound of Samuel's flute fills the long pause, like a soulful background score in a Hollywood movie.

"Did I tell you, Ray, that when I left to enlist, my father refused to speak to me? Here's something that's almost funny: One of the last things he said was that it was bad enough I learned to speak the white man's words in school. And bad enough that I repeated *bilaga'ana* lies to my own people when I translated for the government. But what's worse, he said, was that I would be speaking the white man's words to help them win their war." Jimmie's forehead takes on faint furrows. "What do you suppose he'll think, Ray, when he learns that we helped in the war effort by speaking *Navajo* words?"

With that, Jimmie settles into his bunk. No need to dwell on the past, for this has been a productive day. An exhilarating day.

And when the call comes for lights-out, sleep is understandably elusive for all the men. There is a palpable energy that cannot be extinguished by the playing of Taps or by the diminishing light or by the soft, lulling spatter of gentle rain upon the roof. Excited whispers glide from bunk to bunk, slipping easily through the darkness, progressing with increasing urgency as if slumber is an unseemly imposition.

"A—Ant. *Wol'la'chee,*" come the first hushed words. From three bunks over: "B—Bear. *Shush.*" Then: "C—Cat. *Moasi.*" Followed by: "D—Deer. *Be.*" And: "E—Elk. *Dzeh.*" And ...

AT 2:25 IN THE MORNING, Jimmie awakens abruptly with a dream still fresh in his mind. Not like the puzzling dreams he had experienced before enlisting, but rather, one that echoed events that actually took place, no doubt summoned by his earlier conversation with Ray. It replayed the bitter father-son confrontation a couple years back at a chapter meeting in Shiprock when Jimmie translated for the government.

It was Jimmie's job to translate, clarify, sway, and proselytize on behalf of those leaders, Navajo and non-Indian alike, who saw some form of livestock reduction as either necessary, inevitable, or both. He was a referee, a go-between, a messenger who, as people perceived it, bore only bad news. He became entangled in the melee of ideas, proposals, and mandates, thick as mud after a spring thaw, as he attended meeting after meeting at local chapter houses which functioned as assembly points for government business and social gatherings.

To his chagrin, this dream unfolded not as a memory, but almost as if it were happening all over again. He saw himself and the well-intentioned Commissioner of Indian Affairs, John Collier, take their seats behind a small table, elevated above the dirt floor on a makeshift wooden platform. Collier tried to explain to the assemblage that the soil was eroding, that the herds were growing, that grazing land was disappearing. That the land simply could not support so many sheep and horses. Trouble is, Collier could explain the problem of overgrazing in a hundred different ways, but the people would still fall back on their long-held beliefs that only the supernaturals had the power to make things right.

Collier tried to explain that Washington was not asking, it was *telling* them to cull down their livestock. He pointed out that their tribal leaders had agreed to this.

As Jimmie translated Collier's words, a man pushed his way through the crowd and shouted in Navajo, "And who would those tribal leaders be, the ones who agree? Chee Dodge and his wealthy rancher friends? They are witches, you know."

The voice was angry. Defiant.

Wilson Goodluck.

Jimmie's father parked himself in the front row and looked up at his son. "Are you just going to stand there, Mr. Translator, Mr. Government Dog, Mr. Lick-the-White-Man's-Boots? Or are you going to tell the *bilaga'ana* what I said?"

Jimmie turned to the commissioner. "He says the leaders are witches, Chee Dodge and the other wealthy ranchers. He … he is my father, the man who speaks these words. He doesn't like what I do. But his views aren't so different from many others who live in this area."

"Then by all means, let's continue, if that's all right," the commissioner said. "Tell him—tell *them*—that rain won't bring back the grazing land that's already gone. In fact, a hard rain may well take the remaining soil with it."

Before Jimmie got halfway through the translation, his father cried out, "What good is the soil or the rain without our sheep? We do not live like the *bilaga'ana*, except maybe half-breeds like Chee Dodge. We provide for our animals, and in return, the Holy Ones provide for us."

Again, heads nodded vigorously. Jimmie might as well have talked directly to the animals for all the good it did. Wilson, meanwhile, was just getting started. Like an out-of-control wagon careening down from the crest of a hill, he quickly picked up speed. Even in the gauzy fabric of this dream, Jimmie was not spared his father's wrath.

"You make us promises, you and your fellow thieves in Washington, and what do we get? You promise us a dollar a head if we sell you our goats. Before we accept this insult, your people come through anyway. They kill our goats by the thousands and leave them to rot. Now our babies have no milk. Then you kill our sheep and horses, more than we can eat at one time, so the meat is wasted and again our people starve. Still you ask us to slaughter even more of our animals. Why should we do this? You will come and do it for us anyway.

"And you, Government Dog"—Wilson leveled his glare at Jimmie—"will you help them, your *bilaga'ana* friends? Will you take a rifle and point it at your mother's flock? You, with your *bilaga'ana* education and the money you take from the *bilaga'ana* government, will you kill off your own family's two remaining horses now that you speak for *them?*"

Jimmie sprang to his feet and bounded to the front of the small wooden platform. Speaking in Navajo, his voice took on an angry tenor as he glared back at his father. "Think about your words. You wrap yourself in a blanket of hate when faced with something you refuse to understand. You live in the past. Like it or not, change is coming to the reservation."

"Now think about *your* words," Wilson shouted back, as if he and his son were the only ones in the room. "You have come under the spell of their witchcraft. You chew their lying words and take their worthless money. You turn your back on your people."

The crowd edged forward, eager for more. They murmured words of encouragement each time Wilson spoke. For them, the debate bordered on entertainment.

"No, Father, I respect my people. For our traditions to go on, we must also respect the land." He swept his gaze over the crowd, which grew increasingly restless, especially when Jimmie spoke. "What you all refuse to see is that the whites know many things we do not. There is much we can learn from them." Jimmie took a deep breath and continued to addresses his father directly as the commissioner looked on, not comprehending the rapid-fire Navajo words. "Suppose you were bitten by a rattlesnake and John Collier, here, had the medicine that could save your life. Would you turn away from him? Often the white man's medicine is stronger than that of our own healers. And sometimes, the medicine isn't pleasant, but it can make things better."

"And sometimes," Wilson called back, his voice heavy as wet timber, "the plant that is medicine for some is poison to others. I hope you learn that one day. You are spreading the poison and you do not even know it."

Wilson spit on the ground, turned, and then pushed his way back through the crowd, disappearing through the open door.

The meeting lasted only another few minutes. There was little either the commissioner or his earnest translator could do to change the mindset of the agitated group.

As they collapsed afterward in Collier's car, the commissioner said to Jimmie, "Don't be too hard on your father. His anger, as you know, is not without justification. Hell, I'm not proud of many things my government has done to the Indians. Even now, promises I've made in good faith aren't always backed up in Washington." He stared expressionlessly out the window. Several men who were in the audience walked past the car, smirking and muttering something incomprehensible. "But things have to get better," Collier continued, perhaps trying to convince himself. "The 1940s are almost here, and the next decade holds promise for us all."

"The 1940s," Jimmie repeated, his voice flat, unsure. His brief tenure as a government translator had proven even less satisfying than baking fry bread and cooking sausage at the Ganado hospital. At least there the people there liked what he dished up. He yearned for something more in his future than working dead-end jobs, or being a pariah among his own people.

He looked at Collier with a vacant stare. "Yes, maybe the 1940s will be a better time for us all. We can dream, can't we?"

JIMMIE IS NOW FULLY AWAKE. Sweat glistens on his skin like morning dew. In the streaky moonlight that saturates the far window, Ray lies fast asleep. Same for all the others.

Jimmie scrunches back under his blanket and strains to break free from his tether to the past with thoughts of the task at hand.

The code.

A fresh day is approaching, soon to be followed by many more, each filled with new words to be substituted, and learned, and memorized, and then, presumably, in the heat of battle, summoned in an instant. Lives depending on it.

The code.

It is suddenly clear how every occurrence that has shaped Jimmie's muddled existence to this point, like coils of clay pressed one upon the other to build up a piece of pottery, is trivial and insignificant compared to what is now expected of him and of his platoon.

From this moment on, it is only about the code. The code, and the consequences it could have in shaping the outcome of the war.

CHAPTER 8

JULY–AUGUST 1942

D
ay two in the creation of the code begins easily enough with a review of the previous day's alphabet. After the platoon has mastered the twenty-six substitutions, Jimmie reaches for the pile of printed material that Lt. Colonel Jones left behind.

"We need code words that identify the officers: major general, brigadier general, colonel, lieutenant colonel, major, captain, first and second lieutenant. Any suggestions?"

Ray speaks up first. "Couldn't we just spell the ranks letter by letter?"

George Benally pounces on him like a wildcat on a jackrabbit. "Gee, shit-for-brains, how many marines do you suppose might die before you finished transmitting and decoding 'brigadier general' one letter at a time?"

Ray looks away, embarrassed.

"Listen, Benally," Jimmie snaps, "if you want to try out your new expressions and talk like a drill instructor, I don't care. But you will not talk that way to a fellow marine. You didn't insult your friends on the reservation, if you had any, and you won't do it here."

George merely shrugs, indifferent to Jimmie's disapproval. Perhaps he knows he crossed the line here, but if so, he does not acknowledge it.

Jimmie turns from George to Ray and says, "Insulting though he was, I s'pose you realize there's truth in his words."

Ray flashes a sheepish grin and nods his head. Suddenly, his eyes grow wide and his voice rises with excitement. "Okay, then, how 'bout this: what else shows an officer's rank besides his title?"

"The number of people over him he has to take shit from," pipes up Carl.

Ray ignores the remark and says, "His insignia, of course! A major general, that's two stars. *So'na'ki,* right? A brigadier general is one star. *So'ala'ih.* Short and simple. Now we just follow the rank order and match the officers to their insignias: silver eagle, silver and gold oak leaves, two silver bars, one silver bar, gold bar."

The men erupt into spontaneous applause. Ray gives an "it was nothing" kind of shrug and beams. Charlie excitedly writes down the code words, and the group immediately begins to memorize them. The platoon is off to a very good start.

Next they move on to codifying the names of airplanes and ships. Charlie gets the idea to use bird names for the planes, and names of fish and aquatic animals for ships. "Dive bomber" becomes *gini,* or "chicken hawk." "Transport plane" changes to *astah,* or "eagle." "Battleship" turns into *lo'tso,* "whale." There is a logic to the substitutions, which makes the code easier to memorize and facilitates speed and accuracy in communication.

The following day, they take a shot at military designations. For "corps," they settle on the word for "clan"—*dineh'ih.* For each organization term within the Corps, they choose a clan name that can be spoken in one or two words.

Each day they come up with new code words. And each day they practice the words they have already committed to memory. Even over lunch, they do not deter from their mission. There is no horsing around, no place for small talk.

At four o'clock on Friday of this first week, Lieutenant Colonel Jones walks through the door and asks for a briefing on the men's progress. He listens intently as they proudly take him through their accomplishments.

"I'm delighted at how far you've come," the colonel says, although his expression belies his encouraging words. "In another week or two, when you've added a hundred or more words to the list and memorized them all—"

He is interrupted by a good-natured groan from several of the men, which elicits a rare smile from the officer.

"When you've done that, I'll arrange a … let's call it a field demonstration … for some of the commanding officers. But come Monday, your work on the code will be cut short by a few hours each day so you can begin your regular training to become radiomen. And always remember, when you're training with the other platoons, you will not discuss what you're doing in this room. Any questions?" Again, he does not wait for hands to go up. "Good. Take the rest of today off, men. You've earned it."

Jimmie checks his watch. It is already 1645.

As the colonel nears the door, Charlie calls out, "*I* have a question, sir. When we complete our training here, *then* will we be allowed some home liberty before we, uh … before we ship out?"

Lieutenant Colonel Jones, his hand already on the doorknob, stops abruptly. There is an expectant pause before he turns.

"Well, we'll have to see about that, won't we?" he says cryptically.

EVERY MARINE IN THE 382ND Platoon works harder than at any other time in his life. And it is only week two at Camp Elliott.

The men train with other platoons to learn Morse and panel

codes, flags, blinkers, and field telephone operation. They drill in the basics of radio transmission and repair. They are schooled in every aspect of the Signal Corps, including combat and amphibious assault training. Through it all, they continue to meet in their sterile, windowless room as they expand and memorize the code.

Unlike the other platoons at Camp Elliott, they have no free weekends. Saturdays are spent back in the dungeon, as they call it, where they come up with code words for a general vocabulary of verbs, nouns, and pronouns. They also codify a wide spectrum of language necessary for combat communications, like directional and military terms. On Sundays, they take several hours to practice the mushrooming palette of words.

By the last week in July, when Lieutenant Colonel Jones learns that his Navajos have already put more than 150 words into code, he announces the time has come to try it out in the field using sample messages devised by his staff.

The Navajo marines work in pairs in an isolated area of the camp. Officers from Jones's staff give each sender a series of messages. The sender radios his partner, who is positioned some distance away, as if working within each other's line of sight might somehow compromise the exercise. Beginning early in the morning, they send and receive messages for hours.

Jimmie teams up with Ray. Their first message reads, *Heavy artillery fire. Company C reports many casualties, alert headquarters.* Using the corresponding Navajo equivalent words they devised, this becomes *Many big guns fire; Mexican cat got words many out of action, watchful main house.* That is the thing about the code, Jimmie marvels: if the enemy should ever capture one of the more than three thousand Navajo servicemen *not* in the code program, the hapless prisoner could be forced to translate the Navajo words, but he would not understand the actual message.

Not surprisingly, some mistakes are made. But considering that the men are just three weeks into the program, it is little wonder that Lieutenant Colonel Jones is grinning like a sailor on shore liberty by the time the platoon spills into the mess hall for lunch. They are allowed back to their barracks an hour early, a small reward for their sterling performance in the field.

Jimmie is just settling into his bunk, stretching out and trying to clear his mind of the three codes—Morse, panel and Navajo—when the door bursts open and a military policeman enters, all business.

"I'm looking for, uh, Private Goodluck," he announces, reading from a scrap of paper.

The pockets of conversation stop and everyone looks at Jimmie, who jumps up like a startled jackrabbit.

"I'm Private Goodluck."

The MP walks over to him. "I need you to come with me."

"Come with you? Where?"

"North Island. Immediately. Private."

Clearly, this is not a request. The North Island Naval Air Station, aside from being the major continental US base for supporting operating forces in the Pacific, is security headquarters for the coastline of Southern California, where watchful eyes scan around the clock for Japanese subs and aircraft.

"What did I do?" Jimmie asks, wondering whether he should be frightened or angry.

"I have orders to escort you there," the MP says, his face as impassive as his voice. "You have been identified as the senior member of this platoon."

"*Cheii*," giggles Ray with nervous laughter.

The MP continues. "They need you to confirm your whereabouts this morning."

Jimmie settles on angry. "I was right here in camp, on field maneuvers. Our whole platoon was there. You can ask the colonel."

The MP seems to digest the information before ignoring it.

He adds, almost as an afterthought, "You are to bring two of your buddies with you. Your choice."

Jimmie looks at Ray, who is standing with his mouth agape. "Ray, I don't know what's going on here, but how 'bout taking a little ride?"

"Of course," he says. No laughter now.

"And Carl, your English might be even better than mine. Okay with you?"

Carl nods. "You're not in any trouble, are you?"

"That's what I'm trying to figure out," Jimmie answers as the three of them squeeze into the jeep for the ride into San Diego and the Coronado Peninsula.

NORTH ISLAND NAVAL AIR STATION looks to be a city unto itself. The three privates pass through a heavy iron entrance gate, past Flag Circle, past the guard house. There they wait until a second MP comes along and leads them through four sets of barred doors and into the bowels of a long, musty building.

"Jeez, you must be in a pile of shit," says Carl under his breath as a young MP ushers them into a small waiting room. The metal chairs, drab walls, and lack of reading materials suggest the anteroom is not designed for anyone's comfort.

Jimmie does not acknowledge Carl's wisecrack because one of the MPs is saying to him, "Your buddies will stay here. Private Goodluck, you first. They're waiting for you."

Jimmie opens the door into a long, high-ceilinged room that is only a bit bigger than the massive oak table that stretches in length from nearly one wall to the other. Unlike the anteroom, this space is brightly lit and faintly smells of fresh paint. Seated at the table are a dozen senior officers. They stare at Jimmie as he stands awkwardly by the door and salutes.

"Take this seat," says one of the officers, gesturing toward an empty chair on his right, midway down the table.

As Jimmie pulls out the chair, a lieutenant comes into the room carrying a small machine. Jimmie recognizes it as a battery-operated Armour military wire recorder that the navy has been trying out. The lieutenant sets the recorder down in front of a long-faced full colonel whose name tag identifies him as Fred Beans. Jimmie waits nervously for someone to tell him what this summons is all about.

Eventually, Colonel Beans looks at him and says, "This morning, at about 0700 hours, the Coast Guard began intercepting a series of messages of unknown origin. As a result, the entire California coastline has been put on red alert. Private Goodluck, we're going to play a portion of that transmission and ask if you're able to identify the source."

The colonel searches for a button on the machine. The officers around the table do not follow the colonel's motions but instead keep their gazes fixed on Jimmie. From the machine comes a click, then a voice, barely audible over a symphony of static. In spite of the sound quality, Jimmie recognizes both the voice and the message.

Be'al'doh'tso'lain coh nakiah moasi who'neh bih'din'ne'day ha'ih'des'ee na'ha'ta'ba'hogan ...

For the next several minutes, there follow snippets of other transmissions from the morning's field maneuvers.

The colonel turns off the wire recorder. "Well, Private?"

"Sir, the first voice on the wire is mine. All the others belong to men in my platoon, the 382nd. We were transmitting at Camp Elliott. It was our first field test of the—" Jimmie stops abruptly, looking up and down the line of officers. "You are aware of Lieutenant Colonel Jones's program there, of what we're doing?" Most of the men at the table are equal in rank to the colonel, surely they must know.

In place of a direct answer, Colonel Beans frowns and asks, "Can you translate what was said in the three messages we played?" He hands Jimmie a pencil and tablet of paper.

"Yes, of course, sir."

After no more than a minute, Jimmie passes the decoded messages back to the colonel, who does not look down at what he wrote. Instead, Colonel Beans summons Ray, leaving Charlie by himself in the anteroom. He then asks Ray to listen to the wire and translate the messages. This time, when Ray turns over his written translation, the colonel looks at the paper and then looks at what Jimmie had written, comparing the two. With a slight nod to the other officers at the table, he passes the two translations around.

In similar fashion, the colonel invites Carl into the room and makes the same request of him. Minutes later, three nearly identical sheets of paper are being circulated around the table with only a few inaudible murmurs breaking the silence.

At last Colonel Beans speaks up. "Private Goodluck, we appreciate that you and your fellow marines answered our summons today …"—he looks at his watch—"… this evening. Your CO verified the nature of this voice interception, of course, but now we've seen for ourselves. So that it doesn't happen again, your CO has been advised that we are to be notified in advance of all field maneuvers such as you performed this morning."

"Will that be all, sir?" Jimmie asks. Although greatly relieved, he bristles at the way the matter has been handled. As if he might be part of some enemy conspiracy.

"Yes, we'll return you to camp," says Colonel Beans, his voice no less serious than it has been from the start. "And please understand, privates. What I said about the red alert was no joke. The Coast Guard, they were sure you were Japs."

IN THE DAYS THAT FOLLOW the North Island incident, the twenty-nine Navajo men continue to train side by side with other platoons.

Their work on the code progresses separately and under strict secrecy, mostly during late afternoon and evening.

On a misty morning in early August, they learn they will be heading out on a two-day desert maneuver with two other platoons. Each of these platoons will be divided into thirds and then scrambled into three new teams for the exercise. The brass, apparently, sees it as a good opportunity for Anglo and Navajo privates to interact with one another. It will also reinforce the ideology that, cultural differences aside, they are all marines. The Navajo men view it as a welcome break from the long hours of devising and memorizing code words.

Jimmie looks upon the maneuvers as comparable to a story in a picture book he once read, the fable of Brer Rabbit in the briar patch. The oppressive heat and dryness of the California desert will be quite to his liking. For him and his buddies, the exercise promises to offer a glorious change from the moisture-sodden atmosphere that smothers Camp Elliott. Still, it will be no rodeo, exactly. Each private is allowed only one canteen of water that has to last through both days.

The officer in charge of Jimmie's group (which includes eight other Navajo men including Ray, George, and Carl) is a first lieutenant, a tall and jovial southern lad everyone calls Julep. He hails from Alabama, a town called Huntsville, which he says is known for its textiles and watercress. Jimmie tells him he comes from a place called *Dinetah,* known for its scraggly sheep, rattlesnakes, and poverty, so Julep has every right to boast about the watercress.

Julep scratches his thatch of thinning brown hair with a bony index finger and grunts. His voice is laced with a hint of levity, not bluster, when he says, "Y'all came through boot camp and think you're tough guys, huh?" He reminds Jimmie of Sergeant Carston, his boot platoon's short-lived boxing instructor, only the way Julep says it suggests he has a sense of humor whereas Carston only evidenced hatred and disdain.

"Lemme tell you," the lieutenant chides, "you don't ration that water, you goin' be dead marines come tomorrow night. Me, I got me one canteen, just like y'all. Beg me all you want, but I ain't gonna share it with nobody who runs dry."

With these words of warning, the platoon sets out on bivouac. They trudge over washes, around fields of pink and purple wildflowers, along ridges offering sweeping vistas, and through vast, arid stretches of desert where several varieties of cactus thrive heartily. The young men barely notice the scenery. Mostly they are on the lookout for cactus burrs and the ever-present red diamond rattlesnakes. By noon the first day out, only the Navajo privates are smiling. Some of the Anglo marines have already used up half their water.

While the platoon breaks for midday rations, Ray gets an inspiration. He summons Carl and Jimmie and points out the abundance of prickly pear cactus, a ready source of liquid back home. "Suppose we have us some fun and, when Julep ain't lookin', take our drinks from the cactus instead of our canteens?"

Jimmie and Carl embrace the idea and then quickly spread the word to the other Navajo men in their group. During latrine breaks, they sneak off to cut down the prickly pears without the others catching on. They scrape off the hair-like thorns and then peel back the fleshy skin and suck out the juice just as they have all done at one time or another on the reservation. They easily finish the day's march without even opening their canteens. Next morning, most of them take advantage of scattered opportunities to do it again.

Come noon of the second day, some of the white boys are in rough shape. Lieutenant Julep, looking a bit dehydrated himself, checks with his Indians to see how they are holding up.

"Hey, chiefs," he calls. "Hope y'all got some water left. Gonna be a hot afternoon."

By now, the Navajo privates are used to being called "chief." The word, as far as the young men can tell, is delivered without any derogatory intent. No need for them to explain that the word is not found in the Navajo culture, the closest Navajo term being "headman."

George Benally shakes his canteen. It is still nearly full. "Got plenty of water myself, sir," he taunts. Then, turning to Charlie, he asks, "How 'bout you?"

"I'm in swell shape," Charlie answers. "Barely touched a drop."

Julep saunters off, looking baffled.

A little past two in the afternoon, the lieutenant looks even more haggard. Jimmie walks up to him with Ray close behind and says, "Sir, you got enough water left? I'd be happy to give you a sip of mine." Jimmie holds up his canteen and swishes it back and forth, trying to keep a straight face. The substantial volume of water inside makes an impertinent sound.

"I'm 'bout out," Julep admits, licking his parched lips, "but I ain't gonna take none of yours. How's it you Indians got so much left?"

"Well, sir," Jimmie answers, making it up as he goes along, "us Indians, we're like that picture on the cigarette package. Y'know, the one with the camel? We don't need a lot of water to keep us going. Don't know why that is, maybe we're different somehow. What do you think, Ray?"

Ray, trying not to laugh, assumes a dignified expression. "Maybe it's that reddish skin of ours, holds the moisture inside. Never thought much 'bout it till now." He holds his canteen up to Julep. "Sure you wouldn't like a drink? Barely used none myself."

With a look of annoyance, the lieutenant waves the privates off and lumbers away without saying another word.

Somehow Julep makes it through to the end of the day, though just barely, from the look of him. But several of the Anglo marines have to be revived before maneuvers end the next morning. Water is flown in from the base.

As for the Navajos in the group, they decide not to let Julep in on their little deception, although Jimmie and Ray swear they will never look at a pack of Camels the same way again.

Klagetoh, Arizona
July 18, 1942

Dear Jimmie,

I have no idea where this letter will find you. Are you still in California? I met a boy in Wide Ruins yesterday who just finished training at the naval base in Southern California. He was back home on leave before shipping out with his unit. I wonder if we'll see you when you get your leave.

Much has happened here since you left. The worst was in mid-May—I can barely write about it. Government sharpshooters came to the ranch and killed hundreds of Father's cattle while George and I watched. There was nothing we could do. Here Father asked everyone to go along with the reduction, and he eliminated much of his own livestock, yet the government was not satisfied. We tried to butcher as many animals as we could, but hundreds of carcasses spoiled in the hot sun.

While Father is sad about what happened, he's not angry. He told my brothers and me to look past the mesa that's visible in the distance and think instead of the many mesas that lie beyond. It's good advice, to leave your mind open to what you cannot always see, don't you agree?

Now some other news: Father is chairman of the tribal council once more. He was elected last month and will serve four more years. After getting back to ranching and riding and roping—the things he loves—the call of politics won out again.

As for me, I'm expecting again! My other children are doing pretty well, especially Georgia Ann, who is practically a young lady, and Irma, my wild six-year-old. As for Marvin, Henry, and George, they still need a lot of attention. But they're all a joy to me. I only pray that there are no problems from the birthing this time. Still, the health of others gets my equal attention. Tuberculosis is everywhere, treatment for trachoma has nearly stopped since Pearl Harbor, I fear another outbreak of measles—

But forgive me. You have much to face without hearing problems back home. I wish you strength and courage and good fortune. If you get a chance, George and I would love to hear from you. Maybe you can stop here before you go across the water?

I know you haven't taken up the Catholic faith like us, but I hope you won't mind Father and me asking the Blessed Mother to watch over you.

Fondly,
Annie

Annie's letter is in Jimmie's mail call when he returns from maneuvers. He reads through it twice, feasting on the news from home as if it were fresh-picked piñón. Then he tucks the letter away in his bag, too exhausted to answer right away.

With each subsequent week, the pressure increases. The code vocabulary grows to two hundred words and then to nearly two hundred and fifty. The privates often work late into the night, memorizing and practicing their word substitutions. This, after a grueling day of training in advanced communications, field exercises, and war games.

While the platoon works to improve their speed and accuracy, a Camp Elliott cryptographer comes along and expresses concern about the rate of repetition for several alphabet letters, particularly vowels, that could offer the enemy a partial key to the code. Within days, the privates are ordered to double or triple the code words for letters with high frequency patterns. So the letter *A*, for example, becomes not only "ant" in Navajo, but also "apple" and "axe."At the same time, the brass gives them a new vocabulary list to codify in order to reduce their reliance on letter-by-letter spelling.

Less than two weeks later, they undergo field tests using the expanded alphabet and vocabulary. Once more, they succeed.

"Chiefs, I don't know how you do it, but I'll be a son-of-a-bitch if your code don't work just like you say it does," an officer exclaims to the platoon one afternoon. It is as if the brass looks upon their hard work as some kind of magic trick. A showy stage illusion, perhaps, or a divination that a careful observer might debunk.

"They think we're fucking Houdinis," George snickers to his partner Carl.

"Maybe we are," answers Carl, who probably has not heard that famous name until he left the insulated reservation. "With all the new words they keep throwin' at us, jeepers! Sometimes I wonder myself how the heck we do it."

CHAPTER 9

AUGUST 1942

The waitress winds her way through the tangle of young navy men and marines, most of whom are either loaded or well on their way. Her brazen hips seesaw beneath a black crepe skirt that clings to her shape like the dew on a peach. Every man turns as she breezes past, undressing her with their eyes.

"That'll be a buck, boys," she chirps to Jimmie and Ray. She sets down two coasters, whose large type reads: *Acme, the beer with the high IQ (It Quenches!)*. On each coaster she places a tall draft beer. A tired half smile works its way across her pretty face. If she is aware that these two marines have a ruddier complexion than most of the other servicemen in the bar, she does not show it.

"Thanks, miss," Jimmie says, putting a dollar and a quarter on her tray.

"Thanks yourself," she responds cheerfully, delighted to see more than the usual dime tip on two beers. Or maybe it is that Jimmie respectfully calls her "miss" instead of "honey" or "doll," the way most of the other customers address her.

This is a typical Saturday night for many of the young soldiers in Uncle Harry's, a lively joint owned by an ex-army man from the Bronx with an engaging personality that is half bullshit and half— well, nobody claims to have seen the other half. For the Navajo platoon, it is a rare off-base pass. The privates have scattered to different night spots in the San Diego area, many going from bar to bar. A few—very few—just walk around, preferring to stay away from alcohol and other temptations.

As the waitress sashays off to another table, Jimmie takes a big swallow of brew and wipes the foam from his upper lip. "A year ago," he muses, "six months, even, who'd have guessed we'd be off the reservation, sitting in a San Diego bar in marine uniform, mixing with white guys, being served a beer with no questions asked, and getting a boner while watching a California girl wiggle her ass?"

Ray nearly chokes on his beer. "You sound like George!"

"Tell me it's not true, then." Jimmie grins like a kid tasting candy for the first time. "Tell me you didn't snap to attention under the table."

"Well, I admit I ain't here 'cause I love that music." Rays flashes a coy smirk. Benny Goodman is playing softly in the background, though it is barely audible over the raucous laughter and rowdy conversation. "Have to say, though, I'm more taken with that girl behind the bar. The waitress, she reminds me too much of my older sister, Katherine, take away the milky skin and blonde hair."

"In that case, I sure would like to meet your sister."

A look of mock disgust sweeps over Ray's face. "Heck, no! No old guy with a hard-on is goin' *near* my sister."

They both break up with laughter. After weeks of hard work and constant pressure, they are happy to get out and unwind a little. Actually, Jimmie would not mind getting laid, but that is not the kind of example he wants to set for his shy little brother.

The pair had taken in a film a little earlier. Ray had never been to a movie theater, so they went to a picture called *Casablanca* that everyone back at camp was talking about. Afterward, they decided to stop by Uncle Harry's for a beer before heading back to barracks.

"Seriously," Jimmie says. "How old's your sister?"

"I think Katherine's twenty ... no, wait, twenty-one now."

"And your younger sisters got married before her? Pretty unusual."

"I guess Katherine ain't fallen for no man yet. My sister Lorraine, she let my parents pick her a husband when she was fifteen. My sister Betty, same thing. Nice boys, their husbands. But like I told you, Katherine says she'll never agree to a fixed-up marriage. She's independent. Wants to go into nursing or something. Not that there's much chance of a woman getting any kind of work, 'specially when most guys can't find none. I think maybe Katherine don't know *what* she wants."

A familiar voice interrupts with, "Hey, chiefs, how goes it?" First Lieutenant Julep grins down at the pair. In his hand is a half-empty mug.

Ray leaps up, startled. "Good to see you, sir. Join us?" He points to the empty chair at the table as Jimmie also rises.

"Uh, just for a second. And since we're off base, call me Julep, like everyone else. Ain't my real name, any more than 'Chief' is yours, but what the hell. Say now"—he glances at the mugs of beer in front of the two privates—"I see you boys do drink after all. And not just water, neither."

Jimmie and Ray exchange glances. Jimmie is about to confess right on the spot when Ray says, "Actually, half a glass fills us up for days. Mostly, we come for the peanuts."

"Yeah, right," Julep says dryly, looking now at Jimmie. If the Lieutenant is trying to gauge whether Ray is putting him on, he gets no clues from Jimmie's poker face. Inside, though, Jimmie struggles to maintain his composure. Nobody tickles him like his buddy Ray.

"Anyway," Julep says, "you reservation boys did real good out there last month. Most of the others could barely drag their lily-white asses back to the bus after the second day. From what I been hearing, your whole platoon is pretty damn tough."

"That desert reminded us of home, is all," Ray admits truthfully.

"Yeah? Well, the Corps is your home now." Julep raises his mug for a toast. "Here's to Indians who also happen to be damn fine marines, from what I seen. That's the only thing that matters in the Corps. *Semper Fi,* boys."

"*Semper Fi,*" the privates repeat in unison, raising their glasses also.

Julep clinks his mug against theirs and proceeds to drain the contents. He belches proudly, slams down his empty mug, and then stands to leave.

"Well, I still got people to see and places to be. Just wanted to come over and say howdy. Maybe we'll meet again somewhere in the South Pacific. You're the caliber of men I'd want watching my back."

Jimmie and Ray rise to salute him. Instead of returning the salute, Julep simply extends his hand and they shake. "Best of luck to you both, and to the rest of your platoon. Keep up that gung ho."

As Julep pushes his way through the boisterous crowd and heads toward the exit, the privates sit back down to finish their beers. From a corner of the room comes a round of laughter, piercing through the tumult of drunken chatter.

"See, it's like I was saying before," Jimmie says, distractedly dipping his index finger in beer suds that have pooled on the table. He pushes them around, oblivious to the designs he is making. "Six months ago we were Indians, nothing more. Nothing but hard times back home. Those who tried to leave got treated like shit, 'specially in the border towns. Now here we are, wearing these here uniforms, part of something important, making friends with white guys like Julep, getting *respect* from white guys in other platoons, being treated like regular American citizens and not second-class ones."

"Yeah, I know what you mean," Ray says. "I never been around Anglos much myself, not before comin' here. Just a few traders, schoolteachers, missionaries, and such. I always thought they was somehow smarter and more important than us."

"Whoa, now wait a minute—"

"Think about it, Jimmie. Take the traders. We're completely dependent on them. They say how much we get for wool, or for my mother's baskets or my father's boots. Take it or leave it."

"But don't forget, the traders need us, too."

"Yeah, but they can pick up and leave *Dinetah* any time they please, move to one of the big cities, do somethin' else if they take a likin' to it."

"You got a point, I guess."

"Now the teachers," Ray goes on, "they got the learnin' we need. They're smarter by definition, right? But lot of 'em, and the missionaries especially, they act like our legends, our holy spirits, are below theirs. Nonsense and superstition. To them, that's all it is. It all works on a person to make him feel second-rate, y'know? But now that I been around boys my own age, eatin' meals with 'em, drillin' with 'em, drinkin' with 'em, I don't see 'em as all that different. I mean, there's dumb ones and poor ones and drunken ones and smart ones, just like we got, right?"

"Yeah. I guess I always wanted to be part of a group where the place I come from and the traditions I was raised up with don't get in the way," Jimmie admits. "It's the real reason I joined up, now's I think about it, and that's what the Corps is givin' us, Ray. We're living an Indian's dream. *My* dream, anyways."

Ray nods thoughtfully, lifts his mug, puts it to his lips, and then sets it back down without taking a sip. Overhead, a light flickers, casting eerie shadows on their table. "Thing about that is," he says with a faraway look in his eyes, "what happens *after* your dream comes true?"

The question startles Jimmie. He feels a sharp sense of déjà vu, like he has heard these words before, although he cannot place when and where. Having no answer to Ray's question, he finishes the last of his beer in silence as the Hips return, assertively pressing her assets into the table.

"You guys look awful serious," she notes with a weary smile. "Ready for another?"

"Not me," Ray says. His glass is still more than a quarter full.

"Me neither." Jimmie's brooding thoughts dissolve like sugar in the fluid warmth of the girl's smile. For a moment he wonders if he could ever make time with an ivory-skinned beauty like her. For once in his life, all things seem possible now. "Guess it's time we got back to base."

"Well, you boys take care," she purrs, then glides over to another table.

"Now *there's* something worth dreaming about," Jimmie exclaims, brightening like a shepherd's moon and feeling no sense of shame.

Ray shoots him a circumspect look that quickly transforms into a puckish grin. He slowly shakes his head and quips, "Nuh-uh, Jimmie. You ain't goin' nowhere *near* my sister when this war is over."

CHAPTER 10

SEPTEMBER 1942

On what starts out as just another exhausting day of training, Jimmie comes face to face with the man who dreamed up the idea for a Navajo code.

The all-Indian platoon is drilling under a relentless sun when Lieutenant Colonel Jones summons Jimmie to his office. The others in his platoon look enviously at him as he bounds off. After the obligatory salutes, the officer steps out from behind his desk and introduces Jimmie to a lanky civilian named Philip Johnston. The man—slender, balding, with a neatly trimmed mustache and thick spectacles—is clearly no youngster. Midfifties at least, Jimmie guesses.

Johnston extends his hand to Jimmie and greets him in perfect Navajo with *"Ya'at'eeh:"* The Navajo equivalent of "How's it going?"

"Ya'at'eeh," Jimmie responds mechanically, until it hits him that Johnston is speaking in Navajo. What's more, the civilian pronounces the word with such precise glottal nuance that it is hard to believe it flows from the mouth of a white man.

Johnston smiles at Jimmie's reaction and says, "I grew up on the reservation. My parents ran a mission in Leuppe. I still visit the area when I can."

The colonel's mouth turns up slightly, as if threatening a smile of its own. "Mr. Johnston, you'll discover, speaks fluent Navajo. 'Course, you'd be a better judge of that than me. At any rate, Private Goodluck, I invited our distinguished guest to see how your platoon is coming along. It was his idea, the code program. That's why I've set up a field demonstration for this afternoon. Perhaps you'll show him around in the meantime."

Jimmie is happy to spend a few hours with the man behind their mission. As they walk toward the building that houses the code room, Jimmie asks the obvious question, "What got you thinking about doing this in the first place?"

Johnston explains that he was an army man in World War I. In the forests of northern France, he heard about experiments conveying combat information in Choctaw. Apparently, it met with only limited success. But the Germans took notice of the new language and may well have uncovered its American Indian roots. Johnston mentally filed those facts away, he says, until a couple years ago when he saw a piece in the *Los Angeles Times*. Seems the Army Signal Corps in Louisiana had field-tested communications between Comanche enlistees using their native language. It was discontinued as well, for the same reason as the much earlier Choctaw experiment. In each case, the native vocabulary was too limited to cover the necessary military terms. Then, shortly after the Pearl Harbor attack, according to Johnston, he came up with the notion of adapting the Navajo dialect and found an advocate in Lieutenant Colonel Jones, who promptly booted the suggestion upstairs.

Over lunch in the empty, windowless room, Jimmie asks his visitor why he championed the Navajo language over others. Johnston takes off his spectacles and pushes away his tray, having barely touched his sandwich. His short mustache looks black as pitch against his drawn and pale complexion. The man still has a military demeanor about him, even though he has been a civilian—a civil engineer, he mentions—for many years.

"My admiration for the Navajo people had a great bearing," Johnston says, "but I recommended Navajo—and the marine brass agreed—for one other major reason. Can you guess?"

Jimmie cannot imagine.

"The Navajo reservation covers around twenty-five thousand square miles, right? Some of the most remote, impassable, sparsely populated terrain in America. That's why Navajo country was the only reservation land not visited by hoards of German students in the 1930s."

"Are you suggesting that they came to—"

"Oh, those young Germans feigned various interests in their visits to Indian reservations. But, yes, many of us believe they were following their government's orders to bring home a knowledge of Indian dialects."

Jimmie is incredulous. "How could they understand our language even if they did spend time among the Navajo?" Surely Johnston must know that Navajo has always been an oral language. What's more, it is highly complex and precise, with nuances of meaning that depend on tonal inflections, glottal closures, and pitch variations. This makes it incomprehensible not only to the world at large, but even to most other American Indian tribes.

"Most likely they wouldn't understand it at all," Johnston admits. "Another reason to rely on Navajo, wouldn't you agree?"

Jimmie and his honored guest go on to discuss the program and how the code is progressing. An hour later, the platoon puts on a demonstration of the code in use. When the exercise is over, Johnston removes his glasses and wipes a tear from his eyes, so moved is he by the skill and spirit of the men. Before leaving camp, he addresses the twenty-nine Navajo privates back in their code room, where he can speak confidentially.

"Gentlemen, what I've seen today makes me so darn proud," he says, standing in the front of the American flag. "And not because it validates my notion that the Navajo language can prove helpful in wartime communications, though it's always nice to be right."

A few polite chuckles from the men.

"No, what really tickles me is that you took a reasonable hypothesis and not only made it work, you made it better. In essence, you created a code in English, and *then* put it into Navajo. Well done, men."

A few days later, the platoon learns that Johnston is given special status as a staff sergeant, responsible for administering the Navajo communications program. He will also help with recruitment back on the reservation, for the order has already come down to train more young Navajo men. To teach the code to the incoming group, two men in the Navajo platoon will be selected to stay stateside. Assuming, of course, that the marines can find enough qualified Navajo boys in the hopeful, brooding days ahead.

THE PLATOON IS AWARE THEIR orders will be coming any day, scattering the twenty-nine of them like buckshot as they ship out to join their fellow marines who are, even now, bravely facing the enemy in distant places whose names defy correct pronunciation.

Jimmie, however, harbors little apprehension over what lies ahead. Leaving the safety of the mainland for the sweltering, battle-charged tropics will be a welcome escape from the desperation of the reservation, from the apathy and condescension of border communities, and from the scorn and myopia of his father. And while he loathes the destruction and senselessness of war, he embraces the exigency of *this* war, revels in its potential to keep his homeland safe.

For these reasons, everyone except Jimmie is livid to learn they are—once again—being denied home leave. It is an order, they discover, that applies only to this platoon, to the twenty-nine-man team that holds and nurtures the secret weapon that must be held close and accountable and guarded at all costs.

Still, the men do get some good news: effective immediately, they are all promoted to privates first class, rewarding the Navajo privates with the early raise in rank (and correspondingly in pay) in view of their unique contribution.

In barracks on this evening of mixed news, Ray speaks for most of the boys when he says, "That still don't make up for us not gettin' back home for a spell. I don't think they ever intended givin' us home leave."

"Maybe they're afraid to let us out of their sight," Jimmie points out. He sits on the edge of his bunk, head lowered.

"I don't know," Ray says in a tentative voice. "Anyhow, I just miss ... well, my family, of course, but also ... you know, the food, the desert, the ceremonies, all of that."

Suddenly an idea comes to Jimmie, rough-sketched but bristling with possibilities. He leaps up from his bunk. "Ray's right! That's something we can do. We can do it for us, and for anyone else in camp who's interested."

Ray scrunches up his face. "What're you talkin' about?"

"You said it yourself, Ray. A ceremony! Let's put on a ceremony. We'll invite the whole camp if they want to come and watch. Maybe Lieutenant Colonel Jones will give us his okay for tomorrow night."

George's voice is heavy with sarcasm. "What are we gonna do, beat out the Marine Corps Hymn on Wilfred's drum?"

Now Jimmie's vision blossoms from sepia to full color, like in that *Wizard of Oz* movie he saw in town one night. "Actually, George, that's a good idea too."

"You can't be serious," Ray says. Even George looks at Jimmie as if he is no longer just an old man of twenty-eight, but senile besides.

The whole platoon gets behind him once Jimmie explains what he has in mind. Next morning, when the colonel hears their request, he readily agrees to let them put on an "Indian show"—his words—right after evening mess.

They decide to do a Blessingway, or rather a greatly modified version of it, taking huge liberties in light of their limited resources and the expected patience of their audience. Normally, a Blessingway ceremony stretches out for up to five nights, from sundown to dawn. It requires, at the very least, a Mountain Soil Bundle—the rite's one essential prop—consisting of buckskin-wrapped corn pollen mixed with pinches of soil from each of the four sacred mountains that roughly mark the boundary points of *Dinetah*. Their version, however, will last less than twenty minutes and settle for cornmeal from the mess kitchen.

The group selects Jimmie to serve as a narrator in order to help their fellow marines understand what the ceremony and the songs are about. And should no one show up, they decide the ceremony will go on anyway. They will do it because they need to, because it is part of the heritage that binds them all together, because it may give them strength and comfort and inner peace. Also, it will be a memorable way to end their time together as a platoon.

Normally an experienced singer would perform the ritual—the singer, in healing ceremonies, is also known as medicine man—but the closest they can come is Carl Slowtalker, whose uncle is actually a singer of some renown. Everyone decides Carl will lead whichever chants he can remember, and they will join in on familiar verses.

Samuel Nez goes to his storage cubicle and takes out his wooden flute. Wilfred Smith lifts out the drum he stashed away in a footlocker under his bunk. Jimmie encourages them to bring their instruments to the parade ground, even though drum and flute are not normally used in Blessingway.

When it is time for the ceremony to begin, there is a surprisingly good turnout at the parade grounds, including Lieutenant Colonel Jones himself. The men sit in a semicircle—privates and NCOs and a few ranking officers—where they await this rare evening of entertainment. Even the weather cooperates. The humidity is relatively low, and the breeze off the ocean is as gentle as the breath of a sleeping baby.

In the moments before Jimmie comes forward to address the assembled marines, he experiences a sense of awe, a feeling of being overwhelmed by the irony of it all. Here he has achieved the ascendancy he has dreamed about for so long—acceptance as a regular marine in this close-knit, white-dominated society—and now they are about to put on an "Indian show." But he recognizes that the two cultures are not mutually exclusive. You can be Navajo and a marine just like you can be Mexican and a marine or a southerner and a marine or Catholic and a marine. Go back far enough, after all, and everybody comes from some other place and time. Jimmie sees that every white man sitting out there carries within him a distinctive heritage, a cultural imprint, that helps to define who he is just as his uniform on the outside identifies him as a US Marine. In this regard, Jimmie is no different. He has everything the white boys have, including a defining heritage. And now he and his buddies are going to share their heritage with their fellow marines, not to show off their differences, but to celebrate what makes them the same.

"Uh, we didn't expect so many of you to show up!"

Jimmie talks in the loudest voice he can muster. Behind him, twenty-eight young Navajo men in uniform sit in a circle, leaving an opening to the east. In the center, four upright branches lean inward, joined together at the top with cord. Samuel begins to play his flute to provide background ambiance.

"We're happy you're here to share this evening with us," Jimmie says. "The branches inside our circle represent the *hogan,* our traditional dwelling places. We call this ceremony *ho'zhooji.* It has no exact English translation, but it refers to everything that's good, everything that's in harmony: beauty, success, well-being, happiness, good fortune … stuff like that. In our songs we ask for blessings, so we translate *ho'zhooji* as Blessingway. It's our most important ceremony. The backbone, I guess you could say, for all the others. In it, we tell our creation story, which I'm pretty sure has some parallels to your Old Testament. Anyways, with our orders coming any day now, who among us wouldn't ask the holy spirits—whichever holy spirits you believe in—for their blessing?"

Heads nod. Expressions brighten. Expectations rise, or so it appears. The men have stopped talking and laughing among themselves and are now paying rapt attention as behind Jimmie, Wilfred's drum begins its rhythmic beat, while Samuel's flute darts and dodges like a lightweight boxer, dancing in and around the heavy thump of the drum. Jimmie stops speaking, for the flute and drum need no translation.

After a short time, Carl gets up. He goes over to the branches and marks them with a smudge of cornmeal in each of the four directions. Then he begins to chant.

"*Holagh'ai,*" he sings. "*Holagh'ai, golagh'ai, ye'hi'ye, ye'hi'ye'ee …*"

"He sings to Mountain Woman, to Water Woman, and to Corn Woman," Jimmie explains to the audience. "The inner human forms we give to elements in nature."

Carl picks up the ersatz Mountain Soil Bundle and holds it high as he begins another chant. Then he lowers it to his nose and breathes in deeply, four times.

"The Bundle Carl is holding represents First Man's potent medicine. That's what held the power to produce those human forms I mentioned, two of whom gave birth to a girl. She became

Changing Woman. We believe it was from her body that the four original Navajo clans were created."

The audience watches closely as Carl is joined on familiar refrains by others in the circle. But lest the audience's attention wane, Jimmie makes a hand motion to Carl, signaling him to jump to the Twelve-Word Song that usually ends a Blessingway.

"This is almost always the concluding song," he tells the onlookers. "It reminds us that the Holy Ones will never again be seen in this world, but that their presence is revealed in the sound of the wind, in the feathers of a bird, in a field of golden corn. Their nearness and their blessings can always be found in the beauty and the harmony of the earth. It is good for us to remember that."

Now the Navajo privates stand and reach into their pockets. Each pulls out a sheet of paper. From the audience, a low-level murmur fills in the momentary silence. Words and breaths and chuckles and, from just a few, playful groans of impatience.

In a strong voice Jimmie concludes, "And now, before we leave this place, there is one thing more we want to share with you. It has nothing to do with Navajo ritual. But it has everything to do with the ritual of being in the Corps."

A few whistles and cheers echo forth from the spectators. Jimmie looks at Samuel, who lifts his flute to his mouth. This, in turn, cues Wilfred to begin beating his drum.

Turning back to the assembled group, Jimmie continues, "You won't find the words familiar, but unless we sound worse than I think we will, you'll know the tune."

While Wilfred taps out the cadence, Samuel plays an opening lead-in. He misses several of the notes, but even with the mistakes, the melody is unmistakable to the surprised and delighted audience.

The Marine Corps Hymn in flute and drum.

All twenty-nine voices of the 382nd Platoon begin together, a little raggedy and often off key as they look down at their mimeographed paper. They sing the words—a rough translation of the English lyrics that begin with "From the halls of Montezuma"—that Ray and George and Jimmie had hammered out just hours earlier:

> _Nih hokeh ni'kheh a'na'ih'la_
> _Ta'al'tso'go na'he'seel'kai ..._

And now the audience rises as one, even before all three stanzas have been sung in Navajo, and they join along by clapping and cheering and humming and whistling.

When the song ends, Lieutenant Colonel Jones comes up to the Navajo men and reiterates how pleased he is to have had them at Camp Elliott. He tells them that they have already done themselves proud, that he expects to hear great things about them in the months to come. Men from other platoons come rushing up, gathering around the Navajo privates to let them know how much they enjoyed the ceremony. At this moment, Jimmie and every other young man in his exemplary platoon soar on eagles' wings as they bask in the glow and acceptance of being full-blooded members of two tribes: Navajo and US Marine.

"_Semper Fi,_" they whoop to their fellow marines. "_Semper Fi,_" they whoop to one another.

Two days later they get their orders to ship out and go to war.

JIMMIE PREPARES TO LEAVE THE mainland, painfully aware of how desperate conditions are back home. Letters he has received from Annie, along with letters to Ray from Ray's sister Katherine, hint at the changes that stampede across the sacred land of _Dinetah_.

There is a war-related rise in employment opportunities, but only as long as Navajo workers are willing to relocate outside the reservation and accept far less pay than white workers doing the same jobs. Navajo men have started working as laborers for government and private industry. They are taking jobs with the railroad, sweating away at mining and highway construction, toiling in fields and orchards as migratory workers. They are manning assembly lines to make bombs and grenades. Thousands of others are registering for the draft or enlisting.

On the reservation, wartime rationing is causing goods and services to erode like the land itself. Schools are closing throughout *Dinetah* due to the diversion of government funds and lack of teachers. Silver craftsmen are falling victim to a government freeze on the metal. The weaving of rugs and blankets has come to a standstill because wool is needed for the war effort. Although more money finds its way onto the reservation than ever before—from servicemen and off-reservation laborers who send home their pay, from the leasing of minerals, from the sale of raw materials, like wool—there is little the money can buy. Many people are subsisting on a diet of fry bread and coffee, nothing more. Disease, which has long been a problem, is running rampant as the meager medical services nearly disappear. And through it all, the government-mandated stock reduction continues, etching away the livestock that provides the sole livelihood for so many people.

Jimmie worries how his mother will survive with no wool to weave. She can get by with the sale of her raw wool, perhaps, but the weaving of it has always been her escape from loneliness, from boredom, and more important still, from the resentment and paranoia of her husband.

Escape, Jimmie observes, runs deep within the Goodluck family.

THEIR ORDERS DIVIDE THE ALL-NAVAJO platoon between the First and Second Marine Divisions. Thirteen of the men are apportioned to Signal Company, First Marine Amphibious Corps, Seventh

Regiment. The others, in groups of two to four, are assigned into either Headquarters Company or one of several battalions in the Second Marine Division.

As had been rumored earlier, two men receive orders to stay behind and train the next group of Navajo enlistees—twice the size, it appears, of Jimmie's boot platoon. This will be an all-Navajo platoon as well. The two men selected for the training job, John Benally (no direct relationship to George) and Johnny Manuelito, have both achieved the top percentiles in everything from marksmanship to transmission accuracy.

"I figured you for bein' one of 'em stayin' here," Ray tells Jimmie when he learns that they are both shipping out together. "But I'm glad they ain't splittin' us up." He looks down at his orders and rereads them for maybe the hundredth time. "Day after tomorrow, we're at sea. First stop, Pearl Harbor. I get chills just thinkin' 'bout that."

"I know what you mean. All those men, dead at the bottom." Jimmie swallows hard, readily identifying with those poor navy guys. It no longer matters that they are mostly whites. They could have been his friends. All is possible now.

"Hey, Private First Class Goodluck, looks like you and Ray are coming on my ship," Carl Slowtalker shouts out, orders in hand. "Charlie, too. And George, I think. First Marines all the way!"

For Jimmie, it is a day of learning who is going where, of saying farewell to the Anglo friends he made at camp, of wishing each other good health and success. For some men, like Ray, just leaving the boundaries of the four sacred mountains has been a big event in its own right. Now they are about to leave the mainland altogether, most likely for a long time. And unspoken among them is the fear—the likelihood, really—that not all of them will return.

When their ship steams out from the naval base two days later, Jimmie and Ray and most of the other Navajo radiomen on board are up on deck, watching the California coastline disappear in the distance. Once the ship reaches open water, dolphins leap out of the depths to frolic alongside, their tail flukes undulating in a powerful dance, their streamlined bodies, smooth as satin ribbon, shining like polished silver in the glint of the sun. It is a sight the boys of the desert have never witnessed before.

Jimmie marvels at the antics of the mammals, at the way they seem to keep pace with the ship almost precisely below the spot where he stands, transfixed. But perhaps there is a greater significance here: didn't the Holy People promise they would always be visible in the wonders of nature? This, then, is a sign—what else could it be?—that they are nearby; that no matter how far he and his buddies wander from the sacred land of their ancestors, the Holy People will always be with them.

Almost as a reflex, he touches the small buckskin pouch he stills wear around his neck, its strap intertwined with his dog-tag chains. He presses lightly with his fingers, feeling the sacred corn pollen within, the only tangible tie to his heritage that he will be able to carry with him into battle.

Silently, resolutely, his lips form words of prayer as the ship plows stalwartly through the choppy water and races with the setting sun.

Only those who have traveled together under severe conditions over long distances can understand the tender fellowship which such an association develops. Nationality and race mean nothing. It is the integrity of the human being that counts.

—Evans F. Carlson, Brigadier General, USMC. From his book Twin Stars of China, *Dodd Mead, 1940.*

PART II:

FIGHTING WORDS

CHAPTER 11

OCTOBER 1942

If you could overlook the humidity and the insidious diseases and the mosquitoes and the bats, Espiritu Santo might once have been a tropical paradise. But that would have been before American warships glutted the shimmering blue waters of Mele Bay, before the powdery white-sand beaches became overrun with military personnel and tons of machinery, before the magnificent rainforests had been cleared to build roads and barracks and hospitals and airstrips.

After a brief stop at Pearl Harbor, Jimmie and Ray arrive on this steamy jungle island in the New Hebrides chain. They barely finish settling in with their new unit when a marine—there are no markings to indicate his rank—approaches them.

"Goodluck and ... Begay, right? That you men?" He looks down at a small sheet of paper in his hand.

"We just got here, what'd we do now?" Ray quips, grinning.

"Second Raider Battalion's looking for volunteers." The marine parcels out words as if there is a wartime shortage of them. "You two have specifically been requested to apply."

"How'd our names come up?" Jimmie asks.

"Dunno. You'll have to ask the colonel. If you're interested—I'd think you would be; it's a coveted invitation—report tomorrow at 0800 hours to Lieutenant Colonel Carlson. Anyone can tell you where to find the old man." The soldier hurries off without saluting.

Jimmie can barely contain his enthusiasm. "The Raiders—Carlson's Raiders—are asking for *us!* Can you believe it?"

"Jeez, he's such a legend in the Corps, I almost didn't think he was a real person. Back at camp, he was more talked about than General MacArthur."

This is hardly overstatement, Jimmie knows, for few officers are more admired and resented, desired and dismissed, aggrandized and trivialized, than Evans F. Carlson. He had trained his Second Marine Raider Battalion in the olive grove adjacent to Camp Elliott from late February to early May of 1942. They shipped out to Hawaii for further training around the time the Navajos started boot camp.

Word around camp was that Carlson's earlier military experience in the Nicaraguan jungle and as an American observer in China—where he courted controversy by proclaiming the Chinese Eighth Route Army to be the world's best-led fighting force—helped shaped his vision of creating a special commando unit trained in guerrilla warfare. His highly vocal and divisive stances did not curry favor with military brass, but he eventually enlisted the enthusiastic endorsement of President Roosevelt.

In February of 1942, the all-volunteer Marine Raiders were born. Carlson—with Major James Roosevelt, the president's son, as executive officer—became commanding officer of the first-ever Raiders Battalion. Carlson promised volunteers that, if accepted, they would be "first to fight the Japs." His selection standards were tough. Physical superiority was only the beginning. Carlson scrutinized each candidate's politics, principles, and attitudes about war. Only one in seven volunteers made the cut.

Jimmie and Ray had heard all the stories about Raider training: how the men slept in pup tents, for example, and ate skimpy meals outdoors from mess kits. They were pushed sixteen to eighteen hours a day, seven days a week, all liberties cancelled. They trained intensively in guerrilla-force tactics such as demolition, hand-to-hand combat, amphibious assault, knife throwing, and assassination techniques. At least once a week they marched with full pack seventy miles without rest. And most surprising of all, Carlson eliminated long-established distinctions and privileges of rank between officers and the men under them, insisting they all dress the same, carry identical equipment, and live and train in equal discomfort. The unorthodox leader encouraged his Raiders to think for themselves, to understand the reasons behind every military decision, to push themselves no less than Carlson pushed *him*self.

What Carlson left back at Camp Elliott, long after he and his trainees shipped out, was a mystique, a salience, and beyond that, something far more tangible: a motto, whose call captured the imagination of marines everywhere.

Gung ho.

Every marine knows that gung ho is Carlson's philosophy, his lifeline, his dogma, his battle cry. Every Raider under him lives and embraces it or washes out. Carlson interprets the words—once the rallying cry of a Chinese industrial cooperative—as "work together." Under his doctrine, every member of his battalion is equal, training and fighting as one. Ranks and hierarchy exist mainly behind the scenes; something to placate the paper shufflers in Washington.

In mid-August, while Jimmie's platoon was busy constructing their code, Carlson's Raider Companies A and B made a much-ballyhooed assault landing off Butaritari Island in the Makin Atoll. The highly controversial operation made Carlson and his Raiders a household name. *What I would not give to be a part of it,* Jimmie thought back then.

He can hardly wait until morning to hear what Lieutenant Carlson has to say.

AT PRECISELY 0800 HOURS, JIMMIE and Ray head for Carlson's Nissan hut in the center of a busy conclave about a mile from the main base. From the debris and palm fronds strewn about, the area looks like it was only recently cleared. It is widely known that the Raiders are responsible for their own billeting, so it comes as no surprise to see pup tents still dotting the grounds while more formidable Nissan-style barracks, in varying stages of construction, sit like scattered sets of Tinker Toys. A makeshift sign nailed to two wooden furring strips reads *Headquarters, Second Marine Raider Battalion.* In the center of the sign is a cartoonish drawing of an angry skull. Crisscrossed behind the skull is a Raider knife and a lightning bolt. Lean, young Raiders scurry all around, going about their business with a sense of urgency. Jimmie and Ray report to an unsmiling aide, who promptly ushers them inside the colonel's hut.

"Welcome to Camp Gung Ho," calls a voice from the dimly lit interior. A man rises from behind a desk made from a board that sits astride two columns of cement blocks.

Jimmie and Ray snap to attention and salute, but the man waves them off. "We don't waste time with all that bull crap here," he says, extending his right hand. "I'm Evans Carlson."

The privates introduce themselves. Ray, awash in admiration, bubbles, "It's a real pleasure to meet you, Colonel."

"Oh, is there a colonel in the room?" Carlson says it with a straight face and then points to his green fatigues, which lack any indication of rank. "I don't see anything that shows I'm a colonel, do you? Name is Evans. Or Boss, to my lads. Or Old Man, behind my back."

"We heard a lot about you." Jimmie regrets the words the

moment they leave his mouth. What a dumb thing to say to the celebrated officer.

"And I've heard a lot about you, which is why you're here. Please, sit down."

Even in the shadows the colonel's features are unmistakable: his generous nose; his thick eyebrows, black as burned-out tree stumps; his jutting chin. Perched above Carlson's narrow, tightly drawn face is a short outcropping of silver hair that has the patina of a well-worn *concho*. Carlson is not merely thin; he appears gaunt, head to toe. But from the colonel's neck alone, thick as Ponderosa, what there is, is all sinew and muscle. In Carlson's presence Jimmie looks like a youngster, for from all appearances, the officer is easily pushing fifty.

"First, let me tell you some things about my Raiders," Carlson says. His voice is soft—surprisingly so, projecting from such a muscular body. Carlson goes on to explain the all-volunteer nature of the unit, the demanding training, the unconventional make-up of the six Raider companies under his command, and his notions of shared hardship to unify the men and promote achievements greater than the sum of their individual efforts.

"Permission to ask a question, sir?" Ray jumps in when the colonel pauses to take a long drink from a canteen on his desk.

"Ask any question you want, Begay, but the one thing you may not ask is my permission. Around here, everyone speaks freely, questions freely, says what he thinks."

Ray stammers, "We were—that is, I was wondering, how do you know about us, to ask for us by name?"

Carlson looks directly into Ray's eyes and replies, "You came to my attention through two different people. The first was Colonel Fred Beans. Friend of mine. You may remember him from when you were summoned to North Island."

Jimmie gently bites his lower lip, recalling how angry he was when Colonel Beans asked him to explain the strange language on the tape.

"The second is Major Roosevelt. He's just been named to head up the new Fourth Raider Battalion, but when we were together, he kept me apprised of your platoon's progress. Goodluck, you showed strong leadership at Camp Elliott, and they say you and Begay made a great team. Roosevelt and I, we're able to handpick the men and the equipment and the weapons we want for our missions. Could be this code of yours is a weapon in its own right, if the Japs don't figure it out."

"Don't think those Japs have a chance at decoding it," Jimmie boasts.

"That's why you're here. I'm not much for doing what's been done before, especially when I can do it better. The rest of the Corps, they're like lumbering dinosaurs, slow to adapt. You mark my words, lads, your code won't get much use on Guadalcanal unless I'm the one to use it. My Raiders don't follow tradition. We start it."

Jimmie and Ray exchange glances. They both feel the colonel's dynamic presence. Time seems suspended during this brief period. Jimmie barely registers the construction noise coming from outside the hut or the oppressive humidity that makes San Diego seem desert dry in comparison.

"Now, if you don't mind, I'm going to ask *you* some questions," the colonel says. "You're both full-blooded Indians, right?"

"Navajo, you bet," comes Jimmie's enthusiastic answer.

"It's just that ... well, you both speak American so well."

"We *are* American, sir," Ray says. Then, with a grin: "We got there early."

Carlson forces a tight smile. "Yeah, I guess you did. So let me ask you something." His face grows serious. "The way I see it, the US government treated you Indians ... you *Americans* ... like crap. Helped themselves to your land, put you on a reservation, gave you separate rules, probably screwed you more ways than I know, am I right?"

Jimmie answers, "Yes, sir." *Is this my father talking?*

Carlson points a bony finger at him. "Well then, why are you in uniform? What the heck are you fighting for?"

Jimmie takes a deep breath. "Ray and I are fighting for that reservation land you spoke of, sir. See, for all its problems, it's our home. It wasn't given to us by the government like you might think. It was given to us by the Holy Ones in our stories. When the Japs attacked Pearl Harbor, they attacked Two Grey Hills, where I'm from. They attacked Kayenta, where Ray's from. They attacked our traditions and our way of life and our freedom, just like they attacked yours." He pauses a moment, lowers his voice to almost a whisper. "Look, I'll be honest, sir, I also had other reasons for enlisting. But when you ask what I'm fighting for, I know that real clear now. I'm here to fight for my land."

Carlson remains silent, his gaze piercing and steady.

Ray adds, "That's how I feel, too. Every word of it. See, back home, there ain't much I can make of myself. But here in the marines, I'm part of something bigger 'n me. I can do things with my fellow soldiers I never could do on my own. Defeatin' an enemy who wants to destroy us, what could be better 'n that? An' when the war's over, if I make it through, I'll go back home knowin' I was part of something that really mattered."

Wordlessly, the colonel gets up from behind his desk, sets down a straight-backed chair in front of Jimmie and Ray, and then straddles it. His face is just inches away from theirs, uncomfortably close. Ray looks down, but Jimmie barely moves a muscle.

"You may think these questions are tailor-made for you," Carlson says at last, "but let me tell you, I interrogate every volunteer pretty much the same way. Your answers are from the heart, I can see that. A lot of people in this country—and I include our government—they could learn something from you two."

Carlson reaches into his pocket, brings out a pipe and a pouch of tobacco. "The smoking lamp is lit, lads. Smoke 'em if you got 'em."

Neither Jimmie nor Ray care for tobacco, but they watch as Carlson proceeds to fill the large bowl of his pipe with tobacco and then strikes a match and puffs until he seems satisfied that it is properly lit. The smoke has a sweet, pleasant smell. Jimmie can almost picture himself back home in the sweat lodge.

"What I'm looking for," Carlson continues, "are men who understand and believe in what they're fighting for. Every march, every mission, every battle must have a purpose. I expect my men to understand that purpose at all times so decisions can be made by consensus, not followed through blind obedience. If you join us, you'll hear more about that at our weekly gung ho meetings. You've heard about 'gung ho,' I imagine."

"Don't know a marine who hasn't, sir," Ray says.

"Well, my Raiders are the only ones who understand it and live it, day in and day out. 'Gung ho' is about viewing yourself as part of a team, not as an individual. Become one of my Raiders and you'll learn to stop thinking of yourselves as privates first class, or even as Indians, because no one here will call you 'Chief,' like I know they do in other companies. Here, it goes without saying: every one of my men is a chief."

Ray's face speaks volumes: the wonder in his eyes, the expectant way he purses his lips together, mouth upturned, like a kid with penny candy, like a poker player who has filled an inside straight. He wants what Carlson is offering. The colonel is pulling all the right strings, and Ray will follow him anywhere.

So will Jimmie.

Carlson continues, "It's no secret we're shipping out to Guadalcanal soon, so if you come aboard, your training will be shorter than I'd like. But it will be more intense, more physically and mentally demanding than anything you've ever been through. You lads are tough, but I'll push you to the limit. If you're willing to do what it will take to become a Raider, I'd like you in my unit. I need your answer by the end of the day."

Jimmie speaks up, certain he is also speaking for his little brother. "Don't think we need that much time, sir. Ray and I would be proud to serve under you. Right, Ray?"

Ray bobs his head up and down, Carlson's eager marionette.

"*With* me, not under me," Carlson corrects. He sets his pipe in an ashtray on his desk. "We're a team here, remember?"

Smiles all around. Hands shaken once more. Then Carlson says, "By the way, don't get the idea that I requested you just 'cause of the code. You two are Raiders material, with or without it. But I'd like to arrange a demonstration so I can judge this code for myself." His lamb's wool eyebrows rise up in unison as he asks, "Think you can measure up to one of the navy's decryption machines?"

"You mean to put us up against a code machine? Wouldn't be fair," Jimmie says.

Carlson's face drops.

"What I mean is, we can code and decode in a few minutes instead of, say, the four hours it probably takes using those machines." Jimmie brims with confidence. "See, Ray and I, we're better code machines than that scrap metal you're using."

Carlson stands, clearly satisfied. "That's what I'm counting on, lads."

An hour later, the demonstration begins.

While Jimmie stays with the colonel, Ray hops into a jeep with Carlson's top aide and rides to a palm-fringed location about a mile away. Clicking his stopwatch, Carlson scribbles out a test message and hands it to Jimmie, who begins speaking Navajo into his radio as Carlson watches intently. Ray receives the coded message, and four and a half minutes later, he repeats it back word for word to Carlson over a walkie-talkie.

"Let me get this straight. You translated my words into Navajo, right?" the astounded colonel asks Jimmie.

"If that's all we did, we could do it in seconds. But there's no words in Navajo for lots of those military terms. So first I change the English words into other words or letters, and *then* into Navajo. 'Course, it works in reverse on Ray's end."

"And you do it all by memory alone? How is that possible?"

"Well, Boss, we're pretty good at remembering things. See, our language has never been written down, least not till recently, so for us, *every*thing is memory. Our history, our songs, our rituals, they're told and retold to every generation. We're trained from childhood to remember. It's kind of like this: I'm a talking code machine over here, and my buddy Ray is another talking code machine at the other end."

Carlson welcomes the men once more and then directs Jimmie and Ray to a nearby hut to fill out the necessary transfer papers. As the privates walk away, proud and excited, Carlson huddles with an aide, talking quickly. But Jimmie is still within earshot, so he overhears the colonel comment, "These lads might have the best weapon yet in our arsenal against the enemy. We got to protect that weapon with everything we got, y'hear? We got to do all we can to keep those young men alive."

Chapter 12

November 1942

In life, events don't always work out as expected. In war, they seldom do.

Lt. Colonel Evans Carlson and two Raiders Companies, each with 133 men, including Jimmie and Ray, set sail for Guadalcanal on the last day of October. It starts out as a short, simple mission: to secure an area called Aola Bay for a day or two while the navy lands supplies and personnel onto the beach. Apparently, two admirals have decided to build an auxiliary airstrip there.

After five days at sea in rough, stomach-churning waters, they make their amphibious approach to the island in predawn darkness, crouching beneath the gunwales of their Higgins boat like processed sardines. They land behind enemy lines, fifty miles east of the main airstrip, Henderson Field, which has been taken earlier by Allied forces. Jimmie can barely make out the narrow strip of beach that rings the bay. Neither can he envision the dense and marshy jungle that begins barely fifty feet from where the waves lap at the sand and then stretches out across the island like an impenetrable reproach to all who come here.

111

Before long it is evident they will not be leaving the island so quickly after all. New orders have them marching inland to help destroy a Japanese beachhead party that landed up the coast. In a steady rain, they set out over deep and muddy ravines that transverse the malaria- and leech- and snake- and insect-infested jungle. They take along several native scouts and less than four days' worth of dwindling rations—primarily tea, rice, raisins, and salt pork. "Guerrilla food," Carlson calls it, modeled after the diet of China's Eighth Route Army he so admires.

For Jimmie and Ray, this is their first time wearing "Raider boots"—sturdy Oregon logging boots—along with green and brown camouflage fatigues, a jungle adaptation of the all-black fatigues Carlson himself had originated. After only a few hours, though, the once-crisp fabric mats itself to their stew of body parts as they hack their way through the dense, rotting foliage over evanescent trails.

Carlson, carrying full pack like the rest of his men, seldom rests. Even when his platoons find a rare moment to relax, the Old Man studies maps or consults with others or goes off to scout. Jimmie finds the scent of his pipe tobacco strangely comforting, almost invigorating, like the aroma of fresh coffee brewing at the trading post. When the smoke is noticeably absent, it often means Carlson is up at the point, leading his column with keen senses and a watchful eye.

On their third day out, George Tenne—a genial young boy of Italian background—mentions to the Boss that food rations are running low.

"We run out of food, we'll just have to find the Japs and take theirs," Carlson shrugs.

Luckily, three fresh Raider companies arrive the next day bringing renewed supplies of guerrilla rations. But even before they finish distributing the provisions, the men begin bartering with one another, trading raisins for rice, tea for coffee, chocolate for fatback. To nonsmokers like Jimmie and Ray, negotiations take on a fevered pitch. Their allocation of cigarettes commands a hearty haul of coffee.

Jimmie remains camped with Company C at the bivouac area, but Ray is reassigned to Carlson at the Battalion Command Post. Carlson says he wants a Navajo with him at all times, not only to field messages from patrol, but also to communicate daily with a Navajo counterpart at First Marine Division base camp further west on the island. Jimmie is relieved his little brother will be someplace relatively safe.

After dinner that evening, a few of the men sit around and talk softly, their heads filled with horror stories about the enemy. The ground is soggy from an earlier cloudburst, but that does not dampen the determination of the men, anxious to face the enemy and complete their mission.

Nighttime sounds of the island fill the air. Jimmie hears the siren call of frogs, the inharmonious melodies of insects, the scratching of six-inch land crabs, the soft slither of foot-long lizards. From somewhere far off comes a lone burst of machine-gun fire, not returned. And music, from inside a nearby tent, a soulful tune on harmonica.

The company's second in command, a solidly built, balding officer named Keith McClintock—everyone calls him "Bulldog"— comes around with orders from the Old Man. They are to form combat patrols and fan out in search of the enemy. McClintock reads, *At 0600 hours we head west, toward the Metapona River, radioing back to base every two hours. As enemy is located and destroyed, the Boss will move the base forward and repeat the patrol tactics.*

"Goodluck?" McClintock squats down next to Jimmie. "The Old Man says he wants all communications from our company to be in Navajo. You can do that?"

"That's why I'm here. It's what I'm trained for. Just keep the messages short as possible, and I'll talk 'em in code fast as I can. My buddy Ray will decode it for the Boss."

McClintock is silent for a while. He looks down, pokes at the damp earth with a slender branch that lies at his feet. "Do you believe in God?" he asks finally. "I mean, is the concept of God part of your Indian religion?"

"Can't speak for all Indians. But in Navajo, we got no word for what you call religion."

"Oh." There is disappointment in McClintock's voice.

"That doesn't mean we don't believe. It's more like ... how can I say it? Like a way of life for us, natural as breathing. We have holy beings, who we call the Holy People or the Ancient Ones. We have many names for them. Our ceremonies are really blessings and offerings of thanks, y'see, done in an ordered manner."

McClintock brightens. "Sounds like religion to me."

"Well, for us, the universe is made up of four basic elements: earth, water, air, and fire. They weave together in orderly patterns. Like our rugs. Only in nature there's both good and evil. When the elements are in balance, we describe it as walking in beauty. Anyway, that is for us what religion, I s'pose, is for you."

"I see."

"Do you?"

"Well, I'm not sure. Thing is, it sounds like you believe a greater force controls the universe. I think that's important. So does Lieutenant Colonel Carlson."

McClintock starts to get up and then crouches back down. "Did you know he's the son of a minister?"

"Carlson? Haven't been with him very long, but he seems to be a spiritual person. Never heard him cuss or raise his voice, even when he's angry at somebody. And now's you mention it, it's ironic—is that the word?—that he trains us to kill, to take no prisoners. Yet like you say, he's a religious man."

"Yeah. Well. War's filled with irony, I guess." McClintock sighs and rises to his feet. "Listen, get some rest, Goodluck. And say your prayers. Might not have much time for either after tonight."

"Oh, there's always time for reaching out to the Holy People," Jimmie says, looking up at the officer. "Like breathing, remember?"

McClintock nods grimly and walks off.

For no apparent reason, Jimmie reaches for his knife and removes it from its sheath. In the dim moonlight that filters through the frayed palms, he studies the blade, and through some trick of vision—what else could explain it?—he sees a flaming pyre reflected in the steel. Within the white hot orb glows the face of a soldier, vaguely familiar. But the specter is already too far gone, melting like candle wax before his eyes.

THE TBX RADIO, FOR ALL its bulk and weight, is considered the workhorse of the marines and the navy. It usually takes three men to carry the transmitter, receiver, and hand-cranked generator. A spool of wire attached to a pole serves as the antenna. For the Raiders, who move stealthily and travel light, transporting the TBX on patrols is like dragging an elephant by the tail. Improvements in portability are rumored to be just months away, but these days, the TBX is about as dependable over long distances as front-line communications get.

Like all radiomen, Jimmie knows his gear inside and out. He can take each unit apart and put it back together as swiftly as he can disassemble and assemble a rifle. The radio is his company's lifeline, and as such, it never leaves his side, even when he sleeps. The military has recruited island natives to help lug around some of the equipment, but Jimmie still carries a heavy load. It prevents him from taking much else on patrol. Nothing more than the standard-issue cartridge belt that holds his Raider knife, canteen and cup, first-aid packet, and ammunition pouches. And a food sock, of course—literally, a sock—filled with two to four days' rations of the ubiquitous rice, raisins, and fatback.

Shortly after dawn on November 11, Company C—Jimmie's outfit—moves out. By midmorning they cross a wide field of razor-sharp kunai grass, stepping stealthily in single-file formation through the dense, yellow blades that grow as tall as mature cornstalks. Entering a wooded area that borders the field, the advance guard comes upon a sizeable enemy force and begins an immediate assault, killing a number of surprised Japanese. But the enemy quickly mans their positions and opens up on the Raiders with rifles, machine guns, mortars, and cannon fire.

Five Raiders die during the opening salvo and three are injured. Company C's point positions are driven back to the grassy field, where they immediately seek cover within the dense foliage. The company commander is pinned down by enemy fire, but a stocky lieutenant with the mortar section at the rear has field radio contact with a front column radioman. He acts on his own authority to open fire on enemy positions with a fusillade of 60-mm mortar rounds.

"Goodluck!" he screams. "Where's my goddamned Indian?"

Jimmie is about a hundred yards away, already cranking up the TBX. The gun and mortar fire resonates in his ears. Real this time, not some training exercise. The company appears to be under attack by a sizeable enemy force, yet he feels strangely calm as the generator roars into action. This is what he has been trained to do.

The lieutenant bounds over to him. Jimmie raises the microphone to his lips.

"Arizona, Arizona," Jimmie calls repeatedly in English, alerting the radioman at the other end that a message is about to be sent in Navajo code. It will ensure that a Navajo radioman—Ray, in this case—is summoned to receive.

In an urgent tone the lieutenant says, "Tell 'em we're taking heavy fire from a reinforced Jap company. Request support. Give 'em these coordinates." He scratches the numbers on a scrap of paper and shoves it into Jimmie's hand.

Jimmie looks at the paper, composes the message in his head, and begins.

"Nakia moasi ... bi'ya lin dzeh wol'la'chee a'keh'di'glini tsah'as'zih coh ...

It takes him about ten minutes to finish the communication. On the other end, Ray scrambles to decode the message so he can hand it to the Boss.

Carlson immediately orders two additional companies to reinforce the beleaguered Company C. A few hours later, Carlson himself arrives with a third company to coordinate a renewed attack. By this time, Company C manages to pull back from the grassy field.

Carlson directs Jimmie to radio division headquarters with a request for air support. "Use your code," Carlson insists.

A short while later, two American bombers roar overhead, dropping death on the enemy position. Carlson leaves a fresh company in position and returns to base camp with the exhausted men of Company C. There, after washing thoroughly with lye soap, Jimmie collapses into a restless sleep. But the smell of burning flesh still lingers in his nostrils, while the sound of enemy fire and the screams of the wounded on both sides echo in his ears.

WITH A DAY TO REST and replenish before moving base camp, Jimmie and Ray catch up with one another. They sit together, burrowed between the roots of a banyan tree, inured to the putrescent jungle odors and thrum of insect noises. That is nothing compared to the fungus infections and diarrhea and ringworm and constant threat of malaria that plague all the men on Guadalcanal.

"What happened on your patrol?" Jimmie asks. "Did you take enemy fire?"

Ray pulls his Raider knife from its sheath, turning it over in his hand as if he is looking at it for the first time. "Not like you did, big brother. My outfit must have killed a dozen Japs, though. They were wanderin' around, completely disorganized. I kept my distance from the bodies. If I touched 'em, their *chindi* would come after me."

Chindi, ghosts of the dead: always malevolent, no matter how good the person was in life. It is the reason many Navajos of this day refuse to touch dead bodies, even those of loved ones; why *hogans* in which a person dies are often burned; and why, Jimmie suspects, some individuals with the ability to foretell their own imminent deaths wander off to die alone.

Ray goes on, "Several of the guys around me, they run over to the dead Japs and bring back souvenirs. Anything they can find. One guy in the company, Hal D'Orazio, he brings over a … a …"

For a moment it seems as if Ray is going to cry. "Brings what?" Jimmie asks gently.

Ray clears his throat and sheathes his knife. "He shows me what he took from the Jap's pocket: a letter, all folded up. That funny Jap writing. And an identification packet, along with two photos. One of an older couple. His parents, I'm guessin'. The other is him, the guy D'Orazio shot. In the photo he's smiling, standing with his arm around a girl. And I got to thinkin', here's a kid 'bout my age, with features a lot like my own, people back home who love him, and here he is, under orders to kill as many Americans as he can before we kill him. And we do. We kill him."

Ray is shaking as he continues. "Y'know, it used to be easy to think of the enemy as something large and evil, something … I don't know, not human, I guess. But those photos and the ID with 'em … they changed all that. They made my enemy into flesh and blood. They told me he had a name. Hideo Tanaka, somethin' like that.

Jeez, Jimmie, he was probably no more evil than any of *us*. What I'm tryin' to say is, the letter ... those photos ... they made him human, and I'm havin' a hard time with that."

"It's all right, Ray, you don't have to explain."

"Don't you see?" Ray's voice quivers, rising in pitch. "The photos, they took my enemy and they made him ... *me*."

THE RAIDERS' MISSION ON GUADALCANAL—THE one that Carlson originally said would be just a quick in-and-out at Aola Bay—is being called the Long Patrol, for it lasted nearly a full month.

By now, everyone in the battalion suffers from exhaustion and hunger. Many have malarial dysentery, including Carlson himself, who—in spite of his protestations—has been ordered to fly to the United States on the next transport for treatment. The men, meanwhile, learn a ship is on its way to take them back to Espiritu Santo. They have just broken down the mess hall in anticipation of their imminent departure when they find out that their embarkation might be delayed for up to a week. Nobody wants to set up the mess hall again, and the nearby army encampment is not willing to share their dining privileges, so the Raiders resort to raiding the army chow dump.

Word spreads that fresh supplies have come in for the army boys. A bunch of the Raiders skulk over and survey the scattered crates of food and supplies that are piled high under lean-tos in a jungle clearing. There the men help themselves to cans of meat, fruit, and vegetables. Jimmie and Ray, however, are not content to grab and run like everyone else.

"Y'know what I could really go for?" Ray whispers to his buddy. "Orange juice." Powdered orange juice concentrate has been recently developed, and the entire limited supply heads directly to the military.

Jimmie licks his lips. "Think they got some here?"

"Does a sheep have fleece, big brother?"

The rest of the Raiders have already fled with their booty, but Jimmie and Ray continue to wander like scavengers among the crates and boxes of foodstuffs.

"Think I found it!" Jimmie calls out, scampering like an eager puppy toward a case stamped "Minute Maid." He and Ray work to pry it open when they each feel a point of cold steel pressed against their backs.

"What the hell we got here?" snarls a gravelly voice behind them.

"Turn around slowly, nips," says a second man. "One sudden move, and I swear to Christ, we'll fuckin' kill ya."

"Nips? You think we're—is this some kind of joke?" Jimmie asks, turning slowly to face his captor. The man pointing the rife at him is an army staff sergeant.

Ray also turns as instructed. "Look, we're sorry, we was just tryin' to get some orange—"

"Looks like we got us a couple of *English*-speaking nips here, don't it!"

The other man, a corporal, nods. "Japs in Marine Corps uniforms."

"We're US Marines," Ray practically shouts. "With the Raiders Battalion just up the beach. C'mon, *look* at us!"

The realization hits Jimmie like desert lightning. He and Ray have dark hair, dark eyes, sparse beard, ruddy complexion. To the uninitiated, they undoubtedly *do* look like Japs.

"We're Navajo," Jimmie tries to explain. "Y'know ... Indians. *That's* why we look like we do. But we're Americans, and we're marines. Just march us over to the Raider bivouac. They'll identify us."

The corporal scowls. "Dog-tag number."

"What?"

"Your dog-tag numbers. Both of you. What are they?"

Jimmie and Ray each recite their numbers without hesitation. The corporal checks their tags and then nods to the sergeant. The army officers huddle briefly, weapons still raised.

"Okay, let's go," they agree finally. "But keep your hands where we can see 'em."

Grumbling all the way, the two Raiders march at bayonet point, hands in the air, back to the Raider encampment. Ray later admits he nearly pissed himself out of sheer terror.

"These boys say they belong to you," the sergeant says to a surprised Bulldog McClintock. "You recognize 'em?"

"Are you serious?"

"Either you ID 'em, or we'll shoot 'em right here."

"Of course I know them! They're our Indians, Goodluck and Begay. What, you thought they were Japs?"

"Wouldn't be the first time a couple of slants got into our chow dump." The sergeant sounds almost disappointed at the turn of events. "You better keep an eye on 'em from here on. Next time they might not be so lucky."

With no apologies, the two army officers turn and stomp out.

Jimmie and Ray breathe sighs of relief, but McClintock is furious. "What the hell were you thinking? You're the most valuable property we got around here. Yet sneaking around almost gets you killed. Wait'll the Boss hears about this!"

Jimmie shrugs. Sure, scavenging around the dump was stupid, but it never occurred to him he might be shot for it.

"I just came from a briefing with the colonel," a stern-faced McClintock informs Jimmie and Ray two hours later. "Sick as he is, it's the first time I ever heard him cuss."

Ray freezes, but Jimmie looks up warily. "What'd he say?"

"He says from now on, until we leave this stinking island, you and Begay gonna have a shadow everywhere you go. And I mean *everywhere*—even when you take a shit. 'Course, that's going to piss off George Tenne some."

"Tenne? What's he got to do with this?"

Bulldog takes a cigarette from his pocket and lights it, inhaling deeply. He makes a fish face and puffs out three perfect smoke rings.

"That lucky bastard? From here on, he's your personal bodyguard."

CHAPTER 13

JUNE 1944–JANUARY 1945

On their way to Saipan, Jimmie and Ray come face to face with an old friend.

They are standing on the crowded forward deck of a troop transport heading toward the heavily fortified headquarters of the Japanese Central Pacific Fleet. A voice behind them, familiar in its soft-spoken tenor, gets their attention.

"Goodluck and Begay, aren't you going to say hello?"

They turn and stare directly into the piercing eyes of Evans Carlson.

The colonel, his skin still as taut as a drumhead, has returned to the South Pacific in the role of planning officer for Major General Harry Schmidt.

"I've been keeping track of you lads," Carlson says before Jimmie and Ray can get out a word. "Lot has happened since we were together."

Indeed it has. After the Long Patrol, Jimmie and Ray shipped out to New Zealand on R&R; to New Caledonia, for retraining;

back to Guadalcanal, now under the American flag; and twice more to Espiritu Santo, former home of Camp Gung Ho. The camp's name went away when Carlson left for the States to recuperate. The Second Raider Battalion was reorganized and run strictly according to regulations by a colonel who had little use for Carlson's unconventional methods and gung-ho meetings. Jimmie and Ray felt fortunate when Lt. Colonel Fred Beans pulled them out and transferred them to the Third Raiders Battalion under his command. Within weeks, they shipped out with their new battalion to face the enemy on an island where it rained all afternoon, every afternoon, almost without exception.

Bougainville.

Ray was assigned to H&S Company, while Jimmie was attached to Company K, which headed inland in search of the enemy. Their radio net kept the two buddies in communications with one another, using Navajo code part of the time. A short while later, the Raider companies were unexpectedly deactivated and funneled into the Fourth Marines. There followed four months of noncombat duty, but now Jimmie's and Ray's division is heading back into action.

"It's good to see you, Boss," Ray gushes. "Uh, I mean, sir. Jeez, I miss the way we did things in the Raiders!"

Carlson's smile fades. "Yeah, I miss those things too, but change is inevitable." Stories had been flying that he was bitter at losing his Raiders, but Carlson shows no sign of that now.

"We heard you were at Tarawa when you first came back," Jimmie says. "Word is, you were pretty amazing over there."

"I was merely a forward observer," Carlson says, scowling. "Believe me, I had nothing to do with the success in that battle. Let me tell you something, lads. You want to know how Tarawa was won? How Saipan will be won? Not by me, and not by skilled officers alone. It'll be won by a few courageous men—*enlisted* men—who take initiative when their commanders go down. And it'll be won by soldiers like you and the other Indian lads who do an almost impossible job without error, and without ever shirking their duty, and without complaining."

Moments later, Carlson is called away by a senior officer. Ray whispers to Jimmie, "That little speech would sound corny coming from anyone else, don't y'think? Is it any wonder his men would do anything and go anywhere for him?"

Jimmie is still reeling from the encounter. "Listen, little brother. I myself would go straight into the emperor's bedroom, long as I could walk in right behind the Old Man."

CARLSON'S IDEAS FOR THE INVASION of Saipan and nearby Tinian are built, not surprisingly, on a radical departure from standard operating procedure. He has determined that the marines can achieve tactical advantage, particularly on Tinian, by landing immense forces on small, seemingly inaccessible beaches.

Although Jimmie and Ray make separate landings, they both experience intense shelling. Ordnance rains down with the fury of a tropical storm. Shards of shrapnel and chunks of burning phosphorous turn the beaches into sandy morgues. The fighting rages on for more than three weeks, and it is unlike any combat that has come before. Saipan's honeycombed complex of limestone caves, along with bunkers, concrete pillboxes, and sugar cane fields, provide protection for the enemy's formidable artillery and serve as excellent camouflage for snipers.

Jimmie is assigned to the Twenty-Fifth Regimental Headquarters Company. He lands with his regiment on Saipan's west coast, an area designated as Yellow Beach. The shelling is fierce and there is little place to hide. He digs in behind a sand dune with quiet desperation. When the shooting diminishes, the men are able to move a few hundred yards inland, across the blood-soaked sand strewn with eviscerated bodies. Jimmie retches violently as the stench and sheer horror of it all overcomes him. At the periphery of the carnage, under the paltry shelter of scrub and palms, the company stops to set up base camp.

As part of his duties on the regimental level, Jimmie ferries calls to and from the battalions, and sometimes on up to division headquarters. Having survived the landing and the first hellish twenty-four hours, Jimmie is removed from front line action for the rest of the engagement.

For Ray Begay, assigned to the Third Battalion, Saipan is a different experience.

As Ray later tells his buddy, when he came ashore with his company, the men made their way a short distance to a steep embankment. There they dug in for the night. With one of the new, portable TBY radios strapped to his back and a .45 tightly in hand, Ray hunkered down and prayed. Nearby, Battalion Commander Lt. Colonel Justice Chambers—"Jumpin' Joe," as he was known, for his vigorous stride—waited for his orders from the Marine Force Commander. Those orders came the next morning. Ray, as Chambers's radioman, was the first to know.

The battalion's primary objective was to secure Hill 500, an outsized ridge that dominated the terrain. Its capture would give the marines access to the highest point on the island, nearby Mt. Tapotchau. A company of about a hundred men made the first assault on the ridge. They met intense fire and were ordered to withdraw. They returned to base with half their men wounded, one dead.

In the morning, their captain led a fresh attack with rifles, grenades, and flame throwers. Ray radioed in Navajo code for air support. When the smoke cleared from the aerial bombs and the subsequent ground attack, the marines controlled the hill. The next objective was Mt. Tapotchau itself.

For this mission, Chambers sent a recon patrol led by Sgt. Major

Gilbert Morton. When they reached the top, they were surrounded by enemy soldiers. They tried to hold their position, but the situation was precarious. Deaths and injuries quickly mounted up. Reporting their dire circumstances back to Chambers, they received permission to withdraw after dark, when retreat would be somewhat safer. It was Ray who fielded the messages.

But Morton was faced with a dilemma. To withdraw silently, under cover of darkness, would mean leaving behind his dead and wounded. He feared the wounded would be captured and mercilessly tortured.

"Tell the commander we want to stay and fight it out," he radioed to Ray. "I've talked it over with the men, and everyone's in agreement. We all leave, or none of us do."

Ray passed the message on to Chambers. He, in turn, consulted with Operations Officer Evans Carlson, the Old Man himself, who had joined up with the battalion commander the previous day.

It came as no surprise to anyone that the two men knew and respected one another. Both stand straight and lean as cornstalks—though Chambers has a rounder face and is easily fifteen years younger—and both are courageous on the battlefield. Chambers had been wounded in the Solomons, according to scuttlebutt, but had still managed to single-handedly drive off a party of Japanese soldiers who raided the island hospital where he was recovering.

Chambers told Ray that, because division headquarters wanted a first-hand report on Morton's situation, he and Carlson were going to take some men at sunrise and go up there themselves. Ray would come along as their radioman.

It was June 22 when they headed up the heavily forested flank of Mt. Tapotchau. Sounds of intense fighting from somewhere up ahead carried on the wind. As they neared the besieged unit, a burst of machine-gun fire came from behind. Ray felt pain, white hot. It coursed through his left thigh. He fell to the ground. With the thirty-pound radio strapped to his back, he could not easily move from the line of fire. He squirmed on the ground and struggled to remove the radio.

Chambers and Carlson saw him fall. Together, they rushed over to him, grabbed his arms, and dragged him a few feet to some cover—no more than a small bank of dirt. Then both officers dived for cover themselves.

The machine gun fired again. Bullets flew just millimeters over Ray's head.

"He's not going to survive there," Carlson called to Chambers. "That sniper's got an accurate fix."

Without another moment's hesitation, Carlson ran to Ray and scooped up the boy in his arms, radio and all, as if he were weightless. He advanced no more than a yard or two when the machine gun came alive once more. This time Carlson took fire, multiple rounds of ammunition piercing his right shoulder and leg. For the first time in the entire war, Carlson crumpled, his sinewy body sheltering Ray as they hit the dirt.

Moments later, Chambers's men located and destroyed the sniper. Soon stretcher bearers arrived and, following protocol, began to remove the officer first.

"Take this man before you take me," Carlson insisted weakly, gesturing with his head toward Ray. "Private First Class Begay was wounded before I was."

And so it was that Evans F. Carlson—architect of the Raiders, pioneer of unconventional warfare, early adapter and staunch supporter of the Navajo code, visionary officer who lead by example and lived by everything he preached—again left the fields of battle that he had embraced over two world wars. The seriousness of his wounds suggested that this time, he might not come bouncing back.

Ray admits it is exactly how the colonel might have scripted an end to his colorful career: wounded in the line of duty, saving an enlisted man. So why, Ray asks, does he feel such a heavy burden of guilt over having sustained only relatively minor injuries himself?

RAY FILLS JIMMIE IN ON all of this back at regimental headquarters as he awaits medical transport off the island.

"Do you know what happened to the guys we were trying to help?" Ray asks. "Did Morton's company make it out?"

As regimental radioman, Jimmie knows almost everything going on with the Twenty-Fifth Marines on Saipan. "Yeah, little brother, we took Mt. Tapotchau this morning. A team got Morton's guys out, all the dead and wounded. It was pretty bad. Only five of 'em made it out alive. Morton was one of 'em. He deserves a Navy Cross for sure."

"What about Carlson?"

"In a lot of pain, not that he'll ever let on. Got torn up pretty bad. He's already on his way to the Naval Hospital at Pearl. They'll fix him up, but it'll be a long recovery."

"He saved my life. If he hadn't moved me from that spot ..." Ray chokes back a sob. "And now he's hurt. 'Cause of me."

Jimmie assures Ray he has no reason to feel guilty. But that is something Ray will have to work out for himself.

"They're sending me to New Zealand for a month or two to get better," Ray says. "Guess you know that already. But I'll be back before you know it, big brother."

"Listen, I got to get back to work," Jimmie says reluctantly, putting his hand on Ray's shoulder. The boy looks pale, vulnerable. "I'm going to miss you, but like you say, you'll be back in no time. We been through a lot together, you and me, and it's not over yet."

Ray feebly squeezes Jimmie's hand. "No, it's not over yet," he repeats, unaware of the carnage those words foreshadow.

For these two expatriates from the reservation, there is still Iwo Jima.

RAY RECUPERATES FOR SEVERAL MONTHS in New Zealand and then reunites with Jimmie during training exercises in Hawaii. As part of the Fourth Division, they are based at secluded Camp Maui, along the lush, but often muddy, trail to Hana. There they are housed in wood-framed tents, no bigger than sixteen feet square, staked near rugged terrain that proves ideal for both jungle and amphibious maneuvers. Ray insists he feels fit and ready to go back into battle. He practiced the code silently the whole time he was convalescing, he boasts, creating flash cards with dozens of different messages in English.

In between field maneuvers, training exercises, amphibious landing rehearsals, and high-level coded message drills, Jimmie and Ray rehash some of their experiences on Saipan and fill each other in on what happened during their short time apart. Ray's renewed energy and spirit are clearly evident. He even gained a few pounds during his recuperation. "More mutton in New Zealand than you can shake a fork at," is how he puts it.

In mid-November they are summoned to Ewa Field on the southern tip of Oahu for a two-week-long Navajo code refresher course. It seems the commanding generals of three divisions have finally embraced the code program and have encouraged the Fleet Marine Force Commander to continue its implementation and expansion in the battles to come. At Camp Pendleton—now the country's largest Marine Corps base—new groups of Navajo radiomen are being trained around the clock.

At Ewa Field, meanwhile, old hands like Jimmie and Ray update their Signal Corps skills, memorize additional code terms and shortcuts, and familiarize themselves with new equipment.

These days they have "walkie-talkies" in place of the heavy, outdated radios.

Among the Navajo faces there are several of the men from the original boot platoon, including George Benally, Charlie Yazzie, Carl Slowtalker, and Wilfred Smith. They get together one evening in a vacant Quonset hut to talk about old times and share combat experiences, lapsing into silence only when Charlie mentions that the flute of Samuel Nez has been silenced forever. He was killed a few months earlier coming ashore on Peleliu. A bullet through his neck.

Jimmie and Ray gain some celebrity with their old boot buddies through stories of their time with Carlson's Raiders. "But understand," Jimmie insists, "our experiences were not so different, really, from what other Navajo soldiers must have gone through."

They sit on metal chairs and reminisce as the tales keep coming.

Wilfred Smith explains that, while on New Britain, he had to function as a runner when the radio and phone lines got knocked out. "I was heading back to my company from regimental HQ, dodging sniper fire the whole way. Guess I became disoriented, but eventually I ran into a marine and, of course, he asked me for the password. I must have used an old one because the SOB pointed a bayonet at my back and called me an 'effing Jap.' I might've got myself killed if I hadn't fallen into a foxhole at that very moment. Lucky for me, I fell on top of a sergeant who knew me and straightened things out."

Carl Slowtalker, not sure how much he can believe of Wilfred's story, recounts how on Guam, he was on the radio nonstop for nearly twenty-four hours, requesting reinforcements and ferrying calls back and forth because suddenly every officer wanted to use the Navajo network. "Don't know 'bout you guys, but us Navajo radiomen on Guam were given a special code number. The idea was, if we should be captured and forced to send a phony message in code, we would insert the number in Navajo so's the receiver would know we were making it under duress."

For Charlie Yazzie on Peleliu, the casualties were so heavy at one point that he was pressed into service as a stretcher bearer. That was the day Samuel Nez got killed. "Can you imagine our fathers carrying and burying dead bodies all day long?" he asks, shaking his head. Tongues cluck because many of the men face their own misgivings about that.

And George Benally swears that one night in a foxhole, he heard the chanting of a medicine man, followed by a vision that convinced him his family back home was singing over him at that very moment. "I knew then I'd be safe. You wait and see—the Holy Spirits are watching over me."

When the refresher course ends, the men say their farewells and prepare to return to their units to await the inevitable final push toward Japan.

"I'm grateful we're together again, little brother," Jimmie tells Ray once more as they await transportation back to Camp Maui. They sit together under a thatch of palm trees well beyond the four rebuilt runways of Ewa Field, watching as a F2A-3 Brewster Buffalo fighter comes in low, its gear descended for landing.

"I'm glad too, old man." Ray lands a playful jab on his buddy's arm.

"Still a little weak, I see. Better work on that, so's in the next battle, you don't go and get yourself wounded again."

"Tried it once and found it not to my liking," Ray grins. "Next time it's all or nothin'."

Jimmie fails to find any humor in that.

THE EVENING BEFORE THEY SHIP out from Maui, Jimmie and Ray and several other Fourth Division Navajos—not all are radiomen—get together to perform a shorthand version of the *Ye'ii Bicheii*, or

Night Chant. They improvise masks to transform themselves into *Ye'iis,* deities that represent forces of nature and that function as spiritual guardians. They dance to a steady drum beat and they chant traditional prayers. When they finish, several Cherokee boys get up and do a dance of their own, which in turn inspires a young Zuni lad to sing one of his tribe's sacred songs. Almost everyone feels the need to seek approval and protection from a higher force.

All too soon, morning comes. The Fourth and Fifth Marine Divisions vacate their respective training camps and converge on Honolulu like fleas on a mutt for one last liberty before battle. Jimmie and Ray spend a couple of evenings on the town, seeing Bing Crosby in *White Christmas* one night and a forgettable comedy the next. They hit several bars each evening as well, mostly because that is where their buddies want to go.

In one boisterous tavern they introduce themselves to a fellow marine of obvious Indian heritage. He is a Pima boy from the Gila River Reservation, he tells them, name of Ira Hayes. They chat for a few minutes until it becomes evident that Hayes is more interested in drinking than in talking, so they wish him well and take off. Their departure leaves young Hayes to his moody introspection, which cannot possibly include a vision of his imminent encounter with perpetual fame that is soon to unfold along with a solitary American flag.

SOME OF THE MEN FIRST learn where they are heading from Tokyo Rose.

"Hello, all you boys in the Fourth Marine Division," purrs Rose Toguri over the airwaves. "I hear you're leaving Hawaii, enjoying your last moments on earth as you make your way to Iwo Jima. When the battle's over, the Fourth Marines will be taking roll call in a telephone booth."

Jimmie and Ray have known their destination for nearly a month. Iwo Jima was the subject of coded messages they have been sending and receiving at Camp Maui for Colonel John Lanigan, their regimental commanding officer, as well as for Major General Clifton Cates, the highly decorated commander of the Fourth Division. Of course, there are strict orders to keep their knowledge confidential, though the destination really does not matter much. The coming battles will be costly wherever they are waged.

When the USS *Southampton* pulls out of Pearl Harbor in a fleet convoy seventy miles long, it heads toward the staging area on Saipan where the marines will conduct final invasion rehearsals off neighboring Tinian Island.

One morning, when all communications personnel are assembled in front of a large relief map of Iwo Jima, the chief operations officer announces, "Every man here will memorize every inch of this island before we get to Saipan. You'll also memorize the latest reports on suspected enemy troop emplacements along with instructions on posts and frequencies. Oh, and one more thing," he adds. "From now on, a Navajo will be assigned to each reconnaissance team that goes in to Iwo. When the full-scale invasion begins, our Navajos will be disbursed throughout every battalion. As much as they can, they'll send and receive all orders and critical communications."

Our Navajos. Jimmie evaluates the phrase not as condescending, but as a statement of pride that signals a bipolar awareness of both alienation and acceptance, of separation and assimilation. This ascendency has been a long-held dream of Jimmie's, but here the reality actually goes beyond mere tolerance and approval. Here, for every one of the enemy who wants to kill him, stands a company of fellow marines—mostly Anglos—who have his back, who would put their own lives in danger, if necessary, to safeguard his.

In truth, Jimmie realizes that he and his tribal buddies *are* different from most of their white counterparts in appearance, in cultural and spiritual background, in their use of English as a second language. But they have proven themselves time and again, from boot camp to battle, and the novelty of their differences has been overshadowed by the magnitude of their contributions.

The Navajo code has come a long way from its lukewarm reception, two years earlier, on Guadalcanal. And from all indications, never will it be more depended upon in the maelstrom of battle, or play a more essential role to an outcome of success, than it will in the desperate, agonizing weeks that lie ahead.

Today I will walk out, today everything negative will leave me
I will be as I was before, I will have a cool breeze over my body …
I walk with beauty before me, I walk with beauty behind me
I walk with beauty below me, I walk with beauty above me …
In beauty all day long may I walk.

—Navajo Blessingway, traditional prayer

PART III:

THE SHATTERED VISION

CHAPTER 14

MARCH 1946

Gallup, from all appearances, has changed during the nearly four years Jimmie has been away, although it is difficult to tell if any of the changes are for the better.

As he steps off the train, he is assaulted by the jarring sounds of John Philip Sousa, attempted by a local high school band huddled on the platform. The welcome, certainly, is not for him. To celebrate the individual is not the Navajo way.

Sure enough, the band members spot their prey, a young white man in army uniform, one train car ahead. They run as a disorganized squad toward the army sergeant, all the while continuing their haphazard playing as if the musical notes are ricocheting bullets.

Jimmie cannot leave the station fast enough.

It quickly becomes apparent that the town is stretched at the seams, swollen with life like a pupa ready to burst. The March weather is seasonably cool, yet Indian men mill about in astonishing numbers. There are some Zuni and a few Hopi, but mostly they are Navajo, all largely ignored by the crush of indifferent white people

on the streets. The fact that they are here, these Indians, miles
from their reservation homes, suggests to Jimmie that employment
opportunities on Indian lands may not be any better now than they
were before the war.

Then there is Gallup's main street: Main Street, honky-tonk
as ever. Some of the old signboards are still around. Texaco and
Kodak and Western Union and Coca-Cola emblems stand side by
side with the El Rancho Hotel and the Chief Theatre and the Plaza
Café and the Haas Department Store and Merchants Bank. But
the streetlights look new, and on blocks that sported one tavern
there now stand two or three, their jukeboxes cranked up loud,
spilling music out onto the street. Five or six scrawny dogs lope past
Jimmie. Their coats are matted and mangy. Two of the animals emit
mournful yelps, while a third growls menacingly. From the roadway,
the coughs of car engines and the whinny of horses compete in equal
measure to fill out this urban symphony.

Shortly before the train reached Gallup, Jimmie watched as the
sun marched westward toward terrible places he does not wish to
recall. It marked its departure with a perfect twilight desert sky: a
palette of crimsons and blues and purples, the colors of *Dinetah*. But
here in this ramshackle border town that sits like a donut hole carved
out of reservation land, the sunset is shrouded by the gray pall of coal
smoke that drapes over the community, catlike, and chokes off the
sky. Jimmie tries to inhale the surrounding desert, but Gallup offers
him only the stink of burning coal and stale beer and the collective
ripeness of its bloated humanity.

It has been a hot and tiring two-day train ride from Barstow,
California, where he received his discharge. He carries his bag
with his left hand because his right shoulder still complains of the
souvenir metal he picked up at Iwo. He tries to pay the discomfort
little mind. It will heal soon enough. Besides, he knows he is lucky
to be coming back at all, considering all that he experienced. It has

been close to a year since he last saw combat, but the scars from Iwo Jima have yet to heal. The unbidden memories nearly bring him to tears right here.

The home of his parents, in Two Grey Hills, is still a long journey due north. Perhaps he will be lucky enough to hitch a ride. He is tempted to head first to Tanner Springs, which is closer, for although he is eager to see his mother and assure her he is all right, he longs even more to visit Annie, to draw upon her wisdom so he can put things back into perspective. He devoured her last letter in Honolulu, which came shortly after he left the hospital where he spent several months recuperating. She wrote of her hopes that he might get involved in some of her causes upon his return. It gave him something positive to think about while he was laid up, trying to figure out his life.

Of course, he cannot tell her or anyone else what he did over there, he and his buddy Ray and the four hundred Navajo radiomen who followed his original group, because the code—having never been broken by the enemy—is still classified. Uncle Sam, it seems, might want to call on him again in the future. He prays that possibility will not come to pass, for he has seen enough suffering, enough death and dismemberment, to infect him for the rest of his life.

He knows his father, if he speaks to Jimmie at all, will undoubtedly insist that he undergo an Enemy Way ceremony. Jimmie will actually welcome the three-day ritual, rejoice in its cleansing powers, for in spite of his heady transition into the white world, he has never stopped feeling the familiar pull of his own traditions.

Truth is, he can comfortably live with one foot firmly planted in both worlds. The war has changed so many things, himself included; more than that, it has brought a country together. These should be promising times, auguring new beginnings, new opportunities. So why, he wonders, does he feel a vague apprehension about what is yet to come?

With plenty of time ahead to evaluate his options, Jimmie decides a beer is in order. A full-strength draft for once, not the 3.2 percent horse piss they served at the military slop chutes. Something to both quench his thirst and drown the echoes of battle that still resound endlessly in his head. As he surveys the flourishing array of watering holes in town, it is the plaintive sound of Hank Williams singing "Cold, Cold Heart," more than the flickering Schlitz sign, that beckons to him from a joint just off Main Street.

He wanders in and takes a seat at the shabby bar, going no farther than the stool closest to the door. A heady smell immediately overpowers him: tobacco smoke, mixed with the yeasty scent of beer and faint notes of urine. He runs his hand over the pants legs of his marine dress blues. Bits of confetti, picked up at the station, flutter to the ground. It will be good to store his uniform somewhere out of sight. If only the nightmares of Guadalcanal and Bougainville and Saipan and, most terrible of all, Iwo Jima, could be so neatly tucked away.

Behind the bar is a mirrored wall. Peering back through the smeared and dusty surface is a reflection Jimmie hardly recognizes. His face is drawn, having taken on faint lines, like wire fencing, around his mouth and eyes. His eyes, once clear and alert, appear clouded, desensitized, in spite of having seen some triumphs so longingly evoked in his prewar dreams. But along the way they have witnessed too much revulsion, these eyes: shapes wrapped in tatters of death and fear, atrocities that cast a pall over everything else. At least his hair, still military short, is beginning to grow back with the shine his eyes seem to lack.

It is not just a town that has changed after four years, his reflection tries to tell him.

In the back of the half-empty tavern sit a couple of pool tables, where young white boys in faded T-shirts and jeans are killing time. At the other end of the bar to Jimmie's left, a couple of men who are easily over fifty nurse draft beers. They seem not to notice the weary marine as he sits patiently on his stool, waiting for service.

The bartender, however, is another story. He is slim and bearded, with a scowl fixed on his face like a scar. An anchor is tattooed on his right forearm. He glares at Jimmie with a churlish, penetrating look from halfway down the bar. Then he lines up a dozen or so bar glasses and, one by one, holds them up to the dim light the way a jeweler might inspect a precious stone.

Navy vet, no doubt. Making no effort to come over and offer service.

The bartender springs to life, though, when one of the boys from the back saunters up and asks for a pack of Chesterfields and another draft. The man rings up the sale on the cash register, then picks up his cloth and goes through the motion of wiping down glasses that look to be clean and dry to begin with.

With a trace of annoyance in his voice, Jimmie calls out, "I'd like a beer over here, please."

The barman looks up, redirecting his stony gaze in Jimmie's direction. He slowly puts down the rag and the glass in his hand. He continues to take his time as he ambles over toward the uniformed marine.

"You Injun, ain't you?" he asks, arching one eyebrow.

Jimmie tries his best to act unruffled. "I'm Navajo, yes."

"Thought so."

For the first time, the two men at the far end of the bar look up.

Jimmie waits. The pulse begins to pound in his temples like the prelude to a tribal dance.

The bartender speaks slowly, as if the redskin might not otherwise understand. "We don't ... serve ... no ... Injuns ... here."

Jimmie says calmly, "I'm a US Marine, as you can see, and I'd like a beer."

"Not at this bar you ain't. Some places 'round here, they might ignore the law and oblige you, just for the fun of watching you fall off the stool. Me, I got better things to do."

Jimmie's voice is firm, determined. "You're a navy man, right?"

"Damn straight. Ensign First Class. What of it?"

"I fought for my country just like you did. And like I been saying, I'd like a beer."

"And I'd like your feathered war bonnet. But it looks like neither of us gonna get what we want here today, don't it? What you're gonna get is trouble, less you pick yourself up right now and skedaddle out that door, y'understand me, Geronimo?"

The two men at the end of the bar look on intently. "C'mon, Frank, guy's a marine, for Chrissakes," says the portlier of the two. The other interjects, "Lots of bars pay no attention to that old law 'bout no liquor to Injuns. G'wan, give 'im a beer, whydontcha."

The barman looks over at these customers, narrowing his eyes to little more than slits. "Just 'cause somebody else might serve him don't make it right in my book. Now you boys stay out of this and remember it's my bar where I serve who the hell I want."

The husky man raises his arms in a supplicant gesture and looks at Jimmie as if to say, *Well, I tried.* Then both men resume their downward gaze.

Jimmie stares directly into the bartender's eyes, something he could never have done before acclimating to life in the Corps. "Look, pal, it's been a long trip and I'm just looking for a cold Schlitz."

The bartender breaks eye contact and snarls, "I ain't your pal, Geronimo, and for all I know, you *stole* that uniform—maybe rolled the white guy who deserved to wear it, though in my book, the marines is way overrated anyway. It's time you remember that back here, you ain't one of the *Corps*"—he practically spits out the word— "you're just one of the *tribe.* Now be a good Injun an' go back to the reservation where you belong."

Jimmie wants to cut the bartender's throat. A quick, clean slash the way he was trained to do back on Espiritu Santo. Only through extreme effort does he push aside this frightening impulse. Instead, he takes a deep breath, inhaling his anger like acrid smoke.

Without saying another word, he gets up and walks through the door into the honky-tonk night, into the real world, where some things, clearly, have not changed after all.

HE TAKES A ROOM FOR the night at a dingy flophouse that caters to transients. He does not get a great deal of sleep, for he is still seething over his encounter with the surly barman. During his four years in the Corps, never once was he turned away from any establishment. Back here, it seems, the old prejudices have not gone away.

Next morning he tries to thumb a ride on the rutted dirt roadway heading north out of Gallup. After a futile half hour, he is heartened to see a rusty old pick-up screech to a stop. Behind the wheel is a Navajo man who answers to the name Rides-in-Smoke. He has gone by many names over the years, the man says, speaking in Navajo. The heavy clouds of exhaust coming from the back of the old Ford make it obvious how the fellow came by his current name.

Rides-in-Smoke has clearly been a human being for many years. His long hair is almost all white, tied behind his head in the bundle still favored by many of the old-timers. His face is lined and weathered like the sun-baked earth of a dry wash: bleached terra cotta punctuated by piercing dark eyes that seem to have peered through the ages. In his left hand, a cigarette dangles between his thumb and forefinger. The man earns Jimmie's respect by virtue of his age alone. How blessed it must be to walk in beauty for so many years! Jimmie is grateful for the ride, for the company, even for the update on conditions back home, as disheartening as they turn out to be. He is surprised at how good it is to speak conversational Navajo again. He has almost forgotten it was his first language.

Rides-in-Smoke explains he is heading back to his sheep ranch in Littlewater, having sold wool to a trader in Gallup. This means he will be traveling past the cut-off to Two Grey Hills. So the decision is made. Jimmie will head there first, visit with his mother, face his father. He will put off seeing Annie until later. There is another trip he is also eager to make, to Ray's home near Kayenta. There are no roads leading directly there, so it will be a long and strenuous journey. But that passage will pale in comparison to excursions already taken, to patrols and marches with full pack and radio, to advancements often measured in yards, not in miles.

"Been away long?" Rides-in-Smoke asks.

"Four years," Jimmie says, still distracted by his thoughts. He tries to concentrate, works to keep his mind on the present, his eyes on the flat, muted expanse of desert before him, its familiar peaks and mesas accenting the horizon just as they did in the memories he carried throughout the savage tropics. He has been on this road before, after all, shamefully selling his White Mule between Shiprock and the Gallup county line to any Navajo with money and a thirst for alcohol. The former was in short supply. The thirst was readily available.

"Did you know," Rides-in-Smoke is saying, "they are *still* taking away our sacred land, those war leaders in Washington?"

Jimmie shakes his head, beginning to tune in.

Rides-in-Smoke explains, "Hundreds of thousands of our acres, gone. First they gave some to the Hopis. Then the railroad people held out their hands and helped themselves to land on both sides of the tracks while Washington whistled. During the war, still more land was taken from us, turned into air bases and shooting ranges and bombing targets."

"The situation doesn't look any better in Gallup," Jimmie remarks, now fully engaged in the conversation. "I can't remember ever seeing so many Indians wandering around there, like they have nothing to do."

"That is because they have nothing to do," replies Rides-in-Smoke with a matter-of-fact air. "Many places around there—the air base and the factories where they made bullets and bombs—they gave people work. Men from the reservation flew to Gallup like flies to a barn. Now that the war is over, the jobs are gone. There is nothing even off the reservation anymore. Maybe some part-time railroad and mining work, not much else. No chance for steady pay. At least I have some sheep, though not as many as before. My sheep give me wool, they give me food, and they never make a promise they do not keep."

"Well, maybe next election we can vote in somebody in Washington who might make things better for us." Jimmie's words do not carry much conviction.

Rides-in-Smoke tosses away the stub of his cigarette and grips the wheel tightly as if he is reining in a horse. "Yes, maybe that is true, but we will have to leave our reservation to do it. Indians still cannot vote here. They say we cannot vote because we do not own our own land."

Jimmie knows that New Mexico, Arizona, and Utah had nullified the federal right to vote that was granted in 1924 when all Indians were made—in theory, at least—US citizens. Still, he is shocked that the ill-conceived laws have not yet been overturned, especially now, in light of all the Indians who fought for their country.

I am a US citizen in name only, just like before, he thinks. His irritation begins to percolate. He can taste it, like bad coffee, strong and harsh.

"But in our tribal council elections, a good thing happened," says Rides-in-Smoke. "Chee Dodge thought about leaving the council—he has heart troubles, some say—but the people talked him into running again. Sam Ahkeah got more votes, so he will be the new chairman. But Chee Dodge came in second. He will continue on as vice chairman. I am happy that Mr. Interpreter is staying on."

Mr. Interpreter is what the people have long called Chee. The news lifts Jimmie's sagging spirits. Since it is obvious that Rides-in-Smoke is surprisingly well-informed about news and politics, Jimmie asks him, "How do you know all these things? How do you know what's going on outside of *Dinetah*, and how it affects us here?"

"Hard to say. From the newspaper, maybe."

"Newspaper? You read and understand English?"

"English? Why would an old man like me need to know the white man's language?" Rides-in-Smoke laughs, a hoarse sound not unlike the noise coming from his motorcar. "The newspaper is in Navajo. Started three years ago, maybe. Now it even has pictures. The daughter of my son sounds out the letters, reads it to me, and that is how I know things. Are you still in the army?"

"Marines," Jimmie corrects. "Discharged a few days ago."

"That so." Rides-in-Smoke is quiet for a moment as he negotiates a deep rut in the road. A young child, wearing filthy clothes and covered with open sores, stands on a nearby hillock, watching with little expression as they ride by. Jimmie waves to her, but the girl does not respond. The sight of her fills him once more with melancholy.

"Where did they send you to, these army people?" asks Rides-in-Smoke. "A faraway place?"

"Many places. Islands. Hawaii, of course. Guadalcanal. Bougainville. Iwo ..." He cannot bring himself to say the full name. "Terrible places."

"I heard of Hawaii, I think," says Rides-in-Smoke. "Pearl Harbor, right?"

His response shows how insulated the reservation remains, newspaper or not. "Yes, Pearl Harbor," Jimmie says.

"Did they put all the *Dineh* who went to war on one team? Were there other Indian tribes on your team?"

Jimmie smiles at the old man's innocence. Then again, how could anyone be expected to know how many countless thousands of Indians were fighting alongside mostly Anglo counterparts in World War II?

"During training, twenty-nine of us—all *Dineh*—were in the same group. But once we went across the ocean, we were put on different ... uh, teams."

Apparently satisfied, Rides-in-Smoke asks nothing further as the pick-up bounces along. Jimmie closes his eyes. He tries to digest what he has learned during his first day back and tries to familiarize himself with its bitter aftertaste.

It takes the squeal of bad brakes to jolt him out of his deep funk. Even at slow speed, the old pick-up protests its order to stop with the sound and fury one might expect from a locomotive on the Union Pacific. Rides-in-Smoke has stopped to pick up another hitchhiker—a taut, young Navajo man in his early twenties who is standing by the road in dusty denim pants and jacket. A wide-brimmed hat shades his face from the sun, which pops in and out of billowing clouds.

"Hope you will not mind," Rides-in-Smoke says to Jimmie. "I think it is bad luck to pass anyone by when I have four wheels under me. If I left him, he might die in the desert. Then his ghost would come after me sure as anything."

Turning his attention to the young hitchhiker, Rides-in-Smoke asks, "Where you heading?"

"Shiprock."

"I can take you far as Littlewater."

"Littlewater's good."

The hitchhiker carries a small bundle that he tosses into the back of the pick-up. Jimmie wedges himself against the gear shift to make room for the new man, who introduces himself in Navajo as Thomas Tsosie.

"Jimmie, here, got his discharge from the army," Rides-in-Smoke tells Thomas.

Jimmie does not correct him, for the old man says it like a bragging father. He will not get that from his own father, that is certain.

Thomas seems impressed. "Good for you! What did you do over there?"

Spoke Navajo. Turned it into code the enemy couldn't break. "Radio communications, mostly."

"You're lucky. When I went to sign up, they would not take me. I had no schooling. I could not speak the language of the white man. Then they changed their minds. They put me in a training unit to teach me the words. But I did not learn. Maybe I am too stupid. They said I could not be a soldier."

Jimmie's heart goes out to the young man. While Jimmie searches for words that might take away the fellow's sense of shame at having washed out, Thomas cheerfully exclaims, "Hey, I am good at something. I am very good with horses."

"Now *I* envy *you*," Jimmie says, relieved. "When I ride, the horse feels sorry for me."

Rides-in-Smoke laughs as if that is the funniest thing he has ever heard. Then he says to Jimmie, "I thought you have to be a good rider in the army. The army soldiers chased my father clear across New Mexico on their horses."

"They didn't use horses to fight the enemy." Jimmie tries not to smile. "Too much water, too many jungles." He turns to Thomas and asks him, "Where do you ride?"

"These days, mostly in rodeos. Just came from one at Crownpoint. Heading for another in Shiprock. Now that the war is over, the rodeos are starting up again. They are bigger than before, more contests. And many people come."

As the pick-up rattles past the turn-off to Sheep Springs, it is obvious to Jimmie that nothing along this stretch has changed. If anything, the area looks more barren than ever. Where grazing land had once been visible, only scrub and parched earth survive. The livestock, what little there is, appear undernourished. The *hogans* are still primitive, mud-roofed, some barely able to stand on their own. And motor vehicles, so commonplace in Gallup, are few and far between here on reservation land. Toward the east, in a small depression near the roadway, the sun-bleached bones of cattle lay scattered in random piles, like bodies strewn across the beaches after a marine landing. The reservation, sadly, looks no more hospitable than many islands Jimmie has seen in the South Pacific.

"Now that you have left the army," Thomas asks, "what are your plans?"

"I've been wondering that myself." Jimmie becomes aware that responding in Navajo is taking more thought than answering in English. "Spend some time with my par—with my mother, see old friends. After that, guess I'll have to find a job."

"Don't get your hopes up," Thomas says. "They say there are more men out of work now than there ever were."

"Then I guess there's always ranching, if nothing else." Ranching, though, is the last thing he wants to do.

Rides-in-Smoke, who has been listening in, shakes his head. "Only if you already own the livestock. They will not issue grazing permits for new herds, even to returning veterans. The newspaper told me this. And white ranchers still do not hire Indians."

Jimmie feels as if he has stepped on a land mine in his own backyard. In English he mutters, "I'm beginning to wonder what I came home for."

Both Thomas and Rides-in-Smoke stare at him, not comprehending the foreign tongue.

He hates this feeling of self-pity that has come over him, but here it is. Slipping back into Navajo, he says, "They can't give you something, something you dreamed about all your life, and then take it away from you. *They can't do that.*"

"But they have been doing that from the very beginning," says Rides-in-Smoke. No malice in his voice, just a calm statement of fact. "It is the way things are, dependable as the sacred *Tse bit'a'i* that rises up ahead." He points.

In the distance is one of the sights Jimmie has carried with him throughout the war: the great volcanic "rock with wings" that the whites call Ship Rock for its resemblance (some say) to a nineteenth-century clipper ship. It is easily the most prominent landmark in the Four Corners area.

Rides-in-Smoke makes his point again: "Yes, it is the way things are. Nothing will ever change."

Not long ago, Jimmie would have spoken out against such a defeatist attitude. To believe that things cannot get better would be to deny Chee Dodge's vision of the bridge between the white and Navajo worlds. But back here ... back here he can almost begin to comprehend what has fed his father's animosity toward the US government.

THE OLD TRUCK HITS A deep rut in the road, jarring its three passengers and bursting the dark bubble of Jimmie's gloomy introspection. He resolves not to let the harsh realities of present-day reservation life intrude on the bittersweet delight of his homecoming. Still, he wrestles with the realization that he is more disconcerted now, in many ways, than he was when he left four years earlier. Only this time his doubts and sense of foreboding come from within, cloaked in the guise of his own shifting emotions.

From seemingly out of nowhere, words pop into his head, something he had said to Colonel Carlson back at Camp Gung Ho.

I'm a talking code machine over here, and my buddy Ray is another talking code machine at the other end.

Why has that brash and simplistic metaphor come back to him now? Unless ...

Unless it is presenting him with a reality he has yet to face. The truth, at last: he is not a machine after all, in spite of what he had so blatantly claimed.

He is only human. And he takes little comfort from that.

CHAPTER 15

MARCH 1946

Jimmie stands on the roadway and waves to Rides-in-Smoke and Thomas as the old Ford lumbers off. It coughs clouds of burning oil that trail behind it like a dark omen. Then Jimmie turns toward the west, following the rutted path that will take him to Two Grey Hills.

Along the way, he basks in the familiarity of the world around him: the earth under his feet, dry as kiln-fired pottery. The air, fragrant with smoky notes of mesquite and piñon. The hills farther west, dark and brooding—sentinels that stand watch over Toadlena and Two Grey Hills. But most of all, he revels in the glorious solitude of the place, the all-consuming peacefulness and silence, antithesis to the killing fields of war.

He takes a deep breath, then exhales all of his conflicting emotions, freeing them to scatter on perfumed breezes, though he suspects they will return, unbidden, soon enough. For the moment, he is content to watch a hawk circle lazily overhead, to see small lizards scurry among the rocks, to hear nothing more than the whisper of the wind and the crunch of his eager footsteps on familiar, sacred ground.

In spite of the negativity he has been hearing, in spite of his disappointment over the stagnation at home, it is good, so good, to be back.

HIS MOTHER'S BACK IS TO him as he approaches. She is in front of her *hogan*, grinding parched corn in the old way, on a stone *metaté* laid upon a goat skin. She crushes the corn with a heavy millstone in a rhythmic back-and-forth motion. Jimmie has dreamed of his mother's bread for four years.

"Mother," he says. Softly, reverently, like a word of prayer.

She drops her grinding stone and whirls around at the sound of his voice. "Jimmie!" she squeals as she flies to him, nearly tripping over her own feet.

"I have prayed so long for your safe return, my son," she cries. "And now my prayers have been answered." She hugs him as if she might never let him go.

After a moment, though, she steps back to look at her son. "You have become so thin. But you are handsome in that uniform."

"You look good too, Mother. You haven't changed at all."

In reality, though, she has changed. Her face is webbed with fine furrows, her figure has expanded, her hair is dappled with streaks of white. She still wears a conventional long calico skirt and a high-necked velvet blouse. Not at all surprising, since any modern encroachments would not be welcome in Wilson Goodluck's home. Jimmie looks toward the *hogan* and asks, "Where is ... um, where is Father?"

"Your father should be back soon. He went ... well, who knows where he went. But he will smell my bread baking, I am sure of that. I have to tell you, Jimmie ..." She pauses, gathers her thoughts.

"Your father was angry when you left. You will remember that, I know. He refuses to accept why so many *Dineh* helped the white war leaders. I try to make him understand, but he does not hear me on such matters, any more than he listens to words from the tribal council. The fact that some of our young men died—that *you* might have died—makes him angrier still. What I am saying is, be patient with him, Jimmie."

"I will try, Mother."

"And Jimmie—it might be better if you ..." She doesn't finish her sentence, but her gaze sweeps like a searchlight across Jimmie's dress blues.

"Yes, I should change." He supposes his father will comment anyway on the denim pants and cotton T-shirt, purchased from the post exchange in Oahu.

As it happens, Wilson makes no comment on Jimmie's attire. When he rides in on his favorite horse an hour later and sees his son with Leila at the baking trench, he registers no discernable emotion at all.

"So, the warrior has returned." His steely voice does not reveal what measure of sarcasm he may have intended. He dismounts and walks up to Jimmie, making no physical contact. Then his voice softens noticeably. "I am glad you did not come back as a ghost."

Jimmie, relieved that his father is talking to him at all, says, "It would take more than the Japanese soldiers to kill me. Not that they did not try."

"So you remember how to speak the *Dineh* language after all. I wondered if you might forget it after years of speaking only in the *bilaga'ana* tongue."

If you only knew, Father. If only I could tell you. "I could never forget. I carried my sacred corn pollen throughout the war. I am still Navajo."

Leila rises from the trench where her bread dough, baking in the dirt, is buried under several inches of fiery ashes. "Jimmie looks well, doesn't he?" she asks her husband. She is clearly trying to change the subject.

Wilson slowly walks in circles around his son, as he might do if he were evaluating the impending purchase of a new ram, or a horse. "There will be an Enemy Way," he declares. "You are contaminated by death and war and *bilaga'ana*."

Jimmie has been expecting this pronouncement, so he cannot help but smile.

"Why are you looking this way?" Wilson demands. His voice is sharp, guarded.

"Because I knew you would insist on the ceremony. Because you're right about death and war. I'm filled with negative forces. Maybe the Enemy Way will help bring some balance into my life."

Wilson stops circling. He, too, shows visible signs of aging, but not to the extent that Leila does.

"Does that surprise you, Father?" Jimmie asks. "Did you really think I would come back with white skin, perhaps, or return with a preference for the Jesusway?"

Wilson looks away, his voice now barely more than a mumble. "I thought you might not come back at all. Or that you might choose to live in Los Angeles or Washington or someplace equally … foreign."

Leila signals her son with a pitying look and then nods almost imperceptibly toward Wilson. For the first time, Jimmie begins to understand something about his father. If the man could peel away his ire and bravado, like a snake shedding its skin, underneath would be nothing more complicated than the fear that comes from a lifetime of insecurity.

Jimmie suspects that Wilson might have turned out differently if he had a father to learn from or look up to. But the bastard deserted Wilson and his mother when Wilson was still in the womb. His

mother steadfastly refused to reveal the man's identity. She helped to
arrange the marriage between Jimmie's parents, revealing that their
clans were compatible, but she divulged nothing more. Then a year
later, just before Jimmie came along, she died.

"If you thought I would rather live someplace else," Jimmie
says in a measured voice, "then you don't know me. I would never
be happy in a large Anglo city. The more I've seen, the farther I've
traveled, the more I've longed to return to *Dinetah*. That baked-in-
the-trench bread that smells so good right now—how would I get
that in Los Angeles or Washington?"

Leila jumps at the mention of her bread and hurries to the fire.
Carefully she brushes aside the hot ash to inspect the golden brown
dough beneath.

Wilson, shooing away a fly that buzzes around his head, asks,
"What will you do now that you are back? Now that you have no
more wars to fight?"

"There are always wars to fight, Father. You should know that
by now."

"Hear my words, I—"

"No, you hear *my* words," Jimmie interrupts, offering no apology
for doing so. "Our people still cannot vote. *That's* a war we need to
fight. Our people still cannot get a good education. There's another
war for you. And what about jobs? I've heard they're gone again."
He lowers his voice and continues. "You ask what I'm going to do?
I truthfully don't know. They say there's even less opportunity now
than there was before I left. Maybe all I *can* do is stay and fight
some wars."

Leila smiles, which Jimmie takes as a sign of approval. She
removes the bread from the trench and then flushes the hot, fresh
loaves with clear water, wiping away the dirt and ashes.

"Maybe you finally see the white man for all that he is," Wilson
says. "Lying, devious, corrupt."

"No, Father, it is the white man's policies and politics that are corrupt."

"The war leaders you fought for, they continue to destroy our livestock. You should see how few animals she has left, your mother. And yet they tell us too many remain even now. I do not fear their threats."

Jimmie looks questioningly toward his mother, who nods with a pained expression. He stutters, "They ... they weren't supposed to take so many animals from families with small flocks. I thought ... that is, I was told ..."

Wilson flashes a wicked smile, revealing uneven and missing teeth reminiscent of kernels on a withering ear of corn. A second later, like the pop from a flashbulb, Wilson's smirk vanishes. "What you thought, what you were told: more lies."

"Still, you can't continue to blame every white man because of it."

"And you cannot continue to excuse them."

Leila comes between them with her steaming bread. She divides a loaf in half and her men devour it in appreciative silence. To Jimmie, it is like eating sacred food of the gods. What do Anglos do to bread that makes theirs so starchy and tasteless?

After a time, Jimmie speaks up, his voice calm again. "I must tell you both, I was treated well in the marines. I was ready to give my life for any white soldier next to me, as he would give his life for me."

Wilson looks at his son, his face awash with disbelief.

"I know you cannot imagine that a white person would give his life for a Navajo, but that's how it was. There's a saying in the marines, a watchword: *Semper Fidelis*. It means all marines are expected to be faithful to one another. Not just in war, but in life. It is a clan in its own right, the Marine Corps, much like our clans. I was a part of that, equal with everyone else."

"You think they looked upon you as an equal?" Wilson sneers.

"Your eyes are not open to the world. Your US soldiers like Kit Carson and—"

"You think all whites look at us and see only savages?" Frowning, Jimmie shakes his head. "You're wrong, Father. Not from what I experienced. But you don't wish to open your mind or your heart to what can be, so for now, there is nothing more to say."

WILSON BEGINS THE PROCESS OF purging his son from the contamination of death, war, and *bilaga'ana* the very next day. He leaves on horseback before Jimmie awakens, returning late in the afternoon.

"I went to see Tall Man today," Wilson reports to his wife and son, referring to a locally renowned *hata'ali*—a singer, a medicine man—from nearby Newcomb. "At first he said it is too early in the season for Enemy Way. I told him a boy cannot choose when he returns from fighting a white man's war."

Jimmie restrains from responding to his father's baited remark.

"He has agreed to come in two weeks' time," Wilson adds with a satisfied smirk.

Leila asks, "What will this cost?"

Wilson waves his hand as if the expenses are nothing. "Twelve sheep, plus some additional expenses. What better way for the boy to use his *biliga'ana* money than by emptying himself of their poisons? And after he's cured—"

"*Cured*, father? I pray the ceremony will help bring me back into balance, but there is no cure for what I've been through. Can't you see? It is *war* that has contaminated me. It is having to kill other human beings, seeing friends killed. If your singer can help me deal with that, it's all I ask."

Wilson merely grunts. Then he responds calmly, "Maybe we can both get what we want from the ceremony."

"Maybe so," Jimmie agrees, surprised at his father's willingness to put the issue to rest. "Maybe a little healing is what everyone needs."

THE ENEMY WAY, OFTEN REFERRED to as the War Dance, is performed to negate the effects of war when men return from battle. Jimmie watches the goings-on from a specially constructed ceremonial *hogan*—a temporary arbor, more precisely, made from forked sticks and brush. Tall Man arrives looking every bit of sixty years old. He is not tall at all, but actually rather diminutive. His long white hair is tied back in a bundle. His face, skin like tanned leather, is defined by a square jaw and a strong nose. From a sideways perspective, one can almost envision an eagle's head.

Tall Man fills an earthen jar with water, and then Wilson fits a piece of buckskin tightly over the jar, securing it in place with leather thongs. The singer proceeds to punch holes in the buckskin to resemble eyes and a mouth. This symbolizes the ghosts that trouble Jimmie. When beaten with a pinõn wood tapper during the prayers that follow, the jar produces a dull, hollow sound designed to drive the ghosts into the ground.

On the second day, Wilson rides out in search of a flawless piece of juniper for the rattle stick, the ceremony's most important property. He cuts a yard-long strip of wood and then returns and presents the stick to Tall Man. The singer carves it, blackens it with ashes, and affixes two eagle feathers at the top. Finally, he attaches strips of buckskin knotted with small deer toes so that they hang down from the base.

Throughout the second day and late again into the night, Tall Man taps on his pot drum and shakes his rattle stick and sings the approved songs he has long ago committed to memory. And as Wilson watches, the ghosts that contaminate Jimmie are driven out and banished for all eternity.

At least, that is what Tall Man and Wilson believe.

As for Jimmie, he does take some solace from the ceremony. But he has been away from *Dinetah* for too long, has become too anglicized, perhaps, in the Marine Corps, for he feels a vague disquietude, like an outsider looking in. It will take more than a ritual to restore him to balance, more than a ceremony to fully reconcile him to all the established Navajo ways, now that he has been seduced by life, bristling with possibilities, beyond the reservation.

THE SIGN, HASTILY SCRIBBLED BY an unsteady hand in phonetically spelled Navajo, translates as "Squaw Dance tonight." Jimmie spots it upon returning from the ceremonial *hogan* on the last day of the ceremony. Dozens of similar signs are scattered throughout the area. No need to tell where the dance is being held. Everyone will know. News of a Squaw Dance travels like pollen in the air, for this culminating event of Enemy Way is a major social gathering. This one in particular, as it is the first of the season.

No one can explain why the Navajo people adapted the misnomer "squaw" for the affair since the word is not Navajo and, rumor has it, may even be a vulgar term in the language of another tribe. But here it is, referring to the girls who are essential to this event, with no disrespect intended and none taken. Jimmie knows the reasoning is that contact with gentle, feminine forces on this last night of healing (only young and marriageable women are permitted to dance) can neutralize the negative forces a man carries home from war. What better way to entice the warrior back into balance with the universe?

More than one hundred people pour in to the area surrounding the Goodluck *hogan*. Not only has nearly every family from Two Grey Hills shown up, but also strangers who have walked or ridden from as far away as Sanostee and Shiprock and Tohatchi. It is a rare opportunity to mingle, to gossip and make small talk, to enjoy the gathering of clans that are normally separated by miles and sometimes inaccessible terrain. Everyone comes dressed in their finest clothes, bringing with them a dazzling array of jewelry, much of which has been taken out of pawn for the evening.

Jimmie changes his shirt and pants and puts on a wide-brimmed hat, for no man can be without a hat at a Squaw Dance. Then he wanders outside to look over the assemblage of young women. It has been a while since he has spent any time with a woman; it would be nice to find a fresh face here. There were three evenings with a girl of easy morals in Honolulu, though they were little more than desperate and ultimately forgettable couplings. Before he enlisted, Jimmie had brief relationships with five different young women over roughly an eight-year period. One of those liaisons was particularly incendiary, a girl named Marguerite that he met in Coyote Canyon when he worked as a translator. Aside from his constant travel that kept them apart more often than not, he broke off the relationship when he realized that Marguerite was misinterpreting their physical attraction and mutually satisfying sex as the prelude to an eventual marriage.

He was not ready for a serious relationship then, any more than he is ready for it now. Without knowing his paternal clan (since Wilson never learned his own father's identity), he fears he may never marry. Still, it comes as a relief when a pretty face does catch his eye. She looks no more than eighteen, if that. Jimmie approaches her and introduces himself. Her name, she says with an encouraging smile, is Lucy Tso. When she mentions that she lives just a few miles away, he asks her, "Is Lorraine Tso your mother?"

She nods. "You know my mother?"

"Used to see her at the trading post. When I was little." His eyes open wide with a sudden realization and he laughs. "I just remembered. We've already met."

She looks at him with a puzzled expression.

"Had to be close to twenty years ago. You were in a basket.

Your mother put you down on the counter at the trading post, and someone tagged you with a pawn ticket."

Lucy's expression barely changes.

"Guess you had to be there," he says. "Though now's I think about it, your mother didn't find it too funny either."

They talk until the dance begins. She is the prettiest girl here, but his trading post anecdote certainly called attention to their age difference. In any case, he finds himself hoping she will ask him to dance—at a Squaw Dance, the women ask the men—even though there is no chemistry between them. The only sparks he feels come from a crackling bonfire that is helping to ward off the evening chill.

Soon Tall Man begins to sing, accompanied by steady drumming. After a time, several young girls, including Lucy, get up and sway to the rhythm, bending their knees, their shoulders, rocking on their toes, but never lifting their feet completely off the ground. Jimmie will be asked to dance first and then all the girls will select partners, with the shy ones invariably pushed by their mothers.

At first no woman makes a move toward Jimmie, but then Lucy coyly raises her eyes and walks in his direction. As she approaches, she raises one arm to him, hand extended: the invitation to dance. Jimmie takes her hand for a brief moment and stands beside her. She removes one end of her shawl and drapes it across his shoulders so it covers them both. Then, side by side and arm in arm, they two-step in a wide circle around the fire. Soon other young men are being asked to dance, and though a few may be reluctant to do so, it would be impolite to turn down a young lady.

When the opening dance is over, Jimmie reaches into his pocket and hands Lucy a dollar. She tucks the bill inside the sleeve of her calico blouse. In similar fashion, the other boys hand their dance partners money or small gifts, something of value for their "release," as generations before them have done.

The singing and dancing will go on well into the night, although

Jimmie wishes it were over. He walks aimlessly toward the food table, where he takes a mutton rib, an ear of corn, two pieces of fry bread, and a glass of 7-Up. He eats at the table, standing up, wishing he could make himself invisible. He chews without enthusiasm, reflecting on all that has brought him to this point: his aimless life on the reservation, his acceptance and shared gung-ho spirit in the marines, his close friendship with Ray Begay, his return home to … what, exactly? How can it be that he never felt more alive, more hopeful, more *complete*, than when he was fighting with the marines in those South Pacific hellholes?

The Long Patrol, that was only the beginning. Carlson's words play like talking wind, even now, in Jimmie's head.

The rest of the Corps, they're like lumbering dinosaurs, slow to adapt. You mark my words, lads, your code won't get much use in Guadalcanal, unless I'm the one to use it.

Jimmie knows now that the colonel was right. Carlson was arguably the one officer during the long Guadalcanal campaign who most fully embraced the then-underestimated Navajo code. As the war went on, the code became more accepted and more essential for use in critical communications. Throughout it all, Jimmie felt a part of something vital. He had been respected for his own contributions and had, in turn, admired those who fought alongside him. Anglos, most of them.

But now …

With the Enemy Way almost over, it seems there are still ghosts that have not been driven out and banished after all.

GRAY IS THE LANDSCAPE, THE sky, and Jimmie's frame of mind on the day following the Squaw Dance. His introspection of the past few days has deepened, not erased, his malaise. He is dangerously close to becoming trapped in the same rut he wallowed in before enlisting.

Leila makes no reference to his aloofness at the dance, but she is clearly disappointed in him. Jimmie can see it in her eyes. When he awoke his father had asked him if the ghosts were gone and he answered "yes," because the lie was easier than admitting the truth.

He has some military pay left, but barely enough to carry him through the coming year. Nonetheless, he is anxious to travel, to see Annie and seek out the wisdom of Chee Dodge. And he is eager to head west, to Kayenta, Ray's home, and after that, maybe look up a few platoon buddies like Carl and George and Charlie. Then, if he can think of no more places to go, no more excuses to keep him from taking stock of his own life, what next?

What happens after *your dream comes true?*

Ray had posed that question back at Uncle Harry's during a break from training in San Diego. Or did those words come to him before then? Either way, it was a query Jimmie could not answer earlier and cannot answer now. This is the "what happens?" time of his life, and he is distraught that no response is forthcoming. His future seems as bleak as it was before he found solace in the marines.

"You are deep in thought, my son."

Jimmie's father comes up behind him at the corral and says the words softly. Still, it startles Jimmie. It has been a long time since Wilson used the term "my son." Jimmie had wandered aimlessly over here in an attempt to sort things out, oblivious to the heady scent of manure—like perfume to him after the smell of cordite, of singed and decaying flesh.

"I'm just trying to figure out my life," he mutters, although in Navajo it translates more literally as "I am waiting for my life to come to me."

Wilson squats down and speaks in a slow, even voice. "Now you are free from the contamination of war and *bilaga'ana*. Now you will see more clearly."

"But I'm *not* free from the influence of white men, Father. I know how much we can learn from them."

"All we will get is spit on by the *bilaga'ana*." With great flourish, Wilson brings up a wad of phlegm and spews it onto the ground, more for punctuation than out of necessity.

"Do you know what they do to Indians over in Farmington?" Wilson asks. "Your mother heard this from the trader. In Farmington, gangs of whites—teenagers, mostly—look for old Navajo men. They get them drunk on beer or cheap alcohol. And when their victims are too inebriated to stand up, the white boys roll them onto the street, or off a cliff, or into the river. In the past year, several men died. But one of them was not an old man. He was younger than you. And like you, he had been fighting the white man's war. The boy was killed two weeks after returning from the army. He was killed in the town where he lived all his life. Killed by whites, by *bilaga'ana*, because he was Navajo."

Jimmie tries to swallow and discovers his mouth is as dry as the ground under his feet.

"Tell me that does not make you angry," Wilson insists. "Tell me."

"Of course it makes me angry." Jimmie tries unsuccessfully to keep his voice from rising. "It makes me angry that we join up to fight for our country and then come home to learn that our country does not fight for *us*. It makes me angry that we can't go into a bar or into a voting booth like other citizens. Or find jobs, apparently, any more than we could before. It makes me angry that I find it difficult to defend the things I once believed in."

They can't give you something, something you dreamed about all your life and then take it away from you, he had protested a month earlier. But they *can*, he sees now.

They can.

"You are beginning to understand what I have been talking about all along," Wilson says. A scowl crosses his face like a fleeting shadow. "Even now it is right in front of you." Wilson points to the livestock behind the split-rail fence. "These are all the animals we have left. Barely a hundred sheep, twelve goats, and two horses."

His father had mentioned the family's diminished livestock, but *this* few? "I ... I assumed the rest were out to pasture. These are ... they're half the number of animals you owned four years ago."

"And still the government is not satisfied. Our grazing permit allows for only seventy sheep if we keep the horses. They have threatened to put me in their jail if I do not comply. I say, let them try. We can barely get along with the few animals we have now."

"This isn't right." It is all Jimmie can find words to say.

"This is what white men do to your family while you help them fight their war."

"I came close to being shot by a white man, a sergeant in the army." Jimmie impulsively brings up the incident, the confrontation at the food dump on Guadalcanal. He mentions it because his anger has reignited. It is no longer just a spark of discontent; now, fanned by knowledge and circumstance, it burns with heat and intensity. Wilson will interpret the episode as another example of Indian mistreatment and prejudice by whites, and—who knows?—maybe that is exactly what it was.

Jimmie briefly explains what happened, hearing only the sound of Wilson's breathing. The closeness he suddenly feels to his father is both exhilarating and frightening.

Wilson looks straight ahead as if he is talking not to Jimmie but to the sheep inside the fence. "I am reminded of the teachings of First Boy. 'Do not confuse what you really are with what you are not. Do not try to be someone other than your true self.'"

Jimmie recalls the parable. He has never before considered his years of approval and equality in the marines as indicative of trying to be someone he is not, but at this moment he is not so sure.

"My son, there is something I wish to share with you," Wilson continues. "It is something you need to experience. You will come with me during the next new moon."

"I was thinking of moving on by then."

"You are trying to taste what your life can be. I will open your eyes to possibilities you cannot even imagine. If you still want to leave the next day, I will not stop you."

Jimmie stands and stretches, hands on his hips, back arched. A sheep nuzzles against the corral fence, and Jimmie reaches in to rub its fleece. It is a comforting tactile sensation he has missed during his years away. "What's happening then?" he asks.

Wilson grins, again revealing his imperfect teeth. "It is a monthly meeting I attend. Your mother listens to the lies of the white government. She listens to our tribal council. Like them, she does not approve of these meetings. But you will judge for yourself."

An alarm sounds inside Jimmie's head, loud and shrill. "Is this something illegal?"

Wilson waves his arm. "Misunderstood."

"Another ceremony?"

"A ceremony? Oh, much more than that, my son. It is power. It is understanding. And when the sun rises on the next morning, you will see things in a new way. You will understand what I have been saying all along. You may even discover that we are not so different, you and me."

"I don't know, Father. I really have to go to—"

"Think of it as a new start. The Enemy Way may have driven away your ghosts, but I can see it did not open your eyes. Soon you will see in bright colors what it is you seek. The whole universe will open up to you and you will divine the future."

Wilson lifts his eyes skyward. An almost euphoric expression transforms his face, rearranging his usually dour appearance into someone Jimmie barely recognizes.

"In a few weeks," Wilson says, "you will talk to the gods."

CHAPTER 16

MAY 1946

"Do not be tempted by the magic your father claims he will show you," Leila warns Jimmie as she sits beside her loom. Wilson is watering the livestock, well out of earshot. "It is false magic, filled with deception. Even your friend Annie and her father are working hard to stop the practice."

The practice, Jimmie realizes, involves the cult revolving around peyote, that small, hairy cactus whose plump button of flesh contains eight psychoactive alkaloids including mescaline.

"The 'medicine,' as your father calls it, gives him a feeling of infallibility, of supernatural power," Leila says, shaking her head. "He thinks it will protect him from witches and ghosts, from the sickness and ill fortune they bring."

This comes as no surprise to Jimmie. For a put-upon, disenfranchised individual like Wilson Goodluck, who grew up without knowing his own father, who feels alienated and betrayed not only by whites but by his own leaders, peyote surely offers both validation of his enmity and a seemingly easy pathway to better fortune and unlimited mystical power.

"I always thought other men were not like your father," Leila adds. "I don't understand why the meetings have become so popular these days."

"Different reasons, I imagine. Spiritual enlightenment for some, hope that it will cure illness for others. What Father's motives are, I cannot say," he lies. Gently, Jimmie puts a hand on Leila's shoulder. "Look, Mother. I agreed to attend the next meeting simply to placate Father. I am not easily seduced."

That is a rationalization, of course. In truth, it is curiosity that fuels Jimmie's decision to come along. Curiosity, and the excitement of adventure, of a new experience, of a secretive world where the ultimate danger, he is convinced, can be nothing more than the journey of self-discovery.

Leila says nothing further, but her face expresses great anguish. Jimmie can almost imagine what she must be thinking.

I expected better from you, my son. You, who have come so far, allowing your father to entice you with his questionable ways. How far are you prepared to fall, Jimmie? How far?

JIMMIE SITS BESIDE HIS FATHER on a horse-drawn wagon as they bounce over the uneven trail toward Newcomb. The landscape is barren and pockmarked, the way Jimmie pictures the surface of the moon.

"How long have you been going to these meetings?" Jimmie asks, looking straight ahead.

"Several years. Ever since the tribal council passed a law prohibiting them." Wilson chuckles like a naughty schoolboy. "That is when I knew it was something I would like to try."

"And they still go on, these meetings, even though Navajo law prohibits it?"

"The ruling is not enforced. Not by the useless tribal council. Not even by the white man's government. There have been some official complaints in our district, but nothing more." Wilson swings his hand in the air, as if shooing away a bothersome insect. "It is all nonsense, the fuss about our meetings. Meanwhile, Chee Dodge and his friends get richer. I knew Dodge was not to be trusted from the first moment our paths crossed in Round Rock. I was still a young boy then."

Jimmie turns toward his father at the mention of that small community across the border. This could be his chance to finally learn what happened between Wilson and Dodge, to better understand what fuels his father's acrimony.

"Tell me about it," Jimmie implores. "You've said before that there was some trouble there, and that you were witness. Tell me the whole story."

Wilson scoffs, but his vacuous expression suggests that his thoughts have already drifted back more than fifty years. "Like I said, I was young. No more than fifteen. It was—" He stops abruptly. "You would not understand."

"I *want* to understand. You said it yourself the other day, that I'm beginning to see what you've been talking about all these years. Please, Father. Tell me."

Reluctantly, Wilson does.

OF ALL THE NAVAJO HEADMEN Wilson had heard about as a boy, Black Horse was the craziest of them all. And that was not the only reason he looked up to the man.

Wilson explains to his son that Black Horse was a prominent leader in the Carrizo Mountain region of northeastern Arizona. Individuals from other parts of the reservation considered him to be little more than a defiant, rabble-rousing scoundrel—which, in fact, he was, and proudly so. He and the revered headman Manuelito had previously been of one mind, Black Horse insisted, but Manuelito had grown soft. He had given in to the white man who stole Navajo lands and broke every promise. That is what Black Horse reminded his devoted followers as they gathered around him in a meadow near Teec Nos Pos along the Arizona/New Mexico border.

What brought forth this rancor was news that Manuelito had sided with government agents. He had agreed that Navajo children should be required to attend the government boarding schools established by Congress five years earlier.

This covenant clearly infuriated Black Horse, who talked about the cruelty and brutal discipline meted out daily to the young students as if they were little more than headstrong mustangs needing to be broken. He reminded everyone of how many Navajo children had been kidnapped from their homes and sent to these schools, some as far away as California and Oklahoma, to fill the quotas. He ranted on about how Chee Dodge—who he believed to be a half-breed (but in all likelihood was not)—had been chosen to become Manuelito's successor.

Heads nodded. Mouths frowned. Everyone was already aware that 32-year-old Henry Chee Dodge had been made overall headman of the entire tribe by the Indian Agency and the US Commissioner of Indian Affairs.

Black Horse paced on the grassy field as he spoke, his rhythmic Navajo dialect spilling out like bitter water, falling hard upon the obsequious faction that squatted around him in a wide circle. The nearby mountains, whose slopes erupted with dense stands of tall cottonwood trees, stood watch under a nearly cloudless October sky.

"The government schools fill our children with *biliga'ana* lies," Black Horse shouted, jabbing his finger in the air for emphasis. "They are beaten if they speak our language. They are chained and starved and punished without mercy if they try to protest or escape."

Murmurs of outrage coursed through the small assemblage of men, none of whom needed more encouragement to hate the white usurpers with any greater intensity. The followers spanned a wide age range, but by far the youngest listener was the impressionable young man known as Walks Alone: Jimmie's father.

He had traveled the short distance from Shiprock at Black Horse's personal request, sent through an emissary, who said the headman had heard reports of Walks Alone's experiences at the Ft. Defiance school. The boy suspected he was being recruited solely to stir up the leader's followers, and he was eager to oblige. His mother begged him not to go, but he ignored her, as he often did.

As Black Horse spoke, Walks Alone studied the charismatic figure who paced before him. Black Horse was tall for a Navajo, perhaps nearly six feet. He appeared to be in his early sixties. The skin on his weathered face was the color of saddle leather, its worn patina creasing each time he frowned or narrowed his eyes. Above his scowling upper lip was a neatly trimmed, white-tinged mustache that mirrored the color and density of his eyebrows.

His clothing also made him look different, for it hinted at something more Spanish than Navajo. He wore light-colored pants striped with thin, dark, vertical lines; a dark, bolero-style jacket, fully buttoned even on such a warm day; a colorful kerchief around his neck; and, covering his head, a wide-brimmed hat. Around the headman's neck, hanging loosely below the kerchief, was a necklace made up of many strands of fine beads: turquoise, coral, abalone. Instead of wearing a traditional *concho* belt, Black Horse sported a wide leather waistband that held bullets and a six-shooter, which dangled from a holster at his side. As rumor had it, that very gun may have killed a couple of prospectors, white men, who dared to intrude upon Black Horse's domain.

"Now the agent they call Shipley is making a stand at Round Rock," Black Horse announced to his followers. "I have been told of this by my friend, Left-Handed Thrower, who lives near there. Shipley is forcing families to give him their school-aged children so he can send them away." (As Wilson tells the story, he takes great delight in quoting Black Horse word for word, as if the memory is fresh in his mind, as if he is reliving it in the present).

Black Horse paused, waiting, as the group marked his words upon themselves like corn pollen. The crowd gathered in his anger, made it their own. Several of the men stood and defiantly thrust their fists into the air, turning in circles as they did so, as if looking for someone to fight.

Black Horse looked directly at Walks Alone and motioned for him to stand. He introduced the boy to the crowd and told them he was one of those children taken by force from his mother five years earlier. "The man in charge at the school told Walks Alone he could only answer to a white man's name. The boy was beaten many times. His arm was broken. When he tried to run away, they caught him and brought him back. They locked him in a dark underground place for two days without food. His hands were bound. He was not released until he begged for forgiveness in the white man's language. Is this not true, Walks Alone?"

The young man nodded, his eyes seemingly fixed on a profusion of yellow wildflowers that grew in the meadow. He spoke, shyly at first, his Navajo words becoming more forceful and angry as he continued.

"They said … they said I could not use my own language. I could not carry the corn pollen or repeat the blessings I had been taught. They said I must talk only to their gods, to the Jesus Christ. That I must stop thinking like a savage and learn the white man's ways. And when I did not obey in all things—how could I?—they did to me everything that Black Horse told you, and worse." (At this point in the story, a shudder courses through Wilson's body and he stops speaking. Then, after a moment, he continues).

Black Horse stood quietly while the young man spoke. Then he gently asked him to tell of the brave thing he did to escape the white man's forced exile.

Walks Alone took a deep breath. "One evening, I set fire to one of the buildings. While they were trying to put it out, I ran away. They did not find me. After a short while, they stopped looking. I went home to my mother. She was the third or fourth wife of a man who deserted her—deserted us—just before I was born. I am all she had. Today, you know, the government turns our own people into policemen to help enforce their rules. Today I would not be so lucky to get away."

Walks Alone stepped back and squatted down beside the others. Black Horse resumed his pacing and announced they would ride to Round Rock to challenge the Indian Agent Dana Shipley, who was holed up at the community trading post. This time all the men were on their feet, cheering and hollering. And no one was more vocal than young Walks Alone, Black Horse's newest admirer and now his most ardent follower.

THE MOB RODE INTO ROUND Rock eager for a fight. As they approached the trading post, Walks Alone was surprised to see that it was newly built. The walls were constructed not of logs, but blocks of the local sandstone. The store looked quite impenetrable—even the windows were protected by metal bars—so the gang contented themselves by surrounding the building and shouting scurrilous epithets. After some time, Agent Shipley cautiously ventured out. He was accompanied by the post's clerk, brother of *Dinetah's* leading trader, John Lorenzo Hubbell. In addition, out came three agency-appointed Navajo policemen who were there to enforce the removal of two dozen children for disbursement to government boarding schools. Finally, there appeared Henry Chee Dodge himself. Everyone knew he was co-owner of the trading post—the first Navajo ever to have a stake in the trading business.

Walks Alone had heard of Dodge, of course, not only because Dodge was headman over the entire Navajo Nation, but also because he had claimed for himself some of the best grazing land on the reservation. What's more, Dodge had interpreted for the white government for many years. Reason enough to hate him. (Wilson says nothing about Jimmie's experiences translating for the government. But the truth hangs over them, like Balancing Rock. Perhaps it always will).

Black Horse came forward and followed Shipley, the clerk, and Dodge back inside the trading post. Walks Alone and the other followers waited impatiently as the Navajo policemen stood watch.

An argument must have started up in the store, for after a while the group heard muffled voices followed by the sounds of a scuffle. Suddenly the door burst open and out staggered Black Horse, his arms locked tight around Shipley. He dragged the struggling agent down the steps. By the time the policemen realized what was happening, Black Horse had called to his men, and in seconds they were upon the agent, kicking him and beating him with their fists.

Walks Alone would have gladly joined in the melee, but he could not push his way inside the tight ring of Black Horse's frenzied supporters. He was forced to merely look on as Chee Dodge and the three policemen came running over. After several minutes they managed to free the agent. His face was swollen and covered with cuts. Blood poured out of a gash over his left eye. Dodge and the policemen somehow found a way to pull him back up the stairs and into the relative safety of the trading post. Once inside, they barricaded the doors by piling sacks of flour against them. They covered the barred windows with woven rugs and bolts of fabric.

Black Horse shouted, "Come out or we'll kill you all."

"Kill them, kill them all," chanted his men. Walks Alone, swept up in the emotion, joined in the uproar.

During this demonstration, one of the policemen skulked out the back door of the trading post and rode off on a fast horse that belonged to Dodge. Black Horse chose three of his gang to ride after the policeman and bring him back, but Dodge's splendid horse easily outran the mounts of Black Horse's men.

"Burn it down! Burn them all with it!" shouted the group, and in his murderous rage, Black Horse prepared to do just that. But overhead, heavy clouds rolled in. Soon the men were drenched in a soaking rain. There would be no burning for the time being.

For two days, the intermittent rains did not clear. Black Horse and his men continued to surround the trading post, exchanging occasional bursts of gunfire with the policemen inside. Throughout each day, a group of Navajo women showed up and cooked for Black Horse and his gang.

On the third day of the standoff, the policeman returned on Chee's horse. With him were a group of army soldiers from Ft. Defiance who clearly outnumbered Black Horse's band. There was no shooting this time. Instead, a tense face-off took place between Black Horse's faction and the military. Chee Dodge emerged from the trading post and slipped easily into his role as interpreter and mediator. Using all his persuasive powers, he finally calmed the renegade down. He argued that the whites had many things the Navajos need, like wagons, plows, food. That the two different cultures must build a bridge across the wide divide of their differences.

Black Horse scowled and then spat on the ground. "The *Dineh* do not need what the white man has to offer. The cost to our people is too high."

As the fevered debate continued, Walks Alone edged in closer to better hear what they were saying. His movement caught Dodge's attention.

"Who is this young man with you?" Dodge asked Black Horse.

"One of my group. He has been beaten and tortured by the school you support."

Walks Alone edged up close to Chee Dodge. The leader gave off an unpleasant, flowery scent, a white man's fragrance, Walks Alone assumed. It sickened him. (At this point in the story, Wilson's voice becomes louder, more defiant, as if Jimmie, himself, is Dodge).

"I am Walks Alone. The whites also gave me a name: Wilson Goodluck. Do not forget it. I believe as Black Horse, that you have joined with the whites only to further your own interests. The bridge you speak of is a bridge to your own fortune."

Walks Alone turned and walked back to join the others in Black Horse's group. He was shaking, he realized. Not with fear, but with resolve.

Within half an hour, Dodge's smooth manner and precise translating ultimately defused the stand-off. The defiant Black Horse left peacefully with his band of grumbling dissidents, who were clearly disappointed that there had been no further violence.

"We showed them our strength, our determination," Black Horse said, his eyes flitting over the young man, his invited guest. "For now, it is agreed the parents in Round Rock will not be forced to turn over their children. But hear my words, this is not the end of it. We will be to the white man as bramble is to the wool of our sheep."

And as Wilson relates the story to his son, he says it occurred to him then, in a burst of seething fury, *No, that is not enough. I will not settle for being merely bramble.*

Where is your vision, Black Horse? Bramble is nothing: a small distraction, a minor irritation.

I have far greater ambitions.

I will be the coyote.

WILSON AND JIMMIE REACH NEWCOMB shortly after sundown. The land here is flat and expansive and so uninviting, even the mountains have removed themselves to areas well in the distance. Wilson reins in his horse and stops the wagon beside a large *hogan*. It looks new: log construction, composition roof. A stack of firewood sits neatly in a pile outside the entrance on the structure's east side. Wilson nods to several of his friends who are milling about, but there is little conversation as they enter the dwelling.

The interior, dimly illuminated by two kerosene lamps, is awash with both shadow and expectation. In the center stands a fire pit, fueled by wood and by a heart-shaped bed of white-hot charcoal. Behind the fire pit rises a small altar covered with earth. It is fashioned into the form of a crescent moon. A cross made of sage sits at its center. Directly behind the altar, three men sit against the wall. The center man wears a light-colored shirt and tie, while the other two are dressed much like everyone else, in dusty denim.

"In the middle is the Road Man," Wilson explains to his son. "To his left is Cedar Man, and to his right, Drummer Man."

In a circle along the walls of the *hogan*, the floor is covered with quilts for the assemblage to sit on. The walls are also covered with hangings: Navajo blankets, Pendleton blankets, even bedspreads.

"Father, about that cross on the altar." Jimmie speaks in a low voice as they sit cross-legged on a strong-bordered rug of Tees Nos Pos design. "You mean all this time you've been coming to a Christian ceremony?"

"There are Christian symbols in these meetings for those who find such things important. I am indifferent to them." Wilson proffers a derisive snort. "Upon that cross will sit the Chief Peyote, a perfect specimen we do not eat. It is the only symbol that should matter to you. It will enable your prayers to reach the gods. *Our* Great Spirits, not the *bilaga'ana* gods."

"The Road Man performs the ceremony, then?" Jimmie asks.

Wilson scowls. "It is peyote who performs. The Road Man simply serves."

Soon everyone is seated. There are fifty people, perhaps more. The Road Man takes out the Chief Peyote and places it upon the bed of sage on the altar. He turns and leads a short prayer that welcomes the gods into the *hogan*. Next he consecrates a sage bundle and passes it around. Each person removes a bit of sage, crumbles it in his hands, and then rubs it over his face and arms. The aroma of the sage, along with cedar smoke from the fire pit, is intoxicating.

Minutes later, a bulging burlap sack makes the rounds from person to person.

"The medicine," Wilson informs his son, leaning over and speaking in a whisper. "I suggest only one to begin with. There will be opportunities throughout the night for more."

The sack comes to Jimmie. It smells of damp earth. Inside, brownish-green peyote buttons lie like droppings in a corral. Hesitantly, Jimmie takes one and passes the sack to his father.

Wilson takes a specimen and scrapes the cottony fuzz with a fingernail, holding up the cleaned cactus flesh toward the Chief Peyote as a gesture of offering. Then he pops it into his mouth and chews thoughtfully. After several moments, he spits into his hands and rubs the saliva over his head and body.

After watching his father, Jimmie scrapes his peyote button in the same way. Then he bites into the "medicine," finding that it tastes as bitter as, well, medicine. He has to literally choke it down.

"What will I feel from this?" he asks his father.

"It will depend."

"On what?"

Wilson's answer is sharp, rushed. "Every time is something different. The medicine has many things to show us. What it teaches you will be different from what it teaches me. Now focus your prayers through Chief Peyote. Open yourself to what peyote offers you."

Jimmie waits with uncertain expectations as the Road Man sets out his prayer instruments: a staff, a new bundle of sage, a two-feathered fan, and a gourd rattle. Drummer Man takes out his drum, fashioned from an iron pot with a buckskin drumhead. All are purified by passing them through cedar smoke.

The Road Man sings the opening songs as Drummer Man beats his drum. Long prayers follow, along with more drumming and singing. The minutes march on.

Jimmie begins to experience a state of heightened alertness, as if he has had too many cups of coffee. He perceives a feeling of fullness in his stomach and perhaps something else—nausea, just a hint of it. It roils in his consciousness like distant thunder.

He needs to get up and stretch, but since nobody moves from their squatting or sitting positions, he simply raises his arms over his head, hands interlocked. The mild, nagging pain he should be feeling in his shoulder—it has been with him constantly since his release from the naval hospital—is suddenly gone. The "medicine"?

Gradually, a faint yellow line marches across his field of vision. He blinks, but the streak of color does not go away. It intensifies and shimmers, as if a yellow line of chalk, suspended in air, is being stirred by a gentle breeze. He closes his eyes, but the image is still before him. When he opens his eyes moments later, it has vanished.

He watches as a fire tender approaches the bed of coals with a small whisk broom. He fashions the ashes into the shape of a bird by brushing the heart pattern into a crescent, then adding an eagle's tail of ash below the crescent, in the center.

Soon the sack of peyote buttons comes around again. Jimmie helps himself to another. The taste seems more pungent than before, but he forces it down. Minutes later, the yellow blur is back, and this time the shimmering line looks like heat waves that radiate off parched ground in summertime, but Jimmie feels cold, not hot. He has become like a taut wire in the wind, humming and vibrating. He tries to focus on the Chief Peyote, but his eyes are drawn instead to the hot coals, to the bird made of ashes. He realizes it is speaking to him—speaking!—its voice high and shrill, as if such a feat were an everyday occurrence rather than the hallucinatory delusion it surely must be.

Look at you, says the smoldering eagle. *You who have gone to war, seen death, and brought death to others by using your sacred language. You who have served the white men, the same men who slaughtered your ancestors and helped themselves to your land and laid waste to your people's livelihood by killing their livestock and giving them nothing in return.*

The ash bird's eyes glow redder than the surrounding coals. *You come back to* Dinetah, *but Enemy Way does not help you and the Squaw Dance does not bring you comfort. The white man has given you many chances to die for him, and now he turns away from you when you are no longer useful to him. You have become like a half-breed: no longer fully Navajo, for you have chewed on life in the white world. You were accepted by the* biliga'ana *when you served their purposes, and now they laugh at you They laugh at you!*

From somewhere out of sight, the sound of laughter seems to rise up, sudden and maddening, like a dust devil.

Jimmie cannot resist the ash bird. Although he has not chosen to hear its message, it has clearly chosen *him.* Gone are thoughts of his mother and of Annie Wauneka and of Chee Dodge, the people in his life who provided him with foundation and stability. He sees only the pulsating yellow line.

The yellow line, and the smoldering winged messenger that blisters with the truth.

THE STRIDENT TRILL OF THE Road Man's whistle whipsaws Jimmie back to reality. He shakes his head a few times to clear away his disorientation. His watch reads nearly 5:00 a.m. He feels the fatigue of the long night. The lessons peyote taught him are still fresh in his mind, but the almost euphoric mood he experienced earlier has worn off. He is anxious to get out into the fresh air.

"Is it almost time to leave?" he asks his father.

"It is almost time for breakfast," Wilson replies. "No one leaves until after breakfast."

The fire tender reshapes the ash bird with his whisk broom. Then he gets up and leaves the *hogan*. Meanwhile, the Road Man removes the Chief Peyote from the altar.

"The sage that was under the Chief Peyote will now be given to someone at this meeting," Wilson explains softly. "Someone who is ill, or who needs special prayers."

Drummer Man removes the sage and slowly looks around the circle of people. When his gaze reaches Wilson and Jimmie, he walks forward. Jimmie feels woozy, disconnected, as with great solemnity, Drummer Man offers the sage to him.

"Did you arrange this, Father?" Jimmie asks when Drummer Man walks away.

"They know you have returned from war. You have been given a great honor."

The fire tender returns with the breakfast items of water, corn, fruit, and meat. Jimmie realizes he is famished and very, very thirsty. For the first time there is conversation among the peyote eaters. The mood is upbeat and relaxed.

It seems everyone has changed, in some small but positive way, after the all-night meeting. Jimmie senses harmony within the *hogan*, if not within himself. It is in the air, in the faint echoes of laughter and good cheer, which, like the residual cedar smoke, seem to linger even after the participants file out.

Leaving the *hogan* with his father, Jimmie tumbles out into the bracing morning air. He watches the sun as it yawns above the horizon. By the time they return to Two Grey Hills, that golden orb will be high in the sky, illuminating Jimmie and Wilson together. *We are not so different, you and me,* Wilson had said to him. Jimmie understands as well as fears the import of those words.

But for now, it is a relief to stand, to stretch his limbs and his outlook and his perception of the misguided optimist he had been. He inhales deeply, filling his lungs with the sweet, perfumed breath of the desert.

Overhead, a Gila woodpecker glides by, having flown off from a nearby tree. From somewhere behind the meeting place a horse stomps and whinnies. Everyone, it seems, is impatient to get away. None more so than Jimmie.

Where he is heading, however, he has no idea.

CHAPTER 17

JULY—OCTOBER 1946

The excuse is a flimsy one, but Jimmie delays his travel plans yet again. He shrugs off intended visits to Tanner Springs and to Kayenta. With everything peyote has revealed to him, he finds it easier to stay put, where he can feed on his bitterness like he fed on the bitter cactus itself. They are new and uncomfortable to him, these feelings, yet they grow stronger every day, reinforced and emboldened by his father, who has had a lifetime to bloat on the sustenance of discontent.

Weeks go by. Summer comes with its hot, withering breath that leaves the ground beneath Two Grey Hills as brittle as kiln-fired clay. Jimmie makes no attempt to find work, knowing there is little to be found. His days are spent with meaningless pursuits, wandering among his mother's remaining livestock and gambling with old acquaintances whose lives are as stagnant as his has become.

He continues to attend monthly peyote meetings, in spite of the ash bird who chastens him relentlessly. Its fiery eyes burn into his core in an effort to scorch away treasured memories like a brushfire.

Memories of the buddies he fought beside, most of them Anglos. Memories of the comforts and freedoms he enjoyed, unfettered by the uncertainties and hardships of reservation life. Memories of the dream that his existence would find purpose and meaning at the war's end, that nothing could ever again seem as discouraging as it had appeared before.

Jimmie's spirit, once hopeful and pervasive, has proved no match for the igneous raptor. Its illusory power renders him helpless in all things, except for his ineffaceable feelings toward Ray Begay, or his treasured memories of their time together when they teamed up, seemingly invincible, to make their as yet unheralded contribution to the Pacific theatre of war.

In the time of First Man, First Woman, Talking God, and all the Holy People, it was foretold of the coming of the white man, of his controlling ways, his anomalous beliefs, his sickness, his wars.

For there once existed a being called "Divine Gambler," son of the Sun, his flesh made white, his hair yellow. He left from that place where the Holy Ones dwelled, taking with him the one thing that made him jealous: the People's identity—their values and beliefs and culture. He vowed he would return someday from across a great sea to dominate this red race of people, bringing with him knowledge of the true and only God and an insistence that everyone believe as he believed. When he returned, the Divine Gambler would take away all the Indian names given to mountains and rivers and valleys, replacing them with names of his own. And there would be great hardships heaped upon the Dineh, *who would be destined to live under the one identity set forth by Divine Gambler and his like-skinned followers.*

Growing up, Jimmie had heard the story countless times from his father. He thinks about it again as autumn approaches. His positive experiences as a member of the Corps have become overshadowed by the harsh reality of the present, where the Divine Gambler, it seems, has returned victorious after all.

IN LATE OCTOBER, JIMMIE DECIDES to accompany his father and some of his father's like-minded friends to an upcoming demonstration. The details of this particular protest do not matter, Jimmie tells himself. He is curious to witness whatever rabble-rousing his father has in mind.

Leila does not hide her concern for the change she has noticed in her son. She is clearly agitated when she asks him, "What has happened to you?" Jimmie watches as she sweeps the floor of the *hogan* with such pressure on the broom, the bristles look in danger of breaking off. "Why are you so troubled?" she continues. "If you have become a skinwalker, let me see you take the shape of a wolf or a coyote so I will know for sure. Why else do you take on the wolf's personality?"

Jimmie looks down, unable to meet her piercing eyes. "It's hard to explain, Mother. At one time, I thought the Marine Corps was the best thing that ever happened to me. But I can see now it was all an illusion."

"Do not be misled by your father, Jimmie. Or by the 'medicine' he entices you with."

Jimmie is anxious to walk away, but his mother stands between him and the door. "Those meetings, Mother, helped me to question whether I have been trying to be someone I am not. Perhaps the marines gave me a false sense of belonging. Maybe it was a world where I never belonged. A world where I was nothing more than an idealist, a pretender."

Leila shakes her head, her eyes tearing. "I should not say this, but in truth, it is your father's world that is the illusion." She sweeps the last of the dust outside the door, and then she stands outside, sets down the broom, and turns to her son. "You were always so different from your father in that regard. But now ..."

Her voice trails off. But Jimmie hears her finish the sentence anyway, and not liking what he hears, he walks past her reproachful stare without looking up.

He wanders aimlessly toward the corral, oblivious to the Navajo symphony of bleating sheep and whinnying horses. Does he really embrace the words he said to his mother? All that happy horseshit about belonging ... behind him now? In light of what he has seen and heard since coming home, it seems easier to understand his father's ways than to fight them. Still, he is not fully comfortable with the persona he has assumed. It fits him poorly, like the suits and ties the Anglo businessmen and politicians wear. But for the time being, he finds it easier to cloak himself in it nonetheless.

WITH HIS MOTHER'S ADMONITION STILL ringing in his ears, Jimmie accompanies his father on this journey to ... well, he is not sure where they are going.

The Carrizo Mountains are visible to his left and the community of Teec Nos Pos lies somewhere up ahead. The trail is rough and uneven, carved out of rocky ground covered with ferns and grasses that have long ago turned brown. In his peripheral vision, Jimmie detects a streak of movement far off to his right. Low, along the ground. A coyote, most likely, out to feed in the dusky late afternoon. He wonders if it could be an omen and then quickly dismisses the thought.

They have entered the territory where Black Horse once held sway. The headman has been dead for at least twenty-five years, but his presence and his hubris are still felt and fostered here among individuals who continue to actively protest the incursions of *bilaga'ana.* Wilson Goodluck, clearly, has never severed his ties to this defiant group.

Wilson sits beside Jimmie on the wagon, reins in hand, his jacket collar up in a futile effort to shelter himself from the wind. He has made it clear they must reach their destination before nightfall, for he is not wearing his ghost beads—husks of juniper berries strung together like a necklace—which he believes will protect him from spirits of the night. He is also concerned that the first snowfall of the season might come soon. The gray lamb's wool sky foretells it.

Few words have passed between them on the journey, and Jimmie feasts on the silence as if it were a hearty mutton stew. He mulls over his decision to avoid any further monthly meetings. It is time to see through eyes that are not fogged under a mescaline haze. This outing, however, is different. This will be his first opportunity to witness how his father stands up to *bilaga'ana* injustices. He is vaguely aware that the protest they are racing to join has something to do with the forced stock reduction, for in the four years he has been away, little has changed in that regard.

Except this: Jimmie's former friend John Collier resigned as Commissioner of Indian Affairs early the previous year, his final conflict with the *Dineh* having to do with the brief internment of Japanese-Americans on Navajo land. It seems Collier had pushed to relocate "colonization" camps on Indian reservations, thinking the resulting new communities would benefit the various tribes. The Navajo people, among others, opposed this plan. But that did not stop the government from taking over an abandoned reservation boarding school in Leupp, Arizona, where they interred seventy or eighty Japanese men until federal funds ran out. The wishes of the *Dineh,* as Wilson often points out, never stand in the way of the whims of Washington.

Still, Jimmie can see that things have worsened in Collier's absence. The US government is no longer buying excess livestock, even at unfair prices, as they once did. They are simply killing the animals where they stand in their misguided plan to preserve grazing land. In the eight months Jimmie has been back, he has seen the fields of rotting carcasses—horses, sheep, goats—in such numbers they cannot all be butchered so as to at least provide food for their impoverished owners. The sight of all that maggoty flesh, the repellent smell of decay, the knowledge that unknown diseases are spreading from this carnage, all validate the senseless waste and tragedy that permeates the reservation. It leaves Jimmie feeling more despondent, if that is possible, than he was before the war.

They arrive at a spot just south of Teec Nos Pos as the sky deepens from gray to charcoal. Wilson brings the wagon to a stop in front of a mud-covered *hogan*. It is built in the old style, somewhat resembling a large earthen oven. In front, more than a dozen men huddle close to a glowing fire. Jimmie can feel the power of Wilson's idol growing stronger.

"The place where Black Horse lived—is it nearby?" Jimmie asks his father.

"I cannot say." Wilson seems amused by his son's newfound interest in the outlaw. "Actually, this *hogan* once belonged to a man in Black Horse's inner circle. Old Bead Chant Singer. His daughter lives here now. As for the *hogan* of Black Horse himself, they say he died in it, so of course they had to burn it down."

Jimmie listens carefully as the group discusses the confrontation planned for the following morning. It seems at least two white range-riders have come to the trading post in Teec Nos Pos this very day. They are rumored to have lists of people in the area who hold more than their government-imposed limit of livestock. It is further suspected that, in the morning, the range riders will be joined by Navajo policemen from tribal headquarters in Window Rock, who will work alongside them to slaughter the animals. This scenario

has been happening with alarming frequency. The angry faction is
determined that it will not happen here.

After sharing some of the food they have brought along, the men
sleep, each on their own blanket, all tightly crowded together on the
dirt floor. Slumber, however, does not come easily to Jimmie. He lies
awake for a long while, taking in the desert nighttime stillness, broken
only by the snores and coughs of the strangers packed in beside him.
He glances over at his father, fast asleep, and wonders what angry
dreams might be going through his head. And what angry dreams
might be biding their time, waiting to come to Jimmie as well.

Before dawn, everyone rises in preparation to greet the sun,
which soon creeps over the eastern horizon with an otherworldly
glow, diffused behind a curtain of clouds. No snow has fallen during
the night, but the ground is covered with a crystalline frost. Millions
of infinitesimal geometric patterns spread out like an eye-dazzler
tapestry design.

One after another, the men sprinkle their corn pollen and chant
their blessings. Then they set out together toward the trading post
four miles up the trail, grumbling and muttering in anticipation
of the upcoming showdown. Two hours later, they gather around
the still-darkened post. Wilson and some of his friends build small
campfires. They put coffee on to boil.

From the corral behind the post, horses whinny, waiting to be
fed. Jimmie turns to his father and says, "If the range riders spent
the night here, that must be their horses we're hearing. What if we
take it upon ourselves to reduce *their* livestock?"

Wilson's eyes open wide, as if Jimmie has just spoken the most
admirable words he has ever heard. "You mean … kill their horses?"
He chuckles, low and deep.

"Of course not," Jimmie snaps. "But suppose we open the gate
and chase them off. It won't stop the riders for long, but it should
get their attention."

Wilson looks disappointed at first, but then he chortles, "Well, that is still a good idea. There may be promise for you yet." He enthusiastically repeats Jimmie's plan to the others, who gather around Jimmie as if he were a prophet.

In the faint early morning light, Wilson creeps up to the corral and opens the gate. He approaches the four horses standing inside and claps his hands. The animals need no further encouragement. With loud stamping and whinnying, they head for freedom and gallop, unhindered, toward the open rangeland.

Lanterns glow inside the trading post. Moments later, four white men come tumbling out like sagebrush in a windstorm. One man, comically fastening his pants on the run, shouts, "What the hell's goin' on here?"

"They run off our horses!" cries another man, stating the obvious.

A third member of the group, his girth as big as his voice, calls out, "What's the matter with you fuckin' Indians? The policemen are on their way and you're all gonna go to jail."

The last of these buffoons, the trader, says nothing at first. He steadies his gaze on the troublemakers, many of whom have worked themselves into a clear state of agitation. "No use hollerin' and cursin' at 'em, boys," he says finally. "Most of 'em don't understand much English nohow. They ain't bad people, really. Just don't unnerstand we're tryin' to help 'em. Might as well wait till the policemen get here, and then we'll round up your horses and you can get on with whatcha come fer."

Jimmie saunters over to the white men and snarls, "One of us 'fucking Indians' speaks better English than you do. That would be me."

"A smart-ass, to boot," sniffs the chubby one. "You want to tell us what kind of game you boys is playin'?"

Jimmie turns to the restless group behind him and repeats the question, or the gist of it, in Navajo. He does not seek the role of interpreter here, but how can he escape it? At least this time, he is on the side of his people, not the government.

"Go on, tell the government dogs why we have come here," says the son-in-law of Old Bead Chant Singer. "Tell them what they are doing is not right."

Addressing the *bilaga'ana*, Jimmie says, "You call this a game, do you? Poker is a game. Craps is a game. Basketball is a game."

The three range riders exchange nervous glances while the trader regards Jimmie cautiously.

"You're surprised I know such things? Y'see, I was in the war. Marine Corps, as a matter of fact. And defending my country wasn't a game to me. Neither is defending my way of life. If you leave now and head back to wherever it is you crawled out from, you'll get no trouble from anyone here."

"You know, we got to enforce these livestock quotas for your own damn good," says the first man. "Your animals will starve to death if—"

"Spare me the speech," Jimmie interrupts. "Before the war, I spouted the same horse shit. I know the arguments. These people here, they've heard it all. It's true, I s'pose, that our land can't support more cows and goats and horses. But do you help us to submit to your quotas? Do you offer a fair price for our animals?"

"We don't make the rules," snarls the chubby man. "We just enforce 'em. And in a few minutes there'll be three policemen to back us up—*your* people, sent by your big shots in Window Rock. Now how 'bout you gather up our goddamned horses before the policemen get here, and then stay out of our way?"

But Jimmie hears nothing past "We don't make the rules." He is too focused on deciding how much of this interaction to translate to the group behind him, many of whom know enough English to get an idea of what is being said anyway.

"Enough!" cries someone in the mob, for a mob is what they have become.

"It is time we teach the *bilaga'ana* wolves a lesson," shouts Wilson. Soon everyone is yelling and surrounding the four white men, pressing closer every second. The altercation shows every indication of turning violent.

"At least let the trader go," Jimmie hollers to the group, hoping to be heard over the clamor. "It is not his fault. He is not the one who will kill your animals."

Jimmie rushes forward and pushes the trader through the circle of angry protesters. "Go back inside and lock the door," he shouts. "Do it!"

The trader looks back helplessly and then turns and sets off on a panicked sprint to the trading post.

Seconds later the three range riders are on the ground, futilely trying to ward off repeated blows. Jimmie's father has found a wooden board that he is using to paddle one of the men on his buttocks. Another irate member of the mob is tying the legs of a range rider while someone else sits on the man's back. Now Wilson roughly turns over his victim and, gaining a momentary advantage, raises his paddle high in the air, clearly intending to use the board to strike the man in the head. But the range rider manages to roll out of the way as Wilson brings the paddle down onto dry earth. Jimmie's father stumbles backward, his breath coming in heavy gasps. He looks at his weapon as if it had let him down and then kicks it out of the way. He appears too worn-out to continue.

Jimmie runs over and tries to restrain his father. "That's enough," he says. "You have every right to be angry at the riders, but this is out of control."

Wilson, still breathing heavily, struggles to pull away from his son when someone shouts, "Look!"

A car rapidly approaches from the east. Inside are two Navajo policemen. The mob leaves the three white men writhing on the ground as they run toward the car, surround it, force it to stop. Wilson lopes off to join them.

"Go away, go away!" the group shouts in Navajo. As if being controlled by some unseen force, they move to one side of the car and begin to rock it, gently at first, then putting more of their backs into it as that side rises in the air. Jimmie knows most Navajos respect their tribal policemen and would never harm them, so he is alarmed to see them shouting and rocking the car to the point where it is close to overturning and injuring the passengers.

He cries out to the mob, "Is this not enough? Policemen or not, they are Navajo men inside the car. You're not here to hurt your own people or property."

"What about them?" calls out a voice from the crowd. "Are they not here to destroy *our* property?"

With a groan of resignation, Jimmie throws up his hands and walks away. Who is he to say how far the others should go? Still, there is a vague line between civil disobedience and criminal intent. On this day, the mob is in danger of crossing that line, might cross it still. But Jimmie has neither the will nor the wherewithal to stop them. He is tired of being the mediator.

Eventually, however, the situation defuses on its own. The angry group walks away from the police car, away from the range-riders who rise unsteadily to their feet. As the policemen run over to the two white men, as the trader cautiously peers out of the trading post window, as Jimmie puts some distance between himself and the fracas, the protestors begrudgingly shuffle off to their horses and wagons. There may be repercussions for the group's actions, but Jimmie suspects the Navajo policemen will report that they simply resolved what could have been an ugly situation and let it go at that.

When Wilson catches up to his son, his voice is weary. "You see, we are powerless against the *bilaga'ana*. We can only slow them down. We cannot stop them. Now you see what Black Horse was fighting." He shakes his head, the fury in his eyes replaced by resignation. "For the old ones, it was the Long Walk. These days, it is the killing of our animals that defines our misery. What will it be for the next generation?"

Knowing all of the questions but none of the answers, Jimmie glowers with unseeing eyes and says nothing on the long ride home.

CHAPTER 18

DECEMBER 1946

On the day before Christmas—a holiday that has no special meaning in the home of Wilson Goodluck—Jimmie receives a letter that, like the spinner in a board game, sends him reeling in a whole new direction.

The envelope bears Annie Wauneka's return address. It is delivered to the Goodluck *hogan* by Daughter of Old Hat, a neighbor who lives about a mile up the trail, for such is the mail system here: whoever gets to the trading post first brings back mail for neighbors along the way.

Jimmie tosses the letter aside as if it were a hot ember. The last thing he wants now is to be entrapped in a tug-of-war with Annie and her influential father on one side, his own infamous father and the ghost of Black Horse on the other. But the recent run-in at Teec Nos Pos weighs as heavily upon him as a wagonload of timber wood, so eventually he gives in, tearing the letter open and pulling out the lined paper inside.

Dear Jimmie,

   I am assuming that by now you are finally home. I have been frantic with worry for you, but that's all in the past. I trust this will reach you in Two Grey Hills. I had hoped maybe you would have stopped here by now, or would have written, but …

   Anyway, I'm not writing to scold you. I want you to know that my father is back in Sage Memorial Hospital. They say he has pneumonia this time. His old friend, Dr. Salsbury, says he's very sick. I'm so worried about him! George is watching the ranch and caring for our children while I go back and forth to his bedside.

   You should know Father has asked for you, Jimmie. Twice, now. I told him that since I've heard nothing to the contrary, you surely returned home safely. Still, I don't know what you're doing these days. (What are you doing, Jimmie?) I think Father would like to see you before … before it's too late.

   If you can come, plan to break up the journey by stopping off to rest at Father's Sonsola Buttes ranch. They know your name there. And when you get to Ganado, you'll be welcomed at Hubbell's for as long as you care to stay.

   Would you come soon? Would you do this for an old friend?

   Fondly,
   Annie

The letter flutters from Jimmie's fingers just as his mother comes into the *hogan* to retrieve her Pendleton blanket. Although she is a fine weaver, she does not consider her blankets to be wearable, preferring instead the product of the Oregon mill—a staple at the trading post—to keep her warm on chilly mornings. Jimmie looks up at her with a vacuous expression.

"What is the matter?" she asks.

"Chee Dodge," he answers in a confidential voice, unaware that his father was up and out before sun-up. "Annie wrote he is very sick. The hospital in Ganado."

Leila draws the blanket tightly around her shoulders. "He is an important man, our Mr. Interpreter." She pauses, as if weighing her words. "And although your father strongly disagrees, he has been good for our people because he sees things clearly. If anything should happen to him ..." Leaving the sentence unfinished, she turns toward the door. Then she stops, looks back at Jimmie, and mumbles, "But I suppose that no longer matters to you."

Her remark angers him, not because of her atypical sarcasm, but because she acknowledges what he has not: that he still has strong ties to Annie's father, cares about him deeply, in spite of his recent misgivings. For a fleeting moment he is sailing through time and space, wavering, not knowing whether to fall forward or backward.

Suddenly, impulsively, he snatches the letter and flies toward his mother, catching up with her at the open doorway. Outside, a thin layer of snow gives an illusory appearance of purity and buoyancy. A pair of hawks glides effortlessly beneath the clouds, keen on some unseen destination.

"Mother, I need to take one of your horses and a warm sheepskin jacket, if that's all right. I don't know how long I'll be away. Oh, and can you make some excuse to Father when he finds me gone?"

Leila smiles with such radiance, it practically warms the room. "I will manage your father. I always have." She arches one eyebrow and asks, "So you are going to see Mr. Interpreter after all?"

Jimmie scoops up a change of clothes, grabs some currency from his dwindling packet of military pay, and reaches for his buckskin pouch of sacred pollen.

"I'm going to catch up with my past," he tells his mother, seeking refuge in an indirect answer. "I need to revisit that part of my life when I still believed in the power of dreams."

IT TAKES JIMMIE THREE DAYS to reach Chee Dodge's bedside.

On the day he sets out, he makes slow but steady progress around the southern flank of the Chuska Mountains. There has been a traveler before him on the trail, someone with horse and wagon. The tracks are still faintly visible, peering out from under the dusting of blowing snow. Eager sentinels, they point out the way through the thick mantle of ponderosas and Gambel oak. Jimmie prays the unseasonable weather will hold. This time of year, it is not uncommon for a sudden snowstorm to make the high trail impassable. After surviving the war, he is not amused to contemplate the irony of dying in a blizzard close to home.

By evening, he reaches Chee's ranch near Crystal. Lofty cliffs of thick Chuska sandstone rise directly ahead, while the volcanic formations of the Sonsola Buttes materialize to his right. The wind has picked up, blowing the snow in shifting, inchoate patterns, dusting the desert floor in a floury veneer of white.

Chee's house is immense—reportedly the biggest on the reservation. It is Anglo in style, built with blocks of local sandstone. A covered porch extends out in front, much like the officers' quarters at Ft. Wingate or, for that matter, Camp Elliott, way back when. Off to one side sits a modest *hogan*: the guest quarters. It will offer welcome relief from the cold winds, for the temperature has been plunging steadily for the past several hours.

The small household staff—a man and a woman—greet Jimmie as if he were an old friend. "Do you celebrate the birth of the Baby Jesus?" they ask right off.

Jimmie shakes his head and remembers it is Christmas Day. Many families, like the Dodges, are converts to Christianity. More often than not, they add Christian doctrines to long-held Navajo creation legends. But there are those who simply like the holiday's festivity and amusing symbols. Imagine: horned animals that fly! For many Navajos, Christmas is simply another excuse to have a gathering, a joyful diversion during dreary winters and discouraging times.

Still, the caretakers apologize profusely for the lack of a Christmas tree in this Catholic home. They explain that Chee's wives have not been living with him recently. Jimmie wonders how many wives the plural signifies, for polygamy is not unknown among Navajos, even in this day and age.

The male custodian seems relieved to learn that Jimmie follows only established Navajo beliefs as he does. He attends to Jimmie's horse, and then he brings warm food and water to the guest *hogan*. Jimmie is up and out at sunrise.

Day two takes him south by southwest to Ft. Defiance, which clings to the Arizona side of the Arizona–New Mexico border. There he enjoys the hospitality of a local trader, David Gerber, who is a friend of Chee's. The trading post is gaily decorated for Christmas. A sign echoes "Happy Christmas" in English, Spanish, and Navajo. It occurs to Jimmie that never before has he seen so many notices, in so many places, with Navajo words phonetically spelled. Writing, it seems, has finally come to the reservation in a big way.

On the third day, he follows a more westerly course toward the high desert of the Colorado Plateau and, finally, into Ganado. The community is named for headman Ganado Mucho, whose old *hogan* struggles to remain standing nearby. It has been snowing off and on all day, but Jimmie's sheepskin coat has somehow managed to keep his body relatively warm and dry. His hair is another story. It is damp, flecked with melting snow, some of which insolently trickles onto his forehead and down his cheek.

The hour is late, so he gladly heads directly to the sprawling Hubbell Trading Post a few minutes west of the community. John

Lorenzo Hubbell's hospitality to special visitors has long been legendary. The guest *hogan* here will be more than Jimmie needs and, he suspects, more than he deserves. At least his mother's horse will be worthy of the comfort of the enclosed stable.

Ganado still looks the way he remembers it did before the war: a widely strewn collection of log-construction *hogans* and dirt roads and scrawny livestock. Juniper and piñon pine, their branches crusted in snow, grow in profusion. There are few indications of any building going on. Not homes or stores or services or roads. Like the mercury in a thermometer, uncomfortable thoughts rise up in Jimmie once again. He feels torn between the unyielding pull of Black Horse and the ash bird, and the progressive call of Chee and Annie Dodge. He is unable to see that by tearing himself away from his father's sphere of influence to make the arduous journey to Ganado, he has already chosen a direction. The baggage he carries is cumbersome, certainly, but it takes up no physical space. Even so, he has packed no expectations other than to catch up with Annie and to see—possibly for the last time—the leader who, for so many years, he has held in such lofty regard.

A SIGN TELLS VISITORS THAT Sage Memorial hospital was founded by Presbyterian missionaries in the early 1900s. The campus comprises dozens of buildings—hospital facilities, nursing school and dormitories, dining hall, church, power plant, and private residences—that in many instances bear little resemblance to one another except for their exteriors of either adobe (on all the older buildings) or quarried stone. The self-sufficient little community that is Sage Memorial overlooks a panorama of distant mountain ranges and mesas. It reminds Jimmie that the beauty of the reservation land often goes unnoticed by a people preoccupied with trying to survive on it.

Once offering what was arguably the best medical care available on the reservation, Sage Memorial is still an impressive facility, second only to the new government-run Navajo Medical Center in Ft. Defiance. Jimmie walks toward the main hospital entrance along one of the many paved stone pathways that crisscross the grounds, although on this day the path is little more than an indentation in the snow, trodden into a slippery crust by shoes and boots before him. All around are deciduous trees and shrubs, now dormant, so Jimmie cannot identify many of them. They were planted over the years to transform the desert here into a lush oasis.

Tom Dodge breezes out through the hospital doors just as Jimmie walks up the entrance steps. Jimmie has never met Annie's older half brother, now in his midforties, though he has seen pictures of him at Chee's summer ranch. Jimmie recognizes the lean frame and silver hair, which has been conspicuously cut and trimmed, white-man style. Tom, who gained notoriety as the first Navajo to get a law degree, is now following in his father's footsteps as tribal chairman. Jimmie walks up to him and introduces himself.

"Goodluck, yes, I've heard about you from Annie," Tom says with perfect English diction. He looks smart in dark trousers and a white shirt, both so spotless and freshly pressed they might have come right out of a Sears catalog. "You just came back from giving it to the Japs, right?"

Jimmie squirms, uncomfortable with Tom's choice of words. "I was in the Marine Corps, yes. Got my discharge a couple of months ago." With atypical directness he asks, "Is it all right if I see your father?"

"Question is whether he'll be seeing you, I'm afraid. He's drifting in and out of consciousness." Tom pauses to close his top shirt button, as if he has suddenly become aware of the cold wind. From the main road nearby, an old pick-up sputters past, the sound of its whiny engine unwelcome on these grounds. "Y'know, he asked about you a couple weeks ago. Or did Annie already write to tell you that?"

"She did."

"She'll be back here tomorrow, by the way. Hard for her to stay here every day with young kids at home." He glances at his watch. "Anyway, please go see Father. I know he'll be glad you stopped by."

Tom sighs, his body slumping ever so slightly, like a wilting flower. Lowering his voice he says, "They don't give Dad more than another week. Two at most. He's already talked to Father Haile about last rites."

Father Berard Haile, who heads the Franciscan Order at St. Michael's, has been instrumental in transforming Navajo into a written language. It is widely known that he also worked with Chee Dodge for many years to translate the Bible into Navajo. Finding Navajo phrases and idioms to embrace concepts of the church could not have been easy, Jimmie figures. Another little-known contribution from the man who lies inside, dying.

"I'll stay in the area long as I can," Jimmie says. "That is, if it's all right with your family."

"Of course, Jimmie. I may see you around then. Actually, I'm heading to St. Michael's now. To put ... things ... in order."

As Tom hurries away, Jimmie steps through the door and into the hospital, where he seeks refuge from the chill December air and moves inexorably toward the man who, even near death, is pulling hard, an unknowing pawn in the tug-of-war for the redemption of Jimmie Goodluck.

CHEE'S HOSPITAL ROOM IS A beehive of activity. Attendants scurry about, carrying medical equipment and who-knows-what. Too bad for anyone else in the hospital with the bad fortune to get sick at the same time as Mr. Interpreter.

The dying man lies in bed, face ashen, head elevated. He is hooked up to some sort of breathing apparatus. His eyes are closed, but it is impossible to tell whether he is sleeping or simply lost in thought. There are at least six empty chairs lined up beside the bed. The venerated leader has obviously received many visitors.

"Hello, Chee," Jimmie says softly. "It's me, Jimmie. Been a while."

No response.

A nurse enters, sees there is a visitor, and then exits respectfully, closing a curtain around them. Jimmie looks at his mentor, trying to visualize him in his big chair at his summer ranch, a tumbler of scotch nearby. Not an easy thing to imagine, looking at the pallid man lying there, shrunken and feeble, breathing with the help of a machine.

Jimmie pulls up a chair to Chee's bedside and speaks in a low voice. "I guess you heard I got my discharge from the marines a few months ago. Got no regrets about signing up, though I haven't admitted that lately. Saw terrible things, but me and the other *Dineh* who were there, we did some good, I think."

He wishes he could tell Chee how talking in Navajo undoubtedly helped to save countless lives, but he can never break his promise to keep the code a secret. He is still loyal to the Corps and to his country, in spite of his present misgivings toward the same government that seems to have trouble honoring *its* promises.

Leaning closer to Chee, he goes on. "I don't know if you can hear me, but I'll say this anyway. Being in the Marine Corps opened my eyes to—well, I saw for myself some of the ideas you talked about all your life. Like the things we can learn from the Anglos. In the Corps, I made good friends among the whites. Lasting friends, I like to think. But I have to confess, I haven't had an easy time since coming back to the reservation. I …"

He stops, self-conscious about the one-way conversation. Why share such petty concerns, relatively speaking, with a man consumed by matters of life and death? Still, the catharsis is good for Jimmie. And it is not as if Chee is actually listening and might respond. Jimmie is not asking for advice or seeking absolution, after all; he is simply trying to sort out his own muddled feelings.

"Since I've been back, I've grown angry and disillusioned—the way my father feels, to be honest. Maybe I'm more like him than I ever wanted to be. You'd be disappointed by things I've said, things I've thought, recently. And you'd be right to feel that way. It's just that, in the service, I got a taste of how rewarding life could be. Now it's all gone, like—I don't know, like flashes of lightning, maybe—that disappear before you're even sure where they struck." Jimmie straightens up and glances around the room, taking in but not seeing the sand-colored walls, the dingy curtains, the many get-well gifts that have been brought and sent to Chee by his family and his legion of admirers. So he is unaware, at first, that Chee's eyes have fluttered open, that his lips are moving, almost imperceptibly, trying to form words.

"Can you hear me after all?" Jimmie asks when he realizes the old leader is attempting to communicate. He pulls his chair closer still to the bed and positions himself to where his lips nearly touch Chee's wan face. "Say it again."

From Chee Dodge, a feeble croak, barely audible over the breathing apparatus:

"Rope," it sounds like.

Jimmie holds his breath for a long moment. He hears Chee say "Jimmie," then the word "rope" again, followed by several indiscernible words, ending with "hold it at loss," though that makes little sense.

He is about to ask Chee to repeat what he is trying to say, but the old man's eyes are already closing. Soon there is only the sound of Chee's labored breathing, insistent and mechanical, like a medicine man's rattle, its pleading rhythms arching skyward to stir the ancient spirits.

THE NEXT DAY, ANNIE IS at the hospital when Jimmie returns. Her eyes shine when they focus on Jimmie, and the two old friends greet warmly. There is little privacy at the hospital entrance, so they find a small area off the main wing, an empty classroom used for student nurses, where they can sit and talk. Can it really be four years since they last saw each other?

"Father isn't responding this morning," she tells him. "Two of my brothers are with him now. You know his ... situation?"

"Yes, I saw Tom yesterday. I'm so sorry."

"Well, he lived a long and a good ..." She pauses, her voice choked with emotion. "Listen to me, talking about him like he's no longer with us." Annie forces a smile. "I'm so happy you came. I know the trip is especially hard this time of year."

"Yeah, well, I'm starting to think that, I don't know, that maybe I needed to see your father more than I realized. I sat with him for a while yesterday."

Jimmie finds himself beguiled all over again by Annie's charisma. She was always a big woman, but now she wears her stature differently, as if the weight of her problems—several sickly children, a dying father, reservation-wide health epidemics that have become her own personal crusade—has helped her to carry herself with even more grace and confidence. She wears a patterned skirt with a purple velvet blouse, over which she has draped a fringed shawl emboldened with a Navajo pattern Jimmie does not recognize. Her hair, as he remembers she always wore it, is tied back into a bundle. This is the first time he has seen her wearing glasses, and their bold, oblong frames cry out for attention. It reminds him how lucky he is that his eyesight is still strong. It is merely his foresight, if he is to be honest, that is in question.

Annie looks closely at her friend, the way she might size up an adversary at a chapter house, or a potential buyer for some of her new lambs. "I've never seen you looking so fit," she says finally. "A bit thin, but fit. The military life must have agreed with you."

"Yes, I did find military life agreeable. The war, well, that was something else."

Annie loosens the shawl around her shoulders, for the room is much warmer than the hospital halls had been. "So tell me what you've been doing since you came back," she says. Then, in a playful, taunting voice: "And what's been keeping you so busy you couldn't come to visit."

"You first," he answers, hoping to evade the question. "Tell me about your husband and children, for starters."

Annie sits back and puts her hands in her lap, fingers interlocking. "George is ... fine, though my being away so much, and now staying here with Father, is putting a strain on him. Running the ranch, watching the children. You know. We have help, of course, but still ..."

The way she says this and then stares off into space suggests to Jimmie there is trouble at home.

"Anyway, you wouldn't believe how big the children are getting— all seven of them! Even my youngest, who turned one last fall."

"And they're doing all right then?"

"We manage. Several need extra care. We watch over them best we can. Now the older two, they're asking about their grandfather. They've been here several times to see him. It's only recently that Father has become so ... uncommunicative."

"Speaking of that, when I saw him yesterday, he tried to tell me something. I was talking to him, I thought he was asleep, maybe sedated, but then he opened his eyes and said something I couldn't make out." Jimmie sits up military straight. "I think he knew who I was. I'm pretty sure he called out 'Jimmie.' He seemed anxious to put something into words."

"You couldn't understand any of it?"

"Something about a … rope, maybe? That's what it sounded like." Jimmie scratches his head. "Oh, and something else, something like 'Hold it at loss.'"

Annie's eyes fly open. Her face lights up like the desert nighttime sky. "Not 'hold it at loss.' What he said was, 'Hold it aloft.'"

"Could be, I guess. Still don't get it."

"Come on, Jimmie! He has singled you out. He has included you, and only you, with his own children."

Annie's excitement startles Jimmie at first, but he finds it contagious. He feels uplifted, as if a great secret is about to be revealed.

"I know what he was trying to say," Annie squeals, "because he said the same words to my brothers and me a few weeks ago when he was sitting up and putting his affairs in order."

Jimmie waits for the revelation.

"His words were—I'm sure of it—'Do not let my rope fall to the ground. If you discover it dropping, quickly you must catch it. Catch it and hold it aloft.'"

Jimmie is not sure what he was expecting, exactly, but clearly this is not it. He blinks several times, as if his eyelids are wipers that will clear a wet windshield and bring everything into focus.

Behind her heavy glasses, Annie's eyes are moist. "Don't you see, Jimmie? He's asking of you what he asked of his closest family. He's pleading with you to uphold his ideals, his vision for our people. To carry on for him."

Jimmie turns away from Annie to look out the window. The sky is a brooding gray, the color of ash. In the colorless light, the other side of the glass looks barren and unwelcoming. There are no answers out there, nothing that can stop the uncertainties that run circles through his mind like a restless pony in a small corral.

"I'm flattered your father would include me with you and your brothers," he finally responds, "but I don't deserve the honor. I have no right to—" he searches again for Chee's metaphor—"to hold his rope aloft."

Annie rises to her feet and speaks sharply, her voice forceful and passionate. "Look at me, Jimmie," she commands. "You of all people have earned the right to carry on my father's work. You, who took Father's reins as translator and tried to bring some understanding to our people. You, whose own dreams were not unlike his—or mine."

He looks away, fearing that Annie might see a reflection of the ash bird in his eyes. "You're making me sound far nobler than I am."

Annie puts her hand on his shoulder, holds it there firmly. "Look, I don't know what happened over in the Pacific, or back at home, if that's the problem, but the Jimmie Goodluck *I* know has ideals and vision. And yes, he's human, like us all, and undoubtedly he loses his way from time to time. But he learns from his imperfections. He rises above them and comes away a better person for it."

"Annie, I—"

"Let me finish, Jimmie. I'll never be able to say this again. My father is far from perfect himself, you know. He'd be the first to admit that he drinks too much, that he had—has—a weakness for automobiles and women and diamonds and whatever else his whim might be at any given moment. Believe me, he has many whims. But he never let his flaws get in the way of his vision. And now he approaches the end of his days and he sees there are so many things he'll never get to finish. So he's begging his children—and you, Jimmie, who he also respects—to keep his legacy alive."

Her eyes lock onto Jimmie's as she asks, "Tell me, my friend, would you walk away from a dying man's last wish?"

Before Jimmie can reply, Tom Dodge enters the room and asks Annie to join him at their father's bedside. Jimmie tells her to go ahead, assures her he will think over what she said.

Annie follows her brother toward the door. Without looking back she says, "You don't really need to think it over, you know."

Jimmie can almost see a half smile etching its way across her face, coy and enigmatic.

"I already know your answer, silly man. Too bad it hasn't come to *you* yet."

CHAPTER 19

JANUARY 1947

On the morning of January 7, Chee Dodge leaves this world, the culmination of nearly ninety years as a human being.

Had he and his family not been baptized and had they not become so involved in the ritual and activities at St. Michael's, there would likely be no funeral service, even though he was the ex-council chairman and a revered tribal leader. Until recently, the dead were usually interred quickly, without ceremony, and never in a public cemetery. Furthermore, Navajo burials often enlisted the help of people outside the tribe, since it is ingrained in the *Dineh* to avoid contact with the deceased so their *chindi* cannot come back to infect the living.

But Chee Dodge and his children, like Jimmie and many other progressive Navajos, have no such qualms about death. And since the Dodge family has converted to Catholicism, there will indeed be a mass and funeral befitting a man of his stature. The tribal council, in an unprecedented move, announces they will adjourn for five weeks in tribute to Mr. Interpreter.

The news of Chee's death hopscotches across the reservation, carried over the few existing phone lines and on shortwave radio waves. The information is handed off from one person to another in a relay from town to town, *hogan* to *hogan*. By the next day, few areas of *Dinetah* have not heard about their tribe's great loss.

Jimmie is in Ft. Defiance when the news reaches him on the afternoon of Chee's death. He had come here from Ganado a few days earlier, not wanting to burden the Dodge children by intruding on their remaining hours with their father. Remembering that Carl Slowtalker was from Ft. Defiance, he looked up his old boot camp buddy. Turns out, Carl—who has just turned twenty-three—is back living in the dirt-floor *hogan* where he grew up. He fills the days by helping his parents tend their remaining livestock same as he did before answering the call. He is biding his time, he insists, making plans to leave the reservation for good in order to find work in one of the larger cities. The two ex-marines commiserate some and swap a few war stories, but they have only begun to catch up when news of Chee's death pulls Jimmie back to St. Michael's.

The distinguished red brick church, serving the area since the beginning of the century, is packed with at least three hundred dignitaries and admirers. The requiem mass is led by Father Haile, who delivers the memorial sermon entirely in Navajo. Jimmie closes his eyes and asks the Ancient Ones for guidance, going through the Navajo prayers he knows so well by heart, just as Chee did, according to the leader's family, shortly before his death.

In his heart and mind, Jimmie pays silent tribute to the man he so respected. Chee Dodge: full-blooded champion of the *Dineh*; modern American, wealthy rancher, baptized Catholic, who, for all that, may well have set forth on death's journey with nothing more than a few conventional Navajo chants on his lips.

CHEE'S FINAL RESTING PLACE IS a small veteran's cemetery midway between Window Rock and Ft. Defiance, about two miles from St. Michael's. It had been sanctioned a year earlier by Chee and other tribal leaders. In spite of the outdated taboos regarding death and public burial, the leaders apparently reasoned that white soldiers were buried with honors and special ceremonies, so why not Navajos?

Over the past several months, the coffins of Navajo soldiers from all branches of service have found their way to this special place. Jimmie suspects that this may be the first tangible modification of Navajo custom to come about as a direct result of the war. Chee Dodge, of course, was no war veteran, but there was never any question that he would be laid to rest at this place that he championed.

Solemnly, Jimmie walks on foot to Chee's gravesite alongside the long procession of automobiles—as unusual on the reservation as a marching band would be. Mists dance like sprites on this chilly morning. The ground under Jimmie's feet feels rough against his thin-soled boots. After the church service, Annie offered him a ride in her car just behind the hearse, but he did not accept. He is not family, after all. Far from it.

By the time he reaches the cemetery, the fog begins to lift. It is almost as if the Holy People have decided to look down, unhindered, at the little tableau taking place on earth. With the departure of the haze, the wind picks up, blowing in from the west, off Defiance Plateau. Here on this unsheltered rise of land, Jimmie holds his sheepskin jacket tightly in place against his neck.

Never before has he seen such a medley of American flags in one place. Not on the reservation, certainly. The flags bring back a jumble of memories: reminiscences of early morning revelry at Camp Elliott and camaraderie with his fellow marines and gung-ho meetings with Colonel Carlson and "The Star-Spangled Banner" sung in Navajo and simply marked graves on nameless islands and weeping widows and fatherless children. These recollections, comforting and disquieting alike, come flooding over him in bits and pieces as if he were spinning the dial on a shortwave radio.

At the crest of the little cemetery, Chee's coffin is slowly lowered into the ground. A crush of people press forward to hear the dignitaries make their memorial speeches. But Jimmie draws back, mesmerized by this place, saddened and stirred at the same time, awed and humbled by the concept of a military cemetery for Navajos.

Public burial. With honors. Adorned with flags and flowers and mementos and messages of love. Ghosts be damned.

His eyes gloss over the mounds of earth that sit in uneven rows like loaves of bread at the MCX. On each hillock is a plaque or grave marker, variations on a tragic theme: Died, 1942; Died, 1943; Died, 1944; Died, 1945. Midway, Guadalcanal, Bougainville, New Britain, Saipan, Tinian, Guam, Peleliu, Iwo Jima, Okinawa. Beloved husband, dear brother, thoughtful uncle, loving son …

Carried on the wind are the words spoken by a tribal councilman at Chee's gravesite. Jimmie can make out some of it: "With his death we have lost a great friend, a trusted leader, a capable representative of our interests to the outside world …"

Jimmie shares the loss, feels it deeply, but he grows tired of the rhetoric and the political posturing. He prefers to lose himself in the enormity of this tiny place, to revel in its awesome significance.

And then he sees it, in his peripheral vision: a flutter of familiar colors—orange-red, accents of yellow. The flag of the United States Marine Corps, *his* Marine Corps, fluttering on a pole beside a mound of earth at the end of the row. With a feeling of dread he cannot explain, he slowly walks over to the gravesite and peers down.

In that moment of comprehension in which nothing seems possible and all is inevitable, a name leaps out at him like a rattlesnake whose bite can no longer kill or injure or even sting, so inured is its victim to the unfairness and randomness of life.

Ray Begay, reads the marker, in neat, handwritten letters. *Loving son and brother. Born: Kayenta, Arizona, 1924. Died: Iwo Jima, 1945.*

And below it, scrawled in another hand, two additional words: *Semper Fi.*

JIMMIE STANDS AWKWARDLY AT RAY's gravesite, too numbed to move. He had known about Ray's gravesite back on Iwo Jima, of course. Yet somehow, Ray's family had the boy's body shipped back here. Rather surprising, for considering most Navajos' feelings about death, the majority of young men who fell in the South Pacific remain interred there. Besides, Jimmie had not known about this new veterans' cemetery until now, so how did Ray's family find out?

Tears well up in his eyes. It seems fate has found a way to bring them together again. Big and little brother. Best buddies. Closest friends. Despite their differences in age, despite their short time knowing one another.

Up at Chee's gravesite, the casket shudders under shovels full of earth. The platitudes and prayers are over. As the crowd begins to disperse, Jimmie walks up to Annie and touches her arm. No further gesture of sympathy seems necessary. Annie asks him if he has any plans for the days ahead, and he says yes, he does now, he has somewhere he desperately needs to go. He cannot put it off another day. Then he adds, "But I haven't forgotten what we talked about, what your father asked of me. I'll come visit you soon, I promise."

"I'm counting on it, Jimmie," she says. "You've seen what things are like on the reservation. I could use you with me in the fight."

"I'll be at your door before you know it, Annie. First I have to see if I can turn back into the Jimmie Goodluck you thought you knew."

"You were never anyone else." Then, as an afterthought, she says in her velvet voice, "And I do know one thing. My father would have never bet on a lame horse."

JIMMIE WAITS UNTIL THE CEMETERY is nearly deserted. Then he walks back to Ray's grave.

His body trembles. He cries softly, "Why did you have to be the one who died? Why not me instead of you, little brother?" It is a question he has asked many times over the past year and a half.

The falling temperature pierces his heavy jacket, but he is indifferent to the cold. Toward the east, the heavy skies are smeared with grays and sickly whites: the pallor of death, even above. All around is the smell of earth, and from somewhere far off, a faint bouquet of sage and mesquite. The wind whistles past him, its wintry breath reverberating in his eardrums.

Do not let my rope fall to the ground.

Not the wind, this. The voice is Chee's, every word coming through with a clarity the dying man never achieved in the hospital. Startled, Jimmie looks around, feeling foolish. There is no one close by except for a stray dog that limps past, nursing a wounded paw.

Jimmie squats beside the mound that covers Ray, runs his index finger over the frosted soil. "If it had to be one of us, it should have been me," Jimmie repeats to the wind, to the earth, to the flag that honors the man beneath.

If you discover it dropping ... quickly, quickly, you must catch it!

Again, Jimmie looks over his shoulder. The voice seems to come from everywhere, from nowhere. A trick of his imagination. The witchcraft his father believes in.

He looks back at Ray's grave. "You were so damn young. You joined the Corps to find a better life, as I did, and you lost all chance for any life at all."

Catch it ... catch it ... hold it aloft!

This time he does not lift his gaze from the frozen earth. Still talking as if Ray were listening, he murmurs, "How can your death ever mean anything? You gave your life for your country, but how does it begin to repay you?"

He waits once more for the voice of Chee Dodge, but it no longer calls out. The leader is silent now, silent for all time to come, his spirit already marching on its inescapable journey toward immortality.

No matter. Jimmie knows the answer. Chee has shown it to him after all, as has the wind, the silence of the graveyard, the yearnings of his own heart.

"*I'll* help your country repay you," he says aloud, addressing not just Ray, but all the unseen boys around him who can no longer speak for themselves. He knows now that he must find a way to stop wallowing in the bitterness that consumed Black Horse, consumes his father still. He must do what he can to make the government leaders listen, and then help his own people to see the world and all its possibilities as he and Ray had seen it once.

He stands up military straight, saluting the Marine Corps flag that overlooks Ray's grave. Tears stream down his face. If anyone is looking, he must appear mad, a buffoon, but for the first time in his life, he knows who he is.

"Do you remember what you once said to me, Ray? I'll never forget it. You said, 'I don't want to be a man for nothing.' Lemme tell you, little brother, you died a man. A better man than I've become. And you died for *something*: for the way of life this country has promised *all* of its people. That sure as hell isn't evident back here, but it can be. It has to be. Chee Dodge started the fight, now others will continue it. I swear to you, little brother, Chee's rope won't touch the ground while I live and breathe."

Jimmie reaches for the buckskin pouch hanging on the string around his neck. He opens it, removes a generous pinch of corn pollen, and then sprinkles it in the four directions around Ray's burial mound as he chants a prayer in Navajo.

When he is finished, he runs his hand over the hardened mound of earth as if it were fine silk. "Rest well, my friend. If the only way you can live on is through me, that is how it must be. *Bi'so'dih. An'jah. Wol'la'chee. Moasi. Ah'nah.*"

Pig. Ear. Ant. Cat. Eye.

Peace.

There is no code word for that.

TAKING ONE LAST, LINGERING LOOK at Ray's marker, Jimmie turns and walks up to Chee's gravesite, its freshly tamped dirt a darker color than the frost-encrusted soil surrounding it.

"I'll try my best to honor your wishes," he says quietly. There is so much more in his heart that he would like to express, but it is actions, not words, that are needed from this moment forward.

He puts his trembling hands in his pockets and begins walking back to St. Michael's, where his mother's horse is sheltered in the comfort of an old, weathered stable. If the Holy People are still looking down, they surely see him as an insignificant detail, a smudge against the landscape, one imperfect human being, struggling to accept his heavy burden, striving to find some measure of salvation.

He turns up his jacket collar in an effort to ward off the cold, for he has suddenly become aware of the plunging temperature. He is walking by himself, head leading forward into the wind as he strides with urgent resolve along the uneven road.

But he is not alone.

Ray is with him, and Jimmie's mind is already swirling with possibilities, with the tactics of battle yet ahead, the likes of which no Carlson's Raider has ever undertaken.

Harry, you and I owe these monuments a lot.

—John Wayne, written to Harry Goulding in the
Goulding Lodge guest book.

PART IV:

THE CHANGING

CHAPTER 20

JANUARY 1947

Does anyone still believe that the mesa tops in Monument Valley are stepping stones placed by the Holy Ones so they can reach the earth? Or that the landmark known as Comb Ridge is one of four arrowheads originally used to carve our planet? Or that the formations called "Left and Right Mittens" are really hands left behind by the gods as a sign they will return?

In this day and age, Jimmie assumes most Navajos no longer cling to these notions. Still, as he looks upon the strange and wonderful formations on this sacred land, the myths seem almost as incontrovertible as the picture on a can of peaches.

Tse' Bii' Ndzisgaii, the name of this place. The Changing of the Rock.

With the sandstone and shale found here—the spires and pinnacles and buttes and mesas that rise as carnelian-hued sentinels to overlook the valley—change has been slow, much as it has been for the people who live in the area. Still, for the *Dineh*, accommodation to the times is both inevitable and essential. Jimmie understands this once again, but he does not possess the arrogance to think that he alone can be the instrument to make it happen.

He decides to begin humbly, by trying to orchestrate his own transformation. A skinwalker in reverse: the wolf who becomes a man.

His first stop is Goulding's Lodge and Trading Post, sprawled a few miles north of Kayenta, barely a horse tail's length across the Utah border. The placard in front of the place observes that Harry Goulding started the business as a sheep ranch in 1923. Word has it that Goulding went to Hollywood with only sixty dollars in his pocket and talked director John Ford into coming to Monument Valley to film a cowboys-and-Indians movie—*Stagecoach*, they called it—the first of many shot here.

Ray once told Jimmie how his father had made a pair of Navajo boots for one of the stars of that picture, a newcomer named John Wayne. Then all the movie people wanted a pair—Andy Devine, John Carradine, even Ford himself—so Ray's father finally had to tell them he could not turn them out like flapjacks at a cowboy breakfast, and they seemed a bit put-out by that. But a few days later they came around and asked Ray's father if he would be in their movie. They needed more Indians, apparently, and even though the redskins in the story were Apaches, almost everyone in war paint who was not white was actually Navajo, and that's the movies for you, Ray had laughed.

It was the movies that brought the first business to the area and led to a steady flow of tourists. But in these postwar days, uranium ore is the big draw, and word has it that Harry Goulding has his fingers in that pot as well.

As it turns out, Goulding is not around when Jimmie stops by. One of Goulding's partners, Cal Jenks, speaks to Jimmie in the post's Ware Room, where he is stacking sacks of coffee. Half the space is filled with bags of raw wool, and in another corner, leather saddles, dozens of them, are piled high as if waiting for a rodeo. Jenks tells Jimmie he knows a number of Begay families in the area, but has no recollection of one with three daughters and a son who was in the marines. "Try Oljato," he suggests. "It ain't far. Mebbe the family yer lookin' fer trades there."

Snow falls gently as Jimmie follows the trail that curves like a sidewinder around a low mesa. This was all Paiute country at one time, until the state of Utah moved them north to more fertile acreage. The land then went into the public domain until it was unceremoniously given to the Navajos. A few weeks earlier, Jimmie would have added this widely known fact into his ledger of injustices, but he is no longer keeping a detailed accounting. He has replaced his anger with determination. It is a lighter burden to carry, and a better stimulus to propel him steadily in the right direction.

In just over an hour he reaches Oljato and its adobe brick trading post. A shiny red Texaco gas pump stands in front of the small one-story building, indicating that even here, at the end of a trail in a remote corner of the reservation, the gasoline engine is making vast inroads. Not that Jimmie suspects he is likely to own an automobile of his own any time soon.

As he enters, a bell attached to the door rings with a tinny jingle. The proprietor looks up from behind a dusty counter and greets him in the Navajo language. The man is an easygoing Anglo of about sixty, with warm smile lines around his mouth and a mustache so thick and bushy, it could act as a strainer when he eats or drinks.

Jimmie greets him with a weary hello. "I'm fine with English. Trying to locate a family that lives around here."

"What's the name?"

"Begay."

The trader laughs and sets down a heavy silver buckle, freshly polished. Pawn, most likely. "That's like going to Denver, where I'm from, and asking for someone named Jones."

"Yeah, I know. Had more than a few Joneses in the Marine Corps."

"You served? Good for you. If I was younger and healthier, woulda gone myself, as God is my witness."

Jimmie looks around the dimly lit store at the shelves heaped high with canned goods, sacks of corn meal and sugar, basic hand tools, and various handcrafts. Lassos and saddles hang down from the ceiling rafters. A display of hand-woven baskets, an impressive collection, actually, reminds him of something Ray once mentioned. Jimmie gestures to that corner of the room. "The Begay family I'm looking for? The mother and at least one daughter does this kind of work."

The trader steps out from behind the counter. "You just narrowed it down to two families who trade with me."

Feeling encouraged, Jimmie adds, "And the father, he makes Navajo boots. His son was also learning how. Ray was … was killed in action on Iwo Jima."

"Ah. Samuel and Maria."

The trader reaches up and, almost reverently, takes down two baskets made from sumac twigs that have been sewn tightly together with yucca fiber. Jimmie recognizes the first one as a ceremonial wedding basket, its rim designed to look like the pattern of juniper leaves.

"Maria Begay, Ray's mother, she made the wedding basket," the trader explains. "Probably gave up on saving it for her oldest daughter's wedding, so here it is. Now this one"—he indicates the second basket—"is made by Katherine, that daughter I just mentioned. She could be even better than her mother if she keeps at it."

Jimmie recognizes the name of Ray's sister, Katherine. Her basket is completely different from her mother's. It is jar-like in shape, with two handles of braided horsehair at the top. Jimmie can see how this one will hold water, for it is covered inside and out with a glassy coating of boiled piñon pitch.

The trader sets down the baskets. "Now come over here," he orders. His voice is filled with enthusiasm. Jimmie follows him to another corner of the room where the proprietor reaches up to a high shelf and takes down a pair of rust-colored men's boots crafted in the time-honored Navajo style.

"Samuel Begay made these," he says with admiration. "The tourists insist on calling 'em moccasins, but I say they're works of art. Few people on the rez make these anymore. Looky here: these soles are made from hand-molded, bleached white bull hide. And y'see where the buckskin uppers are sewed into the soles?"

Jimmie looks, but he cannot see it.

"'Course you don't see it!" the trader chortles. "Thread's hidden, so it can't be exposed to wear and tear. Sam told me that's customary, but I never seen nothin' like it. And y'see this here?" He points to the silver button that holds the buckskin together near the top, just below the ankle. "Lookit the control in the etching. Sam's boy made that button. Made a few of 'em before he went off to—well, Ray's death took Sam and the women real hard. You can imagine."

Jimmie's eyes tear up as he says, "Ray was my closest buddy in the Corps."

The trader sets the boots down as if they were fragile. "I didn't know the boy well myself. Never came in here much. But I feel for his family." He sighs, deep and long. "Yup, terrible thing, it was. Folks off the rez got no idea how many Navajo boys gave their lives."

"Can you tell me how to find Ray's family?" Jimmie asks.

"Their *hogan*'s three, maybe four miles from here. I'll draw you a little map, you shouldn't have no trouble. Name's Bill Whisky, by the way." He extends his hand. "Whisky, like the drink."

They shake. "Nice to meet you, Mr. Whiskey-like-the-drink."

"Always a pleasure to shake hands with a serviceman. Say, when you see Sam and Maria Begay, you tell 'em I said 'Hi.'"

"I'll do that."

Jimmie drifts back toward the boots as the trader scratches out a crude map on a scrap of paper. He runs his fingers over the supple buckskin and the handcrafted silver button of the father-son creation. Holding one of them next to his own boots, he checks to see if the soles are reasonably close in length.

"Uh, how much for these here, Mr. Whisky?" he asks.

"Call me Bill. You talkin' cash or trade?"

"Got nothing to trade 'cept some cash."

"Y'know, if you're going to see Samuel anyway, he could probably make you a pair cheaper'n I can sell these to you. Cut out the middleman."

"Don't know as he'd let me pay for them if I asked him. Or if he has any of Ray's buttons left. So I figure you'll give me a fair price for these here."

Whisky runs his thumb and forefinger over his mustache, as if it helps him to think. "Well, to the tourist trade—and we don't get too many who set out past Goulding's—I'd ask ten bucks. But you're a friend of Sam's son. How does six sound? Two-thirds of that goes right to Sam's line of credit here."

Jimmie hands over six one-dollar bills, but he does not put on the new boots. Not to parade in front of Ray's family. "Do me a favor? Keep 'em for me and I'll pick 'em up on my way back."

"Uh, sure," Bill replies as he hands over his hand-drawn map of directions.

Jimmie is practically out the door when Bill calls after him, "Oh, and if Katherine's at home while you're visiting—she's the daughter I told you about, the one that ain't married—best lock up your heart, young man."

Jimmie stops and turns around. "How's that?"

The grin on Bill's face is broad enough to have been classified as "shit-eating" in the marines. "Hell, young man, if you have the good fortune to meet her, I reckon you'll know well enough what I'm talking about."

IT TAKES JIMMIE LESS THAN an hour to locate the Begays' *hogan*. He fears that, by showing up unannounced, his presence will reopen the fabric of their grieving. Then again, he also admonishes himself for not coming sooner. But here he is. Perhaps they can still help one another come to terms with Ray's untimely death.

The Begay *hogan* is a typical six-sided log structure with a separate sheltered enclosure for livestock. A thick plume of smoke drifts up from the hole in the center of the roof. The smell of the burning mesquite is intoxicating on this mild winter afternoon. Jimmie positions his horse outside the *hogan* with the wind at his back. It would be poor manners to go up to the door and knock, so he sits in the saddle and waits for someone to notice him. Two dogs, one black and one white, bark loudly to announce his presence. The reservation equivalent of a doorbell.

Soon the door opens and a woman in her early fifties peers out.

"Are you lost?" she asks. The way she says it, in Navajo: "Are you without direction?"

"Not anymore," Jimmie answers in his native tongue, smiling. He dismounts and walks toward her. "I hope you're not upset that I have come here. See, I was in the marines with … with Ray. You don't know me, my name is Jimmie Goodluck."

"But I *do* know you!" she exclaims, running toward him. "Ray wrote that he called you his big brother. Said you were his best friend. We got some letters right after he signed up, and then again at the end of the war when they … they came all at once." Her voice falters. She dabs at her eyes with the sleeve of her velveteen blouse.

"This is going to upset you. I shouldn't have come." Jimmie
averts his eyes, for Ray's mother comes up very close to him. She is a
short woman, just over five feet, with a trim figure and smooth skin.
The smell of her hair reminds Jimmie of roasted coffee.

"Nonsense!" Maria says. "We were praying you would come and
tell us about our son during the … last part of his life. We need to
hear it." She extends her hand to her son's best friend, palm upward.
"I am Maria Begay. *Tachii'nii* clan. It is good to finally meet the
young man who meant so much to Ray."

Jimmie identifies his mother's clan as he brushes his palm against
hers. "He meant just as much to me. Still does."

Maria touches his elbow lightly. "Please, take your horse to the
shelter. Then come inside and meet Samuel. I have the fire going."

The *hogan* is immaculately clean inside, the way Jimmie's mother
keeps hers. Fragrant dried herbs hang from the rafters, along with
several wide-brimmed hats and a handsome bow. Pots and pans are
stacked neatly by the central fire. On the north side of the room—
the male side—Ray's father is crouched on the floor, surrounded
by scraps of leather and various hand tools as he works on a pair
of boots. Samuel is as stocky as his wife is slender. When he stands
to greet the visitor, he is a full head taller than Maria. Jimmie
recognizes at once the deep-set eyes, the broad nose: a heavier, older
version of Ray.

"Our prayers have been answered," Maria tells her husband.
"This is Jimmie, Ray's friend that he wrote about."

Samuel regards his guest without expression. From all
appearances, he is not surprised to see Jimmie. "You must have
traveled a great distance. We are glad you are here."

"I should have come sooner. I meant to, but …" he trails off,
refusing to lapse into excuses.

"But you have come now, that is what matters," says Maria,
pushing him over toward the stove in the center of the room. "And

you will stay with us for a while." Not a question, a statement. "We are honored."

Jimmie starts to protest, though they all know he would never refuse the hospitality.

"We have much we want to ask you," Samuel says, brushing his hands against the thighs of his pants. "Our daughters will also want to hear what you can say about their brother. Betty lives about a three-day ride from here, but Lorraine is much closer. She will come. And Katherine, she should be home soon. She lives here with us."

"She spends several days a week at the health clinic in Kayenta," Maria explains. "It is all we have for hundreds of miles. She has been trying to locate you, our Katherine. You should know that. She was going to write to the marines to ask them if they could find you."

Samuel chuckles. "She is determined, that is for sure."

"Sounds like a woman I know," Jimmie says, rubbing his hands together. The warmth of the fire feels like fleece, invisible against his skin.

"Your wife?" Maria asks. Her face is a mask of innocence, although Jimmie suspects she is asking—as the whites might say—a loaded question.

"I'm not married. Actually, I was thinking of Annie Wauneka, daughter of Chee Dodge. We've been friends since school."

"Heard he died a week or two ago, Mr. Interpreter," Samuel says. He adds a mesquite branch to the fire. "A good man, I think."

"Yes, I was at the funeral." Jimmie turns away, unable to look in the direction of Ray's parents. "He was buried at the new veterans' cemetery. That's where … where I saw Ray's burial place."

Nobody responds. For several seconds, Jimmie hears only the sound of the wood crackling in the fire pit. The wood, and the whistling of the wind outside that tries, but fails, to penetrate the tight spaces between the logs of the *hogan*.

Maria regains her voice, although it trembles with emotion.

"Katherine convinced us to bring him home to the reservation. 'Bury him with dignity among his own people,' she begged us. 'Do not leave him on the faraway island where jungle animals might disturb his bones.'"

"We knew she was right," Samuel adds. "These are modern times. Not like when I was a boy. Ray should be back in the country he gave his life for. It is a good thing, this new burial ground. I do not believe there can be *chindi* in that place."

"In honor of the best friend of my son," Maria says, fighting back tears, "we must have a special meal. There will be time to talk after that." She looks at her husband and asks, "Do we still have mutton ribs stored in the frozen ground?"

"We do, and I have been saving them for a day such as this one."

"Bring them to me," Maria instructs her husband.

From outside comes the whinny of a horse, accompanied by the barking dogs. "Ah," Maria says. "Katherine is home."

Moments later the door opens and a blast of cool air enters the room, followed by Ray's sister. But it is not the cold air that takes Jimmie's breath away.

"Getting chilly again," Katherine says in Navajo to no one in particular. "It looks like—" She stops abruptly as her eyes sweep over the newcomer. "I see we have a guest."

There is no particular enthusiasm in the way she says it, but Jimmie does not notice. He is too preoccupied with her lustrous, black hair that falls to her shoulders, framing her coppery skin as if an oval of jasper were inlaid in jet onyx. For the first time, Jimmie understands the Anglo expression "flashing eyes"—Bulldog McClintock used the cliché to describe one of his many girlfriends—for Katherine's brown eyes radiate a fire and intelligence that draw him in, envelop him. He is further hypnotized by her full lips which part to reveal teeth as white as primrose. In the past, he was never one to put too much emphasis on physical appearance. But right now, looking at Ray's sister, he is inclined to make an exception.

Standing roll-call straight, he stammers, "Hello, Katherine. I was a close friend of your brother. My name is Jimmie Goodluck."

Katherine flashes the briefest of smiles and then asks quite sharply, "What took you so long to find us?"

Jimmie offers a sheepish look in place of an answer.

Katherine walks to the stove. She removes her sheepskin coat, revealing a Coke bottle figure. Jimmie immediately wonders how she has managed to remain unmarried. Then he remembers Bill Whisky's words—*best lock up your heart, young man!*—and he knows, sure as anything, she has turned down many suitors.

But romance is the furthest thing from his mind, his life being as unsettled as it is. He is here for a purpose. Ray's parents and sisters are looking for comfort, and already he feels a strong kinship to them. Truth is, Jimmie needs to see Ray's family as much as they desperately need to talk to him. So why has he suddenly become so tongue-tied simply because Ray's sister is pleasing to look at? She is his dead buddy's *sister*, after all.

"We told Jimmie he is here now, and that is all that matters," Maria says, rising to Jimmie's defense. "He will be staying with us for two days at least." This time, the way she looks him when she says it, with her eyebrows raised, leads him to believe it is a question.

He nods. At this moment, being anywhere else is unimaginable..

"There will be more than enough time to hear what Jimmie can tell us about our beautiful Ray," Maria continues. "But not until he is fed and comfortable."

Katherine looks at Jimmie critically, as if she were appraising a new coat or a blanket. She switches easily to English. "Ray wrote that they called you *cheii*. You're younger than I thought you would be."

"I was twenty-eight when I enlisted. Compared to almost everyone else in our platoon, I *was* an old man."

Katherine's voice takes on a sharper edge. "We never heard from Ray after he went overseas. Then we got all of Ray's letters at once, dozens of them, written over nearly a three-year period. Did my parents tell you that? How they worried because we never got answers to my letters? Not knowing throughout the war if he even got our mail, or if he was alive or dead, only to find out toward the end that our worst fears had come true?"

"What are you saying?" Maria asks.

"Speak in Navajo so we can understand," Samuel pleads.

"In a moment, give me a moment," Katherine says in Navajo. Again, to Jimmie in English: "I'm asking because at the clinic I met a young woman, a Paiute, who said her best friend's brother was in the war and they got letters from him at least once a week. I never told my parents that. They think the mail delivery was one-way for everyone during the war."

It is not easy for Jimmie to talk in front of her parents in a language they do not comprehend, but Katherine obviously wants it this way.

"We found out only toward the end of the war," he explains. "Our letters home to the reservation were being ... confiscated, withheld, we were never sure. Not everyone's. Only those Navajos, like Ray and me, who had special duties in the marines. I can guess the reasons, though I'm not at liberty to discuss it, even now. Still, it was unnecessary. I stopped writing home when I found out. What was the point? But Ray, he kept on writing letters to you as if they were going right on a mail plane headed directly to your trading post."

Katherine's eyes grow moist while Maria and Samuel Begay clamor more insistently for them to speak in Navajo. Switching back to their native language, Jimmie says, "You have no idea how much your letters meant to Ray. You were practically all he talked about."

"I was asking him why all the mail came at once," Katherine finally explains to her parents. "He said he does not know."

"Speak in Navajo from now on," Maria orders her daughter, "so we can understand everything. But for now, come help me prepare the meal. We have a special guest. Where is our hospitality?"

THE MEAL OF MUTTON RIBS, fry bread, and—a special treat—canned pears is a real feast for Jimmie and, he suspects, for the Begays as well. Over dinner they talk about their crafts—Maria's and Katherine's baskets, Samuel's Navajo boots—and Jimmie expresses his admiration for their respective skills. He tells them about his mother's exquisite rugs and blankets, but says nothing about his father until they specifically ask. He answers simply that Wilson's days are spent taking care of the livestock. Then he changes the subject. His sense of shame rises not so much from his father's belligerence, but from his own fallibility, from his recent weakness in succumbing to his father's anger with—with just about everyone.

It is well after the meal that they exhaust the pleasantries and polite exchanges of information. Finally, the conversation turns to Ray. This is the topic that has been towering over them all from the beginning.

Jimmie tells the Begays how he met Ray while standing in line to enlist, and about how Ray filled himself with water to meet the weight requirement. He describes their budding friendship during boot camp and communications school. Naturally, he omits any reference to the code, though his heart aches to tell them of Ray's contribution to this secret weapon. He wonders if the truth will ever come out in their lifetime.

Over endless cups of coffee, he explains that he and Ray were a team throughout much of the war—communications partners, is how he puts it, glossing over specific details. He talks about how Evans Carlson selected the two of them to join the Raiders, keeping Ray close by his side—here he embellishes the facts a little—as his personal radioman on Guadalcanal. He mentions Ray's distinguished service during the Bougainville campaign and then on Saipan. He tells how Ray was wounded in an ambush and was saved by Carlson himself. Then he goes into detail about how he and Ray were reunited after Ray returned from New Zealand, leading up to their final campaign on Iwo Jima.

There is much more to tell, but by this time the hour is very late. Jimmie is relieved when Maria suggests that they all get some sleep. He insists on sleeping in the livestock shelter, but Ray's parents argue that since he is their honored guest, he must stay in the *hogan* with them. Katherine is silent throughout this debate, for she undoubtedly finds the situation equally awkward. Customarily, many Navajos do not undress to go to sleep, but still …

As things turn out, the wishes of Maria and Samuel prevail, and soon Jimmie falls fast asleep on a luxurious sheepskin Maria has laid out for him across the room from where Katherine sleeps.

It must be a dream, then, that finds Jimmie and Katherine much, much closer together. In the dream, the laughing, taunting voice of Ray reverberates wickedly, sounding every bit as playful as the first time Ray spoke the same words in Uncle Harry's San Diego bar. It chortles, *No old guy with a hard-on is goin' near my sister!*

To Jimmie's delight, Ray's voice has it all wrong.

CHAPTER 21

JANUARY 1947

In the soft, spangled light of early morning, Maria opens the door, framing a slice of sun that spills molten gold over the horizon. Everyone is awake, looking out onto the fresh coating of snow that has fallen during the night. The air is clean and brisk. The clouds that brought the snow are gone, except for a few cottony wisps that slowly drift to the east. When the sun gets higher, this will be a picture postcard winter day, a study in contrasts: the reflective white snow, the emerging browns and greens of winter desert plants, the terra cotta sandstone, the broad patches of azure sky.

After a breakfast of Cream of Wheat, fry bread, and coffee, Katherine asks Jimmie, "Have you ever seen *Tse' Bii' Ndzisganii* blanketed in snow? On a day like today, with sunny skies?" She uses the Navajo name for Monument Valley.

"No, never." Jimmie tries to conjure up a mental picture, but he is certain his imagination is no match for the real thing.

"If you'd like, we can ride over there, you and me. I'm not scheduled at the clinic today."

"I'd like that," he says, wondering if Katherine has an ulterior motive for suggesting the diversion. Whether that thought is cynical or merely hopeful he cannot say.

"Katherine is a good guide," Samuel remarks. "But don't stay too long, you two. There is still much we need to hear."

"Of course, Father," Katherine says in a respectful voice. The Begays are clearly a close-knit family, undoubtedly drawn even closer by their tragic loss.

Katherine, very much a modern young woman, changes into denim pants for the ten-mile ride. A woman in pants is not commonplace on the reservation; Jimmie admires her self-confidence. The rest of her attire is conventional: velveteen blouse, simple turquoise necklace, Pendleton blanket draped over her shoulders. On her feet are Navajo boots, calf-length, in the women's style. Jimmie considers telling her how good she looks but stops himself from saying the words. In some ways, the Japanese were easier to face than Katherine Begay.

Jimmie puts on his fleece jacket over his one clean shirt (wishing he had brought nicer clothes), and then they walk to their horses. The snow is about three inches deep in some spots, less in others. Already the sun is melting the surface layer, leaving small pools of moisture on top of the thin, frosty base beneath. Jimmie shields his eyes with his hand to reduce the glare. In the distance, far to the east, rises the pinnacle known as "Totem Pole," which towers four hundred feet above the desert floor.

Sniffing the air, he inhales the mesquite smoke, sweet and penetrating, that drifts up through the hole at the top of the *hogan*. As the smoke rises on the winter currents, he sees the world through keen, fresh eyes—Ray's eyes, sweeping over the landscape they knew so well, before they refocused on images of war and were extinguished.

For the first half hour, Jimmie and Katherine ride quietly toward the valley. Their horses move slowly, hooves lifted high as they plod through the slush. There is so much Jimmie would like to know about Katherine. He begins by asking, "How did you get involved with the clinic? And what do you do there?"

Katherine looks straight ahead and answers, "I go there because I wasn't born to make babies and baskets as my mother chose to do. I'm here to make a difference." She brushes aside a strand of hair that has blown across her face. "Don't get me wrong, I respect my mother, but we're a different generation from our parents, you and me. I've been lucky to get some schooling. Not all I'd like, but enough to understand the problems here and maybe help a little. If I could afford the education to become a nurse, that's what I'd do. So I do the next best thing and help out where I can." Her horse lets out a loud snort, as if he were making a comment. Katherine ignores it and goes on. "The clinic, if you can even call it that, isn't much. The old Kayenta hospital— well, it was a sanatorium, really—it closed in late '43. The few doctors and nurses who worked there moved on."

"It's terrible, the hospital closing."

"That was only the beginning. Four other hospitals on the reservation also disappeared around the same time. Word is, the hospital in Chinle will shut its doors any day now. That means we'll be down to half the hospitals and doctors we had before the war." Katherine sighs deeply. "Hospitals, schools, it's all the same. Budgets get cut and the money disappears—what little came our way in the first place. Now more people are sick, with fewer places to treat them, and few roads to get them there. Same with teachers and schools."

"I remember stories of children being kidnapped to fill the boarding schools," Jimmie remarks, thinking of his father's tale of the incident at Round Rock. "Now it seems the government doesn't care whether we're dumb Indians or dead Indians."

"You think it's that they don't care, or simply don't know how our needs have changed?"

"What you're asking is whether they're indifferent or merely ignorant. Is one better than the other?"

A fleeting smile dances across Katherine's face. Then it vanishes, an extinguished spark. "At our clinic, we try to educate people, mostly, because we can't do much else. I don't have the training or the materials. So I watch for signs of tuberculosis and other serious illnesses. I try to explain that sometimes only white doctors have the right medicine. You can imagine how that's received, especially by the elders. To them, hospitals are places you go to die, not to get better. And for good reason. By the time most of them agree to be hospitalized, they're too sick to be helped, so they *do* die there. Now the closest hospitals to us are days away, either Tuba City or Shiprock."

"I understand your frustration. Annie Wauneka was telling me that—"

"You know Annie Wauneka?" Katherine twists in her saddle, looking directly at Jimmie for the first time since they set out. "Annie *Dodge* Wauneka?"

"Well, yes, Annie and I are old friends, actually. I worked with her father for a while, too, before the war."

Katherine's whole face lights up, but it is not Jimmie's mention of Annie's renowned father that piques her excitement. "It was Mrs. Wauneka's radio broadcasts that got me interested in helping out at the clinic."

"Radio broadcasts?"

"You know, the ones she does in Navajo. Sunday mornings on that Gallup station." Seeing his puzzled expression, she adds, "Guess you don't know, do you?"

He shakes his head. When he caught up with Annie at Sage Memorial, he wanted to ask what she had been up to, but then the talk turned to her father.

"I have to remember what a short time you've been back," Katherine says. "I have to remember the war didn't stop with Ray's death."

The mention of Ray leads them both to withdraw for a while. In silence, they pass a stand of tall greasewood plants. The shrubs poke high above the melting snow, their thorny black stems and gray-green leaves offering a colorful contrast to the white blanket beneath. Jimmie recalls how his mother chewed a piece of greasewood and applied it to the site of a bee sting when he was seven or eight, after he foolishly poked a hive looking for honey.

"Tell me something about yourself," Katherine says at last. "Where you went to school, what you did before the war."

He tells her about his schooling, his many jobs, his involvement with Annie and her father, his stint with the Indian Service as a translator. She listens with such apparent interest that he keeps on talking, touching on his disillusionment upon returning, but avoiding any mention of peyote or his involvement in violent protest. "I'm trying to put all that behind me now," he concludes. And then he apologizes for talking so much.

"I'm the one who should apologize for prying," Katherine says. "But I'm glad I did."

"Ray talked about you with such affection." The words fly out before Jimmie can hold them back. "He told me many times how smart and how attractive you are. I thought at the time he must be exaggerating. He wasn't."

"Thanks." She says it so matter-of-factly, it is as if she has heard such compliments many times before, and that they hold little meaning for her.

"What's easy for *me* to see is why Ray became so attached to you," she says. "Ray always had a good instinct for people." Her breathing is heavy as she wanders in the labyrinth of some personal memory. Then she adds, "I'm glad he had you for a friend."

And now they enter the heart of Monument Valley, which opens up before them, nature's movie set resplendent in its stage dressing of patchy snow, and there is nothing more mere words can add to the wonder of the moment.

KATHERINE AND JIMMIE WANDER AMONG the dramatic formations, enjoying the solitude and majesty of the place. Jimmie has been here twice before, in other seasons. Each time the sacred valley has cast a different spell, depending on the season and the time of day. But never has it appeared more seductive. Today, an intense light reflects off of the snow. Blue-gray shadows dance off the scattered shrubs and trees onto the white desert floor. Magenta formations of sandstone rise all around in dots and dashes like a topographical Morse code. And above all else, a fascinating woman rides beside him.

As they talk of their interests and of their pasts, both distant and recent, their conversation never strays far from recollections that center on Ray. Jimmie tells Katherine about the time he and Ray sneaked cactus water while on maneuvers. Katherine remembers the first time Ray went with the family to a sheep dip behind the trading post, how upset her little brother became when his father pulled Ray's favorite lamb from his arms and submerged it in the trough filled with the antiseptic solution of water and nicotine.

Jimmie tries to steer the conversation back to Katherine herself, for now he is anxious to learn more about what lies beneath her appealing surface. Over the course of their ride he does manage to learn that she dotes on her sister Lorraine's two children. That she loves watermelon and, oddly enough, likes her coffee strong. That while she made several baskets to please her mother, she has no interest in taking up time that might be better spent working with people. That the smell of roasting piñon is her favorite scent and making cat's cradles on her fingers with string or yarn helps her to relax.

With great reluctance they eventually put Monument Valley behind them and head back toward her parents' home. At one point she looks over and says, "Tonight, you will tell us of my brother's ... last days. We know he died on an island called Eema Jeema—"

"Iwo Jima," Jimmie says softly. How he loathes the words.

"Yes, but we don't know *how* he died, or whether he suffered. I know it will be as hard for you to speak of it as it will be for us to hear, but we have to know."

"I can tell you now he didn't suffer. And yes, tonight I'll tell you everything else that I can."

The most difficult part of the evening will be knowing that, when he finishes talking about Ray, he will have no excuse to stay any longer, no chance to get to know Katherine a little better.

"Y'know, you lost a brother, and so did I," Jimmie says, as overhead, a red-tailed hawk flies in lazy circles. "He was like a little brother to me. And he looked up to me, I think, though I can't understand why."

"Are you always so hard on yourself?"

Katherine's question catches him off guard. "I don't know. It's just that ... I made a promise to Ray. At the cemetery. If he was looking up to me before, I need to believe he's looking down now. I'm afraid I'll disappoint him."

Katherine smiles and lowers her eyes. "I may have only just met you, Jimmie Goodluck, but from what my brother wrote, and from what I have seen so far, I find it hard to believe you could let anyone down."

Her response sends him soaring, and his heart melts like the snow underfoot, which pools into a slushy mass as it draws in the shimmering rays of the late afternoon sun.

THEY SIT AROUND THE FIRE in the center of the *hogan*. Ray's mother and father are across from Jimmie, sitting close together. Maria tightly grips Samuel's wrist. Katherine is well to Jimmie's right, legs drawn back under the fresh calico skirt that spreads out around her on the blanketed earthen floor like the petals of a flower. Jimmie wonders if she might move closer when he pieces together the last days of Ray's life, but he suspects there will be little comfort taken from anyone present, no matter how close the bodies or how tight the grasp of hands.

There is a fifth person present, to Jimmie's left: Ray's youngest sister, Lorraine. Samuel went to get her while he and Katherine were out riding. The whole family expresses regret that Ray's third sister, Betty, lives too far away to join them on this somber night.

"And what about your family?" Lorraine asks Jimmie shortly after they are introduced. "Do you have children?"

Jimmie explains that he is not married.

"Oh," she says cheerfully. "And your clans?"

Clearly she is asking to see if they are related, so Jimmie tells her his mother's people. Apparently satisfied with the partial answer, Lorraine raises her eyebrows and smiles at her older sister. Instead of glaring back, as Jimmie half expects her to do, Katherine blushes and quickly turns her head away.

Lorraine is not as attractive as her older sister. Her face is rounder and darker, her figure less defined. She bears a much stronger resemblance to Ray than does Katherine, and the way she smiles, just like her late brother, sends a chill though Jimmie.

He cautions, "What I have yet to tell you will be difficult for you to hear."

"We must hear everything," Maria says. "We still do not understand how our son died, under what circumstances."

Nor will you ever know everything. Ray's contribution to the code will stay unrecognized even by those who love him most. What Jimmie says aloud is, "All right then, I'll go on. But you must understand, I wasn't with Ray when … the end came." He glances over at Katherine. "I wish I was. I was wounded a short time later and left Iwo Jima, but that was nothing. Ray had his whole life ahead of him. It should be me in the ground."

"Don't say such words, Jimmie," Katherine snaps. Angry, now, her eyes more searing than the blazing mesquite before them. "You don't deserve to die any more than my brother did. It's not your place to question who is with the spirits, or to seek a change of places. *We don't resent that you survived, so why should you?* Be grateful you came back, as we are grateful you came to see us."

Jimmie looks down at the ground. "I s'pose you're right. Forgive me."

"There is nothing to forgive, friend of my son." The words are Samuel's. "Your heart cries out, as our hearts do, for what is lost."

Softly this time, and with compassion, Katherine adds, "You have nothing to feel guilty about, Jimmie. That's all we're trying to say. Will you please go on?"

"Yes, of course." He cups his hands and blows into them, for they have suddenly become cold in spite of the warm fire. He takes a deep breath. The only sounds within the *hogan* are his exhalation and the crackling of the mesquite logs.

He closes his eyes and visualizes that moment when he stood on the crowded deck of the attack transport USS *Bayfield*, Ray by his side, the two of them straining to get their first look at Iwo Jima, which crouched like a cat in the distance, murky and foreboding, a malevolent *chindi* of earth and rock. On the maps, the island resembled a leg of mutton. But seen there, from just off the southeastern coastline, it wrapped itself in the smoke of heavy aerial and naval bombardment, along with enough of its own noxious subterranean discharges, to conceal its shape and accessibility from closer inspection.

Somewhere out there the enemy was lying in wait within their island fortresses, concealed in their secret pillboxes and concrete block houses and caves and tunnels. *What do they see,* he wondered at the time, *when they poke their heads up and look out to sea? Does the armada of the Fifth Fleet, with more than 450 ships silhouetted against the first gash of light, churn some level of fear in them? Are they praying to their gods just as Ray and I are praying to ours?*

The Begays wait patiently for Jimmie to collect his thoughts. He sees it clearly now: his ship disemboweling its LSTs, the landing vehicles which move like lines of ducks, each in their narrow lanes, to propel their precious cargo toward the designated beaches on that bright, indelible morning and then spew them like driftwood onto the black and bloody sands of hell.

"Ray went ashore at about 0920 hours," Jimmie begins, telling all that he knows with the exception of the code, surprising himself at how quickly, urgently, the words come spilling out ...

CHAPTER 22

FEBRUARY 1945

Ray went ashore at 0920 hours, once again teamed with Lieutenant Colonel Chambers in the Third Battalion, HQ Company. He was among the first wave of marines to hit the beach.

Jimmie's orders, on the other hand, had him serving alongside Colonel Lanigan, the regimental commander. That assignment earned him the relative safety of the flagship during the initial assault, fielding messages from all three battalions and relaying orders back. Jimmie wished he could protect his little brother by changing places, but their destinies were sealed: a sand painting set immutably in glue.

Ray's communications counterparts in the other two battalions were two Navajos Jimmie had met in Honolulu: Freddie Yellowhair, a bespectacled young man from somewhere near Tuba City, and a very shy Sidney Sandoval. Though lacking in combat experience, Yellowhair and Sandoval had proved facile with the code in practice back in Hawaii.

It was no secret among the men of the Twenty-Fifth Marines that their regiment had been given the Fourth Division's arguably most difficult objective: to take the steep, heavily fortified quarry cliffs immediately to the northeast of their designated landing area. Further landings were impossible with the beachhead so vulnerable to enemy fire from these cliffs, which dominated the terrain just as the formidable monolith Mount Suribachi—"Sonofabitchi," they all called it—towered above landing areas to the southwest. The battalions had orders to hit the beach and execute a right turn, heading toward the cliffs.

No one thought this would be easy. General Cates himself had commented, "If I knew the name of the man on the extreme right of the right-hand squad, I'd recommend him for a medal before we even go in."

Ray was a part of two marine divisions that landed abreast in consecutive assault waves, fighting the narrow and violent surf zone. The surf turned out to be less formidable than the steep, onerous beach, for the sands of Iwo Jima were actually fifteen-foot-high terraces of powdery volcanic ash. In one of the first radio reports Jimmie received, an officer described moving through the ash as like trying to move men and artillery through coffee grounds.

Enemy fire was light for the first twenty minutes or so. The Japanese held back until the beaches filled up in a chaotic confluence of marines and supplies, all bogged down in the soft, ashen sand.

Then the slaughter began.

The Japanese opened up with machineguns, mortar, artillery, and rocket fire. The men in Ray's battalion fought mostly on their bellies as they attempted to move over the volcanic terrain to their assigned positions.

Fresh waves of marines and heavy equipment came ashore every five minutes or so. But with those already on the beach impeded by the intractable terraces of ash, by heavy enemy fire, by hidden mine fields, and by the mounting loss of officers, organization within many of the troops quickly deteriorated. By all accounts, the carnage on the beach was unspeakable, with few bodies even remotely recognizable as having once been human.

"Jumpin' Joe" Chambers did his best to pull his companies together and execute the orders to move out sharply to the right and take the high ground overlooking the quarry. Jimmie's radio crackled with rapid-fire messages from Freddie and Ray. Both reported difficult advancement and heavy casualties. Jimmie, in his claustrophobic and airless communications room, decoded Ray's message to read, *From Third BTN HQ. Heavy mortar and machine-gun fire from quarry cliffs.* He handed it to a runner to deliver to Colonel Lanigan in his war room on the ship.

A short while later, Ray radioed another message. The Navajo words, when translated, read *Ahead ten ten yards. Loss come together with red soil number one. Space between.* Without a second thought, Jimmie bypassed each word's literal meaning and jumped directly to the code word or letter. What he scribbled down was, *Advanced one hundred yards. Lost contact with First BTN. Gap open between us.* He passed it on to his runner, who had just returned and was leaning against the doorjamb awaiting further messages.

Throughout the morning, Ray's messages remained concise and accurate, but his voice had become taut as fencing wire. Key officers in both active battalions of the regiment had been killed or seriously wounded within their first two hours on Iwo. The men were easy targets for the accurate small-arms fire coming from the very cliffs they needed to ascend and conquer. The fire from automatic weapons was so intense, Chambers later reported, "You could've held up a cigarette and lit it on the stuff going by."

Colonel Lanigan decided to send in his reserve Second Battalion to aid Chambers in taking the high ground along with the quarry and a nearby airfield. After an hour and a half, Ray's battalion had advanced just two hundred yards along the beach toward the quarry.

Jimmie realized he had been on the radio net for six straight hours without relief, but before he could dwell on it, he was buried under a new flurry of orders and messages to and from Colonel Lanigan. One of his communications ordered Company L, with Ray's company attached, to take the ridge line to the extreme right, which included the heavily fortified quarry. Jimmie shuddered as General Cates's words came back to him.

Moments later, Colonel Lanigan committed two fresh companies from a reserve battalion. Now Sidney Sandoval sprang to life, adding another Navajo talker to the regimental radio net. Jimmie could barely keep up.

In midafternoon, Jimmie left the ship with Colonel Lanigan and others to help set up a command post on the island. During the landing, he was out of radio contact while his unit struggled to get settled. The carnage he saw when he hit the beach was more intense than anything he had witnessed before. Overturned boats, tanks, tractors, and other vehicles were in flames or mired in the sand. Bodies and body parts were strewn as far as he could see, the stench of death intermingling with the odious smell of sulfur that the island emitted in great flatulent bursts.

By 1800 hours, after Jimmie had settled into the command post near the beach, he anxiously tried to raise Ray on the radio. No response. He radioed Sandoval, whose battalion flanked Ray's, but Sandoval reported he had also lost contact with Ray. When the radio finally leapt to life a half hour later, the voice coming through was high and strained.

Bi'ne'yei ul'so, Ray shouted breathlessly. *Objective accomplished.* Then, in a flurry of coded Navajo words, he said triumphantly, *Third Battalion occupies ridge and quarry.*

The all-day struggle to overtake the high ground that overlooked the beach and quarry was over.

The victory had come at a terrible cost: Chambers's Third

Battalion lost nearly half of its men, including nineteen officers. And as dusk settled in, the surviving beleaguered troops were still fending off enemy assaults on their newly gained position. So Jimmie was thrilled to radio a new message from Colonel Lanigan that told Chambers his men were being relieved for the night by two fresh companies.

A terse radio message at midnight told Jimmie that Ray and his fellow survivors, weary and shaken, many with bandaged wounds, had trudged a hundred yards toward the rear, well behind the front lines atop the tenuously occupied ridge. There they dug in for the night, a shattered, exhausted battalion, boys who had quickly become men and then, all having lost close buddies in the preceding hours, became boys again, just for a while, crying in their bunkers.

Knowing that Ray was close by, Jimmie felt helpless for not being able to offer him some comfort. All he could proffer was a prayer, and it was with this prayer on his lips that he finally fell into a light, restless sleep, in spite of the sickening odors permeating the air, in spite of the steady bursts of gunfire piercing the darkness, in spite of his unsettling premonition that he would never look upon Ray's guileless face again.

JIMMIE AWOKE SUDDENLY, STARTLED AND disoriented, at 0400. A light rain had begun to fall. Staccato bursts of gunfire broke the uneasy silence from somewhere in the distance.

"Hey, Chief, rise and shine." Gently shaking him was Gerry Weiner, a runner who carried a fistful of messages from Colonel Lanigan.

"Starting already?" Jimmie asked, trying to dissipate the fog in his head.

"Hell, it never stopped," said Weiner, an affable young man who mentioned on the ship coming over that he wanted to be a stock trader after the war. Jimmie had no idea what that involved, but he was sure that with the government-enforced stock reduction on the reservation, it would never catch on there.

Weiner shoved some papers into Jimmie's hands. "Be glad you got a couple hours shut-eye, Goodluck. The boss needs these sent in Indian-talk right away."

Jimmie scanned the orders and saw they were the operational instructions to the battalion commanders for day two. He was heartened to read that Ray's battalion would remain in reserve as the attack pressed on. He wished he could raise Ray on the radio and talk to him, marine to marine, but he needed to keep the frequency open for the active battalions. Soon the steady thrum of messages, both incoming and outgoing, gave him no time to think about anything but his duties. He was on the radio net practically nonstop the entire morning.

At 1430 hours, a breach opened between the First and Second Battalions. Jimmie radioed Ray with orders for his colonel to commit the "Ghouls"—as they glibly called Chambers's battalions—back into action to fill the gap. The depleted battalion to which Ray was assigned had dropped to half of its original strength, and now those who were left were heading once more to the front lines. The bedraggled units moved out immediately, meeting with heavy fire. To make matters worse, the day's intermittent rainfall turned into a steady and heavy deluge, turning the volcanic ash underfoot into a gluey mess.

At 1600 hours, a misdirected air strike from US Navy planes caused serious casualties to a company atop the quarry ridge. Only through a series of furious Navajo radio messages did further casualties from the friendly fire cease.

By 1700 hours, all three drenched and miserable battalions in the regiment were ordered to consolidate their positions and dig in for the evening. For the first time in hours, radio contact was up and running all along the front. And for the first time all day, Jimmie wearily stretched his legs and walked around the command post without a radio in his hand. Colonel Lanigan, in fact, ordered him to grab some K-rations and sack out until the next morning. Jimmie hoped to contact Ray, but the colonel was emphatic. No radio.

Ray, Ray, Jimmie thought while poking unenthusiastically into his first nourishment since early morning. *How long can your luck hold out?*

His answer came the next afternoon.

The dreary skies and numbing rain of the previous day showed no sign of letting up as Jimmie rose in the early hours to send out the day's predawn communications. He began by saying his prayers to Father Sun, although that deity was seldom in evidence on this hellhole of an island.

Jimmie was only peripherally aware that to the south, the marines were still fighting to secure the perimeter around the base of Mt. Suribachi. His primary focus was on the three shattered battalions in his regiment who were directed to make a coordinated drive to push inland. The morning wore on with only moderate gains at best.

At about noon, Ray radioed Jimmie with a dispatch in code from Chambers: *Request rocket support.* Ray's voice again was stressed, either from too little sleep or too little hope. He concluded with coordinates, a hill some eight hundred yards northwest of the quarry.

Colonel Lanigan responded immediately, sending in barrages of rocket fire that drove more than two hundred Japanese from their hillside emplacements. The "Ghouls" trained machine guns on the area, and with little effort they wiped out nearly all of the enemy fleeing their defenses. It was the strongest blow yet against the enemy since Jimmie had come ashore.

Ray radioed Jimmie with the news of this success, and this time his voice was filled with excitement. He broke code for only a moment after the formal message, adding in Navajo, "Enemy's on the run, big brother. Maybe the worst is over."

They were the last words Jimmie heard him speak.

At 1530 hours, according to eyewitnesses, Chambers left a forward observation post with Ray and a few others. Moments later they were surprised by a burst of machine-gun fire from an enemy nest hidden behind a small rise covered with scrub brush.

"Jumpin' Joe," in the lead, fell first. A flurry of bullets shattered his collarbone and tore into his upper chest. He writhed in agony, unable to get up.

The two marines closest to him—Jimmie never got their names—were also wounded, one severely. Ray, according to reports, was right behind them.

Rather than run for cover, Ray advanced toward his fallen commander, seemingly oblivious to the firepower that kept coming, to the round of bullets that pierced his uniform, his chest, his generous heart.

"He didn't even cry out," reported fellow marine Steve Miller. Steve was lobbing grenades at the enemy nest when he saw Ray go down. "Ray never knew what hit him."

Later Steve asked, with tears in his eyes, "What the fuck was he trying to do? Did he think he could get to Chambers before we killed those fuckin' Japs? He was more valuable than any of us, for Chrissakes, didn't he know that? He had the goddamned code!"

What Jimmie will always remember about his last contact with Ray is that his best buddy died speaking Navajo.

FOUR MARINES CARRIED CHAMBERS ON a stretcher to a makeshift medical facility at the regimental command post. Thanks to the immediate treatment, he survived. In short order, he was promoted to full colonel. For his leadership, courage, and fortitude during those opening days of the Iwo Jima campaign, he was later awarded the Medal of Honor.

Every man serving under him acknowledged that he richly deserved it.

The two wounded Anglo marines who were with Chambers also recovered. One was evacuated with the colonel for further treatment. The other went back into action, only to be killed two weeks later in some of the heaviest fighting of the war.

RAY BEGAY WAS BURIED IN a long line of graves on ground that had been cleared of mines just the day before. In another month he would have turned twenty-one.

A cross was placed above his little mound of sandy ash, though he was not Christian. The Marine Corps had no symbol for what he was.

Ray received no posthumous promotion. Because his real contribution was classified, there was no public acknowledgment of his accomplishments.

His remaining pay, along with insurance money, was forwarded to his family in Kayenta, as were his letters, eventually.

Jimmie could not be spared by his CO to say good-bye. Though it weighed heavily on him, there were orders to send, messages to receive. Other lives depending on him.

He never saw Ray's gravesite on Iwo Jima.

AT ABOUT THE SAME TIME they lowered Ray's body into the ground, an American flag unfolded atop Mt. Suribachi. News of this first major victory in the battle for Iwo Jima was radioed to the fleet commander not in English, but in Navajo code.

When a small group of marines raised a second, larger flag a short while after the first, the event was frozen for posterity by photographer Joe Rosenthal. He had come over on the same ship as Jimmie and Ray, although they had not met.

The young flag raiser on the very left of that timeless photo, with his Indian-style blanket tucked behind him into his military belt, with his hands raised in the air, just inches from the long Japanese drainage pipe that served as the flagpole, was the troubled Pima Indian boy Jimmie and Ray met briefly in Honolulu.

When he saw that photo, Jimmie cried for Ray all over again. He cried, too, for the hollowness he felt at having found a little brother, only to lose him so soon. But what he could not explain was that he even shed a tear for that troubled Ira Hayes fellow, the boy on the left in the photo, who, whether he liked it or not, had just become the most famous Indian in World War II.

CHAPTER 23

JANUARY 1947

As Jimmie finishes telling of Ray's last days, he is encircled by moist eyes and quiet cries and clasped hands. Had events turned out differently, if this had been Ray talking to Leila and Wilson Goodluck, Jimmie's mother and father would have never taken comfort from one another as the Begays are doing. Jimmie feels like an intruder on their grieving, although he shares their loss just as deeply.

Lorraine moves over to put an arm around her mother. Katherine seems unsure of what to do, so Jimmie takes a cue and squats on his heels next to her. He makes no physical contact, but his face is close to hers as he says, "Ray was much too young to die, but he was dedicated and brave and, I must tell you, exceptionally good at what he did."

Looking over toward Katherine's parents and sister, he continues, "I cannot stress enough how much Colonel Chambers liked and respected your son, and Ray felt the same way about him. When Ray saw his commander fall, I know he instinctively went to him—I *know* he did this—without thinking about his own safety. That's what made him a good marine and a true hero as well. I can tell you, everyone loved Ray. Other Navajos, whites, everyone. We all watched out for one another. Made no difference what your background was. He was happy being part of the Marine Corps, doing something he believed in."

His words sound cliché, he knows, but sometimes the truth can be expressed in no better way.

Katherine rests her hand lightly on his shoulder. He nearly jumps, so strong is the voltage of her touch. "Thank you for saying that," she says before quickly removing her hand.

He wonders if she feels the electricity too.

Samuel exhales, his long stream of breath heavy with both grief and acceptance. "We're grateful to know that, in the end, our son did not suffer. I hope his spirit found a pathway to the mountain trail on that island, the one to the underworld where spirits live."

Lorraine cries softly. Katherine is silent, yet she makes no effort to move away from Jimmie. So he is quite disappointed when Maria rises and, in a trembling voice, says, "Jimmie, we know this was hard for you, too. You must be exhausted. We should all get some rest."

He nods in agreement. Clearly, there is nothing more to be said this evening. But sleep is elusive to them all, especially to Jimmie, who knows that the rising sun will bring an end to two of the most indelible days of his life.

HE AWAKENS TO THE RICH, heady smells of biscuits and fry bread. The sun is barely up, but Maria has the coffee on and the breads baking. A farewell breakfast. Ray's sisters appear to be sleeping still. Samuel is nowhere to be seen. Probably outside by the corral.

Jimmie steps out into the brisk morning air, tossing off the remaining traces of sleep like a dog shaking off water. The world seems lighter this morning, as does Jimmie's burden. He realizes now just how much he has needed to be with Ray's family.

Samuel is already at work, taking water to the animals. He sees Jimmie and then looks up and says, "Looks like it will be a clear day. A good day for traveling."

"Yes, a good thing for me, especially this time of year."

"My wife is preparing a fine breakfast. She is sad you have to leave."

Jimmie kicks at the thin crust of remaining snow with the toe of his boot. He shares the sadness.

"My oldest daughter, too, I think," Samuel adds, pumping water into his bucket.

A flush of heat radiates through Jimmie's body. "I'll miss all of you as well. Ray was lucky to have such a warm and generous family, and he knew it."

Samuel looks up again at the sky, as if to make sure his first assessment is correct. "Yes, a clear day. Good for traveling," he repeats.

The polite small talk is undoubtedly prelude to something else on Samuel's mind, for coming directly to the point is not the Navajo way. In the awkward pause that stretches between them, only the impatient animals and the squeaky pump handle disturb the calm.

"What are your plans now?" Samuel asks finally, getting to what he undoubtedly wanted to inquire about all along.

The question catches Jimmie off guard. He has thought only in general terms about what he might do and where he might go. Still, his words come out effortlessly, as if the answer has been there all along, just below the surface, like an untapped spring.

"Well, there is not much work on the reservation. And in order to address the things that need changing, I need more education, I can see that. One thing the government has promised to us Navajo servicemen is schooling. Something called a GI Bill. If they keep their word on this—big if—maybe I'll put in for my share."

Samuel pours his bucket of water into a trough as the bleating sheep draw close. "It is good to get an education," he says. He turns to look at Jimmie. Behind the fence, one sheep pushes another out of the way so it can get to the water. "It is even better to be smart."

Moments later Katherine comes out to tell them that breakfast is ready. Katherine, the very personification of Samuel's words.

OVER BREAKFAST, MARIA REMARKS TO their guest, "With respect, Jimmie, you still have not told us everything last night."

"What do you mean?"

"You said you were wounded some days later. If you find it difficult to talk about it, we will understand. But we would like to hear what happened to *you*."

Katherine looks at Jimmie, her eyes wide, her eyebrows arched expectantly. He is more at home with her family, he realizes, than he is with his own.

"Uh, well, not much to tell. I was radioing a message to the command ship. Some mortar shells fell and exploded nearby. Shrapnel sliced into my shoulder. I was carried out to a field hospital at the command post and later put on a ship for the naval hospital in Honolulu. The doctors were good. I slowly got back the movement of my arm."

"After you were released from the hospital," Katherine asks, "were you discharged?"

"Not right away. The war wasn't over yet, remember. The Japanese surrender was still a month away, though we didn't know that then, of course. After the enemy finally surrendered, the Marine Corps kept many of us on active duty, to use as an occupation force. As things turned out, I was never sent to Japan, though Navajos were there." *Using the code even then. Using it for military intelligence, sending back secret reports at night on the effects of the radiation. I know that's true, because some of that intelligence went through me.*

He continues, "They kept me in Honolulu until the end of the year. I had some duties, mostly at ... at night. My days were usually free. They put me on a ship last January. Got my discharge in California a few weeks later and came home."

Feeling more explanation is necessary, he adds, "Look, I know I should have come here long before now. All I can tell you is, when I came home, I was out of balance. I wasn't ready to meet people, to talk about ... the things I've talked about here. I'm not proud of my behavior. I had trouble accepting that things haven't improved around here. Still do. But a few days ago I made a promise. I ask you to judge me not by what I've done, but by what I have yet to do."

Lorraine says, "I can only judge what I see. I can see you're a good man." She flashes a mischievous grin toward her sister. "Isn't he, Katherine?"

This time Katherine returns her sister's remark with a glare. Then she turns to Jimmie, her features softening. "Please take care of yourself, Jimmie Goodluck." She puts a hand on his arm and, this time, she leaves it there for a long moment. "My brother must live on through you now."

"That's a big responsibility," Jimmie says, and he means it.

Katherine does not avert her eyes from his. Her voice is flat and solemn. "Yes. Yes it is."

HAVING RUN OUT OF EXCUSES to linger any longer, Jimmie heads to the corral and leads his horse to the eastern side of the *hogan*. There, by the entrance, he exchanges final good-byes. He promises to keep in touch and to return when he can.

Mounting his horse as the Begays stand together to see him off is hard enough. Turning toward the south and putting Ray's family behind him is more difficult still. But he carries their warmth with him. It covers him like sheepskin on this clear, chilly morning.

He knows his first stop will be the Oljato Trading Post, where his new boots are waiting. He will most likely never wear them, so much does he treasure the handiwork of Samuel Begay and, most especially, the button fashioned by Ray himself.

Still within sight of Samuel and Maria's home, he turns back in the saddle once more to look behind him. In the distance to the east, the tip of Totem Pole pinnacle is the only visible formation that rises from the sacred valley. Its spire of rough sandstone has transformed into a deep gash of garnet in the early morning light, but that will change often throughout the day as the sun and the shadows play tag with this magnificent monument of nature.

The changing of the rock, he thinks. *If rock can change, why not a country? A geographic area? A pathetic and ordinary human being?*

He shifts his gaze to the *hogan* itself and notices that Samuel, Maria, and Lorraine have already gone back inside. But Katherine remains in place, standing tall and rigid, watching him still. He pulls on the reins to turn his horse around so he can look at her a moment longer, lock her image into his memory like a code. But when the horse comes around and he looks again toward the *hogan*, Katherine has vanished, with only his remembered vision of her unreadable smile and the distant echo of her last words marking the spot where she had been standing.

You have to work for something if you want it, not just sit back and say that's the way it is.

—Interview with Wilfred Billey,
code talker, USMC

PART V:

THE ROPE CATCHER

CHAPTER 24

FEBRUARY 1947–JUNE 1948

hat happens after *your dream comes true?*

The question has long haunted Jimmie and has always gone unanswered.

But it is especially relevant at this time. And the response seems obvious, now that Jimmie's mind has compartmentalized the nonsense that once cluttered it like overflowing trash.

You fight to keep that dream alive. You don't let anything—or anyone—take it away from you.

Simple as that.

He begins by writing letters to his congressmen and even to President Truman. He asks why Navajos who were willing to die for their country are not worthy of a VA hospital on or near the reservation, cannot vote for their country's leaders, and cannot get a government loan for a home or a small business. He asks why the reservation schools that our leaders promised were never built, and why Congress denied the increased school funding that was requested by the Bureau of Indian Affairs (as the Indian Service calls itself these days). He asks why Washington sits idly by, knowing the infant mortality rate on the reservation has risen to thirty percent, with half of all newborns dying by the age of five. He asks why Navajo citizens in New Mexico and Arizona—US citizens, all—are ineligible for Social Security or welfare benefits and why there are fewer than five hundred hospital beds and why only a hundred miles of paved road spans the twenty-five-thousand-square-mile reservation.

He asks many questions but gets no answers in reply.

Meanwhile, he takes advantage of his rights under the GI Bill and enrolls at the University of New Mexico at Albuquerque. Before long he is struggling to keep up with his class work, so thoroughly is he immersed in the steady flow of information and altered perceptions. He spends what time he can in the university library, searching the major newspapers for subjects pertaining to the desperate plight of the Navajo people. The "starving Navajos" have increasingly become front page news across the country.

One day in late autumn, as Jimmie settles into a study alcove and works his way through a months-old copy of the *Gallup Independent*, he comes across a short article that hits him like a fist.

Gung-ho Originator and Famed Marine Raider Dead at 61, the headline reads.

The story reports that Evans F. Carlson has died of heart failure in Portland, Oregon. That upon his retirement due to disabilities from combat wounds, the controversial officer had been promoted to the rank of brigadier general. And that in recent months there had been some talk about his running for Congress.

For nearly an hour, Jimmie barely moves in the quiet room as some of Carlson's words come cascading back to him. From day the colonel first met him and Ray: *The way I see it, the government treated you Indians, you Americans, like crap.* From the hell-hole that was Guadalcanal: *You mark my words, lads, your code won't get much use in Guadalcanal unless I'm the one to use it.* From Saipan, where Carlson refused priority medical aid as he lay seriously wounded after taking fire while helping to rescue an enlisted man: *Take this private before you take me ... Begay was wounded before I was.*

Jimmie pays silent tribute to Carlson as a courageous and innovative leader who was idolized by his men yet widely misunderstood by others. And then he recalls a letter Carlson had reportedly written to the family of a Raider who was killed on Guadalcanal. One sentence in particular still resonates with him: *We who survive must work for the objectives for which he died; that tolerance and understanding and harmony may be established in human relationships.* It is the word "harmony" that fixed Carlson's phrase in his mind like a note thumbtacked to a message board. He almost wishes he could write a similar letter of comfort to Carlson's family. Then again, perhaps it is enough that he himself once again embraces many of the values Carlson championed: Tolerance. Understanding. Harmony.

Can anything be worth fighting for more than that?

THE TWO-WORD NOTE SAYS "CALL me." It is signed by Annie in a nearly illegible scrawl.

Standing by the dormitory mailbox at the university, he turns the envelope in his hand and glances at the postmark: *Klagetoh, AZ. December 10, 1947.* It has taken only six days for the letter to make the two-hundred-mile trip to Albuquerque. Mail service, if nothing else, is improving some.

As for telephone lines, they are still a luxury on the reservation, but Annie finds the phone necessary to keep her in contact with governmental and healthcare experts around the country. Jimmie locates a pay phone on campus and gets through to her on his second try.

"What have you been up to?" Annie asks her friend.

Jimmie tells her how he has been trying to keep up with his school work and, whenever possible, connecting with several of his fellow Navajo radiomen by mail. He finds it interesting to learn how their lives have diverged since returning from war.

Wilfred Smith, like Jimmie, enrolled under the GI Bill. He talks of plans to finish college, go on for a master's degree, and become an educator. George Benally, the salty-tongued radioman from Cove, Arizona, writes that he can only find employment in the newly discovered uranium mines southwest of Cove. Charlie Yazzie married a girl he met at a Squaw Dance. The last Jimmie heard, they were living with her parents near Chinle, but apparently Charlie has not adjusted to a life of raising sheep, not after his eye-opening experiences outside the reservation, so the young man has taken to drink and his new wife is frantic with worry. And in Ft. Defiance, Carl Slowtalker left the reservation as he said he might, frustrated and discouraged by the lack of opportunity. He is reportedly hiring on for railroad jobs up in Colorado.

"Listen, Jimmie," Annie says when she can get a word in. The excitement in her voice is barely perceptible over the static on the line. "Here's why I asked. I don't want to come between you and your education, but there's a job opening you should know about. The BIA is looking for a translator."

In Jimmie's opinion, the Bureau of Indian Affairs has changed in name only. It seems to be the same old political dinosaur. So he starts to tell her he is not interested, but Annie's words spill out, one after another, like jelly beans from a jar.

"This isn't like what you did years ago," she insists. "This job is in their Division of Public Health. I can't imagine anyone more qualified than you, you stubborn jackass."

He is annoyed that the BIA controls the money for every program the Navajos need. But that is a fact of life, and the opportunity comes at a perfect time, for he has already grown restless with university life. Albuquerque is too big and too far removed from the languorous pace of the reservation. He is eager to return to *Dinetah,* desperate to make a larger contribution than just writing letters that fall upon deaf ears.

Is it serendipity, then, or intervention from the Great Spirits that has brought him Annie's news about the Health Service opening? Either way, he jumps at the opportunity like a rattlesnake on a mouse.

He interviews for two days in Ft. Defiance at the Public Health headquarters, which is nothing more than a couple of tiny rooms behind the post office building. By the end of the second day, Jimmie is offered the job. He locates a sparsely furnished apartment in town that suits him, although with all the traveling required for his work, it appears he will seldom be there long enough to take off his boots.

Jimmie does not have a moment to meet up with Annie until early spring. They get together, finally, on a sunny day behind Council chambers in Window Rock. She has just come from a council meeting where she has pleaded for more money to fight a frightening increase in trachoma cases. The two old friends sit on a wooden bench and talk in front of the two-hundred-foot-high formation of red sandstone from which the community takes its name.

Jimmie tells her that his work takes him to remote places on both sides of the New Mexico–Arizona corridor where there are few doctors and even fewer healthcare facilities. "I translate for Anglo doctors most of the time. Many of them—and I don't know how I feel about this—are here in a public service capacity to avoid the draft. Well, we need them, so it's okay, I guess. Other times I travel with Anglo nurses who give shots and hand out pills while I try to explain to their stubborn patients why the 'white man's medicine' is necessary."

"It's like I've been telling you all along," Annie says as she pushes her heavy eyeglasses higher on the bridge of her nose. "Now you see for yourself what I've been up against. I've got some traveling coming up myself. Chinle, Round Rock, Kayenta—"

At the mention of that community, Jimmie comes alive, his voice discernibly higher in pitch. "There's a clinic in Kayenta," he interrupts. "I know a woman who volunteers there. Katherine is her name. She's someone very special—the sister of my close buddy, Ray, who died in the war."

Annie's mouth turns into a crooked smile. "Very special as a person ... or very special to you?"

His normally ruddy complexion deepens to the color of the surrounding sandstone.

"Uh, well, both, I s'pose. I haven't seen her for over a year, but we keep in touch by mail." He is certain Annie can see through him, just as he can see through the circular "window" of the arched rock in front of him. In truth, hardly a day goes by in which he does not think about Katherine. He hopes one day, perhaps, an assignment will take him that far west. Meanwhile, he and Katherine exchange letters, keeping the tone newsy and friendly. He has become expert at masking his true emotions behind a facade of noncommittal ink.

"Is she married?" Annie asks, still looking at him with her wry expression.

"No. And don't get the wrong idea."

"Always thought you needed a good woman, Jimmie. What man doesn't?" Suddenly, her smile vanishes, replaced with a look of fleeting anguish.

"Is something wrong?" Jimmie asks.

"No, it's just that I ... well, I may have answered my own question, that's all."

Jimmie lets the subject drop, for her comment is clearly a veiled reference to her own relationship, which, rumor has it, is strained.

All her time away from home cannot help. Being gone for days on end, leaving George to take care of the ranch along with the children ...

Annie looks toward the rock and peers through its opening as if it were a window to the future. "Like I said, I'll be up near Kayenta in a few weeks, and I had planned on checking out the clinic there. Now I have an even better reason to go."

"If you do see Katherine, tell her I'm hoping to get up there myself. Unfortunately, I have to go where the Health Service sends me."

"Anything else I should tell her?" Annie with her coquettish look again, enjoying the direction this conversation has taken.

"That'll be enough." Jimmie's mouth twists into a nervous smile. "Hey, I'm not crazy in love with her or anything, if that's what you're thinking."

Annie throws her head back and laughs, loud and hearty. "There's a man for you," she roars. "Always the last to figure it out."

THE FOLLOWING WEEK, JIMMIE HEADS to Kinlichee to translate for a nurse who is administering vaccinations to babies and small children. She carries a copy of the *Gallup Independent*, and the headline catches Jimmie's eye:

Truman to Ride into Town.

The story reports that the president is heading by rail from Los Angeles to his home in Independence, Missouri, making brief stops along the way. His route will take him through a slice of the Navajo reservation, with rear platform speeches scheduled for the next day in Winslow, Arizona, followed by Gallup in the afternoon, then Albuquerque in the evening.

Jimmie wires his boss to request a personal day. Most likely the president's brief stop will not present Jimmie with a chance to do anything but gawk along with the crowd. Still, as he learned during his Raider days, you don't wait for opportunities, you make them.

Determined to do just that, he hitchhikes to Gallup early the next morning.

With more than an hour to go before the president's scheduled arrival, the crowd has already swollen with dignitaries, reporters, and hundreds of citizens—some Indian, some Mexican, but mostly Anglo—all jostling for position in front of the Fred Harvey El Navajo Hotel beside the station. Jimmie tangles his way along the façade of dramatic, pueblo-style architecture, now dingy from years of exposure to coal dust. The front of the hotel faces the tracks, and he wants to get as close as he can to the proceedings.

Shortly after one in the afternoon the train arrives, sleek and important, only fifteen minutes behind schedule. The yellow and red Santa Fe Super Chief Number 26 pulls forward so that the rear car, grandly festooned with flags and banners, is positioned in front of a makeshift wooden platform which holds the mayor of Gallup, several councilmen, and other dignitaries. Directly behind the platform, a twelve-piece high school band plays "Hail to the Chief" in an asynchronistic arrangement that sounds as if they had received the sheet music only moments earlier.

Soon a door opens at the back of the rear car. President Truman steps out onto the car's generous platform, beaming, his hands in the air as the cheers and accolades of the crowd swell to a raucous din. He is dressed in a dark suit with a blue tie, as if he is oblivious to the Gallup heat. His broad smile and enthusiastic arm movements give the impression of someone going through motions that have been thoroughly rehearsed.

Truman nods to the mayor and then leans over to whisper something to him. Still smiling, the president looks over his enthusiastic audience and holds his hands up again, this time clearly trying to silence the crowd so he can speak. When the president begins, Jimmie cups his hand to his ear in order to make out the all the words.

"What a wonderful turnout Gallup has offered us!" Truman shouts.

The crowd roars its approval.

"I'm heading back to my home in Independence, Missouri, to see the family, and then we go on to Washington to finish the necessary work that has to be done there when the Congress adjourns."

Scattered applause. A few hoots and hollers. The president pauses only a moment and then continues, "I've had a most pleasant ride across Arizona and now, New Mexico. It's beautiful country. And I saw those wonderful pine forests and had a chance to look at the Navajo reservation about which there's been so much talk and about which we've been trying to do so much."

The president pauses again, but this time there is very little reaction from the crowd. To many of the Indians scattered throughout the audience, Truman has clearly not done enough. To some of the whites, the Indians are not worth helping in the first place. Everyone else, it appears, is content with an attitude of mere indifference.

When President Truman finishes his remarks, he introduces his wife and daughter, who step out onto the rear platform to join him. Then he says, "I think your president should be talking *with* you, not just *to* you. I have time for one or two questions."

This opportunity will not come again. Jimmie pushes forward and shouts, "Mr. President! Mr. President!"

Hundreds of pairs of eyes turn to look at him, the president's included. Several of the people standing close to him pull back, as if he were tubercular. From somewhere off to his right, a child wails, crying for her mother.

"Mr. President," Jimmie thunders once more, determined to be heard over the crowd. "I'm a Navajo Indian and a World War II veteran. I proudly fought for my country in the US Marine Corps."

The mayor starts to say something to the president, perhaps to distract him from the Indian rabble-rouser, but Truman gently waves him off and smiles at Jimmie.

"I have the utmost respect for you, son. The Navajo tribe gave us many fine soldiers, and your nation thanks you," he says, as if all Jimmie wants is public recognition.

"Mr. President, with all due respect, I have a question to ask you."

He has thought about this moment carefully. There is much he would like to say, but he needs to pick a single issue and speak out quickly.

"If I have earned your respect by fighting for my country, why is it I cannot vote for my country's leaders?"

The crowd reacts with a mixture of jeers and support, the jeers being in the majority. In the loudest voice he can muster, Jimmie goes on, "Why is it, in this state, that Indians do not have the right to vote like other citizens?"

Two surly police officers lurch toward him. Just as they grab his arms to pull him back, President Truman addresses them in a voice that lacks the assurance of his earlier speech. "That's all right, uh, officers, this … this country was built on free speech and he asks a valid question. Please, let him be."

More jeers from the crowd. Mrs. Truman and her daughter shrink back against the door of the carriage. The president leans toward the mayor, appears to ask him something. The mayor nods his head and they exchange a few words.

Reporters scribble furiously on note pads as the president addresses Jimmie directly, though the affable leader clearly plays to both the press and to the crowd.

"Young man, that's a fair question indeed. As you may know, your federal government guarantees all of its citizens the right to vote. Hell, it's more than a right, far as I'm concerned. It's a responsibility. But states like Arizona and New Mexico have their own ideas."

The president pauses for a second, apparently thinking over what he wants to say next. When he resumes speaking, he jabs his finger in the air for emphasis.

"I can promise you this: I will take up the matter with the governors of both fine states. I can't force them to rectify the injustice, but I can use federal funding issues as a pretty damn formidable stick." The president glances at the press corps and then looks back at Jimmie. "Time is short, son, but I'll do what I can in the hope you can vote in this fall's election."

A few scattered cheers rise up from the crowd. The noise level increases as everyone talks at once. The issue is of minor interest to most of Gallup's citizens, but what is important is that the president has said something of substance in their community.

Truman holds up his hands to quiet the crowd. He clearly wants to add something more. Fixing Jimmie with an engaging smile, he says, "When you do vote, young man, I just hope you remember to vote for *me!*"

The crowd roars its approval. Truman reaches back to grasp the hands of his wife and daughter, indicating there will be no more questions taken at this whistle stop. They wave farewell to the appreciative gathering and disappear—with a sense of relief, it seems to Jimmie—back into the carriage.

As the spectators slowly start to disperse, a dozen members of the press run over to Jimmie. Several have cameras, startling him with the pop of flash bulbs that explode in his face like bursts of artillery shells.

"What's your name?" a portly reporter asks him. Getting no immediate response, he repeats the question as a demand. "For the record, young man, give us your name."

Jimmie stares at him with a flat expression. The last thing he wants is personal celebrity. He is simply working to fulfill a promise, to hold on to a dream, and he has barely begun.

"How 'bout you just call me Ray," he says.

CHAPTER 25

JULY 1948–SEPTEMBER 1949

"Well, I certainly enjoyed meeting your friend," Annie tells Jimmie with a wink. "Katherine and I had a nice conversation."

Annie has returned from her journey to Kayenta and other areas to the west. As she tells it, she showed up at the clinic while Katherine was busy treating a crying five-year-old. The child had apparently fallen while playing, cutting her knee on a sharp rock. Katherine was cleansing the wound and applying a bandage. At the nearest hospital, over in Tuba City, doctors might have closed the gash with a few stitches, but here, antiseptic and a bandage was the best Katherine could offer.

When the mother and child walked out the door, Katherine turned to the stranger who had been sitting patiently for nearly fifteen minutes.

"Hello, my name is Katherine." She spoke in Navajo, for only a few of her patients over twenty-five spoke fluent English, and this woman with the large glasses was clearly in her thirties. Katherine asked her visitor, "Is there a problem I can help you with?"

Annie Wauneka rose from the chair and smiled. "The problem," she said in English, "is that I'm here talking to you, while my dear friend Jimmie Goodluck would give anything to be here in my place."

Annie took in Katherine's look of surprise, grinned broadly, and then introduced herself.

"Mrs. Wauneka!" Katherine sputtered. "I never ... I mean, I'm ... honored."

"Mrs. Wauneka is my husband's mother. Call me Annie."

"I've seldom been without words, but, well ... did Jimmie tell you? It's you, uh, your work that inspired me to volunteer here." Then, in what came off almost as an afterthought, "Um, how is Jimmie?"

"What brings me to see you is a long story, which I'll share over coffee, when you're free. As for Jimmie ..."

Here Annie pauses as she reports the conversation to Jimmie. She scrunches up her eyes, as if weighing how to proceed. "Well, I told her, 'Jimmie is working very hard, he's accomplishing much more than he realizes, and he's talking about you like a lovesick puppy.'"

"You actually *said* that?" His recoil and the look on his face must be exactly what Annie had hoped for, because she breaks into hearty laughter.

"Well, all right, I'll admit I didn't say that last thing about the puppy. But I should have."

They are sitting together on a beat-up couch in the lobby of the Navajo Hospital in Ft. Defiance. Annie is here to study disease and sanitation under Dr. Kurt Deuschle, a young BIA doctor. In spite of only an eleventh-grade education, she seems eager to absorb the thick pile of books Dr. Deuschle has loaned her.

"I can see why you took a liking to her," Annie says. "She's smart, she speaks both Navajo and English, she's self-confident and dedicated, and as you may have noticed, she is rather pleasant to look at."

His sheepish grin is all the affirmation Annie needs. "She's interested in you, too, you big fool. I can tell. But don't let too much time go by. She's not likely to stay single much longer."

Jimmie impulsively moves his hand along the sofa cushion. His index finger finds a hole and sinks into the batting stuffed inside. Changing the subject, he says, "I'm not clear on what you were doing in Kayenta in the first place."

"Ah, yes, the point of all this. Partly, Katherine herself drew me there."

"What?"

"Well, I had other business up there, but the way you talked about her, she sounded like someone I should meet. I've been pushing to get more medical help in that area anyway. I wanted to bring her some health pamphlets to hand out. But I also wanted to see if she might be right for something else I have in mind."

Jimmie sits up straight, curious as to what could be coming next. "What *do* you have in mind?"

Annie takes her left hand, puts her thumb and forefinger together to form a circle, and holds it up to her eye. At the same time she raises her right hand and makes a continuing circular motion, as if turning an invisible crank or handle.

Jimmie looks at her, uncomprehending.

"Movies!" she says, as if it were the most obvious thing in the world. One eyebrow pokes over the rim of her glasses like a caterpillar out for a look around.

Jimmie feels like he has been given an answer without knowing the question. "Movies? Like Humphrey Bogart? Like Greta Garbo?"

"No, movies like Katherine Begay." She chuckles. "Jimmie, the way you described her—and you were right, you scoundrel—I thought she might be perfect on camera for the messages I want to film. See, I do all right over the radio, but come on, look at me. I'm no movie star. Katherine practically is!"

"I still don't understand—"

"Think about it, Jimmie. I can't be everywhere. Neither can you or anyone else in the Health Service. So we pass out printed information, but how many people around here can even read? Here's the thing, Jimmie. We Navajos love movies, right? So I'm going to give our people their movies, and in our own language. Only the stories are going to be about hygiene, about how to understand and prevent and deal with the diseases around here. And Katherine, she's agreed to present these messages. I can't offer her money, of course, but I'm working on something she wants even more." Annie pushes her glasses up on her nose with an index finger and grins. "Something much better than money, actually."

"Like what?" Jimmie regards his old friend with a mixture of apprehension and appreciation.

"Too early to tell you yet. I need to pull in a favor. But if my plan works, I'm sure you'll be among the first to know." Her impish grin again.

"Where will you get the money for film and cameras and the machines that play the movies?"

"I'm working on that, too. Between the BIA and the tribal council, I can probably raise enough to get started. You know me."

He does know her. She will undoubtedly run for tribal council herself before long, so pervasive is her growing influence.

Annie looks at him the way a concerned mother might gaze upon an uncomprehending child. "Consider this an early warning, Jimmie," she says. "Katherine Begay is going to be a familiar face around the reservation by this time next year."

"Meaning?"

"Meaning a lot of young men are going to find her as fascinating as you do." She removes her glasses and leans forward until her face is just inches away from his. In a voice subdued by the very weight of her admonition, she warns, "Don't let someone else pick the prettiest flower in the garden."

SUMMER PRESSES ON.

The corn, scarcely two feet tall, withers on the stalk. A few green shoots poke out from nests of parched grasses, not nearly enough to feed the scrawny livestock. Crops die and animals die and children die for want of water and nourishment.

Through it all, Jimmie works six, often seven days a week, and Annie makes the first three of her movies. Her star presenter does indeed attract attention from a growing legion of eligible males who have suddenly developed an interest in sanitation. Jimmie remains torn between his desire to see Katherine again and the notion that he must stay detached from any serious relationship unless he somehow learns his father's clan. Suppose Katherine turns out to be related to him? This has become his own personal Long Walk; he feels incomplete, alienated, doomed to wallow in self-imposed exile.

Then September arrives, heralding one shred of happy news that brings Katherine and Jimmie much closer together—geographically, at least. Katherine, through Annie's cunning intervention, is invited to enroll with full scholarship as a nursing student at the Sage Memorial Hospital School of Nursing in Ganado.

Established fifteen years earlier by the hospital's medical director, Dr. Clarence Salsbury, it is the first and only accredited nursing school for Indian women in the United States. Annie knows Dr. Salsbury well, for he was her father's long-time personal physician and a key recipient of the wealthy leader's generous philanthropy. Annie had not been shy about reminding the director of her father's contributions. Then she told him about Katherine's volunteer work at the Kayenta Clinic and asked a single favor: to secure one of the few available government scholarships for Katherine Begay. Dr. Salsbury "pulled some strings," as he put it, and Katherine got the nod.

This means Katherine will be nearby. Jimmie can cover the short distance from Ft. Defiance to Ganado in half a day on horseback, two hours or less by automobile. He foolishly rationalizes that this proximity can deepen the friendship between them without leading to anything more. After all, what ties them to one another is their mutual grief over, and affection for, Ray. His father's clan, in this regard, is irrelevant. It makes him realize that creating the code, using it under fire—that was easy, by comparison. It's personal relationships that tear at a man's heart and test his mettle.

Katherine sends Jimmie a letter that is bursting with excitement. She will travel to the school for the start of fall semester and she hopes he will come by and say hello when he can. By return letter he assures her he will visit her. That is, he says, if he can ever get away.

He hitches a ride with a BIA colleague and heads to Ganado on her second day there.

IT IS A BRIGHT AND unseasonably warm autumn day. The Sage Memorial campus looks vastly different from the last time he was here, at Chee's bedside, during winter. Most startling is the well manicured lawn—a highly unusual sight in this part of the country—that reminds Jimmie of the thick, emerald turf around San Diego. He inhales deeply, for the pungent aroma of mowed green grass is the last thing he ever expected on the reservation. And that's only the beginning. Shade trees—elms, locusts, cottonwoods, maples—grow in profusion all around the campus, and most still boast their leaves, although a stand of willows look in need of a drenching rainfall. A sign identifies a large area of dormant bushes as the "Rose Garden," but elsewhere, plantings of flowering shrubs and ground cover appear healthy and thriving. Jimmie wonders where the money comes from to turn the grounds into such a desert oasis.

He heads to the east side of the property and, following a walkway etched within an avenue of trees, he approaches Florence Nightingale Lodge, the nursing dormitory. The rectangular two-story structure is faced with stone blocks and covered with an asphalt-tiled roof. He practically leaps up the three stairs to the front entrance. Inside the entryway, he buzzes Katherine's room.

She comes down after several minutes and greets him with a cheery "*Ya'at'eeh.*" She wears a patterned skirt and a frilly yellow blouse that's far more feminine than anything she wore when they were together in Kayenta. With her lustrous hair down around her shoulders and just a touch of pale red lipstick, she does indeed look like a movie star. Jane Russell in *The Outlaw*, perhaps. In a fleeting moment of conceit he wonders if she has dressed expressly for him.

They walk outside across the bucolic grounds, talking throughout the afternoon like lifelong friends. Katherine brings Jimmie up to date on her family, telling him that Samuel and Maria are busy with their respective crafts, while a few months earlier, her sister, Betty, had her third baby. One topic leads to another, and at one point she mentions the incident that sparked her long-held dream of getting a nursing degree.

"I was twelve years old, thirteen at most, when the accident happened," Katherine begins. "As the oldest of my three siblings, it often fell on me to watch my sisters Lorraine and Betty, and, of course, little Ray, who was barely seven. I guess I was angry that day, resentful at having to run an errand for my mother. She asked me to deliver a basket to the trading post because she was busy helping my father brain-tan a hide of deerskin. She had no choice, of course. If you've ever watched the process, you know it's a lot of work."

Jimmie has a pretty good idea. The hide must be peeled, rinsed, fleshed, dried, and dehaired, after which it is saturated with a mixture of the animal's brain and water. When the leather has softened, the brains are squeegeed off.

She goes on, "As you know—well, maybe you don't—twelve-year-old girls can be pretty self-absorbed. I was not happy at having to walk the two miles to the trading post when I wanted to stay home and play like my sisters got to do. To make matters worse, I had to take my little brother with me to keep him out of trouble. Did Ray ever mention this?" she asks, trying not to cry as she tells the story.

"I don't think so. What happened?"

"We'd walked about a mile and a half when Ray chased after a roadrunner that darted across the trail ahead of us. Don't ask me why, but from the time he was five or so he talked about catching one. Maybe he thought it would bring him luck. This one didn't."

Katherine and Jimmie reach a small man-made pond. There they stand looking out at the water, where water lilies, carefully positioned, beckon like the rare jewels they are in this part of the world. Along the shoreline, cattails dance at the whim of gentle breezes. Katherine has a faraway look in her eyes as she continues, "I guess Ray wasn't paying attention when he ran after the silly bird, because next thing I knew, he was screaming hysterically. He tripped, I guess. He was sprawled face down in a gravelly, dry wash. There was blood everywhere: his elbows, his knees, his forehead. It looked a lot worse than it turned out to be, of course, but as a twelve-year-old girl, I thought he might bleed to death before we got to the trading post. He didn't stop crying the whole way there, and all that blood kept trickling out as I struggled to carry him in my arms. I was frantic with worry, and with guilt too, I guess, because here I was supposed to be keeping him out of trouble. I remember praying to the Great Spirits, begging them to make Ray okay. Thinking back on it, I'm ashamed to admit I was probably more worried about myself, the trouble I might be in, than I was about my brother."

"It's good to know you're human like the rest of us," Jimmie says as two swans glide past, their appearance almost surreal here in the desert.

"Anyway," Katherine says, "as I carried Ray to the trading post, I remember thinking, what if he needs a hospital or a doctor? There are no medical services for hundreds of miles. That's when it hit me: if I were a nurse, I would know what to do. It takes a special person, I believe, to comfort others, to heal them, to help keep them well. Sure, we have medicine men, but what about a medicine *woman,* who can help people who simply need first aid or require medical assistance based on the white man's science? From that moment on, I knew what I wanted to be when I grew up. Of course, I could never have afforded that specialized education, but now …"

Katherine stops in midsentence, insisting she has talked too much about herself. So as they turn to walk slowly back to the dormitory, she asks Jimmie what he has been doing. He tells her of his trials and tribulations with the Health Service and reflects on his short-lived time as a student in Albuquerque before that. Of course, with Ray never far from their minds and hearts, they also share other bittersweet memories that revolve around Ray the way moons circle their planets.

When the sun begins to set, Jimmie reluctantly says he has to return to Ft. Defiance. He promises that he will come again when his schedule permits. He feels an overpowering urge to kiss her good-bye—momentarily forgetting his vow of "friendship only"—but stops himself so as not to seem overeager. Or is it possible rejection he fears? He touches her hand gently instead, almost the way whites shake hands in their gestures of farewell, and he crumbles like weathered sandstone under the devastating sensation of her soft, dewy skin and the force of her unreadable smile.

A FEW WEEKS LATER, A second welcome circumstance comes into Jimmie's life: He steps into a voting booth for the first time.

When you do vote, I just hope you'll remember to vote for me, Truman had said with good-natured intent. Jimmie plans to cast his vote enthusiastically and with immense pride.

At the polling place in Ft. Defiance, the line of Navajos seems to be a mile long. Many of these eager citizens have traveled hundreds of miles to get here, for polling places on the reservation are few and far between. The newly won right to vote is a social event and a day's entertainment for many here; for others, especially veterans like Jimmie who fought for the freedom to elect their country's leaders, it is both an obligation and a privilege of citizenship that has been too long in coming.

Whether Truman's influence played a part, Jimmie cannot say. All he knows is that the Arizona Supreme Court has finally ruled it unconstitutional to bar Indians from voting, so the archaic law has been changed. Across the border in New Mexico, Indians are also able to vote for the first time, thanks to an injunction granted in the US District Court in Santa Fe. But the New Mexico State Legislature still has not passed that right into law as of yet. Neither, according to the *Gallup Independent*, has the state of Utah.

WITH THE ELECTION EXCITEMENT BARELY over, the winter of 1948–49 hits the reservation hard, pummeling the land with one severe blizzard after another. The worst storm strikes in late January, when thirty-five inches of snow bury areas of the reservation. Jimmie is snowbound at home in Ft. Defiance for three weeks. Travel to some places on the reservation will likely be limited for weeks more. The Air National Guard flies in supplies to isolated areas, an act of welfare the press calls a "domestic Berlin airlift." Half of *Dinetah*'s lamb population has died off, along with a quarter of the cattle. This is nature's own stock reduction, and it is devastating.

Jimmie takes comfort in knowing that Katherine, at least, is safely sheltered at the nursing school. Still, he misses her, so when the roadway finally clears between Ft. Defiance and Ganado, he impulsively grabs a ride one morning with an outgoing BIA administrator named Jon Snyder who is heading for a half-day meeting at the Hubbell Trading Post. Snyder drops him off at Sage Memorial shortly after noon, telling him to be ready by five for the return trip. Jimmie rings Katherine's room from the dormitory entryway. No response. Since it is lunchtime, he shuffles through the trampled snow to Café Sage, the dining hall, which carries the distinction of being the largest adobe building in Arizona. Old memories come flooding back. Have fifteen years really passed since he worked here as a fry cook?

The cafeteria-style lunch room is packed with nursing students, hospital workers, and a few visitors, many of whom, Jimmie suspects, have been detained here for days due to the snows. He stands at the door and scans the tables, looking for Katherine. A loud clatter from the kitchen—the sound of metal trays hitting the floor—distracts him for a moment. The air is thick with the smell of frying oil, and something else. Burned toast? It reminds him why he walked away from his job here on a distant winter not unlike this one.

Just as he is about to turn and look elsewhere, he glimpses Katherine near the cashier's station. She is sitting at a small table across from a man who appears to be Jimmie's age, maybe a few years older. He seems a bit sallow even for a white-skinned fellow, but his thick, wavy brown hair and his broad shoulders give him an air of authority, while the starched white jacket he wears reinforces his importance. The man is a doctor.

Jimmie dislikes him at once.

The fellow is talking to Katherine with lively gestures, using his hands as if he finds them necessary to propel the words from his mouth. She appears to be listening intently, diverting her eyes from his face only long enough to sip from a tall cup of coffee. The phony so-and-so flaps his right hand with an effeminate air, and Katherine laughs heartily at something he says. He smiles back, talking still, his hand now briefly touching her arm, then withdrawing, not in a recoil but—Jimmie feels certain of this—with slow, deliberate movement. Jimmie experiences a flash of jealousy, though he knows he has no claim on Katherine. Far from it.

Regretting his decision to come unannounced, Jimmie deliberates whether or not to walk over and interrupt them. They appear to have finished eating, but neither is making an attempt to get up. Jimmie's rational mind tells him to approach Katherine—he has come all this way to see her, after all—but his body responds otherwise, shrinking back from the doorway as if following a mind of its own.

Without further internal debate, he strides sullenly from the building and heads across the hospital grounds toward the roadway. From there he stomps all the way to the trading post, ignoring the numbing cold and the wet snow underfoot. He finally collapses into Snyder's Buick which is parked out front. There he waits for his ride back to reality, to a place where he can cling stubbornly to his principles and not fool himself into pretending that, as a man who does not even know his father's clan, he could ever find happiness with someone as extraordinary as Ray Begay's beguiling sister.

JIMMIE IMMERSES HIMSELF IN WORK and stews in the foul broth of romantic indecision as the days go by in a blur. Accompanying him day and night, like a persistent hitchhiker, are thoughts of his aborted visit to see Katherine. Katherine—a part of his dream, it appears, that is out of his reach. So it is with great trepidation that he tears open an envelope that comes in the mail a month later. He practically holds his breath as he begins reading.

Dear Jimmie,

I was hoping you might come to Ganado now that the weather has improved, perhaps even just for a few hours, but I suppose you must be very busy.

I'm doing well, but the competition is fierce among the nursing students here. There are Indian women representing many tribes, along with some foreign students from places as far away as Japan and China. It's hard to believe that Ray was killed by a Japanese, and now two girls from that country are in my classes. Nice girls, both of them. Of course, we don't talk about the war; it's too raw for all of us.

There is one exception, though. One of the doctors here was a medic in the army. I told him all about you and Ray being in the marines together—he also lost a brother in the war, shot down over Germany, I think he said. I should explain that the students here are on rotation, meaning once a week each of us has lunch with one of the doctors. It's supposed to be a learning experience, but Dr. Weisman and I—he's the former Army medic—we talked the whole time about our brothers. Dr. Weisman leaves next month to return someplace out east, so you won't get to meet him. Too bad, you'd like him, Jimmie.

Well, I better get back to my studies. I would love to see you again. Is everything okay?

K.

He reads the words again: *You'd like him, Jimmie.* He chews them, their bitter aftertaste lingering heavily on his tongue. They mock him, amplify his cowardice, showcase his foolish pride and stupidity. He asks himself, *Supposing the doctor had been a suitor, so what? What have I done to declare my feelings and intentions to Katherine? How did I fight to keep this part of my dream alive?*

He tries drafting a reply, making feeble excuses for not coming to visit. He can hardly wait to see her, he writes. It is the only aspect of his feelings toward her that he feels comfortable admitting.

Then he crumples up the letter he has started and goes to Ganado the next day.

BETWEEN JIMMIE'S JOB AND KATHERINE'S intense studies, they meet only three times over the spring and summer. At least he stops acting like a shy, awkward teenager around her. He no longer conceals the affection he feels toward her, nor does she discourage him. They hold hands during much of their time together, somewhat self-consciously, for they are never alone on the hospital campus. Jimmie limits any further intimacy to brief kisses when they greet and when he leaves. He harbors few doubts, now, that Katherine is as drawn to him as he is to her, but with her final testing coming up, and his own confusion about pursuing the relationship, neither of them brings up the future or what their place together in it might be. Meanwhile, her movies for Annie continue to garner attention from eligible males. Jimmie is grateful—hopeful, more accurately—that she is too busy at school to check out the possibilities.

At last the day comes when Katherine receives her graduation certificate. She distinguishes herself in spite of startling prejudice from the outside world that weighs heavily upon the entire nursing program. Outlandish beliefs, according to news reports, that Indian women do not have the temperament or intelligence to master the rigorous standards.

Jimmie is eager to share this occasion with her, especially since her own family in Kayenta is too far away to attend the little ceremony. Although the graduation is an informal event, Jimmie knows it marks a milestone in Katherine's life.

Dr. Salisbury beams as he hands out the certificates on a makeshift platform in front of the School of Nursing. Then the graduates, all dressed alike in their stiff white uniforms and nursing caps, pose together for photos. Even the plain and unflattering uniform cannot take away from Katherine's charisma and beauty, Jimmie realizes. He eagerly takes her hand and together, they walk across the Sage Memorial oasis, savoring the intermingled evergreen and floral scents that ride on the coattails of afternoon breezes. Katherine is effervescent as they sit on a stone bench in front of a trio of silvery-green Russian olive bushes that Dr. Salisbury's wife introduced to the area. There Katherine breaks her big news: the Kayenta Clinic is going to reopen in a few weeks, this time with sufficient provisions to dispense more than just information. In fact, a certified nurse will be in charge.

"It will be me!" she bubbles. "As soon as the results of my state exam come in."

A wave of apprehension washes over Jimmie. He should be thrilled for her. But it means she will be settling down back in Kayenta, a long and difficult two hundred miles to the northwest. He panics with the realization that he might have already missed his opportunity. Time and distance and circumstance—along with his own vacillation—will surely terminate any chance for their relationship to continue.

Abruptly, he looks down at his hands. They are shaking.

"What's wrong?" Katherine asks, her brown eyes wide open, a look of concern sweeping over her face.

"Nothing," he says. "Nothing is wrong, not anymore." He is determined, for once, not to let his brain impede the words he wants to say, not to let his muscles obstruct the spontaneous decision he has just made. "This is about what's right."

Oblivious, for once, to the presence of anyone else, he turns toward Katherine on the bench, draws her face close to his, brushes a strand of hair from her eyes, and inhales her warmth. Then, summoning far greater courage than he ever needed in the South

Pacific, he kisses her—not in the tentative, lighthearted ways as before—but deeply, without restraint, exploring her lips, her mouth, her tongue, with an ardor that pours from his body like the rays of light from the afternoon sun. For several indelible moments Katherine responds with equal enthusiasm, her body melting into his. Then she pulls back, her questioning eyes sweeping over his face like a searchlight.

"Jimmie, I—" she begins.

Before she can say anything more, he pulls back. He can only guess that she feels betrayed, as if she were caught in the uninvited embrace of a brother or a cousin or a ... a buddy.

"I'm sorry," he stammers, ever the fool. He looks away, wishing for invisibility.

"No, it's not that." Her voice is soft as lamb's wool. Her hand reaches for his face. She extends her index finger to his cheek, turns his head, forces him to look at her. Her eyes are moist. "Don't apologize, Jimmie. I've waited for you to kiss me like that for ... well, for far too long. Didn't you know? Couldn't you tell? It's just that now, with my life changing so, and my future back in Kayenta, I have to ask: can ... can anything come of this?"

He is tempted to tell her how he comes from flawed stock. How she might even be better off if it turns out they are related by clan. But right now, with Katherine in his arms, with her upper body pressed close to his, with the perfumed shampoo scent of her hair and her pillowy lips still inches from his own, even he cannot swallow the bullshit he has been feeding himself like he once fed on the bitter peyote.

"I haven't worked it out yet, but yes, I want something to come of this," he whispers. "More than anything, I want a future with you. Don't you see? I love you, Katherine. I think I've loved you since I first met you and idiot that I am, I've waited far too long to say the words."

And then he holds back no longer. He spills out his heart and shares the misgivings that have haunted him, about not knowing his people on his father's side.

"All right, suppose your father's clan does turn out to be the same as my mother's or father's," Katherine says calmly, her lips inches from his ear. "That doesn't necessarily mean you and I are blood related. And with what, some eighty-six clans, what are the odds anyway?"

His mind races to come up with possible responses. She is probably right, he decides, so he blurts out, "I have no right to ask you this, Katherine. But for the time being, we're going to be far apart from one another. Will you give me some time—a short time, I promise—to figure this out? I need to find a way we can be together without this … this uncertainty hanging over us."

She looks at him with gentle doe eyes. "You know, Jimmie, I am going to be awfully busy for quite a while, setting up the clinic."

He looks at her with a puzzled expression. "Is that your answer?"

"Yes, my darling man. Just as *this* is my answer."

And then her open lips press once more against his, and her right hand snakes around the back of his neck, caressing the skin there, and her soft breasts crush against his chest, and he feels her rapid heartbeat and tastes her moist mouth and he is consumed by the heat of her embrace and that, for now, is all he needs to know.

CHAPTER 26

SEPTEMBER 1949

Arizona's first post office opened its doors in Ft. Defiance in 1856. Now, nearly a century later, that reservation post office still processes only a moderate amount of mail in any given week. So it is unusual for Jimmie to get three letters in a month, let alone in a two-day period.

The first letter is from Katherine, writing to assure him she has made it safely home to Kayenta and that she misses him already. The next day two more letters arrive, each bearing news of a far less pleasant nature. One is from George Benally, advising Jimmie that, as a "Health Service big shot," he ought to be aware of breathing problems that are effecting George and many of the miners he works with. George's situation is not unlike similar reports coming in from other mining communities. Jimmie hopes this letter will pave the way for him to investigate further up at the Cove uranium mines.

But that will have to wait a few weeks, for the third letter is from his mother, who has clearly struggled with phonetic Navajo spelling to tell him his father has been coughing up blood. What's more, the

293

stubborn man refuses to concede that he needs medical attention. Jimmie does not need to see his father to identify the disorder, for tuberculosis has reached epidemic proportions on the reservation. He knows it will not be easy to get Wilson to enter the sanitarium in Ft. Defiance.

After consulting with Dr. Deuschle, Annie's mentor, Jimmie immediately heads for Two Grey Hills. It means time away from his job, but what choice does he have? In spite of his checkered history with his father, he feels obligated to wage and win the war of wills that is certain to ensue. His father's life may depend on it.

"Everyone knows there are only two ways you can be poisoned with the tuberculosis," Wilson informs his son, taking on the same tone he might use with a foolish child. "And that is if you are contaminated by lightning, or if you are sung over by a medicine man who makes a mistake."

Jimmie rolls his eyes and asks, "And which is it with you?"

"Clearly it was neither one."

"There. You see?"

"Which is why this cannot be the tuberculosis. Maybe it is witchcraft. Maybe I angered the Holy Ones. Either way, I lost my *hozho*. Anyone can see that."

According to time-honored Navajo belief, the loss of *hozho*—an ideal state of balance or harmony with the world—brings on illness or misfortune. For centuries, tribal lore has maintained that the cure can be found only by addressing the cause, which is always connected to some negative force of nature. Wilson's generation holds steadfastly to this way of thinking. It would be easier to dissuade a snake from shedding its skin than to convince these believers to seek proper treatment for TB and other rampant diseases. The very idea of germs, after all, is still foreign to most Navajos, although Annie has been working to put Anglo medical terms and concepts into the Navajo language. The phrase she uses for germs—"bugs-that-eat-the-body"—gets laughter at first, but eventually most people gain some understanding of the notion behind it.

Not Wilson Goodluck, though. He is, as always, readily dismissive of new ideas, especially those from the Anglo world.

Jimmie tries to explain to his father that a powerful new medicine is available at the hospital in Ft. Defiance. He may die if he stays home.

"I would die for certain in the place you want me to go," Wilson counters, coughing into a square of cloth. He turns away from Jimmie and closes his eyes, as if the darkness can make his son, along with his son's unwanted counsel, disappear.

Frustrated, Jimmie walks outside. His mother is at her loom, sending the shuttle back and forth with a fervor that suggests her mind is also tangled in the thorns of what to do about her husband. As a youngster, Jimmie loved to squat at her side while she sat at the loom, softly humming to herself, her strong arms tirelessly working the weft.

"He is a stubborn man," Jimmie says. "I work for the Health Service, but I cannot even convince my own father to get well."

Wearily, Leila sets her shuttle on the ground. "Your father is not like others. He walks in the footsteps of Black Horse, even now."

"You would be surprised, Mother. He is not so different from many I have met."

"I am sorry to hear that."

He crouches down beside her and lowers his voice. "Mother, do you know you can also get Father's disease just from living in the same room with him? You may already have the sickness in you."

She shrugs. "He is still my husband. I am not going to walk away. But understand, I am not like him. If I do get the sickness, I will not hesitate to let your white medicine people make me better."

A thought comes to Jimmie suddenly, as if a switch has been thrown to complete an electrical circuit. A few weeks earlier he and Annie had discussed how Navajo medicine men and modern medical science from the white man's world could coexist. "I'm working on the *hata'ali*," she had said. "Our medicine men are starting to realize that tuberculosis is one illness they cannot sing away."

In her words lies his answer.

"Mother," Jimmie says in an excited whisper. "I know what we can do to get Father that new medicine."

He shares his idea with her. She reacts with a startled smile, as if he had just intercepted a thunderbolt and hurtled it back, purged of its inherent evil, into the void above.

JIMMIE RIDES TO THE Two Grey Hills Trading Post where, in a burst of confidence, he calls the sanitarium to make the necessary arrangements. Then he asks Mr. Bloomfield, the trader, where he can find Tall Man, the local *hata'ali* who sang Enemy Way when Jimmie returned from war.

He rides three miles and then sits anxiously on his mother's horse in front of Tall Man's *hogan,* waiting to be recognized and invited in. To help things along, he sings rather loudly, a raucous ditty he learned in the marines. No one around will understand the words, and the decidedly non-Navajo cadence will draw the attention he wants.

After several minutes, Tall Man comes out to investigate. He recognizes Jimmie at once. They make small talk at first and then continue talking inside as Jimmie explains his plan. Tall Man indicates his approval and accepts Jimmie's offer. Then they smoke some Indian tobacco, for it would be rude of Jimmie to leave immediately after conducting business. Finally, the medicine man blesses his guest and promises to appear at Wilson's *hogan* on the second sunrise.

Jimmie makes one additional stop: the *hogan* of Frank Graybeard, a *n'dilnii'hii*—hand-trembler—recommended by Tall Man for his experience with tuberculosis. This meeting also goes well. The rest will be up to the gods.

Back at his parents' home, Jimmie waits until his mother clears away the remnants of the evening meal, stokes the fire, and prepares the room for sleep. Then he speaks to his father while Leila, pretending not to listen, goes about her chores.

"You win, Father." His practiced words fall as easily as sheared fleece. "Since you will not follow my wishes, you should at least have a healing ceremony. You need to know *hozho* again."

Through bouts of violent coughing, Wilson snickers, "I knew you would see it as I see it. But we do not have enough sheep to pay a *n'dilnii'hii* or a *hata'ali*."

"I have money to buy sheep. I've been working four years now."

Wilson waves his hand with an air of disdain. "Government money. *Bilaga'ana* money."

"Money earned helping the *Dineh*."

Wilson snorts.

"Father, I've called on Frank Graybeard. It's all arranged. He'll be here when you rise. He'll find out what's wrong with you."

Wilson starts to protest but then gives up. He nods weakly and closes his eyes. On this night, he is the only member of the family who succumbs easily to sleep.

Shortly after sunrise they are awakened by the sound of heavy footsteps outside the *hogan*. Frank Graybeard paces back and forth beside his horse, waiting to be ushered in, his breath condensing into cottony clouds as it meets the chilly morning air. He is at least ten years older than Tall Man, which puts him in his seventies. Just as Tall Man is not tall, Graybeard has no noticeable beard—not surprising for a Navajo. But his hair is indeed a silvery gray. It falls gently around his shoulders. In the first dewy rays of light, it looks to have been molded from fine strands of pewter. He wears a bright yellow shirt and a garland of turquoise around his neck.

Inside, Wilson lies in an uncertain plane between sleep and wakefulness. Graybeard walks over to him and extends words of greeting as Leila and Jimmie follow behind. Soon the inviting smell of boiling coffee hangs heavy in the room.

"Now we will see what is wrong with you," Graybeard says to his patient. "I will do all I can to help you restore your *hozho*."

Wilson props himself up on one elbow and tries to speak, but he is seized by a spell of violent coughing. He collapses back onto his bedroll.

The hand-trembler, meanwhile, reaches into his pouch, sprinkles corn pollen around Wilson's body, and then closes his eyes, lost in a kind of trance. His lips move almost imperceptibly in mumbled prayer. He is not a medicine man, this seer; he is a diagnostician, whose sole calling is to determine the patient's malady and, consequently, decide on the appropriate ceremony to affect a cure. That, in turn, will ascertain which medicine man the Goodlucks will hire, for Navajo singers often specialize only in certain ceremonies.

Graybeard slowly moves his right hand over Wilson's body, head to toe. As it moves, his hand begins to tremble—slightly, at first, then with greater and greater jerkiness, as if some unseen power is grabbing his wrist and shaking it with violent force. This movement continues for several minutes. Graybeard's hand evidences the strongest tremors when it passes over Wilson's chest.

With his eyes still closed, Graybeard removes his hand and lets it rest peacefully at his side. Only the coffee, bubbling in the pot, dares to disregard Graybeard's concentration. After several more minutes, the hand-trembler opens his eyes and speaks to Wilson Goodluck.

"I have determined the cause of your loss of *hozho*. I am sorry to say you have what the white men call the tubercu—the TB. I believe it has chosen you because you touched a tree cursed by lightning."

Wilson frowns. "What ceremony will cure me?" he croaks, looking at the hand-trembler. "A Blessingway?"

Frank Graybeard rises and looks just past his patient to some unseen point on the wall. "Maybe. But these days, Blessingway is more popular for new *hogans,* new families, and for women who are with child."

Wilson shakes his head. "Nothing is the same anymore."

"I think you should call on the singer, Tall Man," Graybeard quickly adds, sticking to the script Jimmie discussed with him. "He lives over in Newcomb."

"I know Tall Man," Wilson says. "He sang an Enemy Way for my son, here."

"Yes, he is well known for the Enemy Way. But he is also the best singer I know for the Shooting Chant. I think only the Shooting Chant will heal you."

"How soon do you think Tall Man can get here?" Jimmie asks, affecting innocence.

"I can stop by his *hogan* on my way home," Graybeard answers. "There might still be time for him to gather the necessary plants and perform the ceremony at sunrise tomorrow."

Everyone knows the gathering of herbs is a time-consuming preparation. Remedies cannot be prepared in advance and stored away as the white men do with their medicines. The *hataali* must go to where the plant grows, inform the plant who is sick, and then offer it corn pollen and prayers before taking it from the ground.

"Yes, we hope he can come in the morning," Jimmie says. "Tell him my father is very sick. We will give him as many sheep as he asks."

Leila later admits to her son that she could barely keep from laughing to hear her husband become ensnared in the trap that might, Great Spirits willing, save his life.

TALL MAN ARRIVES ON HORSEBACK carrying the supplies of his trade: herbs, rattles, and the items necessary to make one of the hundred or so sand paintings suitable for a Shooting Chant. His supplies include colored sands, crushed rock, charcoal, compressed flowers, gypsum, ochre, pollen, and cornmeal. Wilson is already on his feet, standing unsteadily at the door of the *hogan,* welcoming the *hata'ali* to his home.

"I am sorry to find you with this sickness," Tall Man says to Wilson, who proceeds to cough forcefully into an already bloodied rag. "Frank Graybeard said you were in immediate need of a Shooting Chant, but he did not mention you were coughing up blood."

"It is nothing," Wilson says with another of his dismissive gestures. "The tuberculosis, some try to tell me." He glares at Jimmie, as if his son has made up the disease.

Turning back to Tall Man he says, "But you will make whatever it is go away." It is a question delivered as a demand.

Tall Man frowns and makes a clucking sound. "There are some things I can do for you, and some things others can do better than me."

"What are you talking about?" Wilson snaps.

"I can do the Shooting Chant right now. It will help the Holy Ones to look favorably on you during the part of the cure I cannot do." Jimmie and his mother glance knowingly at each other as Tall Man continues, "I am troubled to tell you, only the white doctor has the medicine that can make the TB go away. I can cure many things, but the TB takes a potent medicine. I do not have anything like it."

"Is this some kind of trick?" Wilson is clearly agitated. "I will find another *hata'ali.*"

Tall Man continues unfazed, his voice neither breaking rhythm nor growing louder over Wilson's protestations. "You will hear other *hata'ali* speak as I do. We have learned that this is one sickness we cannot sing away. Not by the time you are spitting the blood."

Leila speaks up. "Husband, listen to him. Our medicine man and the white medicine man will work together to make you well. Tall Man says he will perform the healing ceremony Graybeard spoke of. And *iika'ah* as well, is that not so?"

Tall Man nods. *Iika'ah* is a sand painting designed to summon the Holy Ones to infuse the sand with their healing power.

"And Father," Jimmie says, "you won't even have to leave the reservation for the treatment. They're using the new medicine at the sanitarium in Ft. Defiance. You'll be with other patients like yourself, all speaking our language."

Wilson's eyes radiate fear and confusion as he asks Tall Man, "You are sure the Shooting Chant and its *iika'ah* will not make me well by themselves?"

"What it will do is make the white man's medicine work better." As if as an afterthought he adds, "Another thing I can help with—it will cost you more sheep, of course—I can travel to the hospital and do a sing to bless your bed and your room."

"I think that's a fine idea," Jimmie interjects. He had suggested it earlier, of course. "And Mother can stay at my apartment. It's very close to the hospital. I'll be traveling for the next several weeks. She can come and go as she pleases."

Wilson glowers. "Who will watch our livestock?"

Leila says, "I will arrange to have the Tah boy feed them when I am with you." Frankie Tah lives just up the trail.

Wilson struggles to weigh his options. "I will think it over," he snarls. "But first Tall Man must perform the Shooting Chant over me. Then we will see."

Jimmie breathes a sigh of relief. Wilson's resistance to treatment has clearly weakened. But for now his father's eyes are only on Tall Man, who takes out his materials to begin the sand painting, the first step toward Wilson Goodluck's reluctant rehabilitation.

THE FT. DEFIANCE SANATORIUM HAS become a busy place since Dr. Walsh McDermott swept in with his team of doctors from Cornell University.

McDermott has just turned forty, yet the graying at his temples gives him an air of greater maturity than his chronological age might suggest. Along with his confident demeanor and seemingly boundless energy, he exudes a presence not always found among research scientists and members of academia and erudite Lincoln scholars. McDermott is all three, as Jimmie has learned, plus a brilliant internist to boot.

This is McDermott's second visit to the reservation. The previous year he was in Tuba City to treat an outbreak of infectious hepatitis at the boarding school. It was there he met Jimmie, who served as his interpreter. In fact, it was at Jimmie's (and Annie's) urging that the Cornell team began to investigate the staggering incidence of tuberculosis that left few Navajo families unaffected.

Now the doctors' return to *Dinetah* is a triumphant one, for they come armed with two powerful new drugs: streptomycin and isoniazid, donated by the E. R. Squibb Company to test the medicines' efficacy. The tribal council had even set aside $10,000 to pay transportation costs for the volunteer physicians. This was pushed through by Annie, for she did indeed win a place on the tribal council—the sole woman this term. She heads the council's Health and Welfare Committee.

Tall Man accompanies Jimmie's hesitant father to the sanitarium, where he blesses Wilson's bed, his room, the hospital itself, even the doctors. Drs. McDermott and Deuschle leave Tall Man to his chants for nearly an hour before they move in to assess Wilson's condition and start his treatment. Jimmie takes the opportunity to stop by Dr. McDermott's tiny office to warn him that Wilson Goodluck will not be a model patient.

"He's not the first Indian who distrusts me and my medicine," the doctor remarks. "Until I came here, I felt just as uneasy about *your* medicine men. A bunch of witch doctors, seemed to me. But hell, I've come to learn that many of the herbs and plants your medicine men use, along with the prayers they chant, may actually help to heal body and soul. Who knows? For some patients, *believing* it will work may be enough." He reaches for a stack of papers and adds, "But just believing is hardly enough when it comes to treating tuberculosis."

"Yet our medicine men still have the only way to restore what we call balance," Jimmie reminds him. "For the patient to improve, I believe both are essential."

"Yes, perhaps they are." Dr. McDermott strokes his chin as if assessing the closeness of his shave. "Well, if the medicine man can help restore your father's emotional balance so our therapy works to restore his body, maybe he'll think less harshly of us white doctors."

Jimmie shakes his head. "Even if you save my father's life, it won't exempt you from his scorn. It will just prove that Tall Man's medicine kept *your* medicine from killing him."

Dr. McDermott looks over his glasses, the frames perched low on his nose. "From what you're telling me, it's surprising that you got him to come here at all."

Jimmie sighs. The business of dreams—of achieving them and keeping them alive when so many disappointments and roadblocks and unexpected setbacks conspire to get in the way—is a tenuous business indeed.

"If you only knew, Doctor," Jimmie says.

CHAPTER 27

OCTOBER 1949

Cove, Arizona, is a small, secluded mining community loosely strewn within a dramatic landscape of magnificent red rock mesas. It is accessible only by horse, and from just one direction—the east—through the area known as the Red Valley. This makes for an arduous journey from any starting point, including Ft. Defiance, some one hundred miles away as the hawk flies.

Jimmie is able to ride as far north as Tsaile in an ill-tempered Pontiac driven by a BIA official heading on to Round Rock. Staring at the Indianhead hood ornament through the windshield, Jimmie wonders whether Detroit will ever come out with a *Navajo*-inspired model: a Manuelito, perhaps, or a Ganado Mucho. He almost chuckles out loud when it occurs to him that there already is, ironically, a Dodge.

At Tsaile he continues his journey on horseback, heading northeast over a mountain trail to the community of Red Rock, then due west through the crimson dale toward Cove. His horse has been loaned by a rancher who often does favors for the BIA in return for "special considerations," whatever they might be. Jimmie asked no questions.

The weather has turned noticeably cooler, the skies are filled with high, wispy clouds, and the sandstone rock formations that rise on all sides color the land in shades of ruby and garnet and magenta. Today, Jimmie scarcely notices. He cannot shake the image of his hospitalized father, resisting to the end. No one, not even Dr. McDermott, can predict how successfully the new medicine will work. But Jimmie is eager to deal now with people who *want* to be helped, like George, his fellow boot buddy and radioman.

Jimmie's dutiful horse stays on a steady course, lugging his rider with minimal complaint through several altitude changes. Eventually, the Lukachukai Mountains appear to the south, their lower elevations blanketed in a soft fleece of Ponderosa pines. The jagged, striated sandstone peaks rise above the tree line like strange heads poking up out of a thick, green sweater. Farther along, the Lukachukais surrender to the ramparts of the Carrizo Range.

Jimmie's assignment requires him to spend several weeks in this area interviewing Navajo miners for inclusion in an ongoing health study initiated by ranking officials of the US Public Health Service. For in spite of mining company executives who insist uranium is safe, the toxic presence of a substance called "radon" is old news. So is the term "radioactive," which has been around for more than twenty years. One after another, so-called experts profess that uranium poses no threat to those who come in contact with it. But recent findings regarding high concentrations of yellowcake dust—uranium oxide—have raised serious warning signals. George's letter simply confirms that government concerns may be justified.

Following directions George has sent him, Jimmie dismounts in front of an isolated *hogan*. Its sun-bleached logs look like they have stood here for decades. He takes no more than two steps before his

old friend from code school runs out and grabs him in a big bear
hug, an act as uncharacteristically Navajo as is George's cussing.

"Shit, man, where you been? Didn't they teach you nothing in
the marines about showin' up when you're supposed to?"

"Hello to you too," Jimmie says. "Thing is, before coming here
I had to take my father to the sanatorium in Ft. Defiance. He has
TB."

"Shit sakes, I'm sorry, Jimmie. I didn't mean nothing by it."

"It's all right, George. Everyone knows you took shrapnel in the
ass and your head's never been the same since."

They both nearly fall down laughing. But George's laughter
quickly changes into a hacking cough that sounds like the backfire
from old Rides-in-Smoke's pick-up. This cough is different from
Wilson's. It is raspier, more staccato. George turns away and spews
out a generous puddle of thick phlegm that lands unceremoniously
on the parched ground.

George has aged visibly since those days in the South Pacific.
His face is drawn, like one might see on a sickly old man. His skin,
once ruddy and glowing, has taken on the yellowish color of new
twigs that emerge from the coyote willows growing along the washes
and streams. George was always a big fellow, with broad neck and
shoulders and a barrel chest, but now he walks with a slight limp and
appears hunched over, as if he is carrying a heavy, invisible weight.

"You look great," George remarks. "Must be getting laid some."

"You look pretty good yourself," Jimmie answers, trying to
sound sincere. "A little pale, maybe."

"Yeah, well ..." George's voice trails off. He looks serious for
a second, and then, like a cloud skittering across the sun, his prior
bravado returns. "Hey, it's nearly sundown. You must be starved.
Got no shit-on-a-shingle for you like the good old days, but coffee's
on and I think I can scare up some fry bread, maybe some jerky,
too."

"You actually *liked* shit-on-a-shingle, as I remember."

"Hell yeah, didn't everybody? Find it hard gettin' used to Indian food again. Can't get the shit *or* the shingle 'round here. Or much else, neither."

He coughs again as Jimmie follows him inside. The place is musty and dank, with a dirt floor and walls loosely constructed of what are now rotting logs.

"This is where I was raised up," George says, sounding apologetic. He blows the dust out of two tin cups.

They head back outside, where George pours coffee from a beat-up pot that sits on the fire. "My father died while I was stringin' telephone wire in 'Canal," he explains. "My mother up and died last year. Got me a brother in Colorado, a sister down in Leupp. They don't want this place. Guess you can see why. Well, even though my mother died here, I don't believe in that old-fashioned *chindi* shit. I figure, why burn the place down when it puts a roof over my head? I ain't gettin' rich workin' the mines, y'know. But somebody is." He takes a noisy sip of hot coffee. "Somebody is," he repeats. "That's for damn sure."

George brings out fry bread and dried mutton, and the two former radiomen catch up on their experiences toward the end of the war. "Didn't know how good I had it in the service, war and all," George concludes. "Not till I came back to this fucking place."

"*I* knew how good I had it back then," Jimmie says, tearing into a strip of mutton. "We were treated like everybody else. There we were all marines. Just marines. Not here, though. Here, most everything's like it was before. Maybe worse." His tone of voice suggests that, this time, he is making an observation, not spewing forth a grievance.

George snickers. "Yeah, we're back to bein' Indians. Fuckin' Indians who can't get a decent job. Not here in Cove, anyway. You want to find work around here, mining's all there is. You work in the uranium mines or you go off-rez. Maybe find some part time for the railroad. But I got a girl here I might marry up with, so I'm not anxious to leave. That means it's the mines or nothin'. Steady work, if you're Navajo. But they treat us like shit."

Jimmie takes a sip of coffee. It is bitter, like George clearly is, like Jimmie not long ago. "That's one of the reasons I'm here." He presses George for more details.

"I better put on another pot of coffee," George says. "Or you're gonna fall asleep by the time I finish bitching."

ACCORDING TO NAVAJO CREATION LEGEND, when the People emerged from the underworld into this, the fourth world, the gods presented them with two yellow substances and told them they must choose. The first item was corn pollen, fine as dust and faintly fragrant, glittering with the color of the sun. The second substance, called "cledge," came from the underworld. It was streaked in rock, perhaps the only color to be found in the dark void that lay beneath the ground.

The People chose that which was new and beautiful to them, which was the corn pollen. The gods were pleased. "You have chosen all that is positive in life," they told the People."You have chosen the Beauty Way. This corn pollen will carry your songs and prayers to us. It will keep you close to us always."

Then the gods grew very serious and they said, "Having made your choice, you must never touch the cledge or remove it from the ground. For if you ever release it, it will become a serpent. It will bring evil, death, and destruction into the world."

For countless generations, the Dineh heeded this advice. The insidious cledge was contained, buried under mountains and mesas and immense boulders.

Meanwhile, delicate pollen from gossamer tassels of corn became a part of every ceremony, every daily ritual.

The gods rejoiced.

*But in areas of the reservation, especially places like Red Valley
and the mountains north of Cove and the rocky mesas to its south, the
serpent lay inert, patiently biding its time, waiting for the People to
forget, waiting for release, waiting …*

*Then came the great war. Then came the Manhattan Project.
Then came the picks and shovels and wheelbarrows, the bulldozers and
dynamite, the surveying equipment and trucks and heavy machinery.*

*For the first time in eons, the serpent stirred. Eagerly, it anticipated
the time, nearing, when it would open its eyes and feed its hunger. When
it would emerge triumphantly into the bright, propitious sunlight of the
Fourth World.*

"GOT ME A JOB AS a mucker when I came back from overseas,"
George begins.

"A what?"

"A mucker. We go in after they blast a section of mine. Break up
the rocks some more with a pickax. Put 'em into cars that carry 'em
out of the mine. Worked for the VCA—that's Vanadium Corporation
of America—up here in the Carrizos. Few months ago, Kerr-McGee
comes around, takes over some of the existing mines, opens new
ones. Got us Indians by the short hairs, they figure, and they're
right, y'know. You want work, you take what they give you. Which
ain't—" George is interrupted by a bout of vehement coughing.

"I want you to go to Shiprock," Jimmie says in a calm voice. "It's
the closest hospital to here and there's a Health Service doctor there
who can check you over. I've met him a few times in Ft. Defiance
and he's good. And because you're my first, I'm going with you.
Then I'm going to find out how many others around here got health
problems like yours."

"Lot of us. Coughing, shortness of breath, headaches. Prob'ly
all the dust."

"They expecting you at the mine tomorrow?"

"Actually, no. They're blasting today and tomorrow. I was planning to spend tomorrow with my girl."

"Like I said, you're going and I'm coming with you, buddy. How 'bout we bring her along? I'd like to meet her."

George eyes Jimmie warily and then grins. "Not this time, friend. How do I know you won't want her for yourself, big-shot government translator like you?"

"Already got me a girl."

George's grin spreads from ear to ear, so Jimmie gets up and preempts whatever his buddy is about to say by telling George he ought to stop talking and get some rest.

"Hey, you wanted to know about my job, *Cheii,* and I'm not done tellin' you. So pipe down and listen the hell up." George refills his cup from the coffeepot, clearly intent on staying put for a while.

Jimmie shrugs and sits back down.

"Now my first two jobs, the mucking was done all by hand. Ball-breakin' work. Bein' a driller's no easier. Use a sledgehammer to pound steel rods into the rock. There's no easy jobs in mining, but believe me, they save the worst ones for us Indians. Still, we're happy for any work at all. Before everyone went bat shit over uranium, Cove was barren as a witch's womb. You saw mostly women livin' here 'cause their men were up in Colorado or Utah lookin' for railroad work. It's the mines keeping the men home these days, and that's a good thing, I guess."

Jimmie drains the last of his coffee, grimaces. "How long's your workday?"

"Until they tell us we can go home. I don't know … ten, twelve, sometimes fourteen hours at a time. Nighttime don't mean a thing to our bosses. You shine a light on the ore and keep working. Y'know, funny thing about that rock. Turn off the light, and it glows. Glows in the dark, like a fucking watch dial."

Jimmie tries not to register his alarm. "You paid by the hour?" he asks.

"Yeah, but Indian wages. Pay depends on the job, of course, and a mucker's hind tit on that pig. When I started, I got seventy-five cents an hour. Can you believe it? Now I'm up to ninety-five cents from Kerr-McGee."

"Federal law sets the minimum wage at a buck and a quarter," Jimmie says, raising an eyebrow.

"No shit, Sherlock. Here I am, some education—no genius, maybe, but smart enough to speak two languages and learn our code, right?—and the only work I can get is choking on dust in a fuckin' hole for miserable pay." George looks Jimmie in the eye and asks, "Say, when you came up here, did you see the mining camp? The temporary housing outside of Cove?"

"Hard to miss. Prefab, looked like. I have to say, they look comfortable enough. How many miners they hold?"

George snickers. "Miners? They hold thirteen supervisors and foremen. That's how many there are. All white guys, by the way." He waits for Jimmie's reaction. "Big surprise, huh? They live at the camp during the week. Eat there, too. All subsidized by the mining company. Us Indians, though, we're on our own for food and shelter. So we often sleep out in the open, covered only with the yellow dust for a blanket. And believe me, there's plenty of dust, 'specially when we go in after they blast. It stays in our noses, our mouths. Gives me headaches sometimes. The white foremen, though, I never heard *them* cough. They hardly ever go into the mines themselves. 'Injun work,' they tell us."

"Did any of the Navajo workers ever think to complain? They—"

Again George waves his hand, cutting Jimmie off in midsentence. "A guy named Michael Doren—friend of mine—couple of months ago he refuses to go in right after they blast some uranium ore. All he wants is for the dust to settle a little. His cough's worse than mine.

Know what his foreman told him? 'Get the hell out of here and don't come back.' The mine bosses, they fire anyone who complains, anyone who don't go in the hole when they're ordered to, anyone who don't stay there till they're told they can come out. Guess there's plenty more cheap labor where we come from. Not only that, the companies got no taxes or health and safety regulations to worry about. They don't pay nothin' to reclaim the land when they're done. They don't even move out the waste. Just dump the tailings off the mesa or pile 'em up on the ground."

Jimmie scribbles furiously on a small notepad that he plucks from his pocket like a stage magician pulling a rabbit out of a hat. This information is too important to commit to memory, finely honed as his memory may be.

"Who was it who said 'War is hell?'" George asks. "Some big-shit Civil War general or something? Shit on a stick, Jimmie, those white guys didn't know nothin'. One thing I learned since fightin' the Japs, it ain't *war* that's hell. Fuck, no."

George kicks at the ground with his boot. Apparently not satisfied that this is punctuation enough, he takes his coffee cup and flings it. It hits the ground with a tinny *thunk*, then rolls on its side until it comes to rest against a chunk of reddish-brown rock. With an uneasy sigh, George shifts his gaze to his startled buddy.

"Hell, my friend, is what comes after."

CHAPTER 28

OCTOBER–NOVEMBER 1949

D r. Dennis Glenn is a thin young man whose slightly stooped posture reminds Jimmie of *kokopelli*, the Hopi fertility deity depicted with a hunched back and a flute to his lips. The doctor presses a stethoscope against George Benally's chest as Jimmie sits quietly across the examining room, which appears remarkably devoid of anything but a jar of tongue depressors, several tubes of some gel, and a blood pressure gauge. The hospital here in Shiprock is small and underequipped—regrettable, considering this is the most populated city within the borders of the reservation.

Jimmie had offered to wait outside, since George obviously does not require an interpreter. Still, George insisted that Jimmie accompany him, adding only that he would excuse his buddy "if I have to pull out my dick and whiz into a paper cup."

The doctor listens carefully to George's breathing. Then he folds up his stethoscope and says, "I'm sending your urine and sputum out for testing, and we'll get a chest X-ray. But based on the yellowcake dust in your nose, and after hearing your chest, I have a pretty good idea what's going to come back." Without elaborating, he asks George, "There any ventilation in the mine?"

George shakes his head. "Not much. They got a pipe going in through the top that's open to the outside, is all. Even so, we usually work deeper in the hole, maybe a hundred feet or more beyond it."

The doctor scribbles notes on a clipboard. "Your foremen ever tell you to wash your hands carefully, change your clothes, anything like that?"

"They tell us to work faster, work longer. That's about it."

"What about food and drink? You bring your own? And where do you eat?"

"Shit yes, we bring our own food. You kidding? We eat wherever we're working in the mine. For drinking, we got a pool of water in the mine where I'm at now. Color of piss. Seeps down through the rock, I guess. At least it's cool. And free."

The doctor glances in Jimmie's direction, his face a mask of concern. Turning back to George, Dr. Glenn asks, "Nobody ever tell you it's not wise to drink that water?" The pitch of his voice perfectly matches his incredulous expression.

"There something you ain't tellin' me?" George sounds more angry than alarmed.

The doctor clears his throat and pulls up a chair. "Mr. Benally, we're coming to understand that uranium mining presents ... well, problems beyond those found in other kinds of mining. Problems that can be offset—to some degree, anyway—by reducing your direct contact with the ore. This means not inhaling the dust if you can avoid it, and certainly not drinking the water in the mine. It means washing your hands often, and not bringing your mining clothes home, or at the very least, washing them right away. Uranium may be mined for war, but we suspect it can do a lot of damage to people long before it gets inside a bomb."

"This stuff can kill me? That what you're saying?" George asks, and this time alarm wins out over anger.

"Not right away, perhaps, but over time … yes, it's possible."

The hush in the room is palpable. "Look, I'm not here to alarm you," Dr. Glenn continues. "There's so much we're still learning."

"Doctor," Jimmie asks, "are the toxic properties of uranium the reason—"

"*Potentially* toxic," interrupts Dr. Glenn, looking reassuringly at George. "All ore is different, and miners will be affected differently. Many won't get sick at all. We just don't know at this point."

"All right, then, are the *potentially* toxic properties of the ore the reason George has been coughing so much?"

George looks from Jimmie to Dr. Glenn, his eyes wide.

"No. That's something else. We'll wait for the test and X-ray results, but like I said, I know what we'll see. That dust in your nose and mucus, it'll show up in your lungs as well. That's what's making you cough. It's called silicosis: scarring of the lung tissue. See, the rock around here is sandstone, which contains silica. When you inhale the dust, it acts like sandpaper on your lungs. Coal miners get something similar: black lung disease. But the fact that the dust and water you're in contact with also contains uranium oxides, well, that could bring on even more serious problems down the road. It's important that you continue with these check-ups on a regular basis."

George warily digests what the doctor is telling him. When he speaks, his words come out slowly, in measured cadence.

"Let me get this straight. What you're saying is there's *two* things going against me, right? One is the mine dust, this silica shit, that's making me cough. The other is the crap in the uranium itself that's mixing *with* the dust, that's poisoning the water, that can get inside me in lots of ways, it seems, maybe making me even sicker. I got that right?"

Dr. Glenn purses his lips. "Close enough."

George reaches for his shirt on the floor by his feet and flings it against the wall. "I had better odds against the fuckin' Japs."

"Mr. Benally, you're going to do all the things I've suggested," Dr. Glenn says, "and you're going to see me every few months. I'll keep a good eye on you."

George responds with a loud snort.

When George is shuttled down to X-ray a short while later, Jimmie says to Dr. Glenn, "I got a look at that Health Service study before I left Ft. Defiance. If I understand the half of it, George and the others could be in for a rougher time than you let on. That so?"

The doctor gestures for Jimmie to follow him into his office. He closes the door behind them and walks over to his desk, selecting a large-bowled pipe from a wooden rack. He pulls out a pouch of tobacco from his pocket and proceeds to fill the bowl as he says, "It's too early to document direct cause and effect, but yes, the dangers are real, and with miners like George, the damage may already be done. Fact is, we're beginning to think that exposure to the radiation coming from uranium-bearing ore—particularly to small, steady doses of it—can lead to lung cancer, especially the virulent oat-cell type. Then there's the uranium oxide he's inhaling every day. It doesn't just affect the lungs. We're finding that, for some reason, it migrates to the bone marrow and stays there, continuing to break down for years, bombarding the tissues."

"Which means what, exactly?" Jimmie asks.

"Which means," says Dr. Glenn as he holds a lit match to his pipe bowl and draws in deeply, "poor Mr. Benally, for all intents and purposes, is quite possibly becoming radioactive—you've heard the term, right?—from the inside out."

JIMMIE SEARCHES FOR SOMETHING ENCOURAGING to say on the journey back to Cove, but words seem hollow and inadequate. George is faced with either unemployment or suffering the consequences of staying at the mine. And from what the doctor said, it may already be too late.

Tragically, George is not the only one. Over the weeks that follow, Jimmie meets dozens of miners who have the same symptoms. Several promise to see Dr. Glenn, but who knows how many will actually make the trip to Shiprock.

Though he tries to remain focused on his work, Jimmie's mind is never far from visions of Katherine. And it occurs to him that he is not all that far away from her now in miles, either. Coming to Cove has brought him nearly half the distance to Kayenta. He further rationalizes that, since there are uranium mines close to Monument Valley and all along the Oljato Mesa, he can talk to miners in the Kayenta area just as he is doing here. It will provide more input for the Health Service study, so his bosses can hardly complain. And so what if they do?

His heart beats like a ceremonial drum as he thinks about seeing his girl again. It has been less than two months since they were together at her graduation, but that seems like a lifetime ago. Soon winter will claim the land and the mountains will likely be impassable for a time. If he doesn't go now, he will not see her until spring, if he can get away then at all.

Having made up his mind, it is hardly material to him whether his decision is rational or emotional. All he knows is that, come what may, he cannot afford to jeopardize his future with the only woman he has ever truly loved.

ALTHOUGH KAYENTA IS ONLY ABOUT a hundred miles west of Cove, the distance cannot be traversed in a straight line unless one has wings. Being merely human, Jimmie has to first ride east out of Cove and then turn south, eventually circling around to the northwest near the community of Round Rock. It is the one place where he might spend the night, rest his horse, and stock up on fresh water for the remainder of his journey. It is also the area where his father rode with the renegade headman Black Horse and witnessed the historic run-in with Chee Dodge and the Indian agent. It will be a little daunting to walk in the footsteps of his father where, as a young wolf running with his first pack, Wilson had whet his appetite for anger and defiance.

Jimmie transverses the mountains through the Buffalo Pass, where the Ponderosas part like theater curtains to leave a space wide enough for a rough trail. By the time he crosses the Totsoh Wash on the western side of the range, midafternoon has already come calling. The drop in elevation makes the early November sun feel startlingly warm. Here in the no-man's land triangulated by Shiprock to the east, Canyon de Chelly to the south, and Monument Valley to the northwest, the dirt road through Round Rock is the most hospitable passage he is likely to find anywhere along the challenging route.

He rides into Round Rock, observing that neither of the two prominent buttes that give the community its name are actually round. Still, with a little imagination, the stones on top resemble cannonballs or something similar.

He seeks out the local chapter house. It appears newly built, with adobe blocks arranged in the hexagonal *hogan* style. Overhead, the sun drops slowly, painting the sky as it goes. As Jimmie admires the sunset from his saddle, three men emerge from the chapter house and walk toward the back of the structure, talking quietly in Navajo. Two of the men look about the age of his father, while the third appears to be at least ten years younger.

Jimmie dismounts, tethers his weary horse to a post, then approaches the men. They exchange names and clans and make small talk for a short while.

One of the men, Hosteen Yazzie, asks what brings Jimmie to

Round Rock. "Just passing through," he answers truthfully. "But I wonder, is the old Round Rock Trading Post still standing?" He has come with no expectations, but it would be interesting to see the place his father has spoken about.

"Nearest trading post these days is down in Many Farms," answers the man who introduced himself as Big Hat. "You looking to pawn something?"

"Just curious," Jimmie says, feeling a little disappointed. "Growing up in Two Grey Hills, I heard about a fight at the trading post here. A long time ago, probably when you were still a child."

Big Hat shakes his head. "I was raised up over in Tuba City."

A glimmer of awareness shines in Hosteen Yazzie's eyes. "You mean the trouble between Black Horse and the Agent Shipley?"

Jimmie nods, encouraged.

"I heard that story too," Hosteen Yazzie says. "From my mother. She told me I was one of the children the agent wanted to carry off. Said I would not be Navajo anymore if he had his way. Maybe I would be a white man today. I would be eating strange foods, living in a far-off place like Farmington or Denver."

Now the younger man speaks up. He has an Anglo name, David Miller. Further evidence that on the reservation, names are still very much in transition, though since the war, most babies have been given Anglo names right from the beginning.

"There is a man who will know about that incident," David says. "His name is Left-Handed Thrower. I think he was around during the stand-off."

"Yes, you are right, he will know," Hosteen Yazzie agrees. "I remember now. He sent word to the headman that the agent was coming here. He is a very old man now. He was there. He saw it all."

This is more than Jimmie had anticipated. Is it possible he will learn more about the event that shaped his father's longstanding pattern of behavior? There are answers waiting to be revealed. He is sure of it.

"Do you know where I might find Left-Handed Thrower?" Jimmie asks.

The men look at him as if he has just asked where he might find his nose. "Of course we know," replies David. "He is right here, inside the chapter house."

Jimmie thanks the men, excuses himself, and then practically flies toward the entrance.

AMONG THE NAVAJO PEOPLE, NOTHING is more revered than old age. So it is with the utmost deference that Jimmie approaches Left-Handed Thrower.

The old man sits by himself on the floor, legs crossed, smoking a long pipe wrapped with strips of rawhide. The elder looks every bit of ninety, and quite possibly he is older than that. Stringy, white hair tumbles down to his shoulders. His eyes are closed as if he is deep in prayer or lost in thought. Scored on his leathery face are deep-set lines that radiate out in a jumble of furrows and whorls and zigzags and intersecting patterns, each fine etching resembling the concentric rings of a cross-cut pine log. Although the old man sits against a wall, his back is straight. Equally surprisingly, there is no evidence of tremor in his hands as he puffs on his pipe. His clothing is rather nondescript—denim pants and a worn, faded shirt, both blue. His solitary piece of jewelry is a stunning necklace fashioned from three strands of shell-like turquoise *heishi* beads.

Quietly, so as not to disturb the old man's concentration, Jimmie sits facing him at a distance. Folding chairs are scattered around the meeting room, and the scent of Indian tobacco hangs in the air. In an opposite corner of the room, two teenaged boys huddle together playing cards. Jimmie waits patiently, his eyes fixed on the ancient soul smoking his pipe.

After about fifteen minutes, when smoke no longer comes out of Left-Handed Thrower's pipe, the old man gently sets it down on the floor. Eyes still closed, he says quietly in the Navajo language, "You have come a long way, young warrior." He intones it not as a question, but as a statement of fact. His voice sounds surprisingly strong and unwavering for such an elderly person.

Jimmie is so startled by the unexpected words that he looks around to see if the old man could possibly be addressing someone else. But there are only the two boys with their cards.

Flustered, Jimmie sputters, "I am honored to be in your presence, my revered uncle." He uses the term "uncle" out of respect for someone considerably older than himself. He introduces himself by telling Left-Handed Thrower his name and his mother's clan.

"And your 'born for' clan?" the old man asks.

"I … do not know. My father does not know his father."

The ancient soul nods, as if digesting this information. "Me, I am called Left-Handed Thrower," he says. "I am born to the Many Goats Clan. Born for the Sticking-up-Ears People Clan."

The old man opens his eyes for the first time. Jimmie sees how they stare vacuously beneath a transparent white membrane.

He is blind!

"Come closer," the old man says. "I do not hear as well as I once did. "

Jimmie moves forward and speaks in a louder voice. "I've heard tales of a famous… argument, I guess, at the trading post here. Back around 1892, the stories say. I understand you were there when it happened."

The ancient man nods again, slowly this time. "Yes, I was a young man then."

"Do you remember what happened there?" Jimmie asks.

Left-Handed Thrower strokes his chin. "I remember some of it. The agent wanted to take children away from here. He wanted them to learn not to be Navajo anymore." He pronounces the tribal name as *Nabehoo*, from the Tewa language of the ancient pueblo people, shunning the generally used Spanish pronunciation. "There was a powerful headman at that time. From the Carrizo Mountain region. He was called Black Horse. You have heard the name." A statement again, recognition of fact.

Jimmie nods his head, forgetting that gestures are futile in front of the sightless elder. "Yes, I know his name from the stories."

"I knew him very well. Better than anyone alive today. It is good that you came to me."

When Left-Handed Thrower grows quiet, Jimmie breathlessly waits for him to go on. Then the old man abruptly says, "I was the one who asked Black Horse to come here. Many called him an outlaw, you know. A dangerous man. He would not let the white men take advantage of the *Dineh*. He came to Round Rock with his followers. I remember there was Limper. And Tall Red House Clansman. And … and Old Bead Chant Singer. As I recall, if it were not for Chee Dodge, we might have burned down the trading post and killed the agent. I was as restless as everyone else in the group. Black Horse had us pretty excited. He was good that way."

There is a scrape of chairs behind Jimmie. The two boys have taken their cards and are scrambling out, leaving him alone in the room with the old man.

"Now I will tell you some things about Black Horse you do not know," Left-Handed Thrower says. "Things most people no longer care about. It is ancient history, like our legends. But you are different. You have a powerful need. I can see that."

Jimmie feels anxious, confused. *What can you see? What can you see through those shuttered eyes?*

"Black Horse was not an easy person to explain. He became a

human being around 1830. Thirty years before my time. He was raised up in the red rock country of the Lukachukai, born for the Bitter Water People. I first heard his name in connection with a murder. Some *bilagaʼana* prospectors in the mountains. I cannot say if he was responsible. It is possible. I myself had never seen a white man when I first met up with Black Horse. I told him I could not hate someone I had not met. But he told me they had done bad things to our people. He said they would do bad things again. I believed him.

"I would have joined up with him like the others, but I had just taken a wife here in Round Rock. She cost me many sheep. I did not want to leave something so valuable alone for long periods of time. When I told Black Horse this, he said to me, 'Why do you let a woman influence what you do and where you go? I have had three wives and I care little about them now that I am headman here. Two of the wives I do not see anymore, even though one has given me a child. I do not have time to raise a child or pleasure a wife. Not as long as the *bilagaʼana* threaten our ways.'"

Left-Handed Thrower smacks his lips together as if he is chewing something. Jimmie holds his breath, spellbound.

"Never did I regret staying in Round Rock," Left-Handed Thrower explains. "I was happy with my wife. One woman was enough for me. I am sorry to say she was called home by the Holy People a few years ago. My time is also coming soon. Then I will walk alone into the desert."

He pauses again, clearly leading up to something.

"But that is not what you came to hear, young warrior. Very well, then. Let me think. The next time I saw Black Horse was during that argument with the agent. My wife helped to cook meals during those two days. Black Horse later told me that if his wives were more like mine, he might have stayed close to home himself. That is what he said, but he could never be tied to one place. The mountains were his home, the red rock valleys. Any place the *bilaga'ana* threatened his people was his home. He lived to be almost as old as I am now, you know."

"When did he die?" Jimmie asks, although he is uneasy about interrupting the old man.

"Oh, a long time ago. Maybe 1915 or 1920. One year is like another. I saw him during the season of the full moon before his death. He was in the Red Valley then. He knew he was dying, just as I will know. He told me that he would not change a thing in his life, except this: he said, 'I wish I had made myself known to my child, to my son. I have watched him grow from a distance, and now I hear he has given me a grandson. But it is too late for me now.' That is what I heard him say with these very ears."

Left-Handed Thrower stops talking and fixes his sightless gaze on Jimmie, as if waiting for the young man to catch up with him.

All around Jimmie rises a static hum, like the sound coming from a shortwave tuned between bands. Beads of moisture form on his skin as if he were in a sweat lodge. He tries to speak up, but all that comes out is a weak bleat. "The name of the son of Black Horse?"

"Let me think. It was a long time ago."

The old man puts his head in his hands. After a minute he looks up brightly, as if he has just remembered. The gesture seems rehearsed, theatrical.

"You know, the boy—well, he was a young man—he was also there at the fight with the agent. Black Horse admitted this to me just before he died. He said it was the only time he spent two full days with his son. During the Round Rock incident, we did not learn that the young man was his son. Neither did that young man, I am certain of it."

"His name?" Jimmie asks again. His breath comes in short gasps.

"You know his name."

Walks Alone.

The static hum stops abruptly. Jimmie sits in stunned silence as the reality of his lineage sweeps over him.

Left-Handed Thrower says nothing, but continues to look in Jimmie's direction through unseeing eyes. New sounds arise, a jumble of words and voices and accompanying sharp laughter that echo through Jimmie's skull like the sounds at a carnival fun house.

You come from flawed stock, they jeer in unison, each voice varying in pitch and resonance. *Flawed stock.* The sound reverberates harshly, flying at him like an accusing finger. *Flawed stock,* it repeats. *Flawed stock … flawed stock … flawed stock …*

And from very close by—perhaps from Left-Handed Thrower himself, though Jimmie cannot be certain as he thinks about it later—in an old man's voice he hears, "Finally you know your father's clan, Jimmie Goodluck. It is the Bitter Water People. Now you can finish your journey, fulfill your dream, and complete your life, for at last you have learned who you are born for. At last you can recognize who you are. Listen, Jimmie. *Listen!* It is the blood of the defiant Black Horse that runs through your veins."

CHAPTER 29

NOVEMBER 1949

I t is a busy day at the Kayenta Clinic. Nurse Begay is working alone—a traveling doctor comes only one or two times a month—and the office has several waiting patients. There is an elderly woman with a bandaged foot, a young mother with a baby in her lap, and a man of about fifty who holds a bandana over an oozing gash in his arm.

Because Katherine is Navajo, many of the old timers reluctantly allow her to administer advice and treatment in accordance with the "white man's medicine." A Navajo in a nurse's uniform is still a novelty on the reservation, but her role in Annie's growing number of healthcare films has elevated her to near celebrity status.

Jimmie comes in and closes the outer door behind him. An attached bell jangles with a tinny sound. He takes in the small waiting room with its three patients. The walls are unadorned except for a flimsy rack that holds a number of pamphlets.

"Have a seat," comes Katherine's voice from an adjoining examining room. Many of the young people here speak English, for school attendance is rising every year. But among her older clientele, Navajo is still the primary language, so she repeats the same three words in Navajo. Then she adds, "I'll be with you soon."

"You're with me now, Katherine," Jimmie calls back. He is nearly ecstatic from hearing the sound of her voice. "You've been with me every day since we parted."

With a loud squeal, Katherine runs into the reception room. She throws her arms around Jimmie, burrowing her face into his neck as he presses one hand against her back and, with the other, gently strokes her hair, reveling in its velveteen touch.

It causes quite a stir among the waiting patients. The young mother smiles warmly as her child squirms in her lap. The man, confused, asks in Navajo what is going on. The old woman quickly looks down at the ground, as if embarrassed by this display of affection.

"I'm sorry I didn't warn you I was coming," Jimmie says, pulling back just enough to look into Katherine's coffee-colored eyes. "Once I made the decision, it would take a letter longer to get here than it took me."

"Had I known you'd be here today I might not have slept the past few days." Flustered, she adds, "You know, in anticipation."

"I have so much to tell you," he blurts out, ignoring the fact they are not alone. He slides both arms around her waist and pulls her closer, but she resists, looking toward the examining room while she pats down her white uniform.

"I have patients," she giggles.

"And I have no patience at all." An idea occurs to him: "Hey, just tell them you have to hurry because the man who walked in has a heart problem."

"Jimmie, I can't make up a—"

"It's true! My heart is going to break if I don't have you all to myself."

"It shouldn't be more than another hour," she says, quickly squeezing and then releasing his hand. She heads back into the examining room.

Jimmie takes a seat next to the young mother. He is startled to hear what sounds like a military code coming from an old Philco radio in the room, until the announcer reveals that the letters LSMFT, repeated over and over, merely mean "Lucky Strike Means Fine Tobacco." The commercial is followed by a rhythmic rendition of "Walkin' My Baby Back Home." Idly, Jimmie reaches up to the rack for a pamphlet that is printed in both English and Navajo. *Tuberculosis and You,* the cover says. He opens it to the first page, but the words, like Johnny Ray's vocal styling, barely register.

All the way from Round Rock he has wrestled with how to present his new information to Katherine. He is relieved, certainly, that their clans are compatible. But the fact that he is descended from a scoundrel—possibly a merciless killer of at least two white men, at best a man who turned his back on his own child and grandchild—how will she feel about that? To make matters worse is his shame at having once aligned himself with Wilson's foolish notion that Black Horse was some sort of hero. How can he inflict his dubious heritage, along with his own weaknesses, on this woman he loves?

The hour stretches to nearly two as three other people walk in to the clinic. Finally, when Katherine finishes with her last patient, she flips the sign on the door to read CLOSED, and then, after embracing Jimmie warmly, she suggests a place where he might stable his horse. It is late afternoon when she leads him to the silver-colored trailer that is her home. She is an independent woman now, finally earning enough money to have a place of her own, as small and as basic as it may be.

In between more kissing and caressing, Katherine works in her tiny kitchen to prepare a stew of *posole* and mutton. Jimmie proclaims it is the most delicious meal he has ever eaten. He manages to steer the conversation away from himself, but she remarks that he seemed distracted throughout dinner. He suggests that they take a long walk into the desert. It is a chilly evening, but considering the time of year, pleasant enough. Overhead, the clouds skitter past a glowing three-quarter moon, which hangs low in the sky like a welcoming beacon.

Katherine changes into denim slacks and a fleecy white pullover sweater. She drapes a Pendleton blanket over her shoulders for added warmth. But any concerns of a chill seem to vanish by the time they stop walking, nearly an hour later, and, still deep in conversation, snuggle close together beneath an outcropping of rock.

Along the way, Jimmie had told her about George Benally and the other miners, and about his father's treatment for TB. Now he needs to unburden himself by revealing his stormy relationship with his father, things he had only hinted at in the past.

He puts his arm around her shoulders and she moves in closer, leaning against him, her legs folded beneath her and off to the side. She listens intently as he describes Wilson's loathing of the *bilagaʹana*, his alliance with Black Horse during the Round Rock confrontation, his history of participating in violent demonstrations against the US government, his propensity for peyote with like-minded individuals, his anger when he learned Jimmie was going to fight "the *bilagaʹana* war." He levels with her about his own disillusionment upon returning home, resentment that led him to feed on his father's angst and to experiment with peyote himself. He keeps nothing from her.

Katherine absorbs his words as if they are raindrops falling upon parched earth. Her only movement is to squeeze his arm as he speaks of things that so clearly trouble him. There is the sound of his wavering voice and the whoosh of light desert winds, but nothing more. They are completely alone in their togetherness.

"There are four individuals who have shaped the life I am hoping to lead," Jimmie continues, realizing the weight of his words only as he says them. "Like the four sacred peaks that mark the boundaries of *Dinetah*. If I ever accomplish anything at all, it will be because of them. Can you guess who they are, Katherine?"

He does not wait for her to answer. "First is my mother, who gave me strength and independence. Then there's Chee and Annie Dodge—I count them together. They pushed me to find the right path. Third is your brother, who inspired me during the short time we knew each other, who proved by example exactly what it is to be a man."

Katherine wipes away a tear with her free hand. But Jimmie finds it hard to look at her as he says these words. Instead, he looks into the distance and forces himself to go on.

"Finally, there is you, Katherine. Knowing you has given my life … well, corny as it sounds, the promise of harmony. You, above all others, have motivated me to work harder, to hold on to my dreams, to uphold a dying man's wish, to fulfill an oath that I've hardly begun to keep. But I know now it isn't for Chee Dodge that I will do these things, or even for the memory of your brother, important as that is to me. It's so that I might be deserving of you."

Katherine grips his arm tighter. Her breath is warm and honey sweet. And heavy, as if she is trying to hold in her own emotions. But Jimmie is not quite finished.

"I didn't tell you all of this before, those things about my father and me, because I didn't like the person I had become. How could I expect you accept it? But there's one last thing you need to know. The most important thing of all: I've finally learned my father's clan. On the way here. Two days ago."

Still gripping his arm, Katherine pulls her head away from his shoulder. A look of alarm distorts her face. "Jimmie, don't tell me we're born for the same—"

"The good news, the wonderful news, is that we're not," he quickly answers, turning to look at her, watching her face brighten like the moon overhead. "It's just that ... well, clan aside, I learned the identity of my father's father." He tells her the name. "And if that changes how you feel ..."

He does not finish the sentence, because Katherine has a new look on her face he cannot read. So he puts his index finger under her chin and tilts her head until his reflection shines back in the mirrors of her eyes. There is a glistening on her cheeks where teardrops trail. In the burnished moonlight, he tries again to read her expression. His heart pounds with the fury of hooves on dry ground as he waits breathlessly for her to say something. He is suddenly aware of the familiar scent of sage, and of the sporadic howls of distant coyotes. Has his perception sharpened, or have his words proven how imperceptive he really is in matters of the heart?

When Katherine does respond, after what seems like an achingly long time but in reality is less than a heartbeat, it is not with words. Her lips, open and moist with the brine of tears, press urgently against his. At the same time she rubs her right hand over the fabric of his shirt, starting at his shoulder, moving it downward toward his chest. He fumbles with his shirt buttons. Somehow he manages to open the top two without breaking the deep kiss. She slides her hand inside his shirt, caressing his bare chest with soft, languorous movements. Now he moves his own hands over the supple curves of her sweater. She murmurs softly and pulls away just long enough to draw her sweater up and over her head. He brushes his lips along the nape of her neck, his tongue gently tracing small circles in a downward-moving spiral while his hands caress the other contours of her body. Katherine's own hands move from the back of his neck to work greedily at his belt buckle. With nervous laughter, they momentarily separate and free themselves from their remaining clothing. Seconds later they are entwined, two earthbound mortals under an unfathomable, star-draped desert sky, oblivious to the falling temperature and their rising blood pressures, embraced in the mutual discovery of joy and abandon. Finally, there is nothing between them but the intense feeling of belonging to one another as they are swept up, giddy and exultant, in the passion of the moment. And for once in his life, Jimmie feels in perfect, blissful harmony with the universe, Black Horse and his father being the furthest things from his mind.

ACCORDING TO LEGEND, THE STARS in the heavens started out as bits of mica that First Man and First Woman laid out on a blanket after creating the sun and the moon. With great foresight and planning, First Man began to place them, one by one, in the night sky that rested on the four sacred mountains. But Coyote, being his impatient self, could not wait for First Man to finish. He grabbed the blanket and flung it up with all his strength, scattering the stars skyward. Most of the stars stuck in the great void in a random pattern, but some fell back to earth and became the Sonsola Buttes, the monoliths beside which Chee Dodge established his ranch.

Jimmie is reminded of this fable as he lies on his back and looks up at the luminous desert sky. He feels lighter than air, almost believing he can reach the stars and hand one to his love. Katherine lies on her side next to him, lightly stroking his arm. The blanket she brought covers them both. They have put their clothes back on, not out of modesty, but because they both realize it is far too cold to be lying naked in the desert like a couple of crazy teenagers.

"Did you honestly think," Katherine asks, "that just because your father has flaws, or your grandfather was ... who he was, that it would change how I feel about *you?*"

Jimmie reaches over and brushes two fingers along her cheekbone, the way he would touch finely polished turquoise. "My grandfather—my mother's father, that is—once told me, 'Even the playful spring lamb will provide mutton in time.' I took it to mean we can't escape who we are, what we're born into. Guess I've always believed that."

"Foolish man. It could also mean our lives have one outcome, which is death, and that we better make the most of what we have while we have it."

Jimmie props himself up on one elbow. "I never thought of it that way."

"Of course you didn't. That's why you need a woman in your life." A smile sweeps across his face. "I do, do I?"

"Remember something I said the first time we met?" Katherine asks, striking a serious note. "You're too hard on yourself, Jimmie. You're nothing like Black Horse, except that you are a leader, as was he. In one of Ray's letters—he was still in San Diego, I think, when he wrote it—he said, 'Everyone considers my best friend, Jimmie, to be the platoon leader.' I saw that quality in you the first time we met. It attracted me to you then, and it has left me uninterested in anyone else since." She chuckles as she asks, "Why do you think I've been so patient for this last year and a half? I was starting to think I might die a dried-up old woman just waiting for you to come around."

"Yeah, I was a fool," he mutters. "In many ways, it seems."

"Look, you were angry when you came back from war. You had every right to be. From what you told me, the marines gave you what you'd been missing on the reservation—respect, equality, *purpose*—and then you came home and, poof! It was gone. Okay, so you tried to change things the wrong way at first. Now accept the fact that you're not First Man, you're not Monster Slayer. And I'm no Annie Wauneka. But I'm doing all I can with my time on this world, and you're doing the same and that's one reason why I love you."

Jimmie flashes a *koshari* grin. "You're beautiful when you get all serious, y'know that?"

"How 'bout when I get all naked?"

"Then you're downright irresistible."

They kiss again and Jimmie adds, "Y'know, since we're being so open with each other, I'll admit I dreamed of making love with you—really, I literally dreamed it—that first night at your parents' place."

"Oh? And was it everything you dreamed it would be?"

"The dreams didn't come close."

As if to prove a point, he pulls Katherine to him, savoring again the intoxicating, soapy smell of her skin, her hair. He can feel the hunger stir anew within him.

"Maybe we should go back to my trailer," she says tenderly. "We'll be more comfortable and a lot warmer, don't you think?"

"I've never felt more comfortable in my whole life, Katherine."

After a moment in which neither of them stirs, Jimmie scoops up the blanket and gently drapes it over her shoulders. Then, hand-in-hand under the bits of mica scattered overhead, they walk slowly back toward the sparse, flickering lights of town.

CHAPTER 30

NOVEMBER 1949

Heading home to Ft. Defiance after two memorable weeks in Kayenta is tough, but Jimmie has his job to think about, as well as his father's recovery. He promised Katherine this would be their last separation, that they would be together by spring. It is a plan he had worked through over the past few days.

He rides toward home with the events of the previous weeks swirling through his mind. They had spent two pleasant days at her parents' *hogan*, where Katherine and Jimmie respectfully slept on opposite sides of the hexagonal room. Still, their ardor was readily evident to Maria and Samuel. The first evening, when Jimmie politely said goodnight to Katherine and moved across the room to sleep, Samuel actually winked at him.

On the days when Katherine worked, so did Jimmie. He visited the Oljato Mesa mine and then ventured over to Cane Valley's Monument No. 2 mine, which, he discovered, is open pit, allowing the radon gas and uranium dust to freely disperse in the air. All this will go into his report.

Naturally, most of his thoughts on the ride home are of Katherine. He knows it would be unfair to ask her to choose between the clinic and him. Furthermore, she has a deep commitment to the community she calls home, whereas his roots are shallow, like those of a cactus. So he is determined to move to Kayenta and marry her, even if it means leaving his job with the BIA, should it come to that.

He draws mental pictures along the way: a small place of their own. An automobile someday. A son and a daughter, perhaps two of each. He knows he will be a good parent, loving and supportive, unlike his own father, who has no idea that throughout his blusterous life, the man he admired most and the man he despised the most were one and the same.

JIMMIE ARRIVES BACK IN FT. Defiance after hitching a ride from Tsaile, where he returned his reliable but long-suffering transportation to its owner and recommended it for an extra bale of hay. He hopes this will be his last long-distance trip by horseback, for there is talk that a paved road will soon stretch all the way to Kayenta, and from there, presumably, west to the Grand Canyon. It will not only make traveling faster and easier, it will also provide construction jobs for scores of unemployed Navajos. An indication, he believes, that some improvements may finally be coming to the long-neglected reservation.

He stops off at his apartment, where he washes up and changes clothes. A few of Leila's things are in the room, a good sign; her presence here means Wilson is still in treatment. Then he heads over to the sanitarium. Marla, the pleasant receptionist, tells him Wilson Goodluck is in the non-contagion ward. Another good sign. Jimmie walks down the hallway and runs into Dr. Deuschle, who emerges from his office with an armful of papers.

"Jimmie, good to see you. Your father's doing well, don't you think?"

"I'm on my way to see him now. Been away a while. The medicine's working?"

Dr. Deuschle takes the index finger of his free hand and pushes his glasses up on the bridge of his nose, the way Annie often does. "With your father, the drug is making a world of difference. It hasn't been easy keeping him here, though. Your mother has had to practically tie him to the bed."

Jimmie is not surprised.

"He's lucky," the doctor says, "whether he knows it or not. We're still learning about the new drugs, and our success rate is mixed. Good news is, we might be able to let your father go home soon. He's not contagious anymore, but he's far from cured. It's essential he continues taking the medicine and gets checked regularly. He lives up near Shiprock, right?"

"Not too far."

"Well, there's a PHS doctor in Shiprock. Dr. Glenn."

Jimmie knows Dr. Glenn, of course, having been there with George weeks earlier. He assures Dr. Deuschle he will make sure his father gets checked regularly and keeps up his treatment.

"Well, good luck then," says Dr. Deuschle as he turns and walks away, his attention focused back on whatever he is holding in his hands.

JIMMIE PASSES THROUGH THE DOUBLE doors at the end of the hallway and looks into the large non-con ward. Beds, many of them empty, are lined up in a neat row along each of the two long walls. Jimmie's mother and father are not among the patients and visitors in the room. Then he remembers there is a solarium down an adjoining hallway, so he heads there.

The room is filled with light. It pours in through the large windows that look out onto the scrub-filled desert and the mesas beyond. The tiled floor is light in color, and the walls are painted in the cheerful yellow Jimmie associates with acacia flowers. The chairs scattered around the room appear to be new, unlike the worn furniture in the doctors' offices.

Wilson, looking bored and restive, sits slumped in one of the chairs near a window. Leila is on the floor beside him, spinning carded wool onto the whorl of a gooseberry spindle. Several other patients in the small room talk quietly or listen to the radio. A newscast in Navajo makes reference to General Eisenhower's presidential aspirations.

It is Leila who first spots Jimmie as he stands in the doorway. She jumps up and runs to embrace him as if he has been away for years instead of six weeks. Together they hurry over to Wilson, whose expression grows more churlish with each step Jimmie takes.

Without any greeting, Wilson launches into a tirade about being held prisoner by the *bilaga'ana*. His Navajo words fly out so fast Jimmie can barely keep up with the rant. Nothing escapes Wilson's criticism: the food, the medicine, the doctors, the rules, the beds, the procedures. All were designed, according to him, to subjugate the *Dineh* in general and humiliate him in particular. It is hard to miss the fact that Wilson's voice has become stronger, and that he no longer coughs as he spews out his harangue.

"I see you're improving," Jimmie says when he can get a word in. "You're back to your pleasant self."

"Your father is doing so well!" Leila exclaims, the way a teacher might praise her young student. "He complains bitterly, but there has been much improvement. And he can be around other people now."

"Other sick people," Wilson gripes. "And do you know they have a machine that can look inside your chest? What kind of witchcraft is that? I saw the picture they took of me. Just bones and shadows. It shows we will be nothing but bones when they are done with us. They are trying to—"

"You should be grateful for the help of these doctors," Jimmie interrupts, having no further tolerance for his father's paranoia. As his voice rises, nearby patients turn their heads. "Most doctors aren't getting paid for their time here, you know. And the medicine that's saving your life? It also has been donated. You're not paying for it, or for your bed here. Maybe it's time you showed some gratitude."

Leila puts a hand on her son's shoulder as a gesture to calm him down, though she says nothing to stop him. Jimmie speaks for her as well.

Wilson glares. "You are not the same boy who came home from war. You did not think I was so wrong then."

"You're right, I am not the same." Jimmie lowers his voice and squats on his heels so their faces are almost touching. Wilson tries to pull back, but he is against a window and has no place to escape. "Now my life goes forward by building on the wisdom of Chee Dodge, not the nonsense of Wilson Goodluck," Jimmie says, not caring if he has pushed too hard.

"You have no right to say such words. I would never have spoken this way to my—" Wilson stops abruptly, like a barefoot man who has just stepped on broken glass.

"To your what? Your *father?* You did not know who your father was, though you worshipped him unknowingly. He chose not to be a father to you, or a grandfather to me. What sort of man is that?"

Wilson opens his eyes wide, not comprehending. Leila steps in, saying, "Jimmie, this is not the time."

"Trust me, Mother, it's the perfect time." Jimmie's voice softens as he speaks to her, but it becomes firm again when he turns back to his father. "You see, Father, I know something you don't. On my recent journey, I passed through Round Rock, where I talked to an old man who met you years ago. He remembers you. He knows who your father was."

"You don't know what you are saying," Wilson says dismissively.

"The old man's name is Left-Handed Thrower. Do you remember him, Father, from when you were at Round Rock with Black Horse? You mentioned his name when you told me the story. He remembers *you*, Father. And he knows the truth."

"No one knows who my father was," Wilson snaps. "Only my mother, and she refused to speak his name. He hurt her very badly when he left her … left us. I hope he was struck by lightning. I hope his *chindi* remains in a burned-out tree for all time. I curse the man who was my father."

"Really? You curse him now, when your entire life has been devoted to him, idolizing him, thinking like him?"

Wilson grows more agitated. "Never! You speak of—what is that *biliga'ana* word?—the bullshit."

"No, Father, I speak of Black Horse." Jimmie searches his father's eyes for a sign of understanding. "Why do you think he sent for you—*you!*—to join him in Round Rock? Because you were his son. He wanted to parade you around like a rodeo horse. But he never wanted to be a father to you."

"This cannot be true," Leila says. "Perhaps there is a mistake…"

Jimmie looks at his mother. "The old man, Left-Handed Thrower, he heard the truth from the mouth of Black Horse himself. As Black Horse lay dying." Then, turning to Wilson: "What do you say now, Father?"

Wilson glances from Jimmie, to his wife, and then back again. He plainly does not know where to turn. "Why do you tell me this?" he bleats. "Why do you hurt me this way?"

Jimmie puts his hand on his father's arm. "I don't say this to hurt you. I say this to open your eyes. All your life you've followed the ways of a man who spewed hatred and violence. But now you can see how imperfect he was. He turned his back on your mother after he had his way with her. He would not even acknowledge you, his own flesh and blood. He *used* you at Round Rock, Father, and then discarded you again. But *you*, Father, even when you didn't approve of my choices, you stayed part of my life. You are not like your own father, any more than *I* am like him. I can see that now. That's why I tell you these things. Because it is not too late for you to live a different kind of life."

Wilson's eyes seem to lose their angry glare. Leila must notice it too, for she comes to her husband's other side, and she also squats down beside his chair. Now nearly all of the patients and visitors in the room look at them. The quiet conversation around the room has stopped. Even the radio has replaced the newscast with a selection by the Percy Faith Orchestra. Fittingly, they are playing "Delicado."

"I am confused," Wilson says. "And I am … too old to think any other way about things."

"You are not so old, Father," Jimmie argues. "The white man's medicine you complain about? It will give you many more years. You could grow to be as old as Left-Handed Thrower. He may live to be a hundred."

Jimmie's father seems lost within himself. Then he says, "You were right about one thing, about the white man's medicine. It has helped to make the Shooting Chant ceremony get me better and restore my *hozho*."

Not quite what Jimmie wants to hear, but coming from his father, it is a predictable response. More than that, it is a beginning.

ANNIE WAUNEKA'S OLD PICK-UP GLIDES to a stop next to the adobe-crusted building in Window Rock that houses the tribal council chambers. She and Jimmie greet each other with the clasp of hands and a warm *"Ya'at'eeh,"* for they have not seen one another since before Jimmie's journey to Cove and Kayenta. This is their first opportunity to steal a half hour from Annie's busy schedule on the council.

They have their favorite meeting place to themselves, the area behind the council chambers building that faces the natural window rock formation. The light snowfall of previous days has stopped, and the weather is brisk but clear. The surrounding boulders glow a deep pink in the dappled morning light. Annie stares at the spectacle with intense appreciation, though she has seen it countless times before. Then she looks at her friend through her thick glasses and asks him about his father. Jimmie tells her about his ruse to get Wilson into the sanatorium and briefly recounts his experiences among the miners, including Dr. Glenn's disheartening prognosis.

Annie makes a clucking sound with her tongue. "So many health problems to deal with, and now this. Maybe if enough people put pressure on the mining companies ..." She leaves her sentence unfinished, as if she already knows how futile that will be. Then she brightens and says, "But tell me about your love life. You haven't said a word about Katherine. Did you see her?"

He merely nods, waiting anxiously for the inevitable next question.

"Do I have to hit you with a stick? How is she? How's her work coming along at the clinic? How was your time together?"

Struggling to put on a mock frown, he answers, "Well, I got up there and found out she's promised to somebody."

Annie reaches out and touches his arm lightly with her hand. "Oh, Jimmie, I'm so sorry. Do you know who ... who she's—"

He bursts into a broad grin. "Me, actually."

"You devil!" Annie squeals, hitting him playfully on the shoulder. "Does that mean there's going to be—dare I say it—a wedding?"

"Yes, by spring, we're hoping. I've decided to make Kayenta my home. With any luck I can still work for the Health Service from there. Anyways, Katherine and I still have a lot to work out."

Annie giggles like a schoolgirl, and her mood stays upbeat even when Jimmie tells her about his encounter with Left-Handed Thrower. "We can't pick our ancestors" is all she has to say about that.

Jimmie grows pensive. "I can't help but wonder, though, whether your father would have asked me to help carry on his legacy if he knew that Black Horse was my grandfather."

"Who says he didn't know?" She says it with a piercing tone and then follows the question with her typically wry, questioning smile.

"Really? He knew all along?"

"Honestly? Don't know if he did or not. Wouldn't surprise me, is all. He was aware of everything that went on around here. But it wouldn't have mattered to him. He judged people on their own abilities. Not by where they come from, but where they're going."

Jimmie can embrace that sentiment now. "Speaking of where you are going—" He pauses, wanting to ask her about her reelection campaign. Word has it her own husband is running against her this time, seemingly as a lark. How deeply she must be torn between her political activism and her family obligations. Jimmie catches himself and rephrases his question. "What—how's the expression go?—what feathers are you ruffling in the tribal council?"

She throws her head back and laughs, hearty and full. "I got them to part with some of that mineral lease money coming in. That took some doing, let me tell you. Last month the council set aside $300,000 for housing and sanitation."

"That's wonderful."

"And then I threatened the federal government. They put in some money, too."

"You're amazing, Annie. The council could use more people like you."

"Yes, there are so many other things we need to wrestle with. Like the mining dangers you told me about and—"

She stops in midsentence and leans forward, her face inches away from Jimmie's. "What did you just say?"

He looks at her with a puzzled expression. "Um, y'mean, 'The council could use more people like you'?"

"Yes! And you're right, of course. Now tell me, who's more like me than you are? Jimmie—*you* should run for tribal council!

"Whoa, now, wait a minute—"

"Frankly, the Kayenta chapter could use a new delegate. By next year you could win over the locals and walk away with the election."

The idea is at once appealing and daunting. "Annie, I don't know—"

"Of course you do. Think about it! You can continue working for the Health Service, and make a real impact on the council at the same time. The extra money's not bad, either. Enough to make payments on a car, I should think. Why, you could drive between Kayenta and council chambers in less than a day on those new roads they're starting to build."

He says he will think it over. And discuss it with Katherine, of course.

Annie looks pleased with herself. "She'll be all for it. I know her, don't forget. Well, not as well as you do by now, I assume." She winks.

Jimmie's head fills with shifting images that change pattern and form as if he were peering into a kaleidoscope. So many changes in his life, starting with his decision to join the Marine Corps. Have eight years gone by already? And now, finally, after his aimless and turbulent return: a soon-to-be wife. A future. A calling. An identity.

"Think of it, Jimmie," Annie says. "You and me in the tribal council: voices of progress and reform, pushing, always pushing, both here and in Washington, to make this a better place."

Her enthusiasm is infectious. "You're right, we could be great together," he says.

"*Great*, Jimmie? 'Great' is the best you can do? Why, together we'll be unstoppable."

CHAPTER 31

APRIL 1950

He walks in beauty.

The woman Jimmie loves is about to become his wife. And because a first marriage at their ages is so unusual here, their wedding appears to be the social event of the year. One can almost hear people saying, *What was wrong with those two to begin with? Oh well, at least they found each other.*

The number of guests who have gathered in Kayenta this weekend seems staggering, though Katherine and Jimmie are delighted. Her entire family has come, including members of her clans who live great distances away. The family on Jimmie's side is far smaller in number, but the turnout among his old friends and marine buddies helps to even things up. Annie is here, naturally, along with several of her children. A few of Jimmie's coworkers at the BIA have also come to wish the couple well. Even the trader Bill Whisky is present, grinning as if he was the matchmaker who put them together—which, in a manner of speaking, he was.

Katherine's mother has been busy preparing the wedding feast and cleaning the *hogan* in preparation for this big day. In earlier times a separate wedding *hogan* would have been built very close by for the ceremony, after which Katherine and Jimmie would have moved in. But times are different now. Katherine's trailer will be their home until they can afford a bigger place of their own.

There is one longstanding custom, however, that Jimmie does wish to honor: the presentation of an offering to Katherine's parents, although they have told him repeatedly that no dowry is necessary. He has no livestock, but his mother does, and she gladly offers up three sheep and two calves. Then he adds gifts of his own choosing, presenting Samuel with several yards of supple leather and, for Maria, a fine turquoise necklace. Normally it would be forbidden for his future mother-in-law to see him so soon before—or, for that matter, during—the wedding, but that custom, too, belongs to another era.

In the hours before the ceremony, Jimmie and Katherine separately bathe and then dress in their best clothes. For Jimmie, that simply means clean slacks, a fresh shirt, and new boots, never worn before: the boots made by Katherine's father, the boots with Ray's buttons. If ever there was a time to put them on, it is now.

At sundown, all is ready.

Jimmie enters the *hogan,* where the floor is covered with sheep pelts for everyone to sit on. Following prescribed ritual, he proceeds in the direction of the sun and sits down in the back, opposite the entrance. His family follows, along with Annie, her children, and his buddies, all sitting to his north.

Next comes Maria, beaming like a woman who has not only married off her last daughter, but one past marriageable age as well. She carries a bag of corn pollen, a wicker jug filled with water, and a gourd ladle. Behind her is Katherine, the stunning bride, escorted by her father.

Katherine chose to be married in traditional Navajo attire,

and Jimmie finds her resulting transformation to be nothing short of astonishing. Her fluted broom skirt is assembled in three tiers, representing the phases of a woman's life. It is made of bright blue velveteen, as is her matching blouse. Her choice of a woven sash belt signifies the sanctity of womanhood. Her jewelry consists of a multistrand necklace, wide bracelets, and long, dangling earrings, all turquoise and silver, given to her by her mother and sisters. Even her hair is done up in the traditional way, rolled and wrapped four times into a bun, then tied with white yarn. On her feet are supple moccasins crafted by her father. Each is adorned by a silver button, designed by her late brother, Ray.

Katherine carries a ceremonial wedding basket in her hands, the one made by her mother. Jimmie recognizes it as the basket Bill Whisky showed him at the Oljato Trading Post. It is the trader's wedding gift to the couple, one they will treasure. Inside the basket is a clay pot containing unseasoned cornmeal mush, also prepared by Maria.

Katherine sits beside Jimmie to his south, with Samuel, Maria, and her sisters next to them. By the time the rest of her family enters, they are all packed together inside the *hogan* like fruit in a can. Some of the guests have no choice but to wait outside, where another blazing fire wards off the chilly evening.

The last person to enter the room is a singer from the Kayenta area, a friend of the Begays known as Pale Mustache. He will officiate the short ceremony. He takes the basket and the water jug and places them in front of the bridal couple as he introduces the ritual washing. Navajo will be the only language spoken here.

Following the singer's instructions, Katherine takes the ladle and pours some water over Jimmie's hands. Then she hands the ladle to Jimmie so he may do the same for her.

Next, Pale Mustache takes the corn pollen from Maria. He sprinkles some of it around the circumference of the pot containing the cornmeal mush, followed by a cross over the top. Then he turns toward the guests and says, "With your permission I will turn the basket halfway around." This, everyone will know, symbolizes turning the wedding couple's minds toward one another.

The singer next instructs the couple to take a bit of the mush from the eastern edge of the bowl and put it in their mouths, followed by a pinch from each of the other directions and then from the center, where the corn pollen has crossed. Once they do this solemn ritual, Pale Mustache announces that the feast may begin.

There will be songs and speeches throughout the evening, but in the eyes of the assembled guests, Jimmie and Katherine are husband and wife. And as everyone rises to enjoy the feast that awaits outside, Jimmie practically floats to his feet, lighter than an eagle feather, lifting his beloved with him so that he can hold her for the first time as his wife.

And the world is as he never knew it before.

He has found his *hozho*.

EVERYONE IS HAVING SUCH A good time, the party looks like it may go on until dawn.

Jimmie and Katherine bounce exuberantly between their guests, barely taking time to enjoy the wonderful meats and breads and desserts provided mainly by Maria, but also by Leila and by some of the other women who have come this night. Maria and Leila are already becoming fast friends. Throughout the day they have been comparing notes on their respective skills of weaving and basket making, and they often lapse into laughter as they swap stories about Jimmie and Katherine as children.

What surprises Jimmie is how easily his father interacts with Samuel. The two men huddle by the fire, deep in conversation. Six months ago Jimmie might have suspected his father was up to something, spreading some kind of poison. But Wilson has become a different person. Still distrustful of the Anglo world, probably always will be. But not hateful anymore. And while Jimmie suspects he and his father will always have their disagreements, Wilson seems to be trying anew to be a real father, for once, unlike his own. Leila confided that Wilson has even begun to regard Dr. Glenn with grudging respect, now that his treatment is coming to an end. And that last month, he willingly accompanied her to the trading post, where he actually spoke a few friendly words to the trader. Maybe the *chindi* of Black Horse has finally let go, Leila said hopefully, leaving in peace the son and grandson he never publicly acknowledged.

Somewhere around midnight, when Katherine gets involved in giggly girl talk with her friends and sisters, Jimmie catches up with his marine buddies. George Benally, Charlie Yazzie, Carl Slowtalker, and Wilfred Smith have all come to share this day with the bridal couple. George, still experiencing health problems, rode over from Cove on a horse belonging to his wife-to-be. Carl and Charlie hitched rides from Ft. Defiance and Chinle, respectively. Wilfred came up from Gallup, where he works as a high school teacher, having recently earned his Master's in Education from the University of Wyoming.

Jimmie asks Carl what brought him back to the reservation.

"I liked Colorado," Carl shrugs, sipping a Coca-Cola. "But the work, it comes and goes. When they get enough white workers, they don't need no Indians. Gets pretty lonely so far from home when the work dries up. And layin' track's no picnic anyhow."

George snickers. "What else was you layin' up there?"

They all ignore him. "So what are you doing now?" Jimmie asks.

"Whatever work I can find. Road construction. Digging wells. Putting up fences."

"You guys should take advantage of your GI Bill," Wilfred says.

"Study engineering, maybe. Or go into education like I did. Nothing we need more of around here than teachers."

"Yeah," Carl agrees. "I should think about that before it's too late."

"It's only too late once you find a wife," Charlie says. Then he looks at Jimmie, suddenly aware of his ill-advised quip. "Aw, jeez, Jimmie, I didn't mean—"

"It's okay," Jimmie laughs.

"It's just that I can't go to college without leaving the reservation," Charlie explains. "And my wife, she won't leave her family. Funny, when you think about it. I go to war and talk code for my country, and then I come back and talk mostly to sheep. I'd go crazy if it wasn't for the tourists. They been coming to Canyon de Chelly like ants to a picnic."

"You hang around the fuckin' tourists?" George asks, his tone incredulous. "Me, I'd prefer the sheep."

"Been gettin' work lately at the Thunderbird Lodge, taking visitors into the canyon three or four days a week," Charlie says. "They like the scenery, I guess. And the stories of how we got our asses kicked there."

Wilfred removes a piece of jerky that was dangling between his teeth like a cigarette. He asks Jimmie, "Now that you're living here in Kayenta, you gonna stay with the BIA?"

"For the time being, anyways. My bosses are pretty understanding about my move. 'Course, it means I'll have to be away from home a lot, but then, who knows what the future holds? So much has changed since the war."

"We changed too," Wilfred says. "I never would have gone for a degree if I hadn't joined the Corps and seen what an education could do. 'Course, the free tuition didn't hurt."

"Yeah, but what the fuck, guys," George grumbles, keeping his voice low. "This ain't the marines anymore where we can get respect and enjoy a few beers with our white buddies. Ain't nobody patting us on the back or covering our asses now that we're home."

Jimmie shrugs. "Look, what we had in the Corps, we may never have again, it's true. But I got an idea that could help us hold on to some of what we did have."

They all look at him curiously.

"We did something pretty special during the war," he goes on. "Not just our platoon, but the boys who came after us. All four-hundred-something of 'em. Us Navajo radiomen need to stick together. Keep in contact. Look out for one another."

"Wait a minute," Carl says. He looks around cautiously, checking to make sure nobody else is close enough to overhear. "What makes you think it'll ever be declassified? I think we're taking our secret with us into the ground."

"Won't happen today or tomorrow, but someday," Jimmie says. "Meanwhile, the important thing is that we all keep in touch. Then when we can talk about it, we should do it as a group. Not that we're better than the other *Dineh* who served in the war, or the other tribes, even. It's just … well, we have a special bond, those of us who went through code school. We should keep it going."

"Y'mean, like a club or something?" Charlie asks.

"Yeah, exactly. Listen, I got something in the mail a while back. From a buddy of mine, Keith McClintock. We were together in the Second Raiders on 'Canal. He wrote about starting a Carlson's Raiders group. His idea is to organize reunions every so often, where we can all get together, talk about old times … y'know, watch each other grow old. He wants to send out letters that keep track of everyone in the battalion … marriages, births, deaths, that sort of thing. And he wants to tell the world about the Raiders and what they did. Anyhow, that's what we should do. Our code work won't stay classified forever."

Everyone heartily agrees. In the meantime, they all promise

to stay in touch. With or without the code, they are bound to one another. *Semper Fi.*

IF THERE IS SUPPOSED TO be a letdown after the whirlwind weekend, neither Katherine nor Jimmie feel it. The guests have drifted away and, for the first time in days, the newly married couple is alone. But their life together is just beginning, so they are still flying like cottonwood seeds on the wind. In another day, Katherine is scheduled to return to the clinic, and Jimmie will head to Tuba City for a two-day assignment.

On a whim, they decide to enjoy the evening at the place in the desert where they first made love. The sky is clear overhead and the moon is nearly as full as their hearts. The temperature has cooled down some, though it is warmer than when they were here in late November. Regardless, they pledge to remain clothed this time.

Beneath the same overhang of rock, they inhale the desert and rehash events of recent days. Annie, who has become as close to Katherine as she is to Jimmie, lassoed the couple over the weekend. She wanted to make sure Jimmie talked to his bride about running for the council.

"You sure you're okay with it if I do try to run?" Jimmie asks as they snuggle together. "I mean, with all the traveling I already do on my job, this will mean more time away at council headquarters in Window Rock."

She assures him she is fully supportive. It is his calling, she insists.

In truth, he finds the idea exhilarating. "But suppose I don't get elected to the Kayenta chapter?" he asks.

"Oh, you'll get the votes," Katherine assures him. "We'll start campaigning at the clinic. And Bill Whisky will help spread the word at the trading post."

That reminds Jimmie. "Did I ever tell you what Bill said to me on my first trip through there? He gave me directions to your parents' *hogan*, told me you were living there too, and warned me to lock up my heart. Those were his words."

"Good thing you didn't listen, then." She laughs, her eyes shining with the luminosity of the stars overhead. "By the way, I'm glad you didn't see that poor excuse for a basket I made for him to sell. It's been gone from there a long time now, thank goodness. Some poor fool must have bought it."

"Some poor fool certainly did." He grins broadly.

Katherine looks into his eyes. "You didn't!"

"I bought it on that first trip, along with the boots I wore at our wedding, the boots made by your brother and father. I loved that basket because you wove it, Katherine. I had only just met you, but I had to have something that your hands touched and shaped."

Katherine nuzzles close. "Well, then, I'll confess something to you. When you left after that visit, I cried myself to sleep. I knew then why I hadn't married earlier. It was because you hadn't come into my life. There were times when I wondered if you felt the same way. And then if you'd ever act on it."

They remain huddled together, neither of them speaking, both absorbed in the intimacy of acceptance and belonging. To break the silence several minutes later, Jimmie looks up at the sky and says, "When I was little, my mother's father told me never to count the stars. Said if I did, I would have too many children."

Katherine looks up to the heavens and giggles, "One, two, three, four—"

"Better stop there," Jimmie says, laughing along with her.

He continues looking skyward, drinking in the stars, when a constellation just above the horizon catches his eye. He points to it. "I didn't pay much attention in school, but with May almost here, that has to be Scorpius."

Katherine looks and then points out a group of stars a little more directly overhead. "See that cluster over there?" she asks.

He studies the celestial display, but the constellation is unfamiliar to him.

Her voice breaks as she says, "That's my brother, Ray. He's up there looking down on us. And he's smiling."

EPILOGUE

MARCH 1958

The screen door slams and his first reaction is to get angry. Then he thinks, *This* is what happens after your dream comes true. What happens, if you fight to hang on to that dream and if you're lucky, is that your life gets fuller and richer.

No. Luck has nothing to do with it. Luck is something that drops into your lap, and he doesn't cotton to that. *Blessed*, that is the word. That is what his life is, and every day is filled with reminders of those blessings: the touch of a tiny hand; the soft sighs from the pillow beside him; the reliable aromas of dried sage and hot coffee and home-baked bread; the sweet, distinct warble of the mountain bluebird; the steady drone of tires on paved road; the love of family; the laughter of friends.

The slamming of the screen door.

"What have we told you, Ray?" he asks in a gentle, measured voice. The boy is out of breath, apparently having run all the way from the road where the school bus dropped him off. "Your baby sister's nursing in the next room."

"Oh. Sorry."

"And anyways, you should close the screen gently anytime you go in or out."

"Okay. Mom here?"

"The baby doesn't nurse herself." He raises his eyebrows, waits for Ray's reaction, the look that says "I shoulda figured that." Same way the boy's namesake used to do.

Today Katherine has evening hours at the ever-expanding clinic, so she is home for a short break before she passes off the babysitting duties. Jimmie tries to be around as much as he can, but his job keeps him away more than he would like. At least a few new highways have spread across the reservation, shortening travel time. He was even able to buy a used pick-up a couple of years back. Hitchhiking is for men younger than he is.

Health Service headquarters remain in Ft. Defiance, and he is able to time most of his visits there around tribal council sessions in nearby Window Rock. Often his job and his political responsibilities overlap, as with the ongoing fight to get medical care and government compensation for the Navajo uranium miners. His friend George, sadly, has been diagnosed with an aggressive lung cancer. The place where George lives, Cove, is becoming a community of widows. The council is pressing the mining companies to enforce safety regulations, to clean up their abandoned mines, to remove the tailings that are making people sick. But in many places, children still live and play with uranium dumps in their backyards. As Jimmie remembers telling his father when he came home from the South Pacific, there are always wars to fight. So the fight goes on, and some progress is being made, but not nearly enough.

Ray asks, "Dad? Can we go out and, you know, can you help me practice—"

"You have any homework?" The question is from Katherine,

who has stepped into the living room. There is no sound from the bedroom, so the baby must be asleep. Annie is six months old.

"No homework, Mom, and it's going to be dark soon."

"All right. But keep your feet warm. There are still patches of snow on the ground." Winter had made a feeble stand the day before, but early springlike temperatures are already hinting at better days to come.

Katherine turns to her husband. "Jimmie, I have to leave in an hour. You'll be back inside then, right?"

"Of course." He looks at Katherine as he has every day for the eight years they have been married. She has a few more lines on her face, as does he, but like a fine piece of sterling, aging only seems to make her more desirable. He thanks the Holy Ones in his daily prayers for leading him to Ray Begay and for the privilege of Ray's brief friendship. which led ultimately to his connection to Katherine.

Other than the fond memories of his little brother, Jimmie does not think much about those days anymore. The code is still classified, but that means little to him. He knows the things that are important have nothing to do with what he did in a war long ago, but what he did yesterday. What he can still do today. What he might do tomorrow with the years he has left. Like Talking God told his ancestors, *Give something to the world and your people will last beyond your lifetime.*

"Dad?"

He puts his arm over Ray's shoulders. "Get your rope and meet me outside. And don't forget to close the screen door gently this time."

Jimmie drives a wooden stake into the thawing ground behind the house, just as Wilson did for him when he was about Ray's age. Leila and Wilson will be coming up to visit in a week, and Ray wants to show off his roping skills. Ray is very close to them, especially to Jimmie's father, who he knows only as a kind, generous, and loving man. Jimmie himself no longer thinks of Wilson in any other way.

Ray runs up to his dad, rope in hand. Jimmie has his own coil of rope, made of fine rawhide. Katherine bought it for him at the trading post on their first anniversary. He is no rancher, has never used it to rope a calf, but he is happy just swinging it around.

"Now watch carefully," he tells Ray, taking the loop in his right hand about a foot below the ring. "Remember to leave enough loose rope between the coil and the loop. And make sure there are no twists in the line, or the coils won't slip off easily when you throw."

Ray looks closely at his father's hands and then steps back. Jimmie raises his right hand and begins to swing the rope over his head from right to left.

"See how smoothly my wrist moves? Remember what I told you: pretend the loop is a wheel."

And now he takes a quick step forward, extends his swinging hand to arm's length and, without interrupting the motion of the loop, lets it fly in a steady arc toward the stake. Ray squeals with delight as his dad's loop ensnares the target.

"Now it's your turn," Jimmie tells his son.

Ray positions himself a little closer to the stake. He holds his rope well, and while his first attempt at swinging the loop is awkward, he gets a little better with each successive try.

"Keep it circling over your head, that's the way," Jimmie encourages him. "Don't let it touch the ground, keep it aloft. Keep it aloft, that's the idea."

Ray doesn't dare to look up for fear of losing his rhythm, but he can surely feel the smoothness of the rotation, the fullness of the arc, for his face breaks out in a wide smile. Ray's self-confidence seems to be growing by the second.

"How's it look, Dad?"

"You're doing great, son. You're gonna be better at it than me. Just keep it going, keep it aloft."

And Jimmie smiles too, bursting with pride and with love, as Ray's rope spins and spins, high above the ground, elevating ever so slightly higher with every rotation, as if it might stay aloft forever, as if it might almost touch the sky.

Author's note

While Jimmie Goodluck is a fictional character, he is, in many respects, a composite of real individuals. In particular, his military experiences as depicted in these pages have been largely drawn from documented incidents.

Many of the people in this story, of course, did certainly exist, although I have used them fictitiously. Chee Dodge and Annie Dodge Wauneka, for instance, were remarkable leaders of the Navajo people during the time period depicted. I have tried to represent them realistically, and to accurately reflect their accomplishments—in some cases, quite literally in this story—or else in spirit and character.

Black Horse was a real headman (and renegade, apparently) as well, though little is documented about his life. The incident between him and Chee Dodge at the Round Rock Trading Post actually took place as described in these pages.

It is my hope that I have accurately represented Evans Carlson and his Raiders, for Carlson was indeed one of the earliest supporters of the Navajo code. What's more, he actually did leave the battlefield for the last time after sustaining injuries while saving an enlisted man. Carlson, along with Col. "Jumpin' Joe" Chambers and other real people, events, and issues coexist in these pages along with fictional characters and situations.

I have strived for authenticity when depicting the military conflicts, relying on research from a huge number of sources. The combat portrayals have been condensed, of course, for it was my intent to show how the Navajo code was used, not to present a thorough military discourse. I in no way mean to trivialize the real lives that were lost or to gloss over the valiant heroes that were a part of the military actions described herein.

As for the Navajo ceremonies that are depicted in this novel, including Blessingway, Enemy Way, the peyote ritual, and others, I have again simplified and compressed many details to give the flavor of how they were part of the fabric of life in the 1940s. All information I have relied upon comes from published and readily accessible sources. Any mistakes or misinformation regarding Navajo ceremonies or customs that result from my novelization rest with me, and I sincerely hope nothing is revealed in these pages that compromises the best interests of the Navajo Nation, for whom I have the utmost respect.

All told, I wrote each page of this novel with a keen eye toward historical veracity, although I have rearranged a few places and dates when it suited the story. In places where I used English dialogue to represent words spoken in the Navajo language, the word choices and phrasing may appear somewhat stiff and formal. This is intentional, for traditional Navajos have nothing in their language to equal the informal and often idiomatic way we Anglos speak. Furthermore, many words used here in English really have no direct Navajo language counterpart.

There are several nonfiction books of varying quality available for those who seek more information on the Navajo code talkers. One of the best, in my opinion, is *Navajo Weapon* by Sally McClain (Boulder, Colorado: Books Beyond Borders, Inc., 1994). A fascinating book on the life of the amazing Annie Wauneka, *I'll Go and Do More* by Carolyn Niethammer (Lincoln, Nebraska: University of Nebraska

Press, 2001), was indispensable to me. So, too, was the out-of-print book *When Navajos Had Too Many Sheep* by George Boyce (San Francisco, California: The Indian Historian Press, 1974), which does a thorough job of describing key aspects Navajo life in the 1940s, particularly the devastating and controversial government-enforced stock reduction. An excellent book of recent vintage on the tragic (and still somewhat unresolved) issue of uranium on Navajo land is *Yellow Dirt* by Judy Pasternak (New York, New York: Free Press, 2010).

ACKNOWLEDGMENTS

I must begin by offering special thanks to several people on the Navajo reservation who generously gave me their time and support. One of the reasons I wrote this story was not only to dramatize a period of our history that is woefully unknown and filled with misconceptions, but also to showcase the reality that, long-held prejudices on both sides notwithstanding, the Navajo people—indeed, all Native peoples—are no different, really, in their lives and aspirations than everyone else in this diverse country. This was clear to me time and again as I crossed the Navajo Nation.

Harry Walters, historian, teacher, and director of the Hathathli Museum at the impressive *Dineh* College in Chinle, AZ, gave me valuable insights into Navajo history and beliefs. Frank Morgan, a Navajo educator, researcher, translator, and so much more, read an early draft of this novel and offered both support and advice on passages that didn't ring true, including tips on Navajo phrasing.

I am especially indebted to Wilfred Billey, a proud Navajo code talker who I'm grateful to call friend. He shared many of his experiences with me and read an early draft of this novel with interest, delight, and encouragement. Many of his observations found their way into my characterizations of Jimmie Goodluck and Ray Begay. The two epigrams that I attributed to him came from our conversations together. Without question, spending time with

Wilfred and his wonderful family was a highlight for my wife and me during two of my numerous research trips to *Dinetah*.

Thanks also to Diane Schmidt, reporter for the *Navajo Times* and award-winning photojournalist, for her photo that graces the cover of this book. It was hard choosing just one, so extensive are her stunning photographic images of *Dinetah*.

Closer to home—in this first case, right *at* home—I must thank my wife, Loraine, who eagerly read many of the more than twenty drafts of this novel and offered sharp insights every time. Then there is my cheerleading team of Marge and Keith McClintock, who told me what I needed to hear, not necessarily what I wanted to hear, and spurred me on to write a better novel. Every writer needs someone like them in his or her corner; I am lucky to have such a dynamic duo. I also wish to thank a number of friends who graciously allowed me to name characters after them, although many of them may not have been aware that I was doing so! And a nod as well to Verna Dreisbach, a dedicated literary agent who understood and believed in this story but finally suggested I bring it into the publishing world myself rather than have *The Rope Catcher* sit on my hard drive and possibly never see the light of day. Maybe next time, Verna.

Finally, I wish to thank my readers who have shared their valuable time with Jimmie, Ray, and the other characters in my story. I hope I have passed on to you, in some small way, my love of the Southwest and, in particular, my desire to bring this period of Navajo history into greater public consciousness. If so, then I, like my protagonist Jimmie Goodluck, have achieved everything I wished for.

ABOUT THE AUTHOR

LARRY STILLMAN is a lifelong writer and former advertising executive creative director. He is the award-winning author of *A Match Made in Hell: The Jewish Boy and the Polish Outlaw Who Defied the Nazis* (University of Wisconsin Press, 2003). This work of narrative nonfiction was a finalist for best adult nonfiction by the Society of Midland Authors. It was also named among the best young adult books of the year by the New York Public Library System and by the National Association of University Presses. It has appeared as a *Reader's Digest* condensation in Portugal, Hungary, and the Czech Republic, and it has been translated and reprinted unabridged in Poland. He travels extensively to the Southwest from his home in suburban Chicago, Illinois, where he lives with his wife, Loraine. *The Rope Catcher* is his first novel.

Made in the USA
Lexington, KY
17 November 2013